Parish the Thought

A Cadillac Holland Mystery, Volume 5

H. Max Hiller

INDIES UNITED PUBLISHING HOUSE, LLC
P.O. BOX 3071
QUINCY, IL 62305-3071
www.indiesuited.ne

The Cadillac Holland Mysteries

Blowback

Blue Garou

Can's Stop the Funk

Ghosts and Shadows

Parish the Thought

For Lovena.

You deserved so much better

One

Deputies from the Saint Xavier Parish Sheriff's Office manned the roadblock meant to keep gawkers away from the crime scene. I left my car in the parking lot of a century-old wooden church where a television news crew was setting up for a live shot. I zipped up my rain jacket and walked down the muddy lane to where halogen lights illuminated the interior of the open trunk of a silver Mercedes C63 sedan. Crime scene technicians from the Louisiana state police were using a nylon canopy to protect a deep pool of blood in the vehicle's spare tire compartment from the cold misting rain and dense fog rising from Bayou Beausejour. I witnessed levels of butchery in the Special Forces that still haunt me and knew this was not a survivable blood loss. I approached a pair of LSP detectives sheltered beneath a nearby cypress tree and listened to their theories about the possible sources of so much gore, and understood why they investigate car thefts and not homicides.

I was no homicide detective, either, and I felt like little more than an onlooker. I left the bored detectives to check in with my supervisor at the state police. Captain Kenneth Hammond had a plastic wrap over the Smokey the Bear hat he wore to keep rain from getting beneath his rain slicker. His expression tipped me off that this case was giving him more stress than usual, so I shouldn't add to it.

"Sorry for the early hour," Captain Hammond grumbled.

"I was up," I said to let him off one of the many hooks he seemed to be hanging from. It was just after four in the morning and I would have been wrapping up my patrol of the French Quarter about then, anyway. "What's this all about? I'd say murder, but the detectives you brought usually don't handle homicides."

"They were the closest detectives when the call came in, and your presence here wasn't my idea." The sight of Judge Cyrus Rogers explained a lot of what he left unsaid. I had recently used the judge's courtroom to expose the combined efforts of an attorney tied to the Dixie Mafia and a local real estate developer to rig the last City Council election. Doing so must have incurred a favor the judge intended to collect.

"Holland. I'm glad you found us out here." The silver-haired judge's voice snapped me out of my thoughts. Judge Rogers acknowledging me gave the parish sheriff a moment's respite from the tongue lashing the judge had been giving him when I arrived. Judge Rogers offered no introductions between Sheriff Mazant and myself. "I didn't call you away from anything important, did I?"

"Always willing to oblige, Your Honor," I assured him. I doubted that he cared in the least what I had been doing when he summoned me to the scene.

"This is my daughter's blood," the judge declared and pointed into the trunk to be sure I saw the reason for his emotional state. "At least we are assuming that it is."

"You couldn't identify the body?" I asked indelicately.

"There is no body, but everyone has a theory. The current favorite is that her body was chained to the spare tire and tossed in the bayou." I doubted this was the case, first because the amount of blood indicated the body was not intact, and second because a corpse tied to anything that floats defeats the purpose of dumping the body. You want to hide a body, not send it bobbing down a busy waterway.

"Is this is your daughter's car?" I asked. Judge Rogers looked at me as if he might reconsider using me for whatever he had in mind.

"Obviously it is. I think someone killed Gwen before they stole her car and dumped it here." I doubted this scenario as much as I doubted those of the auto theft detectives. My dad was a cop and he always said that the amount of blood involved indicated how personal a murder was. Gwen's murderer was likely someone very close to her.

"Okay, why am I here?" I figured I was expected to serve a larger purpose than consoling the judge. Learning why would get us all out of the rain. Captain Hammond's silence left it to the judge to brief me.

"I need you to find who killed Gwen. That much should be obvious," the judge snapped at me again. He then grabbed my shoulders to steady himself. This wasn't a good time or place to remind him that nothing is ever obvious when it comes to murder. "I'm sorry. This has been rough."

"I take it that you believe the sheriff isn't doing enough." I had arrived at the end of the judge's diatribe, so I missed the exact nature of his problem with the local authorities. My statement was an invitation for one or the other of the two adversaries to tell me what was going on. Captain Hammond cleared his throat to let me know not to push things too far.

"This has been coming for years. Sheriff Mazant's Office has never raised a finger to protect my daughter. Now Gwen's husband has finally killed her." Sheriff Mazant offered no rebuttal.

"So, this wasn't a car theft? Is her husband in custody?" I addressed this to the mute sheriff.

"Kirk is missing as well," the judge elaborated before Sheriff Mazant could open his mouth to speak. "Sheriff Mazant should be looking for him right now."

"Then why do you believe he killed Gwen?"

"The Donovans never get their own hands dirty, as you'll find out for yourself. I think Gwen's husband paid someone to kill her and to make it look like a car theft," Judge Rogers declared loud enough for everyone to hear.

"I am at your service." I assured him in hopes of quieting him down. People were beginning to stare.

Judge Rogers turned to Sheriff Mazant. "Are we clear about who runs things?"

"I always did figure the state police would have to handle this." The way Sheriff Mazant's jaw tightened as he responded to the judge warned me that I was climbing into a hornet's nest. Sides had been drawn and he undoubtedly believed I was Judge Rogers' quarterback. "We'll cooperate in any way we can."

"You'll do better than that. You will give Detective Holland whatever he wants from you whenever he asks for it, Sheriff Mazant," Judge Rogers snarled.

"Let's start with getting the car to the crime lab in Baton Rouge," I said and glanced at Captain Hammond. He nodded his agreement and would handle the logistics of getting the car moved.

"We're done here. Come with me, Detective." The judge turned abruptly and stormed up the muddy boat ramp. I barely caught up to him before he began speaking again. "Gwen's only part of why you're here. Drive me into town so I can explain the rest in private."

Two

We had to pass a gauntlet of reporters as we made our way to where I was parked. The TV and radio reporters expected the brush off the judge gave them, and they accepted it as both a part of the job and as a courtesy to a man who was obviously having the worst day of his life. One female reporter, however, decided to stick to us like a tick the entire way to my car. She was not very tall, slender, and in good athletic shape by the way she kept pace with us. Her dark hair was in a ponytail and her voice was quite direct.

"Judge Rogers, what can you tell me about your daughter's disappearance? Does the sheriff believe Kirk killed her?" the woman demanded to know as she fell in step beside him. The judge turned to show her more respect than her questions did his grief.

"I won't speculate about that," he said, but I already knew he had a definite opinion on the matter.

"Who is this that you're walking with? Is he a police officer?"

"This is Detective Holland from the state police. Feel free to pester him all you want, but leave me alone. Detective, this is Crystal Franks. She owns the local newspaper, which makes her someone you need to avoid at all costs." The familiarity between them caught my attention, but I ought not to have been surprised that he knew the reporter by name.

"Any comment, Detective?" she moved to fall in step with me.

"The state police has an entire department that handles making comments. Please direct your questions to them." I knew that I would be expected to abide by the strict code of silence Chief Avery at NOPD and my captain at the state police placed me under after my first couple of comments to the press when I arrived in New Orleans. We left her pouting in the rain.

Judge Rogers also made no comment about the vanity license plates on my supercharged Cadillac XLR. The deep red coupe bears plates that read COP CAR because there is no other way to make it look like one.

You can't mount a light bar on a convertible and the coupe's lack of a back seat for transporting prisoners complicates its use as a patrol car. I drive it because it is very fast and tends to get overlooked by anyone looking for a police car in their rear view mirror. I also lie about having seized it from a drug dealer when I tell the corner boys in New Orleans why they should give up selling dope.

The paved road at the end of the dirt lane led into the biggest town in the parish, as does nearly every other highway there. Saint Xavier Parish is a small link in the chain of thinly populated parishes stretching along the Gulf of Mexico between the Mississippi River and the Atchafalaya Basin. Donovan is the seat of the parish government and the headquarters of the Donovan family's business empire. Judge Rogers was warning more than joking when he claimed that there are more alligators in Saint Xavier Parish than people, and the gators are friendlier. The parish lacks the cultural and political diversity of Orleans Parish and shares a particular sort of rural existence with the place my father left home to escape. It is that timeless dynamic of the haves and have-nots, where your dead ancestors' financial and social positions pre-determine your own opportunities.

Judge Rogers told me how Gwendolyn Rogers Donovan suffered the drunken wrath of the son of one of the state's longest-serving Republican senators before her blood allegedly wound up in the trunk of her own Mercedes. He detailed hospital visits made over the past twenty years, and the unwillingness of a long string of Senator Donovan's handpicked sheriffs and judges to intervene in the obviously abusive marriage. Gwendolyn endured the abuse in exchange for the comfortable lifestyle in which she raised the couple's only child, a daughter named Belle, who was currently enrolled at Tulane.

Judge Rogers began giving me directions along the town's foggy pre-dawn streets once we crossed the drawbridge over Bayou Beausejour. Ornate cast iron light poles still lit the divided main street as we passed a row of bed and breakfasts occupying many of the town's few surviving antebellum mansions. Shops in the downtown's two-storey brick storefronts were almost all named after the town rather than their owners. Our drive ended in front of a sizeable white two-storey Colonial-style home at the edge of town. It abutted the apparently omnipresent waters of Bayou Beausejour and the Intercoastal Waterway.

"Nice place," I commented as I circled the crushed shell driveway to park behind the judge's Lincoln Navigator.

"You can stay here as long as you need," Judge Rogers told me as he got out of the car. "I don't have much use for it these days. I grew up in this house and let my daughter and her family live here while Kirk built them a place out by his family's country club this past year. You will get tired of hearing the terms 'his family' and 'the Donovans' after you've been here awhile. The Donovans own everything of real value, and control who gets to have anything else."

The house seemed like a comfortable place to raise a family, but it was long overdue for an update. The furniture had fallen out of style long before I had graduated from LSU and entered the Army. I wondered if one could still get parts for most of the kitchen appliances. A stack of old DVDs beside the chunky 1990's era JVC television added to the almost museum-quality setting. All the same, the heart-pine floors were well maintained and the over-abundance of badly dated wallpaper was resisting the peeling and seam discoloration of age.

An enclosed sunroom off the living room would provide a clear view of the Intercoastal Waterway once the fog cleared. Hedges blocked the pool and patio from direct view, but I could explore the expansive premises at my leisure. The judge seemed to be uncomfortable in his own house, as if it held bad memories he didn't want to face just then. I was curious to see a number of family photos still hanging on the wall ascending the stairway. One of them was of a young naval cadet in his dress whites.

"I didn't know you had served in the Navy," I idly commented.

"Sixty-nine to seventy-two, as a corpsman."

"Vietnam?"

"Two tours were enough. I served with the Third Marines at Quang Tri."

"I imagine one tour there would have been enough," I was only generally aware of how bad things were going in Vietnam during those years.

Judge Rogers was not interested in swapping war stories. "I will expect frequent updates on what you find, but I promise not to hound you."

We both knew he lacked the capacity to leave me in peace. I took a seat on the staircase and asked him the question that had bothered me since I had arrived at the crime scene.

"Why me, Your Honor? I know you think I can somehow ignore the Donovans' influence here, but there are plenty of experienced homicide detectives available, and you appear willing to accept that your daughter is dead. What are you really asking me to do?" I was not challenging him or refusing to do his bidding.

"I know this isn't what you normally handle, but you have a reputation for getting to the bottom of things," he complimented me. He followed this with what I took to be his real motivation. "I am certain that someone in the Donovan family killed my daughter and I want you to pay the whole lot of them back."

"I'm not in the revenge business, Your Honor." I was not about to take the judge literally.

"Revenge, justice, call it what you will. I want you to make the Donovans' lives miserable until you can arrest at least one of them for Gwen's death," Judge Rogers demanded in his deepest courtroom baritone. He tossed the house key onto the kitchen counter. "And avoid Crystal Franks at all costs. She and my daughter were close friends, and I am sure she intends to try this case in the local newspaper long before you solve it."

"Understood." I assured him.

"I guess that's everything. Please don't make a big mess while you're staying here." I was not sure if this was his way of telling me to leave my dog in New Orleans or not, so I said nothing.

I was not going to leave a seventy-pound pit bull to roam about my own apartment for weeks on end while I was out here. I hoped to be back in New Orleans in less than a month, maybe half that if Gwen Donovan's body and her husband both turned up soon. I also accepted that ruffling a few feathers on the judge's behalf was about the only way I had to fill my time until either a dead body or a live suspect popped up.

Three

I scoped out the house for an hour after the judge left. There were still a few personal items belonging to Kirk and his family, but I got the impression that these were items they never had any intention of taking with them. This included some well-used cookware and kitchen utensils I was glad to have. The heated pool and pool house were located about thirty yards from the house, down a paver stone walkway and within sight of where the bayou merged with the Intercoastal Waterway.

I wanted to give Judge Rogers a decent head start before following him back to New Orleans. I had a lot of things to gather for what promised to be an extended stay. There were also things I needed to do and people I needed to see before I made this my base of operations.

A light tan Dodge Charger patrol car blocked the street end of the driveway as I tried to leave the property. The occupant flipped on the red and blue lights atop the vehicle and shone his spotlight at my windshield as I made my way out of the circular driveway. This was meant to blind me to who was in the car. The cruiser was parked with its grille at a sharp angle, perhaps in anticipation of being rammed. Whoever was getting out of the far side of the sedan obviously had no idea what replacing the front end on a Cadillac costs these days.

The officer turned off the lights atop his car but left me bathed in the beam of the spotlight mounted on his car door as he approached my car. I had the top up on the coupe because of the lingering rain.

"Step out of the vehicle," the cop demanded. He looked to be roughly sixty and stood about my height, but outweighed me by at least seventy pounds of muscle. His hair was cut short and looked to be held in place with some sort of shiny gel. His brown eyes were wary and the edges of his lips showed the tension in his body. His beefy hand was wrapped around the stainless steel Smith and Wesson revolver holstered high on his right hip. I eased out of the coupe very slowly and kept my hands where he could see them as I set my car keys on the hood and turned to face him.

"I'm a state police detective. My name is Cooter Holland," I explained with as little expression in my voice as possible. This was not the time or place to debate jurisdictions with this particular officer. He used his left hand to turn me towards my car and proceeded to pat me down as though he had not heard a word that I said.

"Why aren't you driving a patrol car?"

"This is what I use." The explanation sounded lame even to me. He tugged the badge and ID from my belt and told me to get back in my vehicle. The officer either ignored or missed seeing my Glock 20 handgun wedged between the driver's seat and center console.

He sat in his patrol car to have a ten minute radio conversation before he returned. "Your story checks out. I guess we'll be seeing more of one another. I'm the Police Chief. My name is Chief Theriot. I can spell that for you if you need."

"Oh, I'm pretty sure I can remember who you are." I assured him.

"You'll want to tread real light around here while you're trying to find that judge's daughter. Kirk Donovan is a popular fella and his family draws a lot of water, if you know what I mean. You don't want to start spreading no rumors." I made mental notes that he was aware of why I was in town, and that I assumed Kirk Donovan was behind Gwendolyn Rogers' disappearance. It made me all the more curious about who he had spoken with over the radio.

"I know exactly what you mean. It's why Judge Rogers insisted the local police departments not be who investigates his daughter's disappearance. I'm pretty sure you were sent as a welcoming committee to remind me who runs this town because of that. Tell whoever sent you that the warning is duly noted. You can also tell them that I am not about to fight you, but I am not going to let you interfere in my investigation, either." The line about not fighting him was only half true. I had already decided which hand I would use to strike his windpipe and how to dislocate his left kneecap if the necessity arose.

The smugness crept from his face when he realized I wasn't going to be run out of town as easily as he thought. I didn't use his name or position because I wasn't about to let him believe either of these had any relevance to me. The parish-level sheriff was my only real hurdle, not the town's traffic cop.

"It sure would be tragic if we had to tussle," the police chief persisted. He was just dumb enough to think he'd win because of his size. He wasn't the biggest man I had ever tangled with, but I doubted that he ever fought a man trained to fight the same way I was.

I retrieved my car keys and badge and returned to the sanctuary of my coupe. I started the car and revved the coupe's supercharged engine a bit before I moved the gear shift into drive. He took the hint and backed his patrol car out of my path before I could push it aside.

Four

The Louisiana State Police had hastily assigned me to the discretionary use of the New Orleans Police Department the day I received my detective's badge. This morning was the most time I had spent with my captain at the state police in over a month. I usually divide my time between the cases NOPD's Chief of Detectives, Bill Avery, trusts me to handle and being the co-owner of a Creole-Italian bistro named Strada Ammazarre. My partner, a talented Italian-Iraqi chef, and I trust our maître d to run the place, so all chef Tony has to do is cook and all I have to do is eat and drink for free. My apartment being above the restaurant provides Chief Avery an excuse to discuss work with me over breakfast most days of the week.

"Judge Rogers called me out to Saint Xavier Parish to lead the investigation into his daughter's disappearance," I informed the bulky chief as Miss J, the bistro's sous chef, began setting freshly fried beignets generously dusted with powdered sugar beside the plate of prosciutto-wrapped cantaloupe on the chef's table, which sat in a niche opposite from the cook's line. There is a waiting list for a seat there at supper time, and a pricey menu as well.

"I know. Captain Hammond called to let me know Judge Rogers personally requested that you be assigned," Avery chuckled in the way he does when he is enjoying a private joke.

"What's so funny?" I demanded. Avery finished chewing a mouthful of beignet before he answered.

"The Donovans have as much sway in Baton Rouge as your own momma's family does. I think the judge wants to use you because of that. Captain Hammond sounded like he wants to be as far from this as possible. He was quick to remind me that you are my responsibility and not his." He was laughing because any influence my mother's family's holds in Baton Rouge does not extend to me. Their power lies with the family's male descendants and my connection to the Deveraux family is through my mother.

Avery leaned back in his seat to allow Miss J to slide a four-egg crawfish etouffee omelet and about a pound of shredded hash browns smothered in red gravy in front of him. My own serving of eggs Benedict looked paltry by comparison.

"Well, the judge is expecting me to keep poking the Donovans in the eye until one of them is arrested for his daughter's murder. What do you know about them?"

"Not all that much beyond the fact they own Saint Xavier Parish. Literally. I also know the judge hated that his daughter married into their family. He has had to watch the way her husband mistreats her without being able to do a thing about it. The old man in that family is the one to watch out for. He has the police and local judges in his pocket and decides what passes for justice. If he declares Gwendoline committed suicide, and then dumped herself in the trunk of her own car, that will be their official version."

"I met the police chief on my way out of town. This could get interesting."

Avery sighed at the thought of how messy the word 'interesting' can become when I am involved. I focused on eating my eggs before they got cold.

"Have you told Katie any of this yet?" Avery seemed determined to bring up every possible problem I could have with the case.

"No. Let's face it, there's not much either one of us can do about this. Judge Rogers expects me to live out there until he's satisfied that he knows what happened."

"You need to be looking for a way to make her okay with this," my boss suggested. It was sound advice from a happily married lawman.

Five

Katie was due in court at ten o'clock. I caught her walking into the courthouse from her office and tried to fit everything I needed to say into the time it took to walk the short distance between the lobby and the courtroom. I know how much she hates having her pre-trial rituals tampered with, and noted that her long auburn hair was tightly braided into what I think of as her war bonnet.

"I have a case that means I have to leave town for a while." I tried opening with something she could not ignore. Her pace slowed, but she kept walking. "Judge Rogers' daughter is missing. Her car was found with blood in the trunk and it seems likely she was murdered and her body dumped somewhere out in Saint Xavier Parish."

"That's terrible," Katie frowned and slowed a bit more. "I was in her older sister's class at Sacred Heart. Magdalena introduced us when Gwendolyn started her freshman year. Gwendolyn dropped out of school during her sophomore year to marry Kirk. She was pregnant so there was no big wedding, as you might imagine. I was sadder that she was going to have live in that crummy town than I was that she was pregnant."

"You've been to Donovan?" We had been dating for less than a year. This was not so long that we lacked the ability to still surprise one another with details from our pasts.

"A couple of times. Just so you know, I went to law school with their District Attorney. His name is Henri Gabouri. We called him Milquetoast because he was lousy in mock court. He'll be of no help." She finally stopped walking and faced me.

"Thanks for the tips," I chuckled and made a mental note. I did not like the odds of Henri Gabouri convicting a member of the Donovan family for murder in Saint Xavier Parish if he failed so spectacularly at pretend court in law school. I liked Katie's connection to Gwen even less.

"Hammond made you the lead detective on this?" Katie sounded as impressed as she was concerned. The little she knew of my previous cases probably made my involvement with something this important and sensitive seem unwise.

"Judge Rogers insisted on my being assigned. I get the impression that he will be intimately involved in the investigation." I wanted to emphasize that the judge was the one responsible for our being separated. Katie knew better than to disparage the wishes of any judge before whom she might appear.

"Which means you really have no idea when you will be done or back in town." The succinctness of her at-work voice makes it hard to gauge her emotional reaction to bad news.

"I will drive back every chance I get, and you can come hang out on the weekends." I wanted to offer something positive or at least consoling.

"I work for a living, mister. I don't have weekends," she was quick to point out. Then she laughed and kissed me on the cheek before she opened the courtroom door. She took another step and then turned to ask me one more question. "Are you taking Roux or dumping him in my back yard?"

"I will need the company, and the backup. The locals don't seem real happy to have me around."

"So you've already turned them against you? You are getting really good at this whole pissing people off thing."

"The locals aren't real friendly to start with. You can almost hear the banjos playing when you step out of your car." The reference to Deliverance is an overused cliché, but it is often accurate, which is the essence of a cliché.

"Call me when you can, and do try to play nice with the local cops. I won't count on you making it back for the parade on Saturday. I'll survive, even if you don't." She forced a smile but I knew my presence was still expected. She was riding in the city's largest Saint Patrick's Day parade in honor of having once reigned as its queen.

There was a far greater chance of our relationship surviving my missing the parade than there was of my becoming best pals with the police chief or the sheriff in Saint Xavier Parish. I took her comment about getting along with them as a joke and not as advice.

Six

I decided to visit with Belle Donovan while I was still in town. I was the lead detective in the investigation, so the duty of informing her of her parents' situations fell to me. Enough time had already transpired that someone else she knew might have taken it upon themselves to tell the young woman that her mother was probably dead and the police were searching for her father. Receiving this sort of news is an especially lousy way to start anyone's morning, especially someone as young as Belle.

I made my way to Tulane University and parked in front of Gibson Hall. I headed to the Registrar's Office on the first floor to ask for their help in locating Belle.

"Good morning, Amy." I slid my badge slowly across the counter towards the young blonde woman whose nametag identified her as a student worker.

"Oh, my," she squealed. "Is something wrong?'

Her head snapped around to lock eyes with one of the adult staff. I tried to appear as unthreatening as possible, but the presence of the state police on any college campus seldom proves to be a good omen.

"How may I help you, Detective?" the older woman asked with just the right balance of reserve and respect to let me know she was still making up her mind about the level of cooperation to provide.

"I need to speak with one of your students, Belle Donovan. It is a family emergency. Belle is in no trouble."

"I wouldn't say that, Detective," The woman's nametag read Miss Davis. I had no trouble reading it as she pressed her hands onto the counter between us and leaned towards me until I took one step back. "Miss Donovan has not been in any of her classes since last Thursday. I was actually rather hopeful that you were bringing us news of her whereabouts."

"Have you reached out to her family about this?" I was hopeful they had, because it would give me a date and time someone spoke with one or the other of her missing parents.

"She's an adult and is free to make her own decisions. We would not contact her parents unless we had good reason to think there was something amiss. I'm sure you missed a few classes as a college sophomore as well, did you not?"

"A few," I chuckled. I almost flunked out of LSU my very first semester. "I hate to say this, but something may be amiss."

"Oh?" It was becoming obvious that she was the one doing the interrogating.

"The state police and local authorities are looking for both of her parents. We recovered her mother's car early this morning in a condition that leaves Belle's grandfather very concerned for her mother's well-being." I left plenty of room between the lines.

"What can we do to help?" Miss Davis sounded ready to organize search teams of her own if asked to do so now that she grasped the situation.

"I guess getting her class schedule is unnecessary. Can you steer me towards her dorm?"

"Oh, Belle lives off campus," Amy spoke up and then acted as if she ought to have kept silent.

"Can you give me the address? Do you know her personally?" I tried to not act like I was prying the information out of her. I could likely find the address by pulling up Belle's driver's license on my computer.

"Everyone knows where Belle's place is," Amy sort of laughed as she wrote down the address on a piece of scratch paper. "I guess you'd call it a party house. At least there is some sort of party there every weekend. She usually dates one of the jocks so everyone winds up there at some point."

"So, she's not in a sorority?" I didn't think the sororities likely appreciated the competition for available jocks to window-dress their own gatherings.

"Um, no," Amy giggled. There was a long story behind her response, but it wasn't one that was likely to help me find Belle or explain why her entire family was missing. My sister had not joined a sorority, either, and she turned out fine.

"Do you know where I could find her current guy?" I didn't get the impression 'boyfriend' was the right term.

"You want to talk to Bradley Ladd. They aren't dating, but he knows her best. He eats lunch over at The Boot. Don't call him Brad. He hates that his names rhyme." Amy was very well informed.

"Ah, The Boot," I sighed at my own memories of the bar and grill that sits barely outside of the campus gates. It has fed, watered, and intoxicated many generations of Tulane and Loyola students. This history included my sister and Katie.

"Then I guess you won't be needing directions for how to get there," Miss Davis smirked and returned to doing whatever our conversation had interrupted. I thanked Miss Amy for her help and walked across campus rather than try to find a closer parking space at that time of day.

Seven

The brick building on Broadway houses a pair of local landmarks. The Boot is a typical college bar and grill: a low-ceilinged open space backed by a long wooden bar with its varnish worn away over the years by over-served college students leaning on it for support in the wee hours of the morning, and a small kitchen in the back that pushes out burgers and fried appetizers just as fast as it can. Nobody steps through the door looking for a quality drinking or dining experience. The second floor houses The Mushroom, which was once the best head shop in town. It is Nostalgia Central for alumni, and a must-see for any freshman students who grew up hearing stories about the place from parents and older siblings.

The Boot's daytime bartender was a friend of the lone male bartender at Strada Ammazarre. He was kind enough to point me towards a table packed bicep-to-bicep with athletic looking young men when I asked if he knew Bradley Ladd.

Bradley was handsome in that way frat boys, scholarship athletes, and pre-law students in their twenties tend to be. He probably wouldn't be at Tulane if he had the sort of criminal record it takes to not worry about a detective looking for him. That's why his ambivalent reaction to my presence struck me as more than a little curious.

"Can we talk outside for a minute?" I motioned for him to head through the open French doors facing the tables on the concrete sidewalk.

"Sure thing." He shrugged and set down his roast beef po-boy. The others at the table gave me a sideways glance but kept their heads down in case I had a list of people to question.

"I'm looking for Belle Donovan. I understand you two are close." I saw no reason to give him anything more to work with. I was here to get information, not to share it.

"I haven't seen Belle since Thursday. She said she had something to do that night so we couldn't hang out." Bradley sounded unconcerned, as if this were not an unusual thing for her to do or say.

"No details on what that was?"

He paused. It was a pause I believed had to do with trying to remember details and not a story he was supposed to tell when I asked this question.

"I remember it involved her father. Belle has been writing a paper on her family for one of her journalism classes. She said that her father was making it as hard as possible for her to do her research. He called her a half dozen times on Thursday, and I know their conversations got her pretty upset. Belle would never tell me what was going on. She called Gwen after one, but that didn't do much to calm her down, either."

"You call her mother Gwen? Are you two close, as well?" I assumed he didn't think I was implying anything beyond a friendship.

"It's what Belle calls her mother. She calls both her parents by their first names," he explained and then chuckled a bit. "She always calls her grandfather Rogers 'Grandpa' and her grandfather Donovan 'Chester.'"

"Have you ever met Belle's father or either of her grandfathers?" I wondered.

"Neither of her parents come to the city to see Belle." Bradley may have considered this to be an answer, but I was looking for something more along the lines of Yes or No.

"And she has never taken you out to see them?"

"No, she has not," he insisted a little too forcefully. I saw no reason for him to be defensive either way about meeting Belle's family.

"Well, call me if anything else comes to mind. Better yet, have Belle call me when you hear from her." I handed him one of my business cards. I wasn't going to sit by the phone waiting for either of them to call. I was, though, curious about how little interest he showed in my locating Belle, or concerned about her situation. Bradley was worth having someone follow for a day or so, but it was unlikely Captain Hammond or Chief Avery could be persuaded to assign anyone to do so based on this brief conversation. Bradley struck me as being someone who had been waiting for me to interview him about Belle's disappearance. He also seemed oddly unconcerned that a woman he just admitted to being one of the last to see was missing along with both of her parents. He must not have watched many true-crime shows on television.

I drove past Belle's address. The overflowing mailbox told me knocking on the door was a waste of time. I walked around the house, but there was nothing like the scent of a dead body or anything else out of the ordinary. Belle wasn't even on the list of people I was supposed to find, so I chose not to add finding her to my to-do list.

Eight

I drove back to Strada Ammazarre and explained the situation yet again, this time to my business partner Chef Tony Venzo. Tony and I met while working on a classified intelligence operation in Baghdad from 2003 to 2005. The mission ended in an ambush that nearly cost me my life, and ultimately led the two of us here. The chef listened to my description of the crime scene, to what Judge Rogers was asking of me, and to my apology for having no idea when I would be back without asking a single question or making any other interruption.

"You aren't just to be his face," Tony deduced.

"Eyes and ears, not face," I corrected my foreign-born friend's latest attempt at a colloquialism. "And I think you are right. The judge knows my reputation for knocking things over and probably does have something else up his sleeve. There are state police detectives far more capable of handling this case. Working alone in a place I have never been does not increase the odds of my finding his daughter's murderer."

"What do you think Judge Rogers really wants?" The chef made a series of hand gestures to the cooks working behind me that kept the kitchen moving along.

"No idea. He hates the local cops. He hates his son-in-law and he hates the entire Donovan family. I think he just wants me to be a thorn in everyone's side until it's worth it to them to let me solve the case so I will leave. That's the best I have come with in the short time I've had to think about it." I needed to see if Tony might offer any opinions or ideas, even though his job no longer involves solving any puzzles I share with him. We were a formidable pair of intelligence officers in our day, but my friend has found a new way to channel his intellect and keep his adrenaline running, leaving me to hunt down bad people on my own.

I was surprised to encounter my mother and Roger, the live-in boyfriend she refuses to publicly acknowledge as such, leaving the dining room as I walked out of the the kitchen. She only rarely leaves the home she restored in the Rigolets near Slidell after Hurricane Katrina.

"This is a surprise," I said as she allowed me to give her a small hug, and I shook hands with Roger. My sister and I consider him to be our hero, as he has occupied our mother's attention, which she would otherwise focus upon us. He came into our lives as a dog trainer who worked with Roux after the now cheerful pit bull fatally mauled its previous owner.

"We have lunch here all the time." My mother showed no remorse for this bald face lie.

"Sure you do," I responded. "Why today?"

"Do I need a reason to spend money in my son's place of business?" she challenged me. I was in too much of a hurry to remind her she had never paid for a meal, including this lunch.

"Of course not. I was only curious about why you were in the city."

"Oh, we had some shopping to do," she said and waved a hand like this was not worth talking about. "I hear you have a new case. Are you really looking for Senator Donovan's daughter-in-law?"

"I have been for less than twelve hours. Who told you? Uncle Felix?" I was always impressed with how well informed she was about my life and work.

"Oh, you know I never divulge my sources," she laughed. Roger and I exchanged grins and I let the whole thing slide by. I had work to do. "I only wanted to drop by to remind you what your father used to say."

"My father said a lot of things," I needlessly reminded her of my father's taste for aphorisms.

"This one was to look at the bigger picture to find where all the parts fit." I suspected that she made the trip into the city simply to tell me this. Her making a point to speak with me was now going to be one of the parts I needed to consider in this bigger picture.

"Well, tell your brother I would appreciate his staying out of this, and would also like him to keep the senator on the sidelines."

"I'll be sure to mention it the next time I speak with him. I believe you might see him before I do," my mother promised. She was already headed for the door, satisfied that what she had heard about my being assigned to the case was correct, and to steering me in what she considered to be the right direction.

Nine

Bradley's reaction to the news of both Belle and Gwen Donovan being missing gave me something to distract myself with while driving back to Donovan from the French Quarter. It was barely an hour's drive from the bistro to Judge Rogers' house at a speed only slightly above the posted seventy mile an hour speed limit, but the drive transported me to a whole other place. I explain to tourists who dine in Strada Ammazarre that they need to get out of the French Quarter to see New Orleans, to venture out of New Orleans to experience Louisiana, and to leave the state to enter the South. I had the sinking feeling that I was about to test my own theory.

I drove back to Donovan in my Cadillac CTS-V station wagon because I had so much to drag with me for an indefinite stay. The most important items were the coolers full of beer and groceries. The largest item was the metal kennel I use to transport Roux. I set the cage in the kitchen's dining nook and led Roux on an exploratory tour of the house before locking him back in the kennel so I could finish unloading the car.

I had brought one medium sized duffle bag of clothes, as well as some additional items, including a large rigid plastic case packed with an assortment of weapons. I wasn't anticipating a major firefight, but my PTSD tends to make me over-prepared when it comes to defending myself. A smaller metal case held the cameras I needed to place the judge's house under constant surveillance. I was deeply concerned about the interest the local police seemed to have in my presence.

Establishing a secure perimeter was going to have to wait until I returned from sitting down with the local sheriff. I held little hope that he was going to be any friendlier than Chief Theriot. I fully understood they were both likely to be looking for a way to send me packing, but I was not just another interloper in their world. I was someone they couldn't get rid of with their usual intimidation tactics and they certainly were not prepared for my own intimidation tactics if it came to that.

Sheriff Mazant and his deputies worked out of a cinder block and brick building located a couple of blocks from the courthouse. It was built with high windows meant to provide natural light without any view. The jail windows were made of glass block that no prisoner could break through unnoticed. Captain Hammond's white Acadia was parked in front of the building and I wondered why he was still in town. The double glass front doors were gilt-lettered with Sheriff Edgar Mazant's name on both doors. The lobby windows looked out on the front parking lot and the waxed and buffed linoleum entryway floor tiles dated the building's construction to the late 1960s. The thick laminated glass divider separating anyone coming into the building from the trio of armed deputies greeting them was a post-9/11 addition. The radio chatter between the dispatchers and patrol officers used the local Cajun patois and gave me a headache. I speak four languages with the accent of a native, but I doubt I could ever master this dialect of French.

I introduced myself to the female deputy at the front desk and showed her my ID and badge before she was satisfied that my presence warranted bothering her boss. She buzzed me through the solid steel door to the left of the window and pointed out Sheriff Mazant's private office at the far end of a corridor. A young female deputy was sitting behind the desk outside of Sheriff Mazant's office and I repeated the ritual of identifying myself. She was polite, but she was also in no hurry to allow me to enter the inner sanctum.

"Sheriff? There's a state police detective here to see you," she informed her boss over the intercom. He asked for my name and I heard a muffled conversation over the open intercom line before she stood up to open the door behind her.

Sheriff Mazant was sitting behind his metal desk as I entered the office. He looked to be in his fifties, a full head shorter than six foot and a little overweight, but not nearly as out of shape as Chief Avery. Mazant dressed his department in the stiff coal-black twill uniforms favored by SWAT teams on television and Federales in sunny Mexico. Sheriff Mazant wore the same uniform as his deputies, but his was tailored and its creases were heavily starched. Sheriff Mazant did not offer to shake my hand or bother to step from behind his desk. He simply motioned for me to take a seat in the chair beside a visibly subdued Captain

Hammond.

"I've been expecting you. Chief Theriot tells me you are going to be staying at Judge Rogers' place. You can't sneak around here and not be noticed." Sheriff Mazant seemed rather smug about knowing something nobody was hiding.

"The state police routinely investigates cases such as this and Judge Rogers has asked me to keep him informed of the progress I make in locating his daughter. Where I stay while I do that is hardly a secret, nor is it anyone's business but mine and Judge Rogers' since it is his house." I wanted him to understand I didn't need his permission to do my job.

"Here's the thing," Sheriff Mazant said and gave us both a smug grin. "I didn't really like those other boys from Baton Rouge that were nosing around the scene this morning. They asked a lot of questions about the Donovans I felt had nothing to do with this at all."

"So, the investigation is going to be limited to things that make you feel good?" I challenged him before that piece of my brain that is supposed to check what I say kicked in.

"Are all of the state's detectives smart-mouthed jackasses?" Sheriff Mazant snarled at my captain. The two detectives he mentioned must have also upset his delicate sensibilities.

"Detective Holland is on permanent assignment in New Orleans, Sheriff. He has picked up some bad habits." Captain Hammond spoke up. This was as close to an apology as Sheriff Mazant could expect, and was the full extent of my boss correcting my behavior. "I am glad he came by, though. It is important that the two of you get to know one another and work something out, because he's absolutely correct that Judge Rogers asked me to assign him to this case."

"Is that how you decide who handles cases?" Mazant asked in an attempt to turn my earlier comment around.

"It certainly was this time," Hammond shrugged. He is not noted for his sense of humor, and I have never heard genuine sarcasm cross his lips, but this was clearly meant to be a provocation. Sheriff Mazant's reaction involved squinting his eyes and gnashing his teeth before he let out a calming breath. "I've already pulled those other two detectives, but Detective Holland is staying here until he solves this whether you work with him or not."

Captain Hammond's show of indifference was for Sheriff Mazant's sake, not mine. He stood up and started to leave me alone with Mazant. The look Hammond gave me as he put his back to Sheriff Mazant approached outright glee. Captain Hammond's trust in my ability to wear out my welcome was the most likely source of this private delight. I sensed there was some sort of personal history between Sheriff Mazant and my captain.

"I can deal with having just one of your wise crackers here," Sheriff Mazant decided as he ushered Hammond out of his office. I kept my mouth shut until Sheriff Mazant was back in his seat and began trying to stare me down. "Tell me about yourself, Detective."

Sheriff Mazant couldn't hide that he was searching for any weaknesses he could exploit. I began cherry-picking my way through my resume.

"Well, my dad was the Chief of Detectives at NOPD," I said to let him start understanding his miscalculation in believing he was going to impede me. "My mom didn't need to work because she was the only daughter of Albert Deveraux. You might have heard the family's name if you know anything about Baton Rouge."

"I have heard the name," Sheriff Mazant said in an abruptly subdued voice. Albert Deveraux was legal counsel to a half dozen state governors and dozens of state senators, as were his father and grandfather. My mother's brothers are all political creatures as well, with my Uncle Felix still considered to be the state's best political fixer. I was expected to join his firm after college, but joined the Army instead. He has never forgiven me for that.

"I served in the Special Forces and did some intelligence work in the Middle East before I moved home after Hurricane Katrina and joined the state police." This was a short version of half my life, but it had the desired effect of making Sheriff Mazant see Captain Hammond had bested him in his own horse trade.

"I assume you've handled some other homicide investigations." This was his last chance to keep me in check. I could tell he was hoping I had not.

"New Orleans is the state's murder capital." This was not responsive to his question. I needed him to believe my investigation record included more than the one homicide Avery let me pursue. The truth is, that investigation, into the murder of a convicted cop killer, never made it to court.

"You won't mind if I pair you with one of our own detectives, will you? You can think of him as being your local liaison." Sheriff Mazant did not wait for my response to his question before he used the intercom to summon the detective he had in mind. I actually liked the idea of having a guide with a better idea of how treacherous this terrain was. Knowing he would also be a spy for Sheriff Mazant didn't bother me all that much.

"You have enough crime that you need to have full time detectives?" I meant only a little disrespect. I was at a loss for the sort of crimes anyone felt comfortable committing in a town controlled quite so tightly by one family. Justice has a way of becoming selective and getting replaced with sheer brutality in places like this.

"Detective Chance worked over in Texas before he joined our force. He has solved over thirty cases since he joined us." Sheriff Mazant wanted me to be clear on who he believed should be running this investigation.

"He sounds like a good partner." This sounded like a lie even to me.

The detective Mazant called to his office was a statue. I say this not to be unkind, but the detective had all the personality of a big block of marble. He was a nearly expressionless white guy whose roughly six foot height ended abruptly in a blonde flat-top haircut. He was dressed in a brand new khaki-colored poplin summer weight suit he probably bought at a department store in the mall over in Lafayette and wore home rather than having it properly fitted.

"Detective Holland, is it, this is Detective Chance. You can call him David. Don't call him Dave, he hates that."

"Does he speak for himself at some point?" I asked to get Sheriff Mazant to stop speaking for his man.

"I like this one," Detective Chance declared in a voice he might use if he were choosing a puppy, or something from a pastry case.

"Doesn't matter. You two are partners. Now go find Gwen Donovan's body and whoever killed her." Sheriff Mazant waved us out of his office. He did not seem the least bit satisfied with how his plan to control the investigation was going so far. I was sure he had some calls to make to let the people, or maybe just the one person, actually running his office know where things stood as the first day of Gwen Donovan's disappearance began winding down.

"How are things between your department and the local police chief?" I asked Sheriff Mazant before I left his office. "He introduced himself as I was leaving town this morning."

"We get along fine, but he doesn't have much authority around here. He hands out parking and traffic tickets and serves legal papers and evictions for the DA. Albert was a damn reliable investigator and officer when he worked for this department." Sheriff Mazant sounded fond of Chance's predecessor, and more than a little sad for him. It also made sense that the police chief worked for Sheriff Mazant once upon a time.

"How'd he get from your department to his own?" I assumed he was elected to the office.

"Albert used to be a cage wrestler, probably about twenty years ago. A couple of your troopers tried to arrest him on a DUI up on I-10 and he beat one of them up so bad he never went back to work. The sheriff at the time, Sheriff Dardenne, agreed to fire Albert rather than have the state trooper he beat up sue the department. The city council appointed Albert to be the police chief about six months after Sheriff Dardenne let him go. He married a widow lady from over in Morgan City a few years back and that seems to have made him a lot calmer guy to be around." Sheriff Mazant's casual explanation made my entire day crystal clear. Sheriff Mazant needed to interfere with my investigation into a grisly murder that implicated the son of a state senator, and Chief Theriot figured I was another state cop he could get away with beating to a pulp. Assigning me to this case was some long-awaited revenge for the aggravation I have put my captain through.

"Having David around to deal with the locals might be a good thing," I grinned good-naturedly and extended my hand.

"Time will tell, Detective. Only time will tell," Sheriff Mazant sighed and gave my hand the briefest touch. The detective opened the door and led the way out of the office and through the building. I couldn't ignore the way the deputies glanced at us before burying their heads in something else.

"You a popular guy around here, David?" I finally had to ask.

"Beats me. I don't hang out with these guys very much." I had no idea where to begin dissecting his response and let it drop into the growing file of things to consider later.

"Do you know where we could get a cold beer and figure out how we're going to make this work?" I really needed a drink right then.

"I don't drink on duty," David said. At least he didn't admonish me for making the suggestion.

"How about a nice place to eat?" I knew I was just far enough west on I-10 to get real Cajun food.

"I used to eat at Johnny's, but I broke up with one of their waitresses last week. I don't think I am welcome there anymore," Detective Chance sighed. He sounded a lot more hungry than lonely over that situation.

"You're striking out as a guide, David," I tried to joke.

"My job is catching bad guys, not giving you some grand tour," Detective Chance grumbled with surprising hostility. It was going to be a painfully long investigation if I had to spend every minute with a humorless gargoyle carrying a chip on his shoulder.

"Sheriff Mazant was bragging on you in there. He says you have solved thirty cases since you've been here. What sort of cases are we talking about? Any homicides?"

"Shoplifting mostly. I arrest all the people they catch stealing out at the Walmart store." He was able to muster an impressive amount of pride in his arrest record.

"How about missing person cases? Handle any of those?" I wasn't expecting a positive response to this, and his wrinkled brow confirmed my fears.

"Not many people go missing around here. Most just move on." He endeavored to shrug off the point I was trying to make. He may have been trying to make one of his own.

"So, you're less of a guide than you are a hobble I have to wear while

I'm here." I didn't mean this to be cruel to the detective or his dedication to law enforcement. I was merely speaking aloud what I finally realized was behind Sheriff Mazant pairing the two of us.

"You can always go back to New Orleans," he suggested.

"No, I really can't. You, however, can meet me at Judge Rogers' house promptly at seven o'clock tomorrow morning. Bring every note, photo, and video your department gathered at the crime scene."

The detective didn't have a verbal response to me bossing him around. He displayed an unexpected immediate physical one instead. I didn't expect him to be a guy who would pout, but that was exactly what he did before he turned around and stomped back into the police station. I was going to be surprised if he chose to follow my instructions.

I gave up on the idea of bonding over a beer or a plate of jambalaya and drove to my temporary abode. I changed into jeans and a pullover fleece to clamber among the trees and porch posts to set up the wireless network of perimeter alarms and the array of night-vision-capable wireless cameras that were going to make it possible for me to sleep in any sort of peace.

It was dark by the time I finished testing and adjusting the cameras. I took a moment to check out the pool and pool house. The pool turned out to be filled with heated salt water. I could use it to stay in shape while I was stuck this far from my usual health club. The pool was as close to a silver lining as I had found after being handed a case the locals didn't seem very anxious to see solved, being lodged in a house last decorated when I was in high school, and having the local sheriff partner me with a humorless prick who seemed to be even less popular with his own department than I was.

Ten

Roux woke me at four in the morning. He jumped onto the bed and pushed at me until I opened one eye. The dog and I have agreed upon the times he gets to relieve himself and when I freshen the food and water in his bowls, so moments like this always mean he is warning me.

I pulled my Glock from under the mattress before rolling out of bed on the side opposite from the bedroom door rather than stand up. I checked to be sure there was a round in the chamber and the safety was off before I followed Roux out of the room. He glanced back twice as he led me towards the living room, patiently waiting as I cleared each room and hallway we came to in case the threat was already in the house with us. I knew Roux would have already taken defensive action if that were the case, but doing so is a habit I see no reason to break just because of having a well-trained guard dog.

I crouched before I entered the living room and went from window to window until I saw what had piqued Roux's interest. Chief Theriot was back, or had sent a deputy to watch the house.

I scratched Roux behind the ear to reward his diligence, but chose to simply note the time of day the local police chief planned to start watching me. I could tolerate this for a day or two before I was going to have to dissuade Chief Theriot in ways he wouldn't misinterpret. I didn't feel particularly safe knowing Theriot and his deputies would be constantly surveilling me.

Detective Chance arrived promptly at seven. He brought neither donuts nor coffee, so I offered him none of the coffee and breakfast I was preparing when I let him in the front door. I glanced past him and saw that the police chief's car was gone.

"Did you pass anyone as you pulled in?"

"There was nobody out there when I drove in. Do you think someone is staking you out?" The detective's thin smile seemed to indicate he knew about Police Chief Theriot's pre-dawn visit.

"I saw one of Chief Theriot's cars out there about four. It was still there when I went for a swim at five." The detective froze in his seat when Roux came into the kitchen and began sizing him up. Roux slowly walked around him with his head level with his backbone and his tail slightly tucked. The hair on Roux's back was not bristling so I assumed he saw Sheriff Mazant's man as no more of a serious threat than I did. I introduced them and the detective eased past the big pit bull and stood by the window to watch me cook my chorizo omelet and fried potatoes.

"Isn't it a bit cold for swimming?" Chance asked as he looked out the window and saw the wisps of fog. "Oh, it's heated. I guess you got the deluxe accommodations."

"More like the Ronald Reagan suite," I laughed and gestured towards the dated décor and appliances.

The detective poured himself a cup of coffee, but made no comment either way on whether he had eaten breakfast. I set my plate at the head of the table and pointed towards Roux's food dish when he came begging for a bite of sausage. I took off the sport coat I was wearing to avoid dropping food on it because I knew I would be talking and eating at the same time. I had dressed better than usual because I was going to be meeting people that I needed to impress.

"You have what I told you to bring?" I inquired as I set about eating my breakfast. He had arrived with a metal briefcase and I was really hoping our first day was not going to start out with some sort of wrangling over who was going to be in charge. I was resigned to creating an equal partnership and hoped he was, too.

"I have it here. There isn't much from our end. I guess the detectives you replaced ran everyone off as soon as they got there. All of the forensics evidence was collected by your own department. I have the transcript of the call between our dispatcher and the responding deputy. I also have his incident report and a few pictures he took, but that is all Sheriff Mazant says we have," Chance informed me and set the thin file on the table between us.

"Then I will call Baton Rouge and have everything else sent to us," I shrugged at the slight delay and inconvenience this was going to cause. They say the first forty-eight hours are the best window in which to solve a case, but we only had one suspect and he was nowhere to be found. The case was on hold until he was found, or his wife's body surfaced. Waiting a day or two for the state police reports and analysis was not going to make much difference. "Captain Hammond was supposed to get the car moved to Baton Rouge."

"Actually the Mercedes is still in our impound lot."

"In a garage or just sitting out in the weather?" I could tell that my new partner did not want to answer this and be blamed for anyone else's sloppy handling of the only piece of evidence we had.

"Probably sitting out in the open. Hopefully somebody put a tarp over it," he said with a bit of a sigh. At least he had some grasp of the importance of how to properly handle evidence. We had the car, but we still did not know the actual scene of Gwen's murder and we did not even have our assumed victim's body.

"Have you been able to establish the last time anyone saw any of the family members?" I rinsed my plate and fork before loading them into the dishwasher. I wiped the cast iron skillet out with a wet paper towel before setting it back in the cabinet where I was elated to have found an entire set the night before.

"Mrs. Donovan was seen filling her Mercedes at the BP gas station downtown just after noon on the same Friday that Kirk was supposed to head to Florida for his race," Detective Chance said as we settled in at the table. "Kirk's secretary said he left the office at nine. We know Kirk took his Ford GT for a test drive out on Highway H from between eleven and one. The family owns a large tract of cane fields up there and we have a couple of units block off the highway at either end until he is done. The dispatcher says it is routine for him to practice before he leaves town for his races."

"It must be nice to own your own race track," I grumbled, although this wasn't so much a matter of money as it was entitlement. Detective Chance chose to shrug rather than open a discussion of his own feelings about the Donovans. "And what about Belle?"

"She hasn't been home in over a week."

"Okay then, let's take a look at what you brought with you." I took a seat at one of the chairs at the Formica-topped table while the detective spread out the contents in his folder. I placed the disc with a recording of the dispatcher and deputies discussing the abandoned car in my laptop computer so we could listen to it while we read the printed transcript. I read through the incident report and found that our only witness was a local deep-sea fishing boat captain.

Captain Haskins claimed to have noticed that the car was parked in the same spot for three nights in a row as he passed the ramp on his way to the Gulf. The concerned captain thought the car belonged to 'one of the Donovans,' but he said he wasn't positive. I saw no reason for him to be intimately familiar with the cars any family drove but his own. The dispatcher sent a deputy, and the deputy called for Sheriff Mazant within a couple of minutes of being on the scene. I wondered why he was so quick to ask for his boss.

The deputy's incident report answered this in brilliantly worded police terms. He found the trunk was unlatched when he arrived and "upon inspection I discovered evidence I could not immediately explain." It was one of the best descriptions of a large pool of blood I have ever read. He immediately asked the dispatcher to send Sheriff Mazant to the scene.

Sheriff Mazant responded in a more professional manner than I would have believed he had in him. He dispatched a second car and told that deputy to block the road to the boat ramp. He instructed the first deputy to walk back to the road rather than drive in the mud a second time and further damage any tire track evidence.

Mazant's own written report claimed his first contact with the state police was at eleven forty-five Tuesday night and that Captain Hammond and the two detectives I replaced arrived with a forensic team just before one o'clock. I must not have arrived very long after Judge Rogers made it to the scene, which meant he was determined to replace Sheriff Mazant's detectives before he left New Orleans.

The half dozen images the responding deputy took with his cellphone were snapshots that did not capture much more than the amount of blood pooled in the spare tire compartment. I noted the absence of splatter or blotches to indicate leakage from plastic bags or a rolled up carpet. The photographs made less and less sense the longer I looked at them. My gut reaction was that someone simply emptied a jug of fresh blood in the trunk and walked away. This is why I have come to believe my gut is something of an idiot.

"Do you have a scenario in mind to fit this?" I asked my new partner. I wasn't sharing mine first.

"Nothing fits. That's a popular boat ramp so the car was going to be reported pretty quickly. I am surprised it took so long before anybody thought to call it in. Maybe someone popped the trunk and ran away when they saw the blood. They might not have wanted to call it in for fear they would be accused of killing somebody." That sounded logical. I had no doubt Sheriff Mazant would have held them as a suspect for at least a day or so. "I just don't understand why all the blood is only in that one place. They had to cut the body up to get it to fit in that compartment and make the blood pool like that, but there should be blood all over the place if there was a hacked up body in there. Every time the killer hit a bump it would have splashed blood. Right?"

"That's my problem with it. Let's go look at the car and see if this makes any better sense in person." I sighed and began setting everything back into the folder.

"I'm not counting on it," Detective Chance grumbled mostly to himself as we headed for the door. He was not very happy when he discovered Roux would be joining us.

Eleven

The Mercedes was at a place called George's Automotive. I called Captain Hammond to find out why the car never made it to Baton Rouge. His explanation was that Sheriff Mazant offered to move and secure the vehicle until the state police could arrange to transfer it to the crime lab in Baton Rouge. The offer was too tempting to pass up while standing in the rain at five o'clock in the morning. What I heard was that he leapt at Sheriff Mazant's offer because he believed it would allow him to leave the parish that much sooner.

I wondered if there was any sort of significance in the garage being named after George and not branded with the Donovan name. George himself turned out to be a short guy pushing seventy with a chain smoker's voice that was as cracked and gravely as the surface of his car lot. Someone had thought to pull a tarp over the car either before it was hauled from the scene or after it arrived on the lot. I was relieved to find a low flatbed wrecker was used to move the vehicle. Raising the rear end enough to get it onto the flatbed trailer had shifted the blood pool some. Using a regular style of wrecker would have destroyed the trunk as evidence.

"I didn't know but what you boys was wanting to borrow the wrecker," George said by way of greeting us.

"Not today, Mister George. We came to look at the Mercedes," Detective Chance explained and led me past the elderly man smiling at us from his office doorway. The old man silently lit his latest cigarette as he tagged along behind us. The oxygen tank slung over his shoulder slowed him down a bit.

"Borrow the wrecker?" I asked Chance. It was a particularly odd greeting.

"He lets anyone that needs a wrecker borrow his rather than have to wait an hour for someone from another parish to drive here to overcharge them. I think almost everyone in town knows how to run the thing now. You sign it out and bring it back full of gas," Chance explained. Small town living does have its odd perks. "Chief Theriot sends one of his deputies over to get it when he wants to tow somebody. George gets to charge them for storing the car until they pay whatever fine Chief Theriot comes up with."

"Isn't that up to a judge?"

"The City Council lets the chief set his own fines. He has to budget his own department, and he is given pretty wide latitude about how he does it. Be careful where you park because he charges tourists more than he does locals."

There seemed no point in discussing the concept of "official business" with the detective, so I let the subject drop. I was going to be mindful of hydrants and such, but the police chief was in for a surprise if he arbitrarily hauled my car off. For one thing, he might well have to contend with Roux if I left the pit bull to guard either of my vehicles.

We rolled the still-damp canvas tarpaulin off the Mercedes and set it on the front end of the trailer. The car was unlocked and I had Detective Chance check the reports to see if it was found this way or if Sheriff Mazant had the doors opened. He opened the file and showed me where the deputy had reported that the car was unlocked when he found it. The keys were discovered in the cup holder. It meant we were either lucky nobody ran off with the car when they found it, or that somebody actually did take it for a joy ride from wherever it was originally dumped and left it at the boat dock. It was beginning to look even more like the boat dock might not even be where Gwen was killed. This would mean I was not just looking for a murderer and their victim, but also a crime scene.

I opened the driver's side door and climbed into the car. I had to bend my knees a bit to adjust to the pedals and estimated that whoever drove the car to the scene was not much over five feet six or seven inches tall. Kirk Donovan's driver's license indicated he was six feet two. Gwen was five feet eight according to her license. Belle's license information put her at five feet four. Kirk could have moved the seat after he got out, Gwen might have been murdered near the boat ramp and her body stored in the trunk until a better time to dump her remains presented itself, or perhaps Belle had more to explain than her missed classes. I was barely an hour into the first morning of the investigation and my brain was already full.

"What is Sheriff Mazant doing to find Kirk Donovan?" I asked Chance as we continued to comb the passenger compartment for anything that struck either of us as being out of place or odd in a useful way.

"We have checked all of his known hang-outs locally and put out an APB in case he gets pulled over. Sheriff Mazant suggested that you subpoena the credit card companies in case there is any activity on one of those accounts." Sheriff Mazant's weak efforts were a very clear indication how little he wanted to find Kirk.

"Who was the last person to see him?" I pressed.

"Like I said, Sheriff Mazant told me Mister Donovan's secretary said he told her that he was going to Pensacola when he left work last Friday. He is big into rally racing and takes off early like that a lot of weekends. He has a room full of trophies at his house."

"So, you have already searched his house?"

"Not yet. Sheriff Mazant said to make sure you have a search warrant before I take you to look the place over." Chance hid his face so I couldn't judge his thoughts about that.

"How do you know about the trophies then?"

I counted to five before he responded with something that ought not to have taken so long to say.

"I've seen pictures of him in front of them in the local paper. It seems like he wins a trophy just about every time he races." This explanation sounded plausible, but Chance's awkward pause made me question whether the paper was the source of this knowledge.

"Have you ever been to Kirk's house? Did you handle any of the domestic disturbance calls?" This was a far more plausible way for him to have seen the trophy room.

"I've never been inside, but Sheriff Mazant had me take Missus Donovan to the hospital a couple of times. Sheriff Mazant didn't want her doctors to keep any evidence of what Kirk did to her. I was supposed to bag everything and give it to him," the detective said, with no indication of whether or not he understood his boss suppressing evidence was an illegal act.

My finger touched something with a dull edge under the driver's seat. I moved to lay my head nearly on the floorboard and aimed my flashlight under the seat. The light fell on a rectangular piece of white plastic. It turned out to be a parking pass for Tulane University that I believed would trace back to Belle.

"How sure are we that this is Gwen's car? Could she have given it to Belle when she went off to college?" I showed Chance the pass.

"I suppose she could have, but I have seen her driving this car around town when Belle's been at school. Maybe they share it." That would explain why the pass was not hanging from the rear view mirror, but this left me with the unsettling question of which of the Donovan women was only missing and which of them was both missing and dead.

"Maybe," I had to admit. 'Maybe' was the best answer to a lot of things that were bothering me at the moment. Maybe both women had been in the trunk. That would explain why there was so much blood, and why both of them were still missing. Maybe one of them killed the other, which made sense if I believed Bradley's story about the family's telephone arguments. Maybe Kirk finally had enough of the women in his life and killed them both before he drove off into the sunset to start a new life. Maybe it was Kirk's blood in the trunk and the women had been arguing about which of them got to kill the son-of-a-bitch. I sat on the covered wheel well of the flatbed trailer to consider the overabundance of ugly scenarios running through my head.

"You don't want to count on those credit cards being any help, Detective," George said just loud enough for me to hear him while he watched Chance check out the back seat.

"Why is that?"

"The Donovans deal in cash. They don't use credit cards or borrow money," he said and walked away. It was a handy thing to know, and was something Sheriff Mazant probably already knew as well. Getting Kirk Donovan's bank records might be trickier than accessing his credit card accounts. His accounts were probably in a bank the Donovan family controlled and there was no way of knowing how fully they would comply with any court orders I handed them.

"Find anything?" I asked Chance when he popped his head out of the open passenger's side door.

"Not even a gum wrapper." It certainly did not sound like the car of any college student I ever knew and I gave Gwen credit for dropping at least one or two French fries. The parking pass under the driver's seat might have been planted there if someone had taken the time to vacuum the car's interior. Now even the absence of clues was a clue.

"Then I guess it's time to open the trunk," I sighed and stepped back onto the low trailer. I used the key fob to open the trunk electronically.

The distinct odor of putrefying blood rolled out of the tightly closed compartment and we both took a big step back and paused to let the air clear a bit. I snorted through my nose twice to try to clear the scent stuck in my sinuses. I have lost my gag reflex to this particular odor, but not my mental one. My PTSD always pays a visit and gives me a brief and involuntary slideshow of the very worst blood splatters and IED dismemberments I witnessed during decades of active service in multiple combat zones.

The interior of the Mercedes' trunk was not going to be an image that would haunt me later. It had a lot of blood, but it looked like a careless spill rather than the result of a particularly heinous and vicious act. Those flashes of past eviscerations and executions actually set a few reference points for my examination of this tableau. One thing immediately stuck out when I dipped my gloved index finger into the largest puddle. Very little of the blood was dry, which was entirely opposite my past experience.

"This isn't right," I informed my new partner. He was transfixed at the sight of my bloody finger. It seemed doubtful he would dip his own finger into the trunk to see what I had found.

"What isn't right to you?" he asked without taking his eyes from the bloody blue glove covering my raised finger.

"Let's assume the car sat for days before it was found, and it was here for the better part of another one before we came to look at it," I explained. "Does it strike you as odd that this amount of blood has still not fully dried? In my experience, most of this should be solid by now. I should not be able to swipe my finger through this as I just did."

"What do you make of it?" The novice investigator nodded his head as he asked the obvious question. He saw my point, but could offer no better immediate explanation than I could, which was none.

"It's probably a clue," I declared and went back to dabbing my finger into more of the pooled blood.

We removed our latex gloves and tossed them into a metal drum George used as a burn barrel. I was curious what he might choose to burn rather than merely discard. I helped Chance roll the tarp back into place before I locked the car and dropped the keys into their evidence bag and led the way off the car lot.

The answer to the anomaly with the blood was not going to come from either of us. It was going to take lab work and experts. I did not want to waste my time sitting in Judge Cyrus Rogers' boyhood home waiting on someone else to answer my growing list of questions.

"What now?" Chance asked as we climbed back into his cruiser. The passenger window was smeared by the drool and snot Roux's snout left while he watched us clamber about the flatbed trailer. I pulled a Sani-wipe from my satchel and cleaned the window while Chance chuckled. "I guess one or the other of you is going to make a mess of things anywhere we go."

"How so?" He was absolutely correct, but we had not been partnered long enough for him to really know this.

"Sheriff Mazant checked up on you. He says you are persona non grata at NOPD because of your reputation for working off the reservation." This linguistic mish-mash left me dizzy for a moment, but I had no trouble understanding what his boss thought he had learned from his police sources in New Orleans.

"I get assigned any cases NOPD won't bother with. The investigations usually look like a waste of time, and what I eventually find to look into may have nothing to do with what I was asked to pursue. Sheriff Mazant is right about my having a reputation for upsetting people, but I always find the answers that solve my cases. I was sent here to learn what happened to Judge Rogers' daughter and to rain justice down upon anyone who hurt her. Sheriff Mazant can either help me or try to stop me, but that is what I am going to do. It's up to you to decide whose side to take." I couldn't get rid of Detective Chance, so he needed to know that any trust I placed in him would have to be earned. I also wanted him to be able to repeat each and every word exactly as I said it when Sheriff Mazant debriefed him.

Twelve

Detective Chance dropped Roux and me at the courthouse. I asked him to see if he could track down the charter boat captain who called Sheriff Mazant about the abandoned car. I had a question or two of my own for the man, and I was looking forward to finding out if Detective Chance had any of the same thoughts I did about the captain's statement. Mostly I wanted my new partner to have something to do miles away from where I was, because I absolutely did not want Sheriff Mazant to know what I discussed with District Attorney Henri Gabouri.

The parish's courthouse was dedicated the same year I graduated from LSU. A commemorative plaque in its lobby marks the spot where Huey Long made a campaign stump speech on the steps of the original courthouse. The parish seemed to have an especially high tolerance for benevolent dictators.

"What's with the dog?" There was a uniformed sheriff's deputy with a rookie's way about him manning the lobby metal detector. He spotted Roux as the pit bull followed me through the courthouse doors.

"He's a K-9 officer," I told the deputy. Nothing about my attitude or the slacks and sports coat I was wearing indicated I was a fellow police officer.

"Uh huh." He wasn't buying my story. "The sign on the door right there says we don't allow dogs in the courthouse unless they are service dogs. Like for blind folks."

"You don't consider being a state police officer to be a valuable service?" I caught the deputy off-guard with the question. The only correct answer to this was as obvious as the sign on the door and the mental conflict made his brain freeze up.

"How do I know you're a real state police officer?" The deputy was growing tired of having his limited authority challenged. "And how can I tell it's even a trained K-9 dog?"

"Verblijf. Verschrikken!" I instructed Roux, and loosened my grip on the leash. The burly canine bared its forty-two bright white teeth before he advanced on the young man, who instinctively reached for his pistol. "I wouldn't do that if you value the use of your hand."

"What the hell did you say to him, anyway?" The deputy wisely chose to take a step back rather than draw his weapon.

"Are my dog and I the only ones here who speak Dutch?" I made an exaggerated gesture of confusion towards the amused line of people stuck behind us. I then pulled my jacket aside to show him my sidearm. I pulled the gold detective's shield from my belt and hung it from my jacket breast pocket before either of them set off the metal detector the deputy glumly waved us through.

"Why didn't you just show me that to start with?" the deputy grumbled as we passed him.

"Where's the fun in that?" I reached into the Ziploc bag in my pocket for one of the dog treats I carry whenever Roux is on duty. I felt he had earned two for this performance.

District Attorney Henri Gabouri's receptionist did not expect our visit, but she remained better composed than the deputy when she first laid eyes on Roux. The woman's face briefly betrayed her nervousness before she recovered her polite smile. Still, she seemed relieved to not be asked to shake Roux's hand.

"How may I help you, Detective?" she asked politely as she maneuvered to keep her desk between herself and Roux.

"I am investigating the disappearance of Gwendolyn Donovan and I was hoping your boss could spare a few minutes to give me some background."

"I'm sure he can," she said and disappeared into the inner sanctum for just a moment before she opened the door and ushered us inside.

Henri Gabouri was just short of six feet tall and pudgy, with an unflattering head of short wiry hair and expressive brown eyes that wouldn't serve him well at a poker table. His suit fit him as best it could, but its tailoring became a mess of fabric across his shoulders when he sat down and his paunch tried to squeeze between the buttons on his shirt. Shaking his hand was like clutching a dead fish. I remembered Katie's derisive nickname for Gabouri and thought how well it still fit him.

The female reporter Judge Rogers and I had seen as we left the boat dock was leaving his office as Roux and I entered. She was wearing a floral print dress that displayed nearly equal amounts of leg and bosom. Both seemed to be in fine shape.

"So, we meet again," I said to acknowledge her presence. I made no move to shake her hand or deviate from my path towards Gabouri.

"Who is following whom?" she asked and gave me a coy smile.

"Does your dog bite?" Gabouri asked as he extended his left hand forward with the palm up for Roux to sniff. I lack my dog's sensitive nose and was still able to pick up the scent of perfume on Gabouri's clothes.

"No, he does worse," I said as I watched Roux approach Crystal. He retreated before she could pet him. "He tends to judge people."

"I'm sure we'll keep bumping into one another. It is a small town, after all," she said with a tone that was both playful and sharp as a knife. Gabouri and I remained standing as she sashayed out of the office.

I took the seat Gabouri waved towards in front of his desk. The DA was amused enough by Roux jumping into the chair beside me that I didn't bother apologizing for his behavior or make him get back on the floor. Roux had developed this habit while living with me. I began to keep his nails trimmed after they destroyed an expensive Stickley leather chair.

Everything about the office was scaled to make anyone sitting before District Attorney Gabouri feel small. The desk was too big, the arms of the chairs too high, and the room itself far larger than it needed to be. Gabouri's undergraduate and law school diplomas were flanked by two photographs on the cypress-paneled wall behind his desk. One was posed with his parents when he graduated from law school at Loyola University in New Orleans. The other was taken at The Grove in Oxford, Mississippi during his undergraduate years. He was standing between Ole Miss football royalty Archie and Eli Manning with a beer in his hand. It was understandable that he would memorialize both moments with the same pride as his diplomas and a copy of the Bill of Rights.

"I heard there was a state detective from Baton Rouge here looking into Gwendoline Donovan's disappearance. How may I be of help?"

Gabouri was obviously trying to look well informed and capable of far more than Katie had led me to believe.

"I'm actually from New Orleans. I should also tell you that this case is far more complicated than you may have heard. The entire family is unaccounted for. Gwen is presumed to be dead, Kirk is supposedly in Florida even though nobody's heard from him since Friday, and Belle hasn't been in class since last Thursday." I filled him in on the initial obstacles I had experienced with the investigation. "Your sheriff was quick to hang one of his detectives around my neck, a kid named David Chance. I figure you know him since he is apparently Sheriff Mazant's choice to handle your Walmart shoplifters."

"Odd bird, that one. I believe Sheriff Mazant hired him on Chester Donovan's instructions. He supposedly came over here from Houston. I don't know of any business dealings Chester Donovan has over there. As for those shoplifting arrests, Judge Duvall puts everyone arrested for shoplifting into what he calls a diversion program. It is really just a way for the parish to get free labor to pick up trash and for getting its buildings painted," Gabouri informed me. I got the feeling he was making conversation while he waited for me to justify taking up his time.

"I'm more interested in the lack of prosecution of Kirk Donovan for what Judge Rogers tells me is a long history of spousal abuse. Is anyone else running interference beside Sheriff Mazant?" I did not want him to believe I was implying that he was remiss in his duties for not having prosecuted the judge's son-in-law. It was bad enough that I was already at odds with Sheriff Mazant. I did not want to get on anyone else's bad side as well.

"Everyone that can," the district attorney snorted. "Sheriff Mazant won't arrest him and the judges Chester Donovan makes sure get elected to the bench wouldn't do a thing if I ever did drag him into court. I am not much more than a figurehead around here. The last district attorney was on the Donovan dole for thirty years before he choked to death eating a muffaletta. The new State Attorney General decided it was okay for the Donovans to own all of the cops and judges, but he decided they shouldn't own the whole system, so I got appointed to this job. Now

Sheriff Mazant and judges just go right around me."

"Your predecessor choked to death on a muffaletta?" It was a rather disturbing image.

"Well, he had a reputation for always biting off more than he could chew." Gabouri seemed to enjoy his joke enough that I wondered if he set me up for the punchline. "But, if you want a good one while you're in town, try Jasper's. They're over by the sheriff's office."

District Attorney Gabouri did not strike me as a person I was going to be able to count on for much of anything besides local dining recommendations. There was no reason to even bring up the subject of search warrants if the local judges were just going to swat me down. I would have to ask Captain Hammond to handle those requests through a court in Baton Rouge so I couldn't be hampered by Senator Donovan's hand-picked judges.

"How do you spend your days if you aren't prosecuting shoplifters or wife abusers?" I did not mean it unkindly.

"I read a lot, and I waste time on my golf game." Gabouri shrugged and smiled. There was no reason to hide the fact he was a man without any real function. "Do you have dinner plans tonight?"

"No. Roux and I have a well-stocked refrigerator and are content to fend for ourselves. I want to check out a place called Johnny's at some point, but other than that I am at a loss for where to find a decent meal here."

"Well, for what it is worth, that isn't a place to get what anyone used to dining out in New Orleans would likely consider to be decent food. It's just the diner at the truck stop on I-10. Who even recommended the place to you, anyway?"

"Detective Chance. He didn't really recommend it as such. He said he recently broke up with one of their waitresses and I thought she might have something to say about him if I caught her in the right mood." I actually like dive diners and enjoy the late-night sideshow at a Waffle House. My nocturnal schedule means I tend to patrol at hours when those are the only places to eat.

"I'll bet she will," he chuckled. "Why don't you join me for supper at the country club? It will be a good way for you to meet the real powers that be around here in their natural setting."

"Like a safari."

"More like a rabid petting zoo. It will be at feeding time, so try not to let yourself get eaten alive. I'll meet you for cocktails; I assume you drink if you're from New Orleans. Shall we say, six?" Gabouri stood up and I realized my time was up. He must have had a good book to read or an early tee time. "Do you need directions to the country club?"

"I'm sure I can find it. It will be the big white house with too much yard, right?" I motioned for Roux to let me put him back on his leash and shook the district attorney's hand before leaving his useless office.

Thirteen

Captain Hammond was expecting my phone call, or seemed to be when I reached him on my cell phone as I walked Roux to the judge's house. It was a pleasant day and I felt we could both use the exercise. It would also give me an opportunity to get a better look at the town.

"How are things going?" I imagined him laughing to himself about my situation.

"I heard a story about the local police chief beating up one of our troopers during a DUI stop. What can you tell me about that?" I was genuinely concerned about my safety now that Chief Theriot was having me staked out. I hadn't been in a fist-fight in years and didn't really want to start again with him.

"It was years ago. I graduated with the guy he nearly killed. We still avoid the parish unless they ask for our help. That's kind of why I asked how you were doing," he said with less amusement. I would have been touched that he was worried about me if I weren't equally upset that someone else told me the story before he did.

"Well, the chief has the judge's house staked out, the local DA has no authority, and Sheriff Mazant forced a stone-faced detective on me that he got from Texas. I'd appreciate you calling anyone you know in Houston and asking about a cop named David Chance. I don't think he has been here very long, and the locals don't seem to like him any more than they do me."

"I can do that. Back to my first question, how's the case going?" Hammond must have wanted to believe there was a chance of the case being solved despite so many obstacles in my way.

"I am still trying to find its edges. It turns out the wife and daughter shared the Mercedes and they are both missing, as is the husband who supposedly went to Florida for the weekend. Maybe all three of them were in the trunk of the car. There was enough blood to make me think so." Hammond offered no opinions or comment on that assessment. "I would appreciate it if you sent someone to pick up the car and had our people look at the blood in the trunk again. It is still wet, and that is just not right."

"No, it isn't. I'll send someone down this afternoon. Where is it?"

"A place called George's Automotive," I said and then heard him utter a little guffaw. "What's so funny?"

"Nothing. It's just that George has been around since the last Ice Age. He used to run moonshine in the Sixties and Mexican pot in the Seventies. They tried to catch him chopping stolen cars just a few years ago. He's quite a character." This was also information I would have liked to have had sooner.

"I'm having supper with the local DA tonight. Katie says they used to call him Milquetoast in law school because he was so bad in mock court. Sheriff Mazant and the local judges don't even bother with him, so I don't see much reason to, either. Can you get a search warrant for Kirk Donovan's residence? Have whoever comes after the car bring it with them." I sat down on one of the benches spaced along the downtown's sidewalk to pull my spiral notebook from my shoulder bag and give him the address to Kirk Donovan's new house. Roux sat at my feet and scanned both ways for any obvious threats or stray cats. I had still not broken him of chasing cats, and I was more than a little amazed that the scars on his nose weren't lesson enough to leave them alone. I understood he was just trying to play with them, but there is nothing playful about the sight of a pit bull ten times your size bearing down on you.

"No problem. They should be there by four, does that work for you?"

"My days are unusually open," I joked. "I am thinking about talking to Detective Chance's ex-girlfriend while I wait for news from Sheriff Mazant about his luck with locating the Donovan family. I will consider it to be solid progress when any of them turn up, in any condition."

"Keep me posted. Anything else I should know about?" Hammond prodded.

"I wish there was," I sighed and disconnected the call before my captain said goodbye.

Fourteen

The service plaza where Detective Chance's ex-girlfriend worked was at the intersection of Interstate 10 and a narrow state highway lined with trailers and fifty-year-old ranch-style homes that spoke of a period of prosperity in the parish's past. Parish Highway H, Kirk Donovan's practice track, intersected the smoothly paved road about mid-way between Donovan and the interstate. Highway H was likely the best surfaced farm road in the entire state of Louisiana.

I should have kept in mind that Detective Chance was a Texan when he gave me the name of the diner where he felt he had worn out his welcome. Johnny's was actually Jean E's, a play on pronunciation with the local accent. The diner occupied the better portion of a grimy brick building that flashed its DONOVAN CASINO PLAZA sign in tall neon-lit letters above the flat roof. The sign likely lit the entire lot at night, though there was an abundance of halogen lot lights, as well. It was mid-day and the truck lot was nearly a third full of semi-trucks and their trailers. The gas pumps were busy and Jean E's still had lunch business after two in the afternoon.

I did not think the place was situated to do good business. Anyone traveling east on Interstate 10 from Texas would have stopped at one of the new places where Interstate 49 connected with I-10 and anyone coming from the other direction probably started with a full tank of gas or made a pit-stop in LaPlace or Baton Rouge. The double bank of video poker machines separating the sizeable convenience store from the restaurant gave me my explanation. Every machine was busy chewing through a mix of trucker cash advances, the locals' paychecks, and tourist dollars by the fistful.

I took a seat at the Formica-topped counter running most of the length of the diner to keep the cooks and their food critics apart. The picked-over lunch buffet did not make me feel like I had missed much, and the menu didn't offer much in the way of palatable alternatives. My admittedly limited experience in restaurant management was enough to make me curious as to why there were so many waitresses still clocked in this long after the lunch rush. A few of the waitresses were sitting with customers in the section reserved for professional truck drivers. The manager in my place takes a dim view of that level of familiarity, even with regulars.

"What can I get you to drink?" My waitress was a cheerful red-haired young woman in her mid-twenties. She stood barely five feet-two and carried the extra pounds in her thighs I would expect of a waitress whose diet involved eating most of her meals at work. Her Cajun accent pegged her as a local girl. She was going to be working here until long after her good looks faded if the local businesses were as family-owned as my recent stroll had led me to believe.

"Anything with ice and alcohol, but I would settle for sweet tea," I tried to joke. She grinned and left me to read the two-page laminated menu while she went to fill a plastic tumbler with cubed ice and tea from a tall dispenser half-way down the counter.

"So, what strikes your fancy?" she gamely joked as she set the tea down in front of me. She set her hands on the edge of the counter and leaned far enough forward to strain the plastic buttons on her polyester uniform.

"How about a club sandwich?" I asked more than ordered. I was prepared to change my order based on her facial expression at the thought of what the kitchen would consider to be a club sandwich.

"Fries okay?" she asked with another smile as she stood back and wrote my order on her pad.

"I probably won't eat them." She studied me to decide if I was a health nut or if I smelled the burnt fryer oil.

"Maybe we can share them." She winked before she headed off to give the order to the rail-thin guy working on the other side of the hot window. She refilled some drinks and dropped off checks to other diners in her station before she made her way back to me. "You passing through?"

"Not fast enough. Is there any reason to hang out in Donovan?"

"I guess not. There's going to be a street fair on Saint Patrick's Day and the fire station always has a crawfish boil." She wasn't making much of a sales pitch for either event. "They had to cancel the beauty pageant. The lady that organizes it is missing. I heard all they found was her car full of blood."

"I may have to check out the street fair. It looks like I could be here for a while." I wanted to ask the waitress what her source was for the information about Gwen's Mercedes, but there was enough reason to doubt that she would tell me not to bother pressing the question.

"Did your car break down?"

"No. I'm just here until I find someone." I still wasn't ready to admit to working for the state police. It was obvious she was headed somewhere with this conversation, and I did not want to derail it before I knew what she wanted to learn.

"Well you found me," she laughed. It was an old joke, but the look in her eye came across as being more direct than funny. She was hitting on me. This would have been awkward enough at closing time in some bar, but doing so in broad daylight made it seem particularly strange.

"A detective with Sheriff Mazant's office named David Chance recommended this place. He said his ex-girlfriend works here. I was hoping she might be working so I could say hi."

She wrinkled her nose a bit and went back to sizing me up. "You a cop, too?"

"State police, but this isn't work related."

"It's always work related with you guys," she sighed and turned to handle a guest at the cash register. I had the distinct impression I had just slammed the door on any further attempts at flirtation. I took a sip of my tea to give her a moment to decide what to do next.

The redhead returned, but this time she kept her distance. "I would say 'girlfriend' was a bit of a stretch. Why are you looking for her? Did he say she was easy?"

"No. He was an absolute gentleman about the two of them breaking up, and never said a bad thing about her," I hastily assured her. "Okay, I guess being here is work related. I am trying to understand David a little better. Sheriff Mazant assigned him to be my local liaison, and frankly the guy is weird."

"You got that right." This time she wandered off and I lost sight of her when she went into the kitchen. Detective Chance said his ex-girlfriend was a waitress so I didn't immediately understand why anyone would look for her in the kitchen. My experiences in town to that point made me wonder if she was calling for reinforcements to bounce me out of the place. She returned with my food and slid a napkin under the plate as she set it in front of me. We made eye contact and I waited until I finished eating a piece of the sandwich before moving the plate to read the note on the napkin.

The way the waitress left me the note left me to believe someone might be watching me, so I wanted to be careful about leading anyone to Chance's ex-girlfriend. I pulled out my cellphone and dialed my own telephone number in New Orleans before tossing the napkin over my plate and acting as though I was headed outside to find a better signal to make the imaginary call. The waitress I was headed outside to meet wasn't part of anything I was doing in town and didn't deserve to be caught up in any of this mess. Meeting me behind the trash dumpsters was a good sign she didn't think so, either.

I didn't believe my new partner had the looks or brains to attract anyone whose dating standards required more than a pulse and a bank account. As such, I was unprepared to discover that my waitress was the woman I came here to find, so I suspected this was a joke or a set-up of some sort.

"I'm Nannci," she said and extended her hand as though we'd just met. Her hand was soft, but she pressed my hand a lot harder than I did hers. She also closed the distance between us by a couple of steps.

"I'm State Police Detective Holland," I said back. Telling her either my birth name of Cooter or my current nickname of Cadillac risked starting a discussion I didn't want to have. "Really, all I want to know is anything you can tell me about David that might be handy for me to know. We are supposed to be looking into Gwendolyn Donovan's disappearance and I am still trying to get a feel for the guy."

"I don't know what I can tell you that will help with that. Obviously, I am not going to sing his praises," she said.

"Let's start with how you two met."

"He used to come in for lunch almost every day, and he would bounce any of the truckers who got too friendly with the waitresses. That's usually a two way street, because some of our best waitresses are notoriously friendly with truck drivers. I have to constantly remind the girls that they are here to work and not to be looking for a ticket out of town. There used to be these two guys from Texas that creeped the girls out, but they were always nice when David was around. David and I got to be friendly and it just went from there." This was obviously not going to be a tale of love at first sight.

"How did the two guys creep the other girls out?" This surely had nothing to do with their dating, but the way she said it intrigued me.

"They'd make comments about how pretty girls disappear from truck stops all the time and then ask them if anyone wanted to go see their trucks."

"And what did David say when they said things like that?"

"He'd laugh, but then he'd tell them he had their license numbers in case anyone ever did disappear. They stopped coming in after they saw he was becoming one of our regulars," she said and tapped another cigarette from the pack she pulled from her apron.

"Anyway, back to the two of you. What can you tell me that would give me a good picture of David? I don't want to pry and I really do not want to know how he was in bed," I said and grinned. I did not want this to seem like an interrogation to her.

"Oh, he was polite and all that. He always opened doors for me and brought me flowers. You know, all those things the good guys do." There was an unspoken "but" at the end of her sentence and I made a rolling motion with one hand to encourage her to finish the thought. "Eventually it just started getting weird. I mean really weird."

"What sort of weird? Was he moving too fast for you, was he needy?"

Nannci grinned and shook her head. Katie would have laughed at me trying to act like I know the first thing about relationships. I was recycling questions she once asked me about girlfriends in my own past.

Nannci lit her third Newport while she worked on her response. She had no reason to trust I was not going to repeat what I learned back to Chance. I had absolutely no idea what the detective's reaction would be to her giving me details about their time together. I suspected that his response to my poking into his personal life would not be pleasant.

"It started with him wanting me to call him 'daddy' when we were alone."

"I can see where that might kill the mood," I tried to hide my own discomfort with the image this formed in my head by making the joke.

Nannci took a long drag on her cigarette and her eyes darted around to be sure we were genuinely alone before she went on. I knew a decision was being made to share the honest reasons she considered Chance to be too strange to handle.

"I kind of liked it when he got a little rough with me in bed. I like a guy that takes control, and cops do that, you know? You guys even bring your own handcuffs." She wanted me to be clear that her distaste for Chance had not put her off dating cops, from any jurisdiction or department.

"I get the picture. So why did you finally call it quits with him?" I really hoped it was something outside the bedroom because I knew I was already going to have a hard time not imagining the two of them together the next time I saw Chance's wooden expression.

"I don't know if I should tell you what else went on." She chewed on her lower lip and studied my face.

"It's entirely up to you. I have a clearer picture of the man, but if there is anything you want to tell me, I will listen." I realized that I was interrogating her.

"I put up with his wanting me to call him 'Daddy.' Lots of older guys around here like that. I broke up with him because he got mad at me for slapping him when he tried to spank me."

I blinked before I could catch myself. "He wanted you to role-play being his daughter?"

She shrugged her shoulders, but then explained herself further after taking another long drag on her cigarette.

"I could have stayed living at home if I wanted to play those games. I thought he was going to punch me, but he just pushed me on the floor me and threw my clothes at me. He really seemed to get off on what he was trying to do. I don't think I was the first woman he ever did that with, but I must have been the first one who ever slapped him over it."

Nannci smashed her menthol cigarette against the side of the dumpster and then flicked the butt inside. She gave me a look that seemed to dare me to say anything cute or to try to pass judgement.

"When was that?" I had to say something and it was as neutral of a thing to ask as I could come up with.

"The tag end of last month. I haven't seen or heard from him since." She seemed hurt that he did not try to reconcile. "Does this help you any?"

"Yes, of course. Every piece of information helps," I assured her. I'd lost my appetite for the sandwich waiting for me on the counter. I pulled twenty dollars from my wallet and handed it to Nannci. "This should cover my meal."

"You're sure I can't get you anything else?" she asked and stepped towards me.

"No, I think that covers everything I came here to find out," I said and stepped aside. She brushed herself against me as she walked past and wagged her hips in a way I was sure to notice.

Fifteen

A wrecker arrived at George's Automotive just after four that afternoon. Two uniformed patrolmen followed the trailer onto the lot in their own patrol cars. Chief Theriot drove past barely a minute later, with his radio microphone in his hand. I assumed he had followed the wrecker with its state trooper escort through town.

I did not share my decision to transfer the Mercedes to the state police crime lab with Detective Chance when we looked the car over earlier, nor had I informed Sheriff Mazant of my intention to have it moved after I made the arrangement with Captain Hammond. It still came as absolutely no surprise that the police chief followed the state police vehicles to the car lot or that Sheriff Mazant arrived with what seemed to be half his force to block the gate.

"What's going on here?" Sheriff Mazant asked in a voice that he believed showed he was in command.

"I am sending the Mercedes to Baton Rouge so our crime lab can take a look at it."

"Why can't they come here instead?" he argued.

"Because the State Police Crime Lab does not work for you, Sheriff Mazant. They don't even work for me, but they do work in Baton Rouge." There was no debate. I was the one with jurisdictional authority over the car.

"What sort of answers do you expect them to give you?" Beads of sweat were beginning to form on Sheriff Mazant's forehead despite the cool weather.

"Honest ones, and scientific ones," I intentionally impugned his own people and ignored the blatantly hostile look this earned me.

The Mercedes was already transferred between the two wreckers, but I waved at the tow truck to stop and led Sheriff Mazant to the car. I retrieved the evidence bag holding the keys from the wrecker driver and used the remote to open the trunk. I wanted Sheriff Mazant to see exactly what bothered me.

I pulled a latex glove from my messenger bag and pulled it on before I dipped my right index finger into one of the deeper pools of still moist blood. "See this?"

"It's blood." Sheriff Mazant gave me an exasperated look because he did not see what I felt was obvious.

"When did they first notice this car? Last weekend, right?" I kept waving the finger in his face while he did the math in his head and nodded agreement on the timeline. "If this blood was in the trunk last Friday, it should be dry as a bone by now."

"So, why isn't it?"

"That, sheriff, is why the car is on its way to Baton Rouge." I slammed the trunk lid closed and peeled off the glove. I tossed it into the same barrel where Chance and I had discarded our gloves earlier.

"What could it mean?" Apparently science was not one of Sheriff Mazant's best classes in school.

"It means something is very wrong with the blood in the trunk besides the sheer quantity of it."

"What do you think it means?" Mazant pressed. He needed an excuse to give the senator when he called.

"It means the blood has been tampered with. I cannot explain why anyone would drain so much blood from a body and then go to the effort of keeping it from drying rather than clean it up. They may be trying to throw off the time of death, but hiding the body already did that." I had no theory on any of this. I was hoping the crime lab would give me something useful so I could begin some sort of actual investigation.

"You'll share what they tell you with David?" Sheriff Mazant asked in a tone that sounded a lot like he did not trust me to do so.

"You made us partners," I reminded him.

Sheriff Mazant's expression conveyed that he heard my opinion about that loud and clear. He was not all that happy with his detective either. My moving the car out of Saint Xavier Parish made it clear that his proxy was unable to either interfere with or properly monitor my actions.

I waited until the sheriff and his deputies left the lot to sign for the search warrant Captain Hammond sent with the State Patrol officers escorting the tow truck. They had kept their distance, but overheard the entire conversation. They were both laughing when one of them said that the warrant was likely to set Sheriff Mazant's hair on fire when he learned of it.

Sixteen

There was just enough time for me to take a shower before I was supposed to meet DA Milquetoast for cocktails after I walked from George's lot to Judge Rogers' house. Chief Theriot drove a parallel route one block to my left all the way to the house. I made sure to use the crosswalks to avoid giving the chief any reason to hassle me. I even put Roux's leash on before exercising him in the front yard before I left to find the country club.

The country club was either a former plantation home or modeled on one, with tall white pillars and a deep veranda. The all Black valet staff wore uniforms that were reminiscent of photographs I have seen of private clubs from the Jim Crow era. This club seemed to make a special point of hiring people who would have never been allowed on its grounds otherwise.

"I am here to meet Henri Gabouri," I told the silver-haired host guarding the doorway to the dining room. I was glad I had guessed right about the necessity of wearing a jacket and tie to dinner.

"He is expecting you in the bar, sir." He pointed to a door across the cypress-floored lobby. The sound of a dozen simultaneous conversations gave the nature of the room away from even this distance. I noted that the maître d did not need my name to know my identity or purpose.

Gabouri was standing at the far end of the bar and gave a wave to attract my attention as I entered the room. I felt, but did not always see, every eye in the place give me a furtive glance as I crossed the room. Conversations went on unabated, but the locals definitely wanted a chance to size up the detective who might come calling on them about Kirk Donovan. The membership by and large was in their forties and fifties and entirely white. I spotted one table near the window that was occupied by a half dozen men who may have been members since the 1950s. They were likely the ones running the place and one of them was undoubtedly Senator Chester Donovan.

"About what you expected?" Henri smirked when I was close enough that he was sure I was the only one to hear him. I smiled and shrugged rather than respond out loud.

"You didn't bring Crystal?" I asked, trying to gauge the depth of their relationship.

"She had better things to do. This isn't her sort of place. The testosterone level runs a little high," Gabouri repeated what must have been a joke of hers.

"What may I serve you, sir?" the bartender was a tall Black man in his late fifties who may have worked behind that bar for half his life. It was doubtful that he needed to ask anyone else in the room what they drank.

"Manhattan. Maker's Mark if you have it."

"We can do better than that," the bartender assured me before he stepped away. I listened to Gabouri's welcoming me to the place, but I kept an eye on my drink. The bartender pulled a bottle of Pappy Van Winkle from high on the shelf and gave me an overly generous pour. Gabouri might regret his invitation when he got the bar tab.

"You're going to spoil me," I joked with the bartender when he set the chilled glass before me. He gave me a nod and went to refill drinks for some far less appreciative patrons. I plucked the cherry from my cocktail and savored the mix of sweet maraschino and silky bourbon as I put my back to the room. I locked eyes with the DA. "Which of the codgers in the far corner is Senator Donovan?"

He nearly spat his drink on the bar laughing but recovered before we made a scene. "Blue blazer, gray trousers, back to the window."

Of course the patriarch of the town's predators would be sure to keep everyone where he could see them. He might choose to sit in the corner, but he wasn't about to let himself be cornered. I glanced at him in the mirror rather than turn around. Chester Donovan looked to be nearly seventy years old, using my mother as a gauge. He had closely-cropped silver hair and gray whiskers, and piercing blue eyes that glared at me in the bar mirror.

We locked eyes in the mirror for an instant. He said something to his companions and all but two of them stood up and left the room. I did not take this as an invitation to approach him. The ritual in the mirror simply acknowledged that our future interactions would likely be adversarial. I felt like I was back to dealing with Afghan war lords, where more is communicated through gestures or expressions than by what is said aloud.

"That went well," I sighed as Gabouri struggled to understand what had just transpired.

"Damn, I really wanted to introduce you to the senator," Gabouri pouted.

"Oh, we just met. He didn't need to be face to face to tell me to get out of town." I assured my baffled host. I had seen what anyone in the business of negotiations calls 'the goodbye look' before. He had already used Chief Theriot and Sheriff Mazant to relay the message. I needed to find a way to convince him I was not leaving until I knew what happened to his daughter-in-law.

"And you got all of that from looking at Chester in a mirror?" Gabouri was understandably skeptical of anyone with a skill he himself should possess but never will.

"And more." I took a long sip of my drink before I continued with his education. "He sent everyone else away. He doesn't need anyone else at the table to help him run me off. I am going to assume one or two of them are his bought-and-paid-for judges and the rest are Donovan family members."

"Two of them were judges. Three of them are the senator's brothers. I don't recognize the men still sitting with him."

"The young one is his security detail. Notice how he lets his jacket hang open just enough to show he is wearing a sidearm, and I recognize the older one."

"Really? Who is it?"

"Have you ever heard the name Felix Deveraux?" I didn't mention that he was my mother's brother. I was just testing Gabouri's knowledge of my uncle's reputation. Felix is a political 'fixer' of the highest order, and everything you hate about back room deals and the like are what you would hate about him. His critics tend to forget to credit him when his meddling benefits them. Felix waved me towards their table. I waved back, but I didn't move.

"He's the wizard behind the curtain in Baton Rouge, right?" Almost nobody knows my uncle on sight because being anonymous is how he manages to pull his shenanigans.

"You are correct," I chuckled and patted him on the shoulder before I walked to the senator's table.

I took a seat next to my uncle because I knew he was not going to have a discussion with me that required him to raise his voice enough for anyone else to hear. He still felt I owed him a favor for asking him to intervene in an FBI investigation that was meant to cost Chief Avery at least his job. I wound up resolving the matter myself, but simply asking for Uncle Felix's help had still incurred a favor. This was not going to be a good time for me to have to pay up.

"Mister Devereaux," I greeted him as I sat down. His thick silvery hair always reminds me of Andrew Jackson, but mostly I imagine him to resemble the devil you meet at the crossroads to sell your soul.

"Detective Holland." His lips formed a thin smile and his deep blue eyes were mirthful over the top of his tortoise-shell rimmed glasses. "Have you met Senator Donovan?"

"No, I have not. I am going to have to speak with you at some point," I shook his hand and offered my business card. He handed it to his shadow.

"The senator was just telling us a funny joke when you arrived. Would you care to share it again?" I wasn't sure whether Uncle Felix was deflecting the conversation or just delaying my questions.

"Everyone loves a good Cajun joke," the senator declared. "Sheriff Boudreaux goes to Thibodeaux's house to give some news about his missing wife. He tells Thibodeaux that he has bad news, good news, and great news. His pal thinks for a moment and then asks for the bad news first. Boudreaux tells him his wife's body was found in the bayou that morning. Thibodeaux sheds a tear and then asks for the rest of the news. Boudreaux tells him that the good news is they pulled a dozen blue crabs off her body when they hauled her to shore. He hands eight of them to Thibodeaux and then tells him that the great news is that they will bring more crabs the next day, after they pull her back out of the bayou." This was amusing enough to the senator to slap his own knee and for Uncle

Felix to smile broadly.

"I suppose that will be even funnier if they don't find any on your daughter-in-law," I all but hissed. I knew his message was that he didn't care about Gwen near as much as he did his missing son.

"How is your investigation going?" Uncle Felix hastily asked to break the sudden tension.

"Forward. Always forward," I deflected with one of my father's go-to bits of wit. You are always going forward whether you are headed uphill or downhill. "You know I can't discuss this with you."

"Don't try to act like your department's rules suddenly apply to a loose cannon like you. Just tell the senator what have you learned so far." Felix does not have the word 'no' in his vocabulary.

"I'm not going to discuss the case with Senator Donovan, or with you. The senator may prove be a material witness at the very least," I objected, entirely for the record.

"Come now. You know very well that the senator did not kill his daughter-in-law or hide his only son from you," Felix tried to dismiss either notion with a wave of his hand.

"I do not, in fact, know either one of those things. I can tell you this much, though. Kirk Donovan's entire family are champions at playing Hide and Seek. They are all missing and I haven't a clue as to what is likely to pan out on any of them. I have heard that Belle and Kirk were arguing about some paper on the Donovan family history. Perhaps Senator Donovan could help me understand what Belle's father wanted to keep secret." I was not prepared to hand his client anything useful unless I received something equally useful in return.

"That is a private matter best left between them. The important thing is whether or not you think Kirk killed his wife." Uncle Felix immediately changed the subject.

I needed to bounce the ball back to the senator's side of the court. "You know your son better than either of us. Do you think a man capable of twenty years of spousal abuse might slip up and go too far?"

"I believe your job is to simply locate Gwendolyn, if I am not mistaken. A decision will need to be made about who investigates this further if you discover she was the victim of foul play." Felix was giving me a warning, and not even one of his more subtle ones. "I'm sure you have met the owner of the local paper by now, a young woman by the name of Crystal Franks. You'll want to be very careful what you say around her."

"She ambushed Judge Rogers and me the night his daughter was reported missing. He also warned me to give her wide berth."

"Your promising career could be derailed were you to start speculating about the evidence in the local paper. You need to keep a tight lid on whatever you find." Senator Donovan added his own warning. "We prefer to have any crimes you discover handled in court and not judged by public opinion."

"Of course you want this handled where you have complete control. You own the judges, but not the newspaper," I pointed out. Felix gave a dismissive toss of his hands. The truth is, handling things like bad press and speculative scenarios is how he earns his living. I started to stand up. "Is there anything else to discuss?"

"This should prove to be a domestic matter. You don't need to be poking your nose into our family's history or my son's business matters. Stay in your lane, Detective, and everything will be just fine," the senator finally enunciated the very precise boundaries his minions were supposed to be keeping me within.

"I have assured Senator Donovan that you view this as a missing person case, and that you are particularly discreet. Was I wrong to do so?" I refused to play my uncle's word games. I noticed the senator's brothers were all staring at us from the bar.

"You were only wrong to sell him on the idea that either of you can tell me what to do."

"I also warned him that you are worse than having a corrupt cop assigned to the case," Felix said with neither insult in the way he called me honest nor humor about trying to forewarn the senator. "You have a conscience that makes you see justice and the law as being separate things. I believe you may well be the only person less concerned with what is technically legal in this state than I am."

"Your client needs to understand that I am going to throw every rock he rolls in my way back through his window." I wasn't going to get into a debate over ethics or the written law with someone as challenged by both as Uncle Felix. I finished my drink in one long swallow and stood up to leave.

"We'll keep that in mind. I'm sure he can find some very heavy boulders if need be." Felix raised his glass to order a fresh round and to signal the senator's entourage standing at the bar that it was safe to return to their seats. I knew the senator repeated every word spoken between us, because the way his forehead was furrowed betrayed his growing concern.

"What did your uncle want?" Gabouri asked when I set my own empty glass on the bar beside me. The bartender was quick to replace it with a fresh cocktail.

"Things he knew I wasn't going to tell him. Then he threatened me with things he knew he couldn't do. He just needed to remind both the senator and myself that this is not a routine investigation, and that more than both of our careers may be riding on how it turns out." What I really believed was that this was all just a charade. My uncle wanted to make sure his client stayed on the hook. He needed to look like he had the ability to sway me, but all he really needed to do was get me to limit the scope of my investigation.

"I hope they didn't ruin your appetite. This place has the best turtle soup in the state." Gabouri changed the subject to hide his concern and steered me towards the dining room.

Gabouri's opinion of the soup was a sign that he needs to get out of the parish more often, but it was good, and the trout I paired it with wasn't cooked to mush under a well-prepared almondine sauce. He regaled me with stories about law school and the classmate who had become my girlfriend. I am sure he believed the stories to be far more amusing than I felt Katie would find them when I repeated what he had said.

Seventeen

Chief Theriot used the pre-dawn fog to conceal himself at the end of the Judge's driveway again the next morning. This was apparently going to be a ritual I would need to learn to deal with or figure out a way to disrupt. I am not very patient about dealing with petty annoyances.

I put a leash on Roux's harness and took him on a three mile run through town, intentionally running the wrong way down any one-way streets I could find and cutting diagonally across large parking lots to make following me as much of a challenge and headache as possible for the determined police chief.

We were a mile from the house when I heard a second pair of footsteps, lighter than my own, approaching in the fog. Roux heard them as well and instinctively placed himself in front of me, though neither of us could see who else was out at this early hour.

"Good morning, Detective," Crystal Franks greeted us as we closed to within a few feet of one another. I was wearing a pair of light weight sweats against the morning chill. She had on tight sweatpants and a very small top that barely covered her sports bra. I could see the firmness of her muscle tone and the goosebumps on what Katie would have referred to as her store-bought breasts. Crystal's intent was as obvious as her lack of sweat.

"Gee, what a surprise," I said but still smiled. Roux sat down in front of me, keeping the two of us well apart.

"Oh, I run every morning. Have to keep this old body in shape," she said. The comment gave her an excuse to do a slow pirouette to allow me to study exactly what fine shape she was in. Her raven-dark hair was pulled into a pony tail. This fell along her spine, and between the halves of the tattoo on her back. Black wings ran from the top of each shoulder to the top of her sweatpants. Each wing must have taken hours and involved a lot of outright pain to color in so well.

"Those are impressive. Crow or raven? I can never remember the pin feather thing," I asked. I was fully aware of what they were meant to be.

"Angel. They are angel wings," she said in a tone that didn't see any humor in my comment. "My father used to call me his little angel."

"Is your father still alive?" I was disappointed in myself for getting sucked into a conversation with this woman.

"He may as well be dead," she responded without any further elaboration. "Mind if I run with you?"

"We were actually just about to start our two mile sprint. Join us if you can keep up," I said and prayed she wasn't in good enough shape to make me actually sprint for two miles just to get rid of her.

"Perhaps tomorrow. I live just a couple of blocks from here. Are you sure I can't tempt you off your training for a cup of coffee?" And there it was. Her plan all along.

"Sorry, Roux has to get his miles in or he gets grumpy," I politely dodged her proposition. We would be changing our schedule beginning the next morning.

"The offer stands," she persisted. I noticed she did not start running as soon as Roux and I resumed our own run.

I was dressed in a pair of cargo-style pants and a sweater with the state police emblem on the left breast when Detective Chance arrived for our morning briefing. I laced my Merrell ankle boots on as he briefed me on his visit with Kirk Donovan's secretary the day before. I made no mention of my encounter with the newspaper reporter and he made no mention of any tongue lashing or discipline he had received from Sheriff Mazant over not being the one to tell him the Mercedes was leaving town.

"Kirk's secretary said he told her to go home early when he left the office about nine last Friday," he said.

"So the last time she saw him was as he left the office. Did he call her at all over the weekend?" It was good to have at least one of the members of the family with a definite last time and place of contact.

"He called her later that morning from his house. He wanted to confirm a couple of appointments for Tuesday morning, which she took to mean he was not coming home from Florida until sometime on

Monday. She said his clients have started calling about their court dates and she doesn't know what to tell them."

"I wouldn't know what to say either. Did she know the name of the hotel where he was supposed to stay in Pensacola?" I wanted to see if he had pursued that lead on his own.

"She didn't make the reservations and never asks him which hotel he uses." I wasn't sure what to make of this. At least three people knew where I was sleeping in Donovan, and not one of them even worked for me.

"That's a lot of hotels to cold call," I hinted. It wasn't like either Detective Chance or I were going to Pensacola to look for Kirk Donovan. I already suspected he never made it that far.

"Uh huh," Chance mumbled. Those calls were not getting made unless he foisted the job off on deputies.

"Okay, he was supposed to go to a road rally. Where did he store his race car? Did he have a pit crew of any sort?" I was talking mostly to myself at this point. I could tell that my partner had given neither of these matters any thought.

"I think he kept his car at his house," Chance said without any elaboration.

"Why do you think that?"

"It was in his garage in the pictures I saw in that article about his being into racing."

"Well, let's go check it out," I decided and pulled the search warrants for Kirk Donovan's home and office from the messenger bag I use to carry what I consider to be my work essentials. It has spare magazines for my pistol, a first aid kit capable of handling a range of terrible injuries, a good digital camera and voice recorder, a flashlight, a multi-tool and some other odds and ends you never need until you suddenly do. My sister used to joke that it is my security blanket, and knowing I am prepared for almost anything does help mitigate my PTSD.

"Who signed those?" He sounded surprised that I was able to obtain the warrants.

"An honest judge in Baton Rouge," I answered his immediate question and the one he didn't know how to ask. I wasn't going to discuss my distrust of the local authorities with him. He was one of them.

We drove to the Donovans' new home in my station wagon, and I needed the local detective's help with directions to the address. He seemed to be very familiar with the location for someone who said he had made only a couple of trips there in the dark.

The sizeable home faced the twelfth fairway on the country club's golf course and backed onto a canal that linked to Bayou Beausejour. The home occupied at least two lots so the nearest neighbors were not very close by. The house was built in an older Acadian style. The home's exterior was covered in weathered cypress lapboards, with a hipped metal roof and its tall windows protected from heat and storms by a wrap-around porch. The four-car garage was detached and sat perpendicular to the house on a paver-stone driveway.

I looked through the windows on the garage doors and saw only one car, a Lexus sedan.

"No race car," I noted. The garage was unlocked, which was curious, so we combed through the neatly arranged space. The Lexus was registered to Kirk Donovan, but we both already expected this was Kirk's personal car. Gwen's Mercedes was sitting in the crime lab, so that only left room in the garage for a golf cart and the car Kirk was supposedly driving.

I found an impressive rolling rack of tools and noticed that one of the empty bays was equipped with a hydraulic lift. This was enough to convince me Kirk handled his own maintenance, so we weren't likely to find a pit crew to interview. The photos on the wall above the toolbox and the shop manuals showed Kirk's late model Ford GT. It was a car priced in the low six-figures, which should have made it a difficult thing to hide. Someone had tried to conceal the spare tire from Gwen's Mercedes on a rack of tires meant for the Ford GT. It caught my eye because it was a different sized tire. This answered the question of where the missing spare tire was, only to replace that question with a new one of why it was here.

The back side of the driveway switched from paver to poured concrete where it became a boat ramp. There was a short wooden dock at the back of the property, as there were behind most of the adjacent homes. Those all had boats tied to them, or boats sitting under covers on their driveways. We found an empty boat trailer on a pad close to the water's edge, but no boat.

I added the lack of a boat to my growing list of things to investigate about this family. They had an unusual capacity to lose things or to leave them in curious states. I held a secret hope that they didn't even own a boat so I wouldn't have to try to find it. The expensive rack of fishing rods and large tackle boxes we discovered just inside the back door after I picked the lock killed that possibility.

We were in what would usually be called a mud room, but this space was far too clean and organized to be described that way. I paused to put the lock-pick back in my messenger bag while Chance decided whether or not to say anything about what I had just done. We had a warrant for the house, but Chance was obviously deeply uncomfortable with my having burglary tools in my bag.

The entire house looked like a model home and felt utterly devoid of human habitation. There were no pets or even a pet door. The house smelled of scented candles. The few photographs sitting on the side-tables and hanging on the living room walls were all shots that had been professionally posed. They looked like the sort of photos that come in picture frames when you buy them. Everyone was smiling, but nobody seemed to be happy or comfortable in their assigned position.

There were no clothes in the washing machine or in the dirty clothes hampers in any of the bedrooms. We checked Kirk's closet and dresser and found that all of his clothes seemed to be present. Kirk's Nomex racing suit, fireproof gloves and shoes, and racing helmet were missing, along with one small bag from his shelf of luggage. The likelihood that Kirk had gone to a race increased with this discovery, but this also added to the mystery of his present whereabouts.

Even more intriguing was the complete lack of clothing in Gwendolyn Donovan's closets. There was an impressive collection of ball gowns and other formal wear in one closet, but her day-to-day clothes were gone from their closet and her dresser drawers. A complete set of empty luggage sat on a shelf in the otherwise barren closet, which begged the question of where her clothes had gone.

Every bed was made. Every trash can was empty, and each had a new trash liner. Mail from Saturday and the past few days was piled up in the mailbox, but there was little to speak of beyond one department store bill and some junk mail. I assumed most of their bills were on auto-pay and the statements went to Kirk's office or whoever handled the family's money.

"This place was cleaned before we got here." I was stating the obvious when we reached the kitchen. The extent of the housecleaning exceeded that of any maid service I knew of, and my mother has a world-class housekeeper. I doubted whether a crime scene tech could prove anyone lived in the home.

"It sure looks that way," Chance agreed. He was leafing through the mail for something to do.

I opened the refrigerator and found all the confirmation I needed. There were no leftovers, produce, or dairy products left to spoil. There were a few jars of pickles and other condiments and the freezer was enviably stocked with good cuts of meat and seafood. The dishwasher looked brand new. Its empty interior was spotless and dry.

"Show me those trophies," I finally said out of sheer exasperation.

Detective Chance led me to Kirk's office without realizing this was a trick. He ought not to have known which room was the office if he had not been in the house before. Chance had not left my side since we entered the home, so theoretically he had no way to find the office on his own.

The drawers to the desk were locked, but I was not inclined to bother picking any of those locks because I believed the drawers were going to be as cleaned out as the rest of the house. It was just a means of frustrating whoever forced them open.

I did pick the lock on Kirk's impressive trophy case and sought to build a profile of Kirk Donovan as a race car driver. The photographs in the case indicated Kirk began racing in a modified 1980s-era Ford Mustang before he leapt to the expensive true race car. His earliest trophies dated to almost fifteen years earlier and were from races in nearly every corner of the country. The trophies were not particularly expensive. They varied in size as his early years didn't involve many trips to the winner's circle. There was an odd change in the style and quality of the trophies during the past few years. My new partner claimed he did not see the difference when I asked him what changed between the early trophies and the later trophies.

I spotted a consistency in the color of the gold and the size of the base of the later trophies. It was far more varied at the start of his hobby. I was intrigued that he also seemed to consistently place second or third in every race in these later years. Not even top race car drivers accomplish that. None of the trophies were for the same race twice within even a few years, which is rare among drivers on the amateur circuit. He seemed to race at least six times a year, but the races began moving closer and closer to home. None involved more than a long day's drive.

I turned one of the most recent trophies upside down and found that it was made by a company barely half an hour away. I turned all of the trophies over and found a dozen more. A race organizer in Kansas can surely find a trophy maker closer than Morgan City, Louisiana.

"I don't think you need to touch everything the man owns to find out what happened here," Chief Theriot scolded me from the doorway to the office. I was startled, but not in the least bit surprised, by Chief Theriot's sudden and unwelcome intrusion. He had not followed us here, I was sure of that.

"Well, Chief Theriot. What an unnecessary surprise," I shot back. "You do realize you are outside of the city limits right now, right?"

"I got a report of a possible break-in," he tried to excuse himself.

"From whom? The neighbors are all at work and Detective Chance here wouldn't report himself committing a crime. Would you, David?" It was a rhetorical question, but Sheriff Mazant's detective still felt obliged to shake his head. "I believe you are the one trespassing."

"I'm not going to argue jurisdictions with you. I just wanted to be sure the place is secure," Theriot mumbled.

"This place is not just secure, it is sanitized. Someone has already been through here making sure there is nothing to find," I complained. He seemed to be as confused and surprised as we were. It wasn't an act.

"I don't see how. Anyone coming in would have set off the alarm system," Theriot said and betrayed knowledge I wasn't sure he should have for a house he was not responsible for patrolling.

"Did we?"

"No," he admitted.

"Then I guess someone either forgot to set it before they went into hiding or someone knew the code and came through here with a fine toothed comb to make sure we did not come away with any clues," I suggested.

"Then you didn't find anything," Theriot asked in an obvious attempt to learn what we found despite the diligent efforts to scrub the place down. Detective Chance shook his head and gave away our secret.

"I wouldn't say I came away empty handed. What do you know about Kirk's racing?" I asked. Theriot seemed to know a lot of things I saw little reason for him to know.

"He was good. Just look at all those trophies. I guess it was a way to blow off a lot of stress," Theriot fumbled for a neutral response.

"What sort of stress did Kirk Donovan have, Chief?" I said it more dismissively than I meant it. I was hoping he would defend his own response with at least some gossip.

"He handled a lot of family law. That can get pretty heated." Theriot's response was more than I imagined I would get, and opened a new avenue of exploration. He was absolutely correct about the stress involved in practicing family law. It is a specialty not many attorneys or judges want any part of.

"We're about done here. If you don't mind letting yourself out that would be great," I told the chief and closed the trophy case with the last trophy still in my hand.

"Like I said, I just wanted to be sure everything was secure. We got a call." Chief Theriot repeated.

"No, you didn't, but it's always nice to see you. I guess I will see you about four tomorrow morning, right?" I said and nudged him out of the office and on his way with a small shove to his shoulder.

"You saw me out there this morning?" he laughed.

"And yesterday morning. One of these mornings I might get tired of being spied on. Just so you know," I said with as little menace as I could behind the obvious threat.

"What do you think it would take to make me stop?" Theriot shot back. He was genuinely looking forward to an altercation between the two of us.

"Be a shame if I mistook you for a burglar casing the house, wouldn't it?" I made sure to look him square in the eye when I said this. It took a moment, but he gulped and blinked.

Detective Chance burst into laughter he didn't even try to suppress. At least I knew whose side he was on.

Eighteen

I asked Detective Chance to stay and make a list of every race Kirk Donovan received a trophy from, including the date and place, without telling him where I was headed with the trophy in my hand. He suggested having one of the department's deputies handle this sort of menial work, but I told him I was only going to work with him and needed him to do a thorough job. He obviously knew I was looking for a means to get away from him to pursue a lead he might be grilled about later.

Brenner's Trophies in Morgan City was a small operation that seemed content to be the place locals purchased trophies handed out at cook-offs, ball games, and school athletic competitions. You could get a personalized trophy to be the Best Anything or Anyone you cared to be for the right price.

Like a second place rally car driver.

"I was wondering when someone would finally come around and ask about this," Lenny, the young but balding owner of the long standing family-owned business all but laughed when I set the trophy on the counter between us.

"How so?"

"Kirk was through here a few times a year to get a trophy made for some race he wanted people to think he went to. He always asked for second or third place because people only remember who took first place."

"He wasn't one to settle for a mere participation trophy then?" I tried to keep the mood light despite the gravity of what the young man had just told me.

"We wound up with a couple of designs Kirk liked. He would order the one he wanted and give me the name of the race and details he wanted on the plaque." That explained why so many of the trophies seemed to resemble one another.

"And he has been doing this for a couple of years?" I needed to hear this confirmed for the record.

"I could check back in the books if you like, but I am comfortable saying he's had an account with us for at least three years now." I was at a loss for any other questions he might provide the answer to, but went ahead with a couple just to fill the time.

"Did he ever say why he wanted the trophies?"

"No, and I never asked him why he was having them made, either. That seemed like a really good way to lose the business." He was likely right in that assumption.

"Did he ever hint what he was really doing with his time?" This struck me as being possible. Kirk was beginning to sound like a guy who liked to bend rules, and people who bend rules need to brag to somebody about it.

"Again, I never asked. I assumed he was having an affair. It was the best reason I could come up with," the shop owner shrugged. "My wife would kill me if she thought I was doing this for a lot of guys around here."

We both had a nice laugh at that, but it left me to be the one find to Kirk's motivation for this strange ruse.

Nineteen

Tony, Katie, and my sister Tulip arrived on my doorstep as I was settling into my after-work ritual of three fingers of Elijah Craig bourbon over just as many ice cubes and rummaging through the packaged meals I had brought from Strada Ammazarre. I was going to need to either grocery shop or get the cooler refilled over the weekend at the rate I was eating.

"We bring wine and lamb chops," Katie declared as she hugged me. Chef Tony and my sister Tulip were carrying the bags containing an evening's worth of relief from my loneliness. I had no idea how much I missed Katie until she kissed me. Roux is far sloppier in his affections, and I suspect his licking me is just his way of making sure he gets fed.

"Good timing. I was looking for the can opener when you knocked," I jested. Tony was appropriately appalled.

"I don't trust you to escape this place on Saturday so I talked these two into coming to see you tonight," Katie explained as she accepted a glass of wine from Tulip. They were smart enough to bring their own wine glasses and opener.

"I will be there," I protested. "I have lots of time to be anywhere but here until something breaks in this case."

"No leads?" Tulip spoke up. Her law practice is civil, but I had begun referring a lot of criminal clients to her when my idea of justice began to veer from the laws Katie still tries to uphold. My girlfriend and I avoid talking shop when we are alone.

"Every lead points to more possibilities than facts, which does nothing to narrow the scope," I allowed myself to openly complain. I had refused to let Chance know I was flailing about in the investigation so badly.

We moved into the living room and Katie snuggled against me on the loveseat while Tony and my sister tried to leave enough separation between them on the sofa that I would not be reminded they were dating. Roux rested his head lovingly on Katie's feet.

"That doesn't sound very good," Katie sighed. She understood this was my way of admitting there was no way to know when I was going to get back to New Orleans.

"Today I discovered Kirk Donovan has been buying fake racing trophies for the past three years. I don't know if it means he wanted people to believe he was a good racer or if he just needed them to believe he was racing. He might have been having an affair for all I know. I don't care, but now I have to figure out if it has anything to do with his disappearance. We searched his house this afternoon, but someone had already been through it to be sure there was nothing to find. There wasn't even a computer in his office, and the beds looked like they have never been slept in."

"What are they trying to hide?" Tony wondered aloud.

"More importantly, who is 'they'?" Tulip asked. Hers was the question needing answered first.

"Well, 'they' probably includes Uncle Felix. He made sure we bumped into each other last night when I had dinner with Gabouri. He and the senator tried to put a scare into me to limit the scope of the case." Everyone's eyes widened upon learning of Felix's involvement.

"Tell me about the house." Tony chose to ignore Felix's warning, as he knew I would.

"Supposedly Kirk and Gwen raised Belle in this house, and then he built a new one after she went to college. They left a lot of things here and the new place literally looks like a model home where nobody has ever slept a night." I had no luck gauging Tony's reaction to any of this. Katie and Tulip began looking around the living room with a new perspective on my temporary accommodations.

"Maybe we should take a look," Tony finally said and grinned the way he used to when we worked together. I think I had failed to understand how much he enjoyed this part of his job when he worked for Iraq's secret police.

"What, right now?"

"Oh, let's. It will make our dinner conversation so much less boring," Tulip half-joked.

"Fine, let's take the wagon," I sighed and watched Katie grab one of the unopened bottles of wine from the kitchen before she headed towards the garage. Tony brought a six pack of Abita beer from the fridge for the two of us to share. Nobody objected to Roux joining us as he jumped over the back seat to settle into his kennel. I didn't want to leave him alone with our lamb chops, anyway.

"Don't open any of that until we get there. The local police are looking for any reason to hassle me, and explaining your having an open container in a car headed to a possible crime scene you shouldn't be at won't be a pleasant call with Captain Hammond," I warned all of my companions.

I gave them an abbreviated tour of Donovan and pointed out the well-lit country club as I drove past. I kept an eye in the rear view mirror for Chief Theriot or one of his deputies. I was beginning to suspect Sheriff Mazant was using the local cops as well as his own detective to inform him of my movements.

"Nice place," Katie mused when I pulled to a stop outside of Kirk and Gwen Donovan's garage. "If you are into expensive homes, I mean."

"Who needs this much house?" I retorted to her subtle criticism of the coziness of my two-bedroom bachelor pad above Strada Ammazarre.

I picked the lock on the back door once again and walked ahead of everyone to turn on every light in the house. Roux began to sniff his way through each room on his own, finally taking a guard's position where he could look through one of the front door's side-light windows. The rest of us moved from room to room looking for anything that might provide some glimmer of insight into the new home's missing occupants. I put the trophy back in the display case when I reached the office.

I sat at the desk and toyed with the cables someone removed from whatever computer once sat on the desk, which was likely a laptop of some sort, before I began working on the locks on the drawers. Tulip and Katie turned their attention to the bedrooms and bathrooms, while Tony began dissecting the kitchen. Tony and I were equally impressed with Kirk's man cave, a wood paneled room easily the size of the living room and furnished with a full-size billiard table and his arsenal of expensive skeet and hunting weapons. I was tempted to pick the lock to look at the Beretta shotguns. The entire process took half an hour and then we convened in the living room to discuss what each of us discovered and the opinions we now had about Kirk Donovan and his missing family.

"The file drawers in the office were all empty, as I expected. I haven't found a wall or floor safe anywhere and the security system is pretty basic, which is probably why someone had such an easy time turning it off," I said to open the discussion.

"The kitchen has a lot of new things, but it looks like someone has been cooking," Tony declared.

"You two are such guys," Katie mocked us from her seat on the dark leather sofa as she passed the open bottle of wine to my sister. They looked like a pair of fashionable winos. Neither of them had brought a glass with them and they both knew better than to use any in the house.

"Which means what?" I challenged. It was a difficult charge to defend myself against without better context.

"Kirk Donovan is a guy who was content to live in his father-in-law's house for what, twenty years, before he built his own house? He had the money the whole time, but he didn't build this until after his kid went to college? The master shower has dual shower heads and a huge Jacuzzi tub, but there are no pictures in the bedroom of the happily married couple that would use them. In fact, the only pictures of Kirk and Gwen are where other people can see them. His closet is as large as Gwen's and the daughter's bedroom doesn't look like she is making many trips home from school. You tell me what all that says." Katie was fully in her prosecutor mode. She has a special talent for presenting any set of facts in a way that will lead even an unreasonable jury to the verdict she sets her sights upon.

"We're just guys, remember?" I wasn't seeing it.

"The guy was getting ready to divorce his wife. This is one huge bachelor pad waiting to be unveiled. Cozy fireplaces in here and in the master bedroom, gourmet kitchen and wine cellar, pool table in his man cave, but not even a sewing room for his wife. There is nothing in this house that indicates Gwen was anything more than tolerated," Katie summed up. Tulip raised the bottle to toast their mutual negative

84

assessment of Kirk and Gwen's marriage.

"And do you have any theories on why her stuff is missing with her luggage still here?" I was sure they did, but I just wasn't sure if it was going to be any better than my own.

"No theories. I can tell you exactly what's going on. She piled everything she had into trash bags and crammed them into her car to get out of here as quickly as she could. Using luggage takes up valuable space when you're bailing out," Tulip advised me. "I have helped more than a few of my friends get the heck out of Dodge, as Daddy used to say."

"That makes sense. The last time anyone saw Gwen was almost exactly in the middle of when her husband was supposedly racing around the sugar cane fields north of town. She probably thought she was playing Beat the Clock." I mulled it over. The idea was logical and fit the facts, and even provided a good reason for having pulled the spare tire out of the trunk. That would have made room for at least one or two additional trash bags of clothes. It just didn't explain the blood.

"I'll bet he already has a mistress, probably more than one. He's probably parking his race car in someone else's garage when he is supposed to be winning all those trophies," Tulip said with a slight slur to her voice. My sister is too easily intoxicated, but I know she has no tolerance for infidelity when she is sober, either.

"But do you think Kirk would kill Gwen to get rid of her? I'm sure there was a pre-nup limiting what he'd lose if he just shoved her out the door. I like your idea about her bailing on the guy, but I still have a trunk full of her blood to explain and there were no bags full of clothes found anywhere near the crime scene." I took another drink from my beer bottle while the two women bandied about a theory to explain the crime scene.

"Husbands kill their wives for considerably less," Katie opined from professional experience. "Isn't there a history of domestic violence in the relationship?"

"I didn't tell you that," I pointed out.

"I talked to Judge Rogers this afternoon. He poured his heart out about Gwen's marriage." Katie admitted. I was glad it was her shoulder the judge cried on because I had no idea what I would have said. Katie had only recently divorced her narcissistic first husband, but he had the sense not to physically abuse her. That may have been because she wasn't going to take it, but it also may have had to do with her father being an NOPD cop from the Irish Channel. He would not have let what Gwen endured happen to any child of his more than once without responding in kind.

Roux barked twice to get my attention. "Hang on, we have company."

I motioned for everyone to stay seated as made my way to where Roux was standing at attention by the back door. One of Chief Theriot's police cruisers was creeping slowly up the driveway with its lights off.

I half anticipated this would happen when I agreed to bring my guests to the house. Their opinions were immensely helpful, but none of them had any jurisdiction or authority to be searching the house. Katie had the best cover, but Tony had absolutely no excuse for being there. Neither of my bosses were likely to view him as a law enforcement consultant, though Chief Avery was familiar with the background the two of us share. I headed out the back door to intercept whoever it was before they got out of their car. I let Roux join me because his running loose was a proven way to keep them there.

"Official business." I waved my badge high over my head as the cruiser's high beams abruptly lit the driveway and nearly blinded me. Roux circled the station wagon and then circled behind the cruiser. I heard a yelp from inside the vehicle when the heavy pit bull leaped out of the dark to rest his paws on the cruiser's open driver's side window. "Roux, play nice."

This was not one of his formal commands but he knew what I wanted and walked to sit next to me. The car moved no further up the driveway.

"What are you doing here?" Chief Theriot demanded over his loudspeaker.

His bluster about looking forward to a fight apparently did not extend to taking on a pit bull. There had been plenty of time for word of Mazant's courthouse deputy's experience with Roux to get around. That growl and those big white teeth were going to be in the poor kid's dreams for a long time to come.

"No, Chief. The question is what are you doing here?" I retorted. "We have had this conversation. You need to get back inside your own jurisdiction and let me do my job."

"Why are you out here at this hour of the night?" he demanded. It was barely eight o'clock. People were beginning to emerge from their houses to watch the circus.

"It's not my bedtime," I mocked him. "Again, you are trespassing on a crime scene and need to leave. This is not a request."

I envisioned Chief Theriot balancing the odds of his continuing to lose ground in this debate against his need to be seen as someone you didn't mess with. The scene I was intentionally making threatened to undermine his authority among the locals. He wisely chose to back out of the driveway and hastily leave the neighborhood. I heard a few cheers from across the way before everyone went back inside.

"What was that all about?" Katie asked as I returned to the cozy position I had been enjoying before Chief Theriot interrupted our conversation.

"Chief Theriot has an appetite for picking fights with members of the state police. He crippled one of Captain Hammond's classmates years ago and only got a slap on the wrist. I get the impression he wants to improve on his fight record before I leave town." This was one of the many things I had hoped not to have to discuss with Katie.

"That would be a very stupid thing to do," Tony needlessly reassured the two women I knew were likely predisposed to believe this.

"I'm glad you're here, Tony, because I have a way to get some room to operate, but I need your help." This comment, and Tony's smile in response, only deepened our female companions' concern for my well-being. "Let's go eat. I don't want any of you driving through this parish late at night. My plate is already full of missing people."

Chief Theriot knew I had company with me; I was also sure that he did not know who they were. My guests had driven to Donovan in the bistro's Ford Raptor pickup truck, so tracing those license plates would only have lead Theriot back to me.

His deputies followed the truck as it left my house after dinner and headed back towards New Orleans. The deputies undoubtedly reported how many people left the house, but it was unlikely Theriot knew how many guests had arrived. It was crucial that he not know one of my guests was still in town.

Twenty

Theriot took his usual pre-dawn position outside the judge's house while Tony and I went over our plan one last time. The primary purpose of doing surveillance is not merely to watch a subject. The purpose is to learn your subject's daily routine and habits. My first early mornings in town were spent building a routine that was meant to lull Theriot into believing I was the one of us who was predictable. I had created the routine just to set this trap.

My plan to rid myself of Chief Theriot's shadow was drastic but simple. His ham-fisted attempts at intimidating me and his willingness to leave his jurisdiction made it almost pathetically simple to lure him into an ambush.

Roux and I left the house at our usual time. Theriot began following me as soon as I left the driveway and started towards downtown. Tony also left the house on foot. I ran a bit slower than usual so Tony could follow the tail-lights on Theriot's cruiser as the lawman inched along behind me. My usual path cut across a church parking lot to a one way street running back the way I came. It made the police chief lose contact with me as he circled the church and doubled back. The first wrinkle in my routine came when I ran past the church and continued into town. I knew the plan was likely to work when I glanced back and saw the chief had his turn signal on as we approached the church parking lot.

I ran straight ahead on the town's main street until I reached George's Automotive. I made my turn to the right at the next corner and pulled Chief Theriot in my wake while Tony located the garage's loaner wrecker. He was remiss about signing it out before he drove out of town.

Roux and I distracted the police chief for another half hour before we returned to Judge Rogers' house so I could take a shower. I debated on bringing Roux for the next part of my plan, but chose to leave him kenneled in the house rather than have to worry how he responded to Chief Theriot's reaction to what was about to happen. I needed to avoid killing Donovan's Chief of Police if at all possible. I was less confident that I could control Roux if he believed Tony or I needed him to defend either of us. I had seen his handiwork before and did not want Theriot's blood on my hands.

The police chief backed out of the driveway as I approached his cruiser in the Cadillac wagon. The positon he had taken in the driveway made it unlikely that he knew the dog was not with me. I was leaving home hours earlier than he was accustomed to, and that alone guaranteed he would follow me.

My left turn at the street signaled my intention to go back to Kirk Donovan's home a third time. Chief Theriot may have had a moment's panic that I was working on a clue found the night before. I didn't believe he was involved in sanitizing the crime scene, but I knew he was a key player in Senator Donovan's plan to keep me from proving Kirk orchestrated his wife's disappearance.

I pulled to the back of the driveway, as I had the night before, and parked perpendicular to the garage doors. Theriot once again chose to block the driveway by parking his cruiser almost two thirds up its length. The way I parked left a clear path between him and the boat ramp beyond the driveway. The distance from his front bumper to the water was less than thirty yards. I casually pulled the telephone from my pants pocket and tapped the first number on its speed dial.

"Go for it," I said and hung up. I slid the phone back in my pocket as I moved towards the safety of the back porch. It blocked my view of Chief Theriot, and his of me, as I slid my Glock from its holster and waited for the impact.

Tony had parked George's wrecker behind a Chevy Suburban half a dozen houses away before I led the Police Chief into this trap. He backed up and steered slowly into the street before gunning the engine. Chief Theriot turned his head towards the sound of the wrecker's massive Duramax diesel engine. I don't think he grasped what was happening until Tony hit his rear bumper at thirty miles an hour and used the heavy metal cattle guard and winch on the front of the wrecker to propel the cruiser forward. The air around me filled with a mixture of tire rubber being burned away as Chief Theriot tried to brake and the sound of the wrecker's engine laboring mightily to shove the Dodge Charger forward. Chief Theriot must have had a fleeting thought that turning on his siren and flashing red and blue lights would make my partner desist, but they only made the unholy pairing of bumpers look like a parade. Holding his foot on the brake and leaving the transmission in park was never going to be enough to stop what he eventually realized was the inevitable outcome.

The cruiser hit the water with enough momentum to nearly reach the channel before it began to sink. Tony made a hard left turn to avoid following the Chief into the canal.

The sound of the powerful wrecker tearing apart the cruiser's drivetrain shook the neighborhood from its usual slumber. None of them were dressed in time to see Tony make his escape.

I holstered my pistol and waved at the knot of curious neighbors gathering at the street end of the driveway before I began a slow walk to where the Police Chief's car was beginning to sink beneath the murky waters.

Chief Theriot waited for the water level in his car to reach the bottom of his open window before he opened his car door. I was impressed that he knew the proper method for exiting a submerged vehicle. Allowing the cruiser to fill to this level equalized the water pressure between the interior and exterior so he didn't have to fight the door to get it to open.

I think we were both caught by surprise when he dropped into deep water immediately after he he exited the cruiser. It appeared to be sitting in more shallow water. He surfaced again and we shared a befuddled look at the way his ruined vehicle sat in the canal. It was obviously not floating, but it also was no longer sinking.

Twenty-One

Captain Hammond was torn between suspending me and pinning a medal to my chest when Sheriff Mazant called to inform him of what he described as an 'incident' at the Donovan residence. He has always hated that my position within his department is the result of Uncle Felix's deal making, but his dislike of me was inconsequential compared to the level of his loathing for Chief Theriot. My having humiliated and nearly drowned Captain Hammond's nemesis, and doing so with multiple eye-witnesses willing to state I had nothing to do with either one, temporarily made me a hero in Hammond's eyes.

The stunt Tony and I pulled had unexpectedly advanced the investigation by two important steps. The reason Theriot's cruiser did not sink as expected was because it had come to rest atop Kirk's missing Ford GT. The added weight pushed the ruined sport coupe further into the canal's muddy bottom. It took a pair of wreckers nearly an hour to tug it loose and bring it to dry ground one again.

Kirk's missing computer was in a briefcase on the floorboards of the swamped coupe, along with a suitcase containing his racing clothes. He was wearing jeans and a T-shirt with the name of what I assumed was a local fishing camp named Camp Dumaine silkscreened on it. It looked new. The week his computer had spent in brackish water meant there would be nothing gained in trying to find what was on its ruined hard drive. The important thing was that I finally located Kirk Donovan. Finding his wife and daughter had a new urgency, and a new wrinkle. Kirk was no longer a viable suspect in Gwendolyn's disappearance, but she was now a person of extreme interest in his death.

I wrote a statement Hammond could feed the press that we both hoped would not create any fresh interest in a missing person case most people outside of the parish didn't even know existed. I needed to locate Gwendolyn Donovan, but I didn't want to announce why just yet.

Captain Hammond brought the preliminary forensic report on Gwendolyn's car with him. He handed it to me without comment and hid his face behind a coffee cup as I read the curious, and unwelcome, findings about the blood evidence. The blood matched Gwen's blood type. That proved to be the only good news in the report.

My fleeting hope of being able to solve a clear case of murder/suicide collapsed with the reality of the lab's analysis of the sticky blood in the trunk of Gwen's Mercedes.

The blood in the trunk was a mixture of corn syrup and human blood, at nearly a five to one ratio of syrup to blood. This was why it never was going to dry. It was going take another couple of weeks before they could confirm whether or not the blood matched her DNA.

"I have to read this as saying Gwen is still alive." The judge's daughter being alive stopped being good news the minute Kirk Donovan's body was found in his car. The irony of the Ford GT being what kept Chief Theriot's car from sinking had already lost its humor value.

"I can't view it in any other way. At the very least someone intentionally faked her death to cover up the disappearing act. She is still missing, but that doesn't mean she is on the run." Captain Hammond sounded like he was trying to feed me positive points to pass to her father. He patted me on the shoulder and headed towards the portable podium Sheriff Mazant was surprisingly quick to offer. One of his deputies made sure the octopus tentacles of wires and cables from the dozen microphones on the podium would not obscure the Saint Xavier Parish Sheriff's Office emblem on its front. Sheriff Mazant was intent on enjoying his unearned moment in the limelight.

I telephoned Judge Rogers shortly before Captain Hammond stepped before the cameras. I doubted that the sad news Hammond was about to present was worthy of a live news feed, but I needed to inform Judge Rogers of the development before he began getting calls from reporters looking for a statement about his son-in-law's untimely death. Kirk Donovan's death was about to change the entire focus on finding Gwendolyn, and I was expecting to hear Judge Rogers express some regret about being so insistent on my handling the investigation.

"I wanted to be the one to tell you about the first breaks in your daughter's disappearance," I informed the judge. I knew there was a courtroom full of people waiting for his return from the recess this call necessitated. I did not want to send him back to the bench in a vindictive mood. "Kirk Donovan's body was located this morning, in his car in the canal behind the new house. He was alone and it is far too early to begin to speculate on how the car wound up in the water. I also have the results from the crime lab about the blood found in your daughter's car. It is Gwen's blood type, but it appears someone mixed something with the blood to make it look like far more blood than was actually lost."

"Are you telling me that my daughter may still be alive?" the judge demanded. "And that now it is her husband who is dead?"

"Yes, sir." The connection between the two realities was not mine to make at that moment. I waited a long moment for him to do so.

"That makes her a suspect in Kirk's death instead of the other way around," the judge sighed.

"I am going to continue to handle this as being three separate missing person cases, Your Honor. We have found Kirk, and I presently have no reason to believe he was murdered. It will be a few days before the coroner tells us how he died."

"You're humoring me, Detective Holland," Judge Rogers argued. I wasn't inclined to rub his face in the role reversal.

"No, I am not. I try to find solutions that match the facts, not to bend the facts to make my job easier. Gwen and Belle are still missing. That is all I can say for certain. They may both be dead and either or both of them may have played some part in Kirk being in the canal, but I have no evidence of either. The only thing I can positively tell you right now is that anyone who had money on Kirk being abducted by aliens lost their bet."

Judge Rogers's chuckle was a sign that he appreciated my attempt at humor, but he was quick to get back to business.

"I should still hire Gwen a defense attorney." This was much more familiar ground for him. "Any suggestions?"

"Only one, and I hate the guy," I replied. "But we both know Dan Logan is the best attorney to defend a case that will be tried in the media. Senator Donovan is going to start doing exactly that in the next few minutes."

"I'll call Logan when we hang up. Should I give him your number?"

"He knows my cellphone number. I'm going to have start giving him updates instead of you, though," I said as apologetically as I could. I was never comfortable with the arrangement he believed we had anyway. This was my first call, and now it should be my last.

"I understand," he huffed. "Thank you for everything you have done, and thank you for not jumping to conclusions like this old man did."

"You're not an old man, Judge. You're a father. For what it is worth, I truly hope Gwen is alive and well and was miles away from here when Kirk went in the water." It was the truth. It was also a truth that overlooked a lot of things I didn't want to discuss with him, such as Kirk Donovan's missing boat and Belle's absence.

I hung up and wandered over to find a place to stand in front of the cameras beside Captain Hammond and Chief Theriot. I had changed clothes after my earlier run-in with the police chief and was looking very official in a dark necktie and a blazer with my gold badge dangling from the breast pocket. I even combed my hair one last time before the cameras began to roll.

"Thanks to a joint effort on the part of the Donovan Police Department and the State Police, the body of Kirk Donovan was recovered from the canal behind his property earlier this morning. A 2006 Ford GT was discovered in the process of using a vehicle provided by Chief Theriot's department to simulate our combined theory on Mister Donovan's disappearance. An autopsy will be performed, and it is premature to speculate on the cause of death. At this time we ask that your thoughts and prayers go out to the Donovan family and that their privacy be respected in this time of grief." Hammond made it through the brief statement without laughing or breaking into a cold sweat that would alert the media as to how much more there was to this story than the tragic drowning of a state senator's only son. Asking that the victim's widow and daughter be left alone was also far less interesting than saying the search for both of them was a separate ongoing investigation.

I noticed Crystal Franks in the small knot of reporters. She was taking a lot of photographs, which was about all there was to do because she wasn't getting any more of a statement from Captain Hammond or myself. I still had hundreds of questions for Crystal about Gwendolyn Rogers, but they were going to have remain unasked. Getting answers from her would come at the price of answering questions of her own.

Chief Theriot now found himself in the often discussed space between a rock and hard place. My captain had credited him personally for the successful conclusion of an entirely fictional joint investigation into the disappearance of a state senator's son. The press release did not mention Sheriff Mazant, nor did it thank Detective Chance. Theriot knew he had just been bested by someone he had seriously underestimated. I held but faint hope Chief Theriot was prepared to concede, and the way he glared at me suggested that only the first round in our fight was over.

Twenty-Two

Dan Logan is one of those people you spend time with and then go home and take a long shower. He is, though, one of the very best criminal defense attorneys south of I-10. He arrived in New Orleans from Brooklyn as part of the carpetbagger wagon train that rolled across the Gulf Coast after Hurricane Katrina. He built his local reputation by getting what prosecutors considered to be slam-dunk cases before Katrina dismissed in the aftermath of the storm. NOPD's evidence storage facilities flooded to the rafters after the floodwalls collapsed. Logan needed only to petition the courts to make prosecutors present physical evidence to get cases tossed out on evidentiary grounds. I suggested him to Judge Rogers because I knew he was the sort of attorney someone in Gwendolyn Donovan's situation needed in her corner when my uncle began a whisper campaign to portray her as a homicidal housewife. Hers would not to be a case for the mild-mannered or civil-tongued to tackle.

I was able to mix business and pleasure by having Logan meet me at Tulip's office on Saturday morning. Katie's parade float would pass directly beneath the balcony outside of my sister's law office on Magazine Street. Katie and I were supposed to meet at the end of the parade, so this arrangement left me enough time to watch the parade and discuss the case. The attorney was still trying to act casually about defending Gwen, but keeping a judge's daughter out of prison promised to cloak Logan in a legitimacy that no amount of freeing drug dealers ever would.

"Judge Rogers claims you recommended me. I'm not sure what to make of that," Dan chuckled nervously as he set his briefcase on one of the chairs facing Tulip's desk. I had the balcony doors open and was paying more attention to the activity below than to his arrival. He still looked like an oversized cherub with a head full of slicked-back hair.

"It's going to be a nasty case if it ever gets to court."

"Why wouldn't it get to court?"

"Your client is still missing for one thing. She might be dead for a second, and for a third there are arguments to be made for self-defense or some sort of battered wife syndrome." I stepped back into the office and offered Logan one of the Michelob Ultras my sister keeps stocked in her office fridge. She only drinks expensive beer and wine when she drinks for free at Strada Ammazarre.

"Are you telling me how to do my job?" Logan laughed at the idea.

"We are not even having this meeting, so there's nothing to tell," I reminded him.

"Oh, that's right. You are the lead investigator," Logan nodded his head and took a swig of his beer. "Tell me then, what else are we not discussing in this meeting that never happened?'

"I need you to help me find your client. You can look for her as though she is alive and I will keep looking for her body. Contact her friends and learn whatever you can about her marriage from her father. Gwen is only a person of interest right now, but Kirk was the prime suspect in her disappearance until we pulled his body out of the bayou." I had no qualms about crossing ethical or professional lines with this arrangement. I needed at least one ally besides Roux, and I had yet to meet one in Saint Xavier Parish. Chief Theriot and Sheriff Mazant were both running interference for Senator Donovan, and Detective Chance was still as much of a mystery as he was the morning we met. I didn't trust him. Worse yet, I did not know what threat he might actually pose to my investigation.

"Fair enough." Logan decided. "Tell me, though, do you think she is alive?"

"I am beginning to. The day Judge Rogers had me assigned to this case, I found out I was looking for the entire family. We found Gwen's abandoned Mercedes, and then Kirk's racing alibi fell apart. Belle hasn't been seen or heard from in over a week. So far Kirk is the only one of three who has turned up, and he's dead. I don't know what to expect when either of the two women are found." I wasn't about to share specific details of the case with him. I was only illustrating how much more was involved than Gwendolyn Donovan's vanishing act.

"You're still going to say that if he didn't kill her then she probably killed him. Being a cop must be one of the easiest jobs on the planet," Logan roared with laughter.

"Yours is a lot easier. I am paid to find facts. You only need to make people doubt them," I pointed out. I could hear a band playing and stepped onto the balcony to find the parade was under way. "That's all I have. I'll see you in court, Mister Logan."

"Let's hope not, Detective Holland," he said with a grin as he grabbed his briefcase on the way out the door.

Twenty-Three

Katie had a change of clothes stashed in a gym bag on her float. She ducked into the restroom in a café at the end of the route and changed into a Saints jersey and jeans from her strapless formal gown, which I was glad had not left her with a chest cold after four hours of exposure to the brisk March weather. This new outfit was also more appropriate apparel for a long day of sustained drinking at Parasol's in the Irish Channel. We were supposed to find my sister and Tony in the drunken mob that stretched shoulder-to-shoulder for blocks in each direction from the landmark bar. Newcomers who moved into the Irish Channel after Hurricane Katrina had complained to the City Council about this raucous post-parade drinking tradition, only to be encouraged to move. Before Katrina this street party was seen as a good reason to buy a house nearby.

"I saw Hammond's press conference yesterday," Katie said as I used the flashing lights and siren on my Cadillac coupe to press into the crowd so we would not have far to walk. "I don't suppose sending us back to New Orleans without Tony had anything to do with that patrol car winding up in the canal."

"I'm glad to hear that," I assured her as I parked at the corner of Second and Constance Streets. My front bumper was well into the intersection, but nobody was going to be doing anything but walking on either street for far longer than we would be there.

"Glad to hear what?"

"That you don't think Tony had anything to do with what happened." My smirk told her that she would never get a straight answer to the question she knew better than to ask.

"This means Judge Rogers' daughter becomes a suspect now that the husband you thought killed her has turned up dead." I was surprised that Katie wanted to discuss the case so badly. This was a perfect time and place to leave both of our jobs behind.

"She won't be unless I find her alive," I tried to point out. "Judge

Rogers has hired Dan Logan to represent her. He needs to start building her defense in case she is alive."

"Dan Logan, that pig?" Her response made me glad I didn't mention that it was my idea. Katie's professional experiences with Logan have been considerably different than mine. Hers were among the cases that were dismissed after Katrina.

"One and the same. Senator Donovan has Uncle Felix on retainer. How do you think this is going to play out? Felix is going to start a whisper campaign against Gwen to poison the jury pool. She needs someone who plays just as dirty in her own corner." I grabbed Katie's hand and began nudging and elbowing a path forward.

Tulip and Tony were standing on the porch of one of the tightly packed shotgun style houses that define the Irish Channel neighborhood. The couple living in the house were offering free boiled crawfish from a massive aluminum pot simmering in the postage stamp-sized front yard to any drunken revelers walking past. The pickets of the low iron fence running along the undulant brick sidewalk were topped with raw cabbage heads. The green orbs looked like spiked heads after some medieval battle.

The Hibernian parade through the Irish Channel is famous for throwing what amounts to a meal in addition to the cheap plastic beads like those tossed at Mardi Gras. Years earlier, the city council had considered banning float riders from tossing heads of raw cabbage, carrots, and red potatoes into the densely packed and intoxicated spectators because of the number of conked heads and broken car windshields the often equally intoxicated float riders left in their wake. Tradition and compromise won out and now the leafy green projectiles are handed over the side of the floats as they pass, or tossed underhand rather than launched blindly into the packed spectators lining the route. The hardball-sized raw potatoes have remained as dangerous as ever.

"Whose house is this?" I asked my sister as I plucked one of the crawfish from her bowl. She lives in the neighborhood, in a quieter part of it anyway, and it seemed reasonable that she might know the name of whoever's food she was eating.

"Beats me. The guy in the Abita cap waved us over and handed us each a bowl and a beer. How do you refuse an offer like that, brother?" She deftly tucked her beer between her knees and managed to peel one of the crawfish one-handed without dropping the bowl or her beer. Tony was sitting on the step at her feet with his beer at his feet and the bowl in his lap. It was easy to tell which of them grew up here. "Did you lock up when you left my office?"

"I even sprayed disinfectant. Thank you again," I laughed. Katie started to say something and then thought better of continuing to discuss work. I was glad about this because I was going to have to head back into bayou country the next afternoon. I still had no idea when I was going to get to come home again, and my plans for how we would spend the weekend did not include arguments.

Twenty-Four

Captain Hammond greeted me at the state police crime lab in Baton Rouge on Monday morning. I very intentionally failed to invite Detective Chance to this meeting, despite my agreement with Sheriff Mazant to share exactly the sort of information I was about to receive. I intended to deliver a file with most of the details of the state police's initial conclusions to Sheriff Mazant once I drove back to Donovan. There were some things that it was best that he, and the senator he would share the report with, not know just yet.

Kirk Donovan's Ford GT sat in one of the forensic bays. The normally brilliant white clear-coat paint was covered by the thick coating of mud gathered during its two weeks in the canal. We cringed at the damage the undercarriage of Chief Theriot's Dodge Charger had caused to the roof of the coupe. Both of the Ford GT's doors were open to accelerate airing out the interior of its swamp-water pungency. The driver's side window was found to be open when the vehicle was towed from the canal. That gave the crabs and catfish free run of the interior and Kirk Donovan's corpse. I saw no purpose in looking at the photos of the grossly violated body Hammond warned me the preliminary coroner's report contained.

I did glance inside to confirm whether there was enough water in Kirk Donovan's lungs for the coroner to conclude he drowned. Kirk's three-point racing harness was still latched in place when he was pulled from the vehicle. The lab techs reported that the catch operated perfectly when they tested it, which meant Kirk should have been able to unlock it himself and swim through the open window of his car in the amount of time necessary for his sports car to sink below the surface. There was a temptation to view the evidence in terms of a murder-suicide, but the supposed homicide victim might not be dead. That left little besides murder to explain his death.

"I thought you might like to know that Theriot still hasn't filed a complaint against you," Hammond informed me as we walked around the car. We wore latex gloves, but neither of us touched the Ford.

"Does that surprise you?"

"A little," Hammond admitted. "I imagine he is going to want someone to replace his patrol car, if nothing else. Theriot can't prove you had anything to do with what happened, but even I know you were involved. Stunts like that usually give me a reason to have a detective suspended or pulled from a case."

"But, that isn't going happen because I have to be the one to handle the investigation." I understood his dilemma. Captain Hammond needed to find a way to maintain professional standards, but he was still enjoying Chief Theriot's comeuppance. "Should I goad Theriot further or apologize?"

"I want you to be careful about starting any wars, because there is no cavalry to send to your rescue," my boss warned me. I assumed doing anything short of this was okay. "I would also like you to dress a little nicer. I don't have to tolerate the outfits Bill Avery allows you to wear."

I was wearing pressed, but still rather baggy, cargo-pocketed tan khaki pants with my non-regulation ten-millimeter Glock pistol in a nylon holster on my thigh. My detective's badge hung on a hand-braided leather lanyard over a dark blue pullover hoodie sweatshirt with the words State Police silk-screened on it. My ankle-high Merrell steel-toed work shoes weren't on my captain's list of approved footwear, either.

"I would wear a suit and tie, but I never know when I am going to have to pull somebody out of a canal," I pointed out, but didn't argue with him.

"I'd settle for a damn necktie," he sighed and changed the subject. "There are two sets of files in what I gave you, as you requested. I assume your plan is to keep the top one and share the other with Detective Chance and Sheriff Mazant."

"Was getting this a problem?"

"Let's just say it isn't something the medical examiner is willing to get in the habit of doing." I needed the preliminary report to suggest Kirk Donovan's death was an accident or suicide. It was my way of denying the local cops and Senator Donovan anything to support an accusation that Kirk Donovan died at the hands of his wife. I was convinced they would use anything suggesting foul play to justify any harm that came to Gwendolyn when she was apprehended. This made my being the first one to find her all the more important.

There were a few clues suggesting foul play in Kirk's death. The coupe's manual transmission was in neutral when it came out of the water. It was barely plausible that Kirk knocked the car out of gear trying to stop it. It made far more sense that someone standing outside of the car disengaged the transmission to make the coupe easier to roll into the canal. Kirk's corpse had no bruising where the restraint harness held him in place at the time of impact and the windshield did not crack, meaning the car entered the water at a slow pace. The evidence certainly favored the theory that a third party sank the car over suggesting his death was suicidal or accidental.

"I understand perfectly. I just don't want to feed anyone's taste for revenge until the toxicology results come back and the medical examiner makes his final decision." Hammond still frowned slightly, despite my assurances. Talking the coroner into this stretched his personal code of ethics to its limit. "You need to understand the dynamics at play down there. We assume Senator Donovan has his hand in everything that happens, but it is more likely that the day-to-day stuff is handled by people on his payroll. That would leave him free to say he had nothing to do with how Sheriff Mazant went about finding his son's murderer."

"He would only need to let them know he doesn't want a trial." Hammond did understand that much.

"We'll see. Is there anything else I need to know before I head back to the lion's den?"

Hammond nodded and then made sure to stand close enough to me that his voice barely rose above a whisper for the rest of his briefing. It was a little unnerving at first.

"I can't get a straight answer out of Houston on why David Chance left their force. They said it was an involuntary separation and that he was not welcome to reapply. I can't get anyone to confirm he was fired for a specific reason, but they made it very clear they shoved him out the door and locked it behind him. I sent two detectives over there to see what they can find out from anyone open to talking off the record. I'd say you need to watch your back until I hear from them."

"I'm already ahead of you on that," I said and lifted the hoodie far enough to show him I was wearing body armor and carrying a second pistol under the bulky garment. He finally grasped that my wardrobe decisions were based on my safety, not just my comfort.

"Do you still have that dog with you, as well?" he asked in a far more neutral tone of voice than usual when the subject of Roux came up.

"He's the best cop partner I have ever had," I said and caught the brief smirk that crossed his lips. "I still want to get him certified as a K-9 dog."

"Sheriff Mazant claims you've already taken care of promoting him. He attacked a deputy?"

"No, Roux did not. The deputy refused to believe he was a police dog, so we had a demonstration."

"In the lobby of the courthouse." Hammond seemed amused about the incident up to that point.

"The matter was laid to rest," I shrugged. He was not going to tell me send my pit bull home, but he was obviously still building a list of reasons to oppose Roux being given official designation.

"That's all I have. Do you need anything else from me?" Captain Hammond was already bounding on the balls of feet, ready to get back to whatever he would rather be doing than having this discussion.

Twenty-Five

Sheriff Mazant seemed to have been waiting all morning for me to check in with his department. His concern continued to leave me with the impression that he was following someone's orders to know where I was and what I was doing.

"Getting a late start this morning, I see," The sheriff said without much humor as I entered his office. Detective Chance joined us and took a seat in one of the chairs in front of Sheriff Mazant's desk while I took my time pulling the medical examiner's report out of my messenger bag.

"I had to meet with Captain Hammond in Baton Rouge," I told them without sounding the least apologetic or making any excuse for not including Detective Chance. "Here is a copy of the state crime lab's preliminary report. The coroner needs Kirk's toxicology results to make any further judgements, and they haven't taken the car apart yet, but right now this looks like a typical accidental drowning."

"People don't typically drive expensive cars into the canal behind their house," Sheriff Mazant was quick to point out. He pushed the unopened folder to one side without opening it as a way of showing his displeasure with the way the investigation was headed.

"But those who do typically look like this." I very calmly responded and opened the folder to the autopsy pictures. He started to say something and then realized I would have some smart comment on that as well and changed the subject.

"What do you intend to do while you're waiting for the final report?" This was a loaded question.

"Locating Judge Rogers' daughter is the only reason I am on the case at all." I wanted to remind both of these men that I did not see Gwen as the wife of their local prince, but rather as the child of someone I knew personally. "I also need to know more about their marriage."

"David will help with that. Just tell him who you need him to interview." Sheriff Mazant was lousy at obstructing justice. Getting my interview list was a shortcut to knowing who needed silenced.

"I'll split my list with him to save time. I'm sure he knows more people to talk to about this than I do, anyway." I turned to Detective Chance and gave him my most partner-like smile. "Why don't you take care of interviewing the senator and Kirk's relatives to see if he discussed any marital problems with them?"

"Um, sure," Detective Chance mumbled and glanced at Sheriff Mazant. Mazant recognized the move I had just made, but he could do little to counter it.

The Louisiana State Senate was in session so the senator would be in Baton Rouge during the week. Most of Kirk's uncles and cousins worked in various family businesses that were conveniently, for me anyway, dotted about the parish and well away from Donovan. The people I wanted to interview all lived in town. Not one of them was named Donovan.

"Well, good. Let's meet at the judge's house at five and compare notes," I said and left the office before either man could say another word. I even shut the door behind me. This was as much to create a barrier as it was to give me an audible warning if either of the men decided to follow me. I estimated the pair would spend the next hour or two combing through the forensic report Sheriff Mazant tried so hard to dismiss while I was in his office.

Twenty-Six

I headed directly to Kirk Donovan's law office. I was not expecting to get much more from his secretary than had Detective Chance. I accepted that I was likely to come away empty handed since there was literally nothing his secretary could divulge about any of Kirk Donovan's cases outside of a grand jury. DA Milquetoast was not likely to convince a local judge to empanel one of those any time soon for that purpose.

My best hope was that flowers and a shoulder to cry on might have the same effect on the secretary's tongue as a subpoena. I brought sixty bucks worth of lilies to her and expressed my sympathies about her employment situation while she busied herself with filling a vase and arranging the flowers atop her filing cabinet.

"Have you been looking for another job?" My intention was to remind her that any loyalty to her boss was going to go unappreciated.

"I've actually been very busy during Mister Donovan's absence, so I haven't had time to give it much thought," she said rather candidly. Her name was Martha and she had likely worked for him throughout both of their careers. She was in her mid-fifties, but still kept a trim figure, and her dark hair was only beginning to show its first silvery roots. Her brown eyes had a gleam that must have driven guys crazy in her younger days. She dressed well, maybe as much to look good as to show off the salary Kirk Donovan paid her.

"Really," I said as if to be polite, and waited a beat before giving my epiphany-like response. "Well, sure, there must still be cases headed to court that are now in limbo."

"Exactly," she sighed and smiled at me as I took a seat on the sofa under Kirk's diplomas and a framed photograph of Kirk and his family rather than in one of the chairs by the desk. "I mean, it's not like any old lawyer could handle what he does. Most people just turn their backs on young girls in those situations."

I let this hang in the air for a moment rather than snap at it like a hungry fish on a lure. I noticed a cross hanging on a gold chain around her neck. This was no simple confirmation cross. It held a few diamonds and looked to be antique.

"It sounds like you two were doing the Lord's work, helping children like that." I spent years doing interrogations and very early on learned to use leverage. I would get more from her by getting her to brag about Kirk's work than by making her defend it, even if I had no idea what it was he did to help young girls.

"Yes, sir. He probably handled just about every one of those marriages in the parish. Other attorneys even referred cases to him. Mister Donovan and Judge Aubuchon got things done." I was having a very difficult time maintaining a neutral but curious expression.

It occurred to me that she had nobody to talk to except anxious clients and that she never sensed anything might be morally amiss with what her employer and the judge did. Nothing she had shared so far indicated they had done anything illegal, either.

"Which marriages were these, again?" I wasn't about to stop her from telling me anything she was willing to share, but I needed to know what we were even talking about.

"Well, Mister Donovan would find good Christian men willing to come here and marry young girls who got themselves pregnant. He always seemed to find some nice grown man who would provide a proper home for the poor girl and a child he could claim as his own," she was only too happy to tell me. "Mister Donovan was always willing to help young ladies from around here to save their reputations."

I wasn't going to challenge her understanding of how pregnancy actually occurs, and I certainly did not want to burst the noxious bubbles her careful wording set aloft in the darker corners of my mind.

"Protect their reputations?" She made it sound like young men didn't have the same problems.

"The law in Louisiana says that if a really young woman wants to get married they need their parents and a judge to give their blessings. Mister Donovan and Judge Aubuchon have made helping these girls and their families their life's work." Her face went soft and I sensed she might subscribe to True Romance Magazine or be a big fan of Hallmark Christmas movies.

"And there were there a lot of these marriages for Kirk to handle?"

"I don't know what a lot would be," she said.

I could understand that. Decades of doing nothing but this sort of legal work would dull one to any sense of scale, or to question its causes or effects.

"I thank you for sharing your time with me, Miss Martha. I had no idea just what sort of legal work Mister Donovan did here. It's simply tragic that young children get caught in the middle of all that's gone bad in society." I reached across and patted her hand and she smiled at me as though we shared common moral beliefs. That was another one of those balloons I needed to avoid popping. "I imagine more than a few parents of these troubled girls worry that their daughter's wedding will be postponed."

"Some of the calls I get," she started, but then trailed off before finishing the thought.

"Now, threatening someone over the phone is a crime. If there's anyone you need me to visit and tell to treat you properly, just let me know." I had found what I hoped was a chink in her armor. She gave me a grateful smile, but no names crossed her lips. One or more might well present itself the longer these cases languished. Pregnancy has a timetable all its own, and I was guessing the town had a lot of ticking clocks.

I decided to leave the office before I learned anything else. I needed to stand in bright sunlight and burn off the shadows and dark images my imagination was forming before they became lodged in my head. I had plenty of such things to deal with without adding new ones.

Twenty-Seven

Martha's disclosures about the nature of Kirk Donovan's law practice spun my arrow of possibilities to the district attorney's doorstep. I was especially interested to learn anything I could about Judge Aubuchon's involvement. I still clung to a dimming belief that District Attorney Gabouri was aware of at least some of what went on in the courthouse.

"Ah, Detective Holland. To what do I owe today's visit?" Gabouri was grinning as he ushered me into his office and out of earshot of his secretary. I held my tongue until we were alone in his office and I had accepted his offer of a pre-lunch tumbler of Blanton's bourbon. I don't know if my facial expression prompted the offer or if this was part of his normal daily routine that came from being a bump on the local judicial log.

"What do you know of Kirk Donovan's law practice? My understanding is that he has built an underage marriage mill with one of the judges." I didn't want to give him any more than I knew for sure, but also wanted to give him enough so he would think I could tell when he gave false or incomplete answers to my questions.

"I'd say that is an accurate description of Judge Aubuchon's courtroom. I don't think any bribes are involved. More's the pity on that."

I didn't see the judge not being bribed to send pregnant minors to live with strangers as being particularly redemptive. Judge Aubuchon must have been getting something in return if his was the only court Kirk Donovan used to handle the cases. Maybe wielding a rubber stamp for the senator's son was simply his role in the local political patronage system.

"How long has this been going on?"

"Kirk took over his daddy's practice as soon as he passed the bar. The senator began handling underage marriages when he took over from his own father. It seems to be their part in the family's enterprises. The senator's brothers handle different parts of what goes on here. Billy runs everything to do with supplying the oil platforms, Ronnie takes care of property management, and Rob handles their sugar cane and cotton gins."

"Did Kirk handle the legal work for all of them?" I swallowed a long pull of bourbon to help digest my deeper understanding of the Donovans.

"Kirk did a little bit of work for them, but I would say that the Donovans' legal issues tend to get settled late at night and out of court. You don't want to tangle with any of them if you can avoid it, because it is all for one and one for all with that family."

"That why you haven't pressed your luck with them?" It was an impolite question to ask of a man so generous with his fine bourbon, but I was curious.

"Luck isn't what it will take to beat them. I have a file on each of them, and sooner or later one of those files is going to get thick enough to outweigh the consequences of tangling with the senator and his lackeys." His plan sounded like the sort of nonsense a man who drinks bourbon alone before lunch would dream up.

"What about the judge?" I hoped he kept a file on everyone on the senator's speed dial.

"Barry Aubuchon has been the family court judge here since I was in diapers. He was good friends with the DA I replaced, and he owes his job to the senator. The three of them used to be part of a group that ran a summer camp for poor kids. They still hold a beauty pageant for our young girls every Saint Patrick's Day."

"So, the Donovans are civic boosters?" Philanthropy didn't strike me as being synonymous with the Donovans.

"Beats me. The camp closed down while I was still in college. The pageant is still going on, though it won't this year since Gwen Donovan ran it. The DA and the judge used them to find the kids living in bad home situations," Gabouri explained, then elaborated. "By that I mean the kids were being abused or their parents could not afford to raise them."

"What happened to the kids?" I wondered aloud.

"Usually the girls were married off and the boys put up for adoption.

The senator, and then Kirk, handled the paperwork and everything was made nice and legal in Judge Aubuchon's courtroom." Gabouri trailed off as he explained this, as though he wanted to change the subject. But I was intrigued.

"Just how many children did they put through this?" I stood up and topped off my bourbon before casually refilling Gabouri's empty tumbler.

"I have no idea. Fewer now than when the senator ran things personally. Even so, too many kids in this parish are calling folks uncle that aren't any blood relation at all. I don't agree that the best solution to a bad home life is giving a kid a worse one. Some of the girls we're talking about are fourteen or fifteen years old. The boys are the same age or younger, and they always wind up living with families from somewhere else. It was that way when I was growing up, and I wish to hell I could find a way to put a stop to it now." Gabouri made fast work of his drink, but this time neither of us refilled his glass. We had hit the limit of his morning cocktails, and of what he would share with me on the subject.

"Do you think maybe somebody tried to? Has anyone ever threatened Kirk's life over a case?" I saw ample motive in what I now knew of his practice.

"You can't kill a Donovan and get away with it. They'd destroy your whole family and everyone here knows that."

"That doesn't really answer my question," I pressed.

"What you are suggesting is unlikely. By the time Kirk presents the paperwork to Judge Aubuchon everyone has agreed to the deal," Gabouri shrugged and set the heavy glass on his desk. I noticed a ring in the finish I had overlooked on my first visit. This was not the first glass he had set in that spot, and by the look on his face it would not be the last.

"Thanks for your hospitality, and your help in understanding the Donovans. I'll keep you posted on anything you might want to add to your files." I set my glass next to his and tried not to sound too patronizing about his plan of attack.

Twenty-Eight

Judge Aubuchon's chambers were three floors above the parish courtrooms. Aubuchon handled civil matters in the smallest of the three courtrooms. Another courtroom handled local municipal offenses such as speeding tickets and local code violations, and the largest courtroom was reserved for criminal trials. That judge only held sessions on Mondays and Thursdays, and this being a Monday, the hallways were lined with clusters of lawyers, clients, and anxious family members.

Judge Aubuchon was working by himself in his chambers. His secretary was either running an errand or perhaps didn't work on the days his court wasn't in session. This didn't strike me as a parish where he might be afforded a paralegal or law clerk.

Judge Aubuchon was as heavyset as Chief Avery, but in a good ole' boy way that drew attention to his sweaty brow and the way light bounced off the scalp he had his barber keep shaved smooth. The judge glanced up from the stack of legal briefs on his desk and studied me over his half-frame reading glasses.

I waved my badge at him. "Good afternoon, Your Honor. I'm Detective Holland from the state police."

"You here about whoever broke the windshield on my car?" he growled. "It costs a fortune to replace any of the glass on a classic car." He surely knew broken windshields fell to the local police to investigate, so I wasn't sure why he thought the state police might take an interest.

"No, sir," was all the more I could say before he removed his reading glasses and leaned back in his wooden chair.

"You that New Orleans detective?" I took this is as my cue to enter his office.

"Yes, Your Honor. I was hoping you might be willing to discuss Kirk Donovan." I needed to pursue this topic without stepping over whatever line the senator had drawn around his son.

"You'd want to speak with his secretary about his cases," he brushed me off, politely but directly.

"Miss Martha was the one who suggested I speak with you," I fibbed. "I would appreciate a quick lesson in underage marriages."

"I can't imagine why that would have anything to do with Gwen killing Kirk," the judge grumbled. I had to take the bait even though I saw the trap.

"It's not clear that Gwen had anything to do with her husband's death. Our medical examiner is inclined to view Kirk's death as being accidental. I am focused on the evidence that Gwen might still be in some sort of danger herself." The clock was ticking on how soon Senator Donovan learned of the reluctance by the state police to view Gwen as a murder suspect, but now he would learn of it from both Sheriff Mazant and his hand-picked judge.

Judge Aubuchon leaned forward and waved towards the chairs across from him. I took a seat and held my tongue as class began.

"Juveniles can get married with the consent of either their parents or a judge. It's not a big deal, and young folk getting hitched is an accepted part of growing up around here. I wouldn't expect someone from New Orleans to understand." The judge was not open to any debate on the subject.

"How young are the girls we are talking about?"

"Girls younger than eighteen need their folks' okay, any younger than fourteen means I would have to give my blessing as well," Judge Aubuchon said this with all the emotion of explaining jaywalking.

"How old does the groom need to be to marry a fourteen year old girl in Saint Xavier parish?"

"Same law applies everywhere in the state. It would be handled the same in New Orleans." He made no effort to hide how much my questions were irritating him, but he also didn't answer my question. I assumed that the law's minimum age requirements applied equally to the bride and groom.

"How often do Romeo and Juliet show up looking to get married?" I couldn't see two teens getting married in Donovan would work out any better than in Shakespeare.

"Most of the grooms are older than the bride. I expect a husband to be able to provide for his wife," the judge said, but then tried to close the door he had just opened. "I also expect a couple to stay married. I've been married to my wife for forty seven years, since we were both seventeen. We got married while I was home on leave from the Army."

"How many girls under eighteen would you say get married here in a year?"

"I don't keep track. Do you really think this has anything to do with Kirk being dead or his wife still being missing? I got other things to do than sit around making conversation with you," Judge Aubuchon said and picked up the brief on his desk to emphasize the point that I was interrupting his work.

"Probably not," I admitted. "Thanks for your insight. There was just one other thing, though."

"What's that, Detective?"

"The district attorney tells me that you and Senator Donovan used to run a summer program for the local kids. Why'd you stop?" I was sure this had nothing to do with my investigation, but I had the notion that his response might tell me a bit more about the men involved.

"We got too old. Young men are better at keeping up with young boys," he said and almost smiled, as though some favorite memory came to him. I let the subject drop, but left the office curious about why nobody else stepped in to take over the program if it was so good for the community. Luckily the answer to that question was another one of those things that I wasn't going to have to come up with before I could go home.

Twenty-Nine

Captain Hammond called early the next morning and said we needed to meet without Sheriff Mazant or Detective Chance being in the loop. I knew about his nearly visceral distaste for New Orleans, but suggested we eat lunch at Strada Ammazarre all the same. I could tell Sheriff Mazant and his detective that I had business matters to handle in the city without raising any of the suspicions another trip to Baton Rouge or trying to meet with Captain Hammond anywhere near Saint Xavier Parish would create. It would also give me an excuse to put the investigation aside long enough to see Katie and check in with Tony.

I arranged for us to have lunch at the chef's table in the kitchen, on the off chance Senator Donovan was using his security detail to keep me under surveillance. Sheriff Mazant and Chief Theriot's deputies lacked the skills it would take, but Uncle Felix knew how to keep an eye on me. I didn't worry as much about anyone following me on the highway as I did about someone posing as a hungry tourist being seated near us in the dining room.

"I finally learned the details of what led to David Chance's termination over in Houston," Hammond said to get straight to the point once we had placed our pasta orders and our server left us to enjoy our garlic bread sticks and tea.

"You don't seem real happy about it," I commented in reaction to Hammond's somber voice and almost pained expression. I don't think either of us had thought Chance's backstory was going to be pleasant.

"It seems the detective may been having an affair with a sixteen year old girl."

"Ugh," I cringed.

"The story is that he responded to a domestic abuse complaint. The sixteen-year old was married to a thirty-eight year old. She claimed he was loaning her out to his buddies, and that he took a belt to her any time she complained."

"How did that morph into an affair with Chance?" I was still not fully prepared to accept child brides were this wide-spread of a problem.

"The story goes that Chance took the girl to one of those homes for abused spouses and became a little too close to her, to say the least. She wound up going back to her husband a couple of months later. She took off on the husband a half dozen more times, but she didn't run off to be with your new pal. She ran off to stay with some kid named Bradley Ladd. He was a few years older, and he had recently inherited a house and business from his dad. Her husband asked Detective Chance to drag her out of Ladd's house and take her home every time she decided to leave him. Something happened the last time Chance dropped her off at home, and the husband shot the girl in what he claimed was self-defense. The husband said she attacked him with a kitchen knife."

"Did the jury buy his story?"

"They didn't have to. The husband was shot dead in an armed robbery about a month later."

"Who did they arrest for that?" I hoped we were near the end of this sordid tale.

The arrival of our meals gave me an excuse to sit on the fact that Bradley Ladd was involved in my case. It was an interesting thing to know, but this peripheral detail surely wasn't going to matter much.

"Officially the husband's shooting remains unsolved, but Chance kept trying to sell the district attorney on his theory that Bradley Ladd killed the husband. That's what got your partner fired."

"I could see that," I had to admit.

"The district attorney told him to drop it. The detective was already trying to make a case that the same boy killed his own father, so the DA started to worry about this being an obsession and not a provable case. The kid's father died in a home invasion while he was celebrating his eighteenth birthday in South Padre Island. Bradley had a solid alibi, but he also just happened to have turned old enough to inherit his father's estate."

"How does that explain what led to Chance working for Mazant?" This was all I could think to say while my brain digested the story.

"I can't tell you for certain how or why he got hired, but he definitely got fired in Houston. Bradley Ladd sued the police department, saying he was being harassed by Chance, so they fired Chance to settle the case as quickly and quietly as they could." Hammond grinned. "Here's the cherry on the cake. Guess where that sixteen year old girl and her husband got married?"

My boss began tapping his fingers on the table.

"Saint Xavier Parish?"

"Yep." Hammond had only begun telling me his story. "The groom already had two convictions involving child molestation. One of his attorneys must have told him that you aren't raping an underage girl if you marry her first. His parole officer gave him permission to travel to Saint Xavier parish to marry the then twelve-year old girl in Judge Aubuchon's courtroom."

"I am going to make a guess and say that the groom retained Kirk Donovan to grease the wheels."

"You are correct. Judge Aubuchon and Kirk arranged a mail-order bride for a sexual predator, but everything about the girl's marriage was done as legally as an attorney and a judge could make it." Hammond managed to smile and scowl at the same time. "Here's something else you need to keep in mind. Senator Donovan made a personal recommendation to Sheriff Mazant that he hire Detective Chance two days after the detective was fired in Houston."

"Any idea what became of the girl's parents?" This was deeply tragic, also a bit too tidy and convenient. I was hoping that the parents could explain the full circumstances behind the marriage.

"I did a little digging and found that the girl's mother was married in the same judge's courtroom when she was only fifteen and five months pregnant with her first kid, a boy. The father was only nineteen."

"What else did you discover about Chance's time in Houston?" I sensed he still had a few more details to share.

"Chance briefly lead Houston PD's fugitive task force. Finding people is what Chance does best. He would probably have been told to find Gwendolyn Donovan if you weren't already put in charge of the case."

"I can tell you that he isn't impressing me with his bloodhound skills so far. I think his orders are to pour sand in my gears. He has lied to me on a couple of occasions about things that hardly mattered, and the witness interviews he has turned in are an indication he was told not to find anything that might actually help solve the case. Based on what you're telling me, I think he might have his own search going for Gwen." I hadn't given the detective credit for being capable of such deceit until right then. In fact, I had come to believe he was an idiot incapable of playing me for one.

"Be careful. That's all I can tell you. Where do you stand right now?" Hammond was going to spare me a lecture on filing my daily reports. I had filed them the first two days, and then lost the sense of urgency to do so once the trail grew cold.

"I tasked Chance with finding the family's boat. I figured he might have some connections at the local marina, and the sheriff should know who would fence such a thing. I am still looking for both Gwen and Belle, but honestly, I have no idea where to even begin looking if they are just hiding out. My next step is to learn how Gwen's blood found its way to the trunk of the Mercedes, and why she staged her death if not to cover for killing Kirk. Whoever helped her stage that scene may have an idea where to look for one or the other of the missing women." I could tell by Hammond's expression that he recognized the sound of wheels spinning when he heard them.

"My best advice on your detective problem is to keep him in sight, but about an arm's length away from you. You are very likely right about his running his own investigation. You may as well keep letting him do the heavy lifting for you with the locals." Hammond was done eating. This meant he was done being in New Orleans. He thanked Tony for the meal and handed our waitress ten bucks as a tip as he left the kitchen.

"Problems?" Tony asked as he took Captain Hammond's place at the table.

"As always, but none I can't figure out a way to handle," I tried to convince both of us. "Luckily I have experience working with murderous psychopaths."

"Surely you are not talking about me," Tony laughed and returned to the cooks' line. I laughed, too, but I wasn't kidding around any longer.

Thirty

I had a couple of hours to fill before Katie could join me at the bistro. My choices to fill the time were to hang out with my sister and listen to her recount my mother's latest rant, or to speak with Belle Donovan's adviser about a question which had begun to tug at my thoughts. It was an easy choice, and Troy Foristell had an hour free in his schedule to speak with me, so I headed to Tulane.

"I'm not sure what I can tell you, Detective," he was quick to apologize as he let me into his office. Troy was a stocky guy in his early thirties who dressed casually so his wards would feel they were talking to a peer rather than to a grownup. "I would not say that Belle has availed herself of my advice and counsel nearly as much as most students."

"Would you say she is a private person or that she is getting her advice from someone else?" I asked just to make conversation.

"She lives in her family's shadow, that much is for sure," he opined. "Belle's father makes the final decision on her course schedule. Her mother bought her a house so she wouldn't be distracted by having a roommate."

"I understand the house is something of a party place on the weekends," I tried to lead him.

"The first thing I tell the parents of my advisees is that Isaac Newton's theory about every action having an equal and opposite reaction will apply to their children once they leave home. The sort of pressure Belle's folks put on her was bound to find an inappropriate release sooner or later."

"I have heard that Belle and her father were arguing over a paper she was writing for one of her journalism courses. Do you have any idea what the paper was about?" I asked. This had made its way to the top of the short list of conflicts in the family I considered to be worth pursuing. I wasn't going to get any straight answers about the nature of the arguments that repeatedly sent Gwen to the emergency room until I was able to speak with her directly.

"That was one of the few things she did talk with me about," Foristell said and leaned back in his chair before elaborating. "She was supposed to write about her family's history during the Civil War. Professor Smyth uses the assignment to teach his journalism students about research sources other than the internet. A surprising number of families have letters and journals of their ancestors from the period, but what he wants is for the students to learn how to do their research the old fashioned way. You know, by going through old newspaper archives or the records at the historical society where their family lived during the War."

"And Belle?"

"Her family must have saved every scrap of paper from the day they set foot in Saint Xavier Parish. She said she the local museum had letters and journals of everyone in her family alive at the time. It turned out, though, that her father insisted on editing the final draft of her paper. She claimed he was trying to white-wash her family's history."

"How so?" I pressed.

"No idea. She wouldn't let me read the paper. She was headed home to see her father to talk about it the last time I saw her," Foristell shrugged apologetically. I could tell he was as interested in reading the paper as I was.

"When was that?" I had a date in mind that I hoped wasn't the day in question. Foristell rummaged around on his desk and found his appointment log.

"Thursday afternoon, two weeks ago," he told me and dashed the slim hope I was still clinging to that Belle had a solid alibi for the day her father died and her mother went missing. Belle's advisor had just made Belle my prime suspect in both of those incidents, if only because she was the one most likely to still be alive.

I compartmentalized Belle Donovan as I drove downtown towards the bistro. There was nothing I could do with what I had just discovered until I found either Belle or Gwen. I couldn't let what Belle found in the archives become a loose tooth distracting me from pursuing other clues. I also wanted to believe the Civil War was done claiming casualties.

Katie and Tulip were both waiting for me in my apartment when I returned to the bistro. Katie greeted me at the door and we shared a long kiss. I went months without speaking to my family while in the Special Forces and doing covert intelligence work overseas, so it is always a surprise to me to find how hard it is to be apart from this person for longer than a day. My sister and mother perceive my affections for my sister's former babysitter as a sign of recovery in my long battle with PTSD.

"What did you learn at Tulane?" Tulip inquired from the living room. Katie and I moved to the sofa, while Roux and Tulip settled into the armchairs.

"I could ask you the same thing," I tried to joke. It fell flat, so I filled them in on my interview with Belle's advisor. They agreed that I shouldn't let myself get distracted with whatever Belle found, but Katie also suggested I pay a visit to the parish historical society to see if they might provide a clue.

"Do you really suspect the daughter?" Katie pressed me.

"It is the obvious thing to do, but I don't think a college term paper is enough motive for murder," I shook my head and leaned forward. "Everyone seems very intent on keeping me from learning anything about her father, which makes me think his death and maybe his wife's disappearance have to do with either his work or something else between the two of them."

"What sort of practice did Kirk have, anyway?" my sister asked.

"He handled underage marriages." I told her without any elaboration. Katie took care of that for me when she told me what she pulled from the local courthouse grapevine.

"That is barely the tip of the Donovan family's iceberg on that subject," Katie assured me. "Kirk seems to mostly be known as the son of a state senator. He went to work for his father as soon as he graduated from law school, and all their law firm handled was child custody cases and any underage marriages that happened in Saint Xavier Parish. Senator Donovan has always led the fight against any legislation meant to make it harder for anyone under sixteen to get married."

"I think Kirk and a judge named Barry Aubuchon are using Sheriff

Mazant to run what I can only describe as a marriage mill for underage girls." I told the pair. I wasn't going to get in any trouble for having this discussion, because none of what we were talking about appeared to have a direct bearing on the case I needed to not discuss.

"What purpose could that possibly serve? How many people want to marry anyone under sixteen?" my sister wondered.

"There are over ten thousand such marriages each year in the United States. More happen in some other countries we would never compare ourselves to for anything else. Delaware is the only state that won't allow marriages under sixteen years of age, but judges in Tennessee have approved multiple marriages of brides as young as ten years old," I informed her. I had Googled the subject of child marriages after Captain Hammond told me why Detective Chance left Texas.

"Ten year olds? Why would a ten year old even want get married?" Katie made her own challenge.

"They don't. Their parents marry them off to get rid of them." My stark response silenced the room. "Girls are considered to be a burden in a really poor family. They always need more medical care, they cannot do much in the way of physical labor, and their kids won't contribute to their own family's future. Marriage can also be used as an end-around to get out of a rape charge. A guy rapes a ten year old, but the charges get dropped if he marries her. It makes for one less single mother or kid up for adoption. Imagine waking up next to your rapist every day for the rest of your life. The parents let it happen because they view their daughter as damaged goods."

I hadn't wanted to discuss what I learned, because I knew Katie and Tulip wouldn't be able shake any images of child brides out of their own heads, either. There was going to be heavy drinking later.

"So, you're telling us that Kirk and the judge married off girls who had already been sexually abused for years." Katie asked me to confirm.

"Apparently that's the case. From what I can piece together, Sheriff Mazant gets an anonymous call about a young girl who is the victim of some sort of sexual abuse. I haven't figured out what happens next, but eventually the girl is married off to some middle-aged guy from who knows where and the family goes back to living like their child never existed. Occasionally it is one of their sons who gets put up for adoption." This was thin as an actionable accusation, and entirely useless as the basis for opening an investigation. You don't get to charge people with following the letter of the law. All this conversation did was ruin our appetites for dinner.

"I'd say that marrying off people's children provides a lot more reasons to want Kirk dead than an argument over Belle's school work," Katie tried to reassure me. I had to wonder how much of Kirk's specialty in the law Gwen ever discussed with Judge Rogers. I also wondered how strong Gwen's own stomach was for her husband's line of work. Maybe she had finally reached the point that she could no longer be party to legalizing child abuse. Perhaps she wanted to stage her escape in a way that might expose her husband's role in the parish's dirty little secret.

I consciously choose not to share what Captain Hammond shared with me about Detective Chance. I seemed to have no choice but to work with the detective. I did have a choice about whether or not to give the two women I loved the most in my life any more reasons to worry about my safety than they already had. I chose silence over tears.

Thirty-One

Saint Patrick's Day dawned with a light drizzle, which dissipated the usual morning fog along the bayou enough to expose the presence of yet another one of Chief Theriot's vehicles lurking at the end of the driveway. The chief himself had not taken this watch since his baptism. His deputies chose to drive away when they first laid eyes on me rather than track Roux and me on our morning run. Chief Theriot just wanted to remind me that he was going to be a presence in my life so long as I was one in his.

The courthouse parking lot was already buzzing with activity when Roux and I jogged past about six o'clock in the morning. Carnival rides were being set up, including a small Ferris wheel. A flatbed stage was being wheeled into place, and blocking the steps to the courthouse. The dispensing of justice was suspended for the day, so this didn't really matter. The stage would be flanked with the tents and trailers of quite a few food and crafts vendors. I felt no inclination towards buying any of their kitschy souvenirs to help remember my time spent in Saint Xavier Parish.

I was going to have to accept that finding anyone to interview would be difficult on a day that most of the local businesses were either closed or running on a skeleton staff. I might well find many of the people I wanted to interview in the throng, but none of them were likely to want to talk with me in public.

My phone rang just after eight o'clock. Detective Chance's name popped up on its caller ID.

"Good morning, Detective." I half-sighed.

"And to you, Detective." He sounded unusually chummy this morning. "I just wanted to call and let you know that Sheriff Mazant has assigned me to patrol duty at the festivities downtown. You might as well join in, because you won't get much else done today."

That made it official. Roux and I had the day off whether we wanted it or not. Now I had to decide if I was going to spend it in Donovan or

New Orleans. It was tempting to head back to the city and at least have lunch or dinner with Katie, but a different part of my mind considered the investigative possibilities in a town too distracted to notice my digging around. I still needed to find Kirk Donovan's boat and what it was that Belle argued about with her father before she disappeared.

It was the second of these matters that I thought I might have some luck pursuing despite the town being in party mode. I decided to take the advice of Belle's advisor and Katie to peruse the Saint Xavier Parish Museum. The place was likely to be open and trying try to draw in as many tourists as possible. Museums don't count on a lot of repeat local business. Donovan was barely an hour's drive from New Orleans, which did most of its celebrating the weekend before Saint Patrick's Day, and a shorter drive than that from Baton Rouge and Lafayette. It wasn't too far for anyone from these places to drive to pass a good time, and I figured the town would be packed even though it was a weekday.

The home that served as the local museum, with its antebellum porches, fat pillars and white stucco over brick exterior, was built a full generation before Louisiana seceded from the Union. It occupied close to four acres at the edge of downtown. The grounds were dotted with small historical cottages. These were all brought in from other plantations that were being torn down, and from lots in town that were developed into other things. There were a couple of former slave quarters, and the home of a locally famous writer, whose name time had wiped from the memory of most readers. It seemed ambitious for such a small parish to have such a massive historical complex. It took only a few minutes inside the main building to grasp that all of this was nothing more than a shrine to the Donovan family.

One of the smaller cottages on the property was supposedly their first home and, if true, theirs was certainly a swift rise from rags to riches. The cottage was dated to 1815, and the plaque out front made only passing reference to Jasper Donovan having served in the British military.

I wondered if Jasper was among the deserters after the brutal defeat Andrew Jackson handed the British during the battle for New Orleans during the War of 1812. Their undisciplined initial retreat offered a brief opportunity for Private Jasper to escape any further attempts by Crazy King George to get him killed, and to make good use of what amounted to his free passage to the United States.

The carefully crafted family history on display in the main house revolved around the family's rise to influence thanks to Duncan Donovan, Jasper's youngest son. Duncan's ascent to power began as the overseer for a small plantation in nearby Terrebonne Parish. He was able to purchase the entire operation upon the death of the owner during a yellow fever outbreak. The volunteer historian leading my tour was at a loss when I asked who financed such a purchase by someone making as little as the average overseer was paid. It was the first thing I added to my mental list of things that Kirk Donovan might not want his daughter to disclose.

The inexorable approach of the War Between the States bolstered the positions of Duncan and his son, Bradford. Major landholders in Saint Xavier Parish signed contracts for the Donovans to protect their interests while they quietly slipped off to England for the duration of the war. Most had been in favor of the state's secession, only to lose their taste for war when it came time for their own sons to serve. The father and son leased the properties left in their care to the Union Army for winter quarters and sold the absentee owners' crops and livestock for pennies on the dollar. The loss of multiple years of cash crops and the property damage left in the wake of tens of thousands of Union troops camped for months on end bankrupted most of the families who trusted the Donovans. Duncan and his son not only failed them, but held binding contracts for their services these families could no longer afford to pay. The guide almost gleefully told us of how the Donovans foreclosed on the contracts so that, by the end of Reconstruction, the Donovan family held title to the most fertile farm and pasture land in Saint Xavier Parish, including the very home we were touring. Jasper Donovan lived long enough to see Bradford elected to the state senate in Baton Rouge. He was the first in the still unbroken string of Senator Donovans.

The family's history was polished to make them look like savvy businessmen rather than backstabbing double-crossers. I did not bother to ask the tour guide to speculate on the current Senator Donovan's ability to use his political position to steer lucrative contracts to his brothers and their influential friends. It was almost certain to be how the family maintained its power over the parish and in the statehouse. Few of the tourists around me were listening, anyway. They had paid to see the lavish interior and the stunning exhibits, such as the complete sets of Miles Mason chinaware and Chawner and Company silver used as table settings in the mural-lined dining room. I had to wonder if Duncan or his son took these expensive collections as further payment from the landholders they had impoverished.

The tour gave me a number of places to view as potential flashpoints between Belle and her father. The Donovans quite obviously spent as much time covering their tracks as they did white-washing the present. If what Belle's advisor at Tulane said was true--that the family had kept very meticulous records of its transactions over the course of the family's meteoric rise in the late 1800s--there was plenty for Kirk to fear his daughter might divulge.

Thirty-Two

I gathered up Roux from Judge Rogers' house before heading downtown to find something for the two of us to share for lunch. My mind was still percolating with the fresh list of unexpected things to consider after observing the Donovans' best version of themselves.

The parking lot was jammed solid with people and the scent of dozens of good things to eat. A cloud of blue smoke rose from the bevy of grills filled with every imaginable kind of meat and, being in the heart of Cajun country, a few things most tourists had never previously considered to be food. Roux paused in mid-stride and looked up at me with an expression of gratitude mixed with deep hunger I had never seen before. Both of our diets were about to take a serious hit. I am adamant about not feeding Roux table food, but most of this Cajun charcuterie would never find its way to my table in the first place. Making an exception did not set a precedent.

A zydeco band was playing on stage. The roped off dance area was packed with Cajun two-steppers and those content with flailing about in joyful abandon as a fast-paced fiddle and the rhythmic scratching of a spoon across a chromed wash board cast their spell. I could feel the energy in my own spinal cord begin to shuffle my feet. I instinctively glanced down at Roux to see if the music might resurrect any of the triggers he once displayed from hearing ultra-high notes. It took a professional dog trainer considerable time and work to break him of the compulsion to look for a fight at the pitch of an ultrasonic dog whistle. This was no place for a seventy-pound pit bull to have a murderous relapse.

It took a long moment for me to recognize that Detective Chance's ex-girlfriend was the redheaded ball of fire in a sparkly dress giving the fiddle such a workout. The rosin on Nannci's bowstring threatened to set the place on fire as she and the trio of much older musicians around her played their set of traditional zydeco tunes mixed with a couple of novel covers of popular songs. It was a pleasant surprise to find Nannci had a marketable skill beyond truck-stop waitressing. Nobody shifted their attention from the stage when the only ambulance in town left the festival, with its siren blaring and red lights flashing.

I stopped to buy deep-fried boudin balls drizzled with freshly-made remoulade sauce, two links of grilled alligator sausage, and an ice-cold Abita beer before leading Roux behind the vendor trailers. I paused to enjoy my lunch and to feed Roux one of the sausage links before making my way behind the stage. I wanted to compliment Nannci on her performance before she got swallowed up in the crowd.

I was surprised to find Sheriff Mazant, Detective Chance, and four husky young men I assumed were sheriffs' deputies standing near a massive pot of boiling water being stirred by the district attorney. Another knot of young men stood nearby with Judge Aubuchon, all of them holding cold beers in their hands. It took a moment to realize both groups wore identical T-shirts, with the image of a gigantic hot dog and the words 'Man Bites Dog' on them. It made finding the gathering of lawmen all the more strange.

"Hello, fellas," I interrupted. "What's this all about?"

Gabouri looked up at the sound of my voice and smiled. "We're raising money for the Chronicle's Christmas Fund. The local paper hands out toys to grade school kids every year, so we have a hot dog eating competition pitting the courthouse against Sheriff Mazant and his deputies to help raise money. If you want, my secretary's out front to take your bet on exactly how many hot dogs you think the winning team will eat. Whoever comes closest takes home one hundred dollars. The rest goes to the fund, and we usually guilt the winner into giving back the hundred dollars. Crystal and I have to be the judges, because all of the actual judges are in the competition."

"Sounds reasonable," I laughed.

"I'm sure you remember Crystal." Gabouri pointed to the now familiar local reporter. Crystal wore a ball cap with her thick pony tail flopped out the back. The jeans she wore emphasized her trim figure and her 'Man Bites Dog' T-shirt was knotted to show off the even tan on her toned midriff. "She also has to cover the event because she's their only photographer. There is only one other reporter on staff, but she usually has a couple of interns around as well. In fact, Kirk's daughter worked for her last summer."

"I could see where juggling all of that might pose a problem," I also admired the woman's efforts, and the cooperation this group was showing for the moment. Tomorrow would pit Gabouri against both sides taking part in today's eating challenge. They had set aside that animosity for the sake of some kids that would otherwise have no reason to look forward to Christmas.

"You're going to miss the big event this year, though," Detective Chance informed me.

"Oh, what is that?"

"Gwen Donovan always organizes the annual beauty pageant to raise money for the Donovan Foundation. It is like our own miniature Miss America contest for the young girls from around here."

I truly wished I didn't understand why not seeing dozens of young girls in bathing suits caused him such disappointment. I did not feel I was missing anything.

"How young are we talking about?"

"They break it up into age groups. There are seven to ten year olds, eleven to fourteen year olds, and then the fourteen to seventeen year olds. They would do a bathing suit competition and then a talent show," Sheriff Mazant weighed in. Now I knew I wasn't missing anything of interest to me.

"What talent does an eight year old in a swim suit usually demonstrate?" I had a hard time not sounding judgmental.

Chance studied my face and then grinned. "You're right. It really is just a way to get the prettiest girls to strut around in a bikini for an hour. It draws quite a crowd and raises a lot of money for the Donovan's foundation."

"And what does the Donovan Foundation do for the community?"

"I haven't the slightest idea," Chance said, shrugged indifferently, and went to stand with his teammates.

I glanced at the rather scummy boiling water and tried to estimate the number of bloated, pinkish-gray hot dogs tumbling in the aluminum pot. Someone likely used the same pot to fry their Thanksgiving turkey, and Lord knows how pounds of crawfish and shrimp had passed through it.

The music stopped and the crowd began to clap as Nannci and her band made their way off stage. I stepped away from the boiling pot to intercept Nannci as she swept past me.

"You were great!" I heard myself gush like some fan-boy idiot as she led the band past me. She turned her head and shot me a big smile.

"Yeah, we're so great that we get the two o'clock slot," she laughed. I was slow to understand the self-deprecation in her response. Her band got to have its moment on stage well before the headliner even had to show up.

"Do you ever play in New Orleans?"

"We're just another band from out in the bayou in that place." She made a point I couldn't argue.

"Are you going to stay and watch the hot dog eating competition?" I needed to stop talking, but I couldn't think of any better company in town with which to watch this spectacle.

"Nah, I've seen those guys stuff themselves quite enough," she said, and was gone before I could say another word.

I tugged on Roux's leash and led him around the trailer to find a place to one side of the stage. I wanted to get a good view without being jostled too much by the sizeable crowd. It would be bad if the dog eating competition were interrupted by Roux physically taking a chunk out of somebody.

The band's equipment was carried off stage and replaced by folding chairs and a pair of cheap banquet tables. Gabouri used a microphone to encourage the crowd to gather in front of the stage. It seemed like this might be what everyone in town came to see. Even the Ferris wheel stopped. Sheriff Mazant and his deputies took seats behind the table to the right and courthouse employees occupied the table to the left of the district attorney. I had no idea how many of them were selected for having large appetites, but it was likely the criteria Sheriff Mazant used to pick his own team.

The rules were country simple. Each team would be provided all of the hot dogs they could stomach in a continuous feeding and the team that could keep the most down won bragging rights until the next year. You were eliminated if you took a break to do anything besides gulp down water from one of the bottles sitting at the ready beside each contestant. No buns or condiments were allowed and contestants were to only feed upon the now luke-warm wieners. I felt sick just thinking of eating such a mess, but Roux sat at my feet and I could tell he was waiting for one or more to fall off a table and roll his way.

Gabouri swung an old school bell and the dozen men began grabbing handfuls of hot dogs from the platters at their fingertips and shoving them into their mouths two or three at a time. I wondered about the false sense of urgency in this production, as I had heard no time limit stated in Gabouri's listing of the rules. My understanding was that the spectacle would last until the last man literally could not stomach another piece of meat. I was only guessing that a time limit was placed on how long anyone had to hold them down before being allowed to throw up. This was a lot to ask of even a seasoned Cajun's digestive tract.

The audience pressed forward as the number of hot dogs consumed passed what any of the rapt spectators would have dared try to eat. The wild facial expressions on stage became increasingly feverish as each man tried to gauge where his team's count was compared to the other. There was no reason to shove more than one unnecessary bite down your own throat. I backed away as the thought came to me that one of the deputies might abruptly purge into the audience.

It was Judge Aubuchon who suddenly set both hands on the table and began to cough up his last bite of food. I was concerned that some of the water I had just watched him gulp down went down his throat the wrong way. I found as much humor as everyone else in the crowd at his momentary distress, a situation the district attorney played for laughs by gently patting the judge on the back. He was very careful not to alleviate the aged judge's distress. One of the competition's other strange rules must have been that one of his own teammates must handle administering the Heimlich maneuver if it became necessary.

It finally occurred to me that Judge Aubuchon was actually choking. His reddened face was shifting to a paleness I recognized as the last color before it would begin to turn blue. He swung his hand and knocked over the bottle he had just drunk from, but it did not appear that he was reaching to take another drink. Aubuchon gave the district attorney a look of real fear and seemed to be pleading for some relief the competition's judge wasn't at all interested in giving while he was still getting laughs from the crowd.

I let loose of Roux's leash and elbowed my way through the crowd. I leapt aboard the stage at the closest point I could, almost directly in front of Sheriff Mazant, and ran towards the stricken judge. I heard Roux bark and looked down to see he was keeping pace with me, but was unable to find the space he needed to jump up on the stage. I was content for the moment just to know where he was.

I shoved District Attorney Gabouri aside and took the judge in my arms to attempt to apply the pressure beneath his diaphragm that was necessary to dislodge any bite of meat blocking his airway. The judge gave me a crazed look and shook his head. I gave two solid jerks to no avail and then felt the judge pushing me away. I was at a loss to what to do, but the judge didn't have any more time to waste.

He opened his mouth and frantically pointed to the back of his throat. His mouth was empty. His tongue, though, was unnaturally swollen. I realized that it must be what was blocking his airway.

I ran both hands around the judge's waist, which did not turn up an epi-pen. This now looked more like an allergic reaction to something the judge just ate, and dying was going to be the man's own fault if he didn't think to carry an epi-pen with him. The judge really didn't have the time for me to engage myself in this sort of internal dialogue. I was staring into the eyes of a man confronting his own mortality.

I swung the messenger bag off my shoulder and dumped its contents on the table to find the first aid kit that fills about half the thing. I began carrying the medical kit with me as soon as I began patrolling the streets of New Orleans. It became my fetish against being wounded as badly as I was in Iraq. It had everything I needed for the worst situations I could imagine ever being in, and almost nothing for a minor cut or a bug bite. I opened the first aid kit and snatched a sealed bag from its compartment. Only someone with my set of personal paranoias would carry a first aid kit that included the capacity to perform a cricothyrotomy, a proper tourniquet, a compress bandage with a blood clotting agent, and enough plastic wrap to seal a sucking chest wound.

I ripped open the package and plunged the large bore syringe into the judge's throat, feeling the tough trachea membrane give way before I attached a ribbed air hose. I had a very brief worry that I was going to look like a crazy man if it turned out the judge only had a piece of meat caught in his throat.

I was nearly as relieved as the judge when he took a breath. It sounded horrible coming through the plastic device I had just inserted. I wrapped the device's Velcro attachment around his neck to hold it in place and watched him calm down. I was not concerned with the depth or quality of the old man's breaths, just that they kept coming. His color began to improve, so I moved out of his space.

I heard a cheer go up from the crowd and turned to see that the judge and I had become the featured attraction on the stage. The hot dogs were forgotten and Sheriff Mazant and his deputies were already clearing a path for a patrol car to back through the throng. Sheriff Mazant must have grasped that there wasn't time to wait for another ambulance to be called to the scene. The deputies also cleared enough space for Roux to leap aboard the low stage and run to me, at the ready to do anything I asked of him.

I looked at each of the other contestants, worried that any of them might also have an allergy to one of the ingredients in the world's most famous mystery meat. Everyone seemed to be fine, and DA Gabouri hastily promised the crowd a re-match would be part of the town's Fourth of July festivities.

"What the heck all do you have in there, anyway?" Sheriff Mazant asked as he handed me four loaded ammo clips for my Glock sidearm which had also fallen from my messenger bag.

"Let's just say that the old maxim about the Army always fighting the last war just saved the judge's life." I wasn't going to try to explain to him what it was that compelled me to carry around a personal sized field hospital, or admit how surprised I was that I still had the muscle memory from my decades-old combat medicine training.

"Go with the judge. I'm sure he will want to thank you the first chance he can talk again." Sheriff Mazant shoved his hand in mine and gave it a hearty shake. For this one brief moment I was not an interloper in his town.

Thirty-Three

I rode to the hospital in the back seat of the patrol car with Judge Aubuchon. Sheriff Mazant's deputy sped through town with its lights and siren clearing a path. I think the deputy drove a little faster because he clearly seemed unnerved by Roux watching him from the front floorboards. I waited for the orderlies to wheel the judge into the emergency room on a gurney before I opened the cruiser's front passenger door to let Roux out. I snapped the leash on his harness and then hung my badge on a lanyard before following the judge's path into the hospital. I had no idea what health protocols there were about dogs in hospitals. I hoped shoving my State Patrol badge in people's faces might get most of the hospital's policies waived temporarily. I was only a bit sorry that I had taken Roux to the festival at all.

I needed to stay close to the judge until I had a much clearer idea of what had just transpired. There was no way he intentionally entered a contest to eat anything that would cause such an allergic reaction. The first thing I needed someone to learn was a list of his known food allergies, but that would just lead to the bigger question of how that ingredient made it into Judge Aubuchon's stack of hot dogs. Most likely every hot dog contained the same extra ingredient, but the judge was the only participant allergic to it.

I mentally narrowed the list of possible suspects down to anyone in Saint Xavier Parish familiar with the judge's food allergies. I was glad it was a fairly small place, because that meant I might wrap up interviewing everyone living in the parish in just a couple of years.

"Call Sheriff Mazant and have him put the judge's hot dogs in an evidence bag and send it to me here," I instructed the deputy. He seemed grateful to have something to do now that we were both left to stand around. I turned my attention to the reception desk and had her point me in the direction of the judge.

The judge was still in the emergency room, but just in one of the curtained-off treatment bays and had not been rushed into an operating room. An intern carefully extracted the breathing tube I had so unceremoniously jabbed into the judge's throat. Nurses began setting up a variety of equipment to monitor his vital signs and rummaging around for his wallet and cell phone. They were checking him into the hospital and needed to go through the wallet and phone to find a contact number for his next of kin.

"You the guy did this?" the young doctor asked as he turned towards me and tossed the plastic tubing into a trash can beside the gurney.

"Yes." I didn't know if I answered a question or admitted to practicing medicine without a license.

"Whether he will ever say so or not, you saved the judge's life," he said and gave me a wry smile. I guessed the judge had been his patient in the past.

"What happened?" I hoped the doctor saw this sort of thing often enough he could immediately diagnose it. This was a place full of odd things to eat.

"We are treating it as an allergic reaction. I'm pumping him full of antihistamines, which will give him a nice nap if nothing else. I didn't find anything stuck in his throat and his medical records shows no history of seizures." I took some relief from having an actual doctor make the same snap diagnosis I did.

"Maybe he knows something that will help clear this up when we get him settled into a room and he has a chance to rest a bit. Seventy is not the best age to have something like this happen to you."

"I'll bet not," I said and left him to his work. I was not going to be able to speak with the judge, or get the doctor's final diagnosis, until the next day. I only needed to stay at the hospital long enough for Sheriff Mazant to transfer the suspected source of the allergic reaction to my care, and then hand it off to the state's forensic technicians. Hopefully they would find the culprit ingredient behind the judge's near-death experience.

"You're working today?" Captain Hammond all but laughed into the phone when he took my call.

"I wasn't until Judge Aubuchon had an apparent allergic reaction to a hot dog," I assured him. "He's at the local hospital and I need you to have someone swing by and pick up an evidence bag of hot dogs. I need to know if they were spiked with something to cause this. The judge was in an eating contest, but he was the only one who went down."

"That doesn't sound very random." This was one of the very few times my captain and I ever agreed on anything. "You're still at the hospital?"

"Yeah. Sheriff Mazant is supposed to be sending over the rest of the judge's hot dogs and I might stick around to see if I can speak with the judge when they get him into a room. Do you know if he has a family?"

"Never married. I don't think I've even heard of his having a girlfriend," Hammond mused. I saw no reason for him to keep up on the judge's love life. "It will be interesting to see who shows up to see him."

I took this as being his way of telling me that was something I should let him know, whether it mattered in what I was there to do or not. A big part of my captain's job was collecting pieces of information about anyone he might ever have to deal with. It was one of the few habits of his I already embraced before joining the state police.

"I'll let you know what happens," I assured him.

"And I will get a car there as soon as I can. Be patient. They'll be coming from over in Breaux Bridge." I assumed sending a car from the closest regional headquarters meant he wasn't prepared to route anyone on patrol to handle my request. He must not have seen any urgency on the lab work.

I thanked him and hung up. I looked around the empty reception area and felt the wheels in the back of my head start in motion. I had the lab report on the blood found in the trunk of Gwen Donovan's sedan in my bag. It explained why the blood never dried, but I still had no idea how Gwen might have collected or stored so much of her own blood. I doubted Kirk would have ignored a jug of human blood in the family refrigerator, no matter how well Gwen tried to hide it or explained it away.

"Excuse me, do you have a blood bank here?" I asked one of the receptionists. Her attention slowly shifted from the book she was reading to me, and then to Roux.

"You can't bring a dog in here," she stated flatly. She was about fifty and probably not new to the job.

"Police business." I showed her my badge.

"This is as far as you two get, unless you have a search warrant and that dog is looking for evidence." I had met my match.

"I don't have a warrant, but I just need to speak with someone about a medical issue. Can I leave my dog with you while I run down the hall for just a minute?"

"You can go sit down," the woman said. Her tone had grown rather frosty. "I will call for someone to come speak with you."

I walked Roux back into the waiting area. We took seats where I could watch for either Sheriff Mazant's errand boy or the State Patrol unit. It was going to be interesting to see who arrived first, as neither of the drivers was likely in a hurry to do my bidding.

I finished signing for the evidence bag Sheriff Mazant's deputy delivered as a sharply dressed man about my age approached. He wore a dark suit and tie rather than a white coat. It immediately suggested that he was an attorney and not a doctor. That, in turn, told me that my visit was anticipated.

"Detective?" he asked and extended his hand.

"Detective Holland, with the state police. I am the state's lead investigator into Gwendolyn Donovan's disappearance." I raised my badge so he could see it was real. "And you are an attorney, and not a doctor, if I am not mistaken."

"What gave me away?" He was going to try to be casual and friendly. I prefer that to attorneys who want to try to take control of the conversation. It was also a sign that he was not entirely sure why I was asking to speak with one of the hospital's employees.

"Let's just say I am used to being approached by attorneys," I joked back to signal I wasn't going to be a by-the-book detective he would need to debate.

"You are not investigating her husband's death?" Now I knew why he was really sent to speak with me.

"Kirk's body was found while I was investigating his wife's disappearance. I am going to assume you are here because what I need answers to involves a member of the Donovan family," I informed him.

"As such, you surely don't want the hospital accused of withholding any evidence or assistance."

"And you surely do not expect us to waive HIPAA regulations until you produce a warrant." He had a better argument than I did, but I really only wanted help with a logistical question.

"My question is of a general nature. I hoped to find a professional to answer a question or two, and to learn about how you handle domestic abuse cases."

"We handle them on a case by case basis, that's how." I really wished my sister or Katie were with me instead of Roux. The bites they would take out of this guy were far more acceptable than those Roux would take if I gave the command.

"Yes, but some of my questions are about procedures, not specific patients." I was not good at guessing which loophole he would try to squirt through, but I did anticipate that one.

"So you say. The hospital would be in a much more helpful position if you were to come back with a warrant to ask your questions. You are obviously pursuing a lead on someone the hospital has treated in the past, and we would prefer not to dance on the thin ice of helping your investigation when it might involve a patient's rights covered by HIPAA." He was courteous, but no less of a roadblock than the woman who called him instead of a lab technician.

"I understand that you need to protect anything involving a Donovan. Hiding them behind HIPAA will only work for so long."

The way the attorney narrowed his eyes before he turned away without further comment told me our next meeting would begin on even less friendly terms.

Thirty-Four

"Of course you hit a brick wall. You know you're going to hit one no matter which way you turn out there," Katie sighed. I called her to hear a friendly voice after the hospital's attorney left me hanging.

"I guess I'll need to get a warrant." It was beginning to seem that I was trapped on a one-step-forward/two-steps-back treadmill. Every question, potential lead, or intentional lack of cooperation added days to how long I would have to remain in Donovan.

"You're also doing that thing again," Katie gave an even louder sigh.

"Which thing is that?"

"You are pulling new cases out of your case like it is a Russian nesting doll. You only needed to find out what happened to Gwen. That turned into tracking down the entire family. Then you found her husband was either murdered or killed himself in his own backyard, and now you think someone has tried to kill a judge. Do you even try to limit this stuff?"

"I follow leads," I defended myself, probably needlessly. She knew my apparent capacity to create work was not intentional.

"Read some Robert Frost before you go to sleep tonight. Two roads diverged in the yellow wood, lover, and you can always choose the well-traveled one."

"Can, but probably won't," I admitted.

"I know that. It's part of what I love about you." Katie hung up before things got any mushier.

Thirty-Five

The State Patrolman who came for the evidence was kind enough to offer me a ride home from the hospital. We arrived to discover four cars parked in front of Judge Rogers' house. They all bore Louisiana plates, but I did not recognize any of the late model autos. It took only a moment for me to hear the distant sounds of a pool party. I rolled down my window and had my driver confirm that he also heard splashing water, decent reggae music, and at least four voices in the near distance.

I had him park sideways in the driveway to prevent anyone from getting past us. I opened my door slowly, trying to try to avoid alerting the trespassers to our presence. I tugged Roux out behind me and gave him only a short length of leash. I didn't really care if a bunch of kids were here to skinny dip, but I was irritated none of them had bothered to ask permission. My real concern was that one of them might be drunk enough to injure themselves and then try to sue the judge, who very likely would have had a problem with everything I was prepared to ignore.

I decided against approaching the intruders from the direction of the house. They undoubtedly knew someone was living here, if only because my coupe was parked in the open garage, and were already expecting someone to eventually shoo them away. I did not see a boat at the end of the judge's dock, so everyone in the pool must have arrived in one of the cars. Roux and I skirted the tree line and approached the party from behind the pool house.

"Zwemmen!" I whispered and released Roux's leash. This was his favorite reward command, and he wasted no time running to the pool.

I had to run to keep up so I could be in position to hold everyone in the pool when the brown blur of a dog hit the water in his usual belly-flop style. He began to swim towards the nearest human. The boy wanted no part of a dog swimming towards him with its mouth wide open and teeth bared. The kid lacked the ability to tell sheer glee from imminent attack.

"Everybody, get in the deep end of the pool. Now. All of you, in the pool as well," I waved the red dot of my Glock's laser across the patio before any of the teenagers sitting and standing there could think to run. Roux was already using the concrete stairs in one corner of the shallow end to leave the pool and join me. His presence was more persuasive than the firearm and soon the deep end of the pool held eight sulking college-aged youths. I was relieved they were all wearing swim suits. I could place an age on the swimmers because I knew two of them well enough that I would not have wanted to see them naked.

Bradley Ladd tried to hide himself behind two of the other young men. Jennifer Deveraux chose to try to embarrass me and swam to the edge of the pool to begin to raise herself out of the pool as seductively as she could muster at twenty. I nudged her back into the water with the toe of my boot before her bikini top broke the surface of the water.

"Line up along here," I ordered the group as I holstered my handgun and used my hand to wave an imaginary line along the edge of the pool. I called Roux to my side and told him to sit down, which he did after shaking himself dry. I pointed to Bradley and Jennifer and then to the area beneath the diving board. "You two. Over there."

They quickly, but sullenly, followed my directions. Both of them seemed to realize that knowing me was not going to do them any favors. I kept my distance from the edge as I addressed the remaining group.

"Tell me your name and where you are from." I said it only once and then pointed to the nervous swimmers in turn. There were five boys and one other girl to question. I didn't really care what any of their names were, because I intended to send all of them home. I planned to scold the pair I knew before I sent them packing as well. All I really wanted to do was put a little fear into the trespassers.

"Fred Jackson. I live in Lafayette."

I motioned for the beefy young man to get out of the water and pointed to his clothes. I did my best to afford him some privacy as he got dressed.

"Duncan McGee. I'm from New Orleans."

I motioned for Duncan to get out and get dressed as well. Fred had enough common sense to sit down when he finished getting dressed.

Nobody was going to try to outrun Roux, and only two of the people still in the pool had any reason to believe I might not shoot them.

"Mitchell Ursin. I'm from Donovan."

He waited for me to give him the same directions and then hustled across the concrete to get dressed and join his glum companions.

I now faced the only other female in the pool. Her bikini was sized to fit someone as trim as my niece, and wearing it was meant to draw attention to every place where it was just a bit too small. She was definitely an eye-catching petite blonde, even with her disgruntled expression. There was none of the fear in her face that even my niece had the sense to show. What I read was closer to an expression that seemed to say I was deeply inconveniencing her.

"My name is Belle Donovan. I live here." The way she said that last sentence left no doubt as to who she believed was trespassing on the judge's property.

"Nice to finally meet you, Miss Donovan. Kindly join the other two down there." I waved her towards Jennifer and Bradley and then motioned for the last two boys to get dressed without bothering to get their names. I waited until the last boy to climb from the pool was dressed and then sent the five of them on their way. The State Trooper could see me from his cruiser so I gave a wave that released him to go back to real crime fighting.

I sat down on the end of the lounge chair closest to where the last trio was still treading water and clutching the edge of the pool. I wasn't entirely sure how to approach them just then so I placed Roux on guard duty and went to the pool house for three large towels. I dropped the towels in a dry spot and motioned for them to get out of the pool.

"Get your stuff. We're going inside," I ordered, and then marched the silent trio around the house, with Roux in the lead. I unlocked the front door and we gathered in the living room. I left Roux to guard the center hallway and told the detainees to get dressed before I stepped into the dining room. Their state of undress was awkward enough without one of them being a relative of mine and the other female being a possible murder suspect.

I called for them to join me at the large antique dining table. I took a seat at one end and took a moment to study Jennifer and her friends. Belle was wearing a more circumspect expression than the one she wore in the pool.

"Let's start with how the three of you know one another." This should have been an easy question. My real purpose in asking this was to see which of them would try to lie their way out of trouble.

"Bradley and I met at Tulane. Jennifer's grandfather, who I guess is your uncle, works for my grandfather." I should have anticipated Belle doing all the talking. She came from a family whose word was law in Donovan. Belle's explanation may or not have been true, but it was now the response the other two would give me if allowed to speak for themselves.

"Fine," I said and then pointed to Bradley. "You can call your father to come get you."

"That would be a neat trick. He's dead." I felt like an idiot for forgetting that, but then realized I had not betrayed that I knew anything about his past.

"Why don't you let them spend the night and go home in the morning? That was what we planned to do anyway," Belle immediately suggested.

"Because that is not how I am going to handle this," I told her. I wasn't about to surrender control to Belle, if only because she was obviously quite used to getting her way. "I have no intention of charging any of you with trespassing, but none of you are going to get off as lightly as your pals. I know that every single one of you knew you didn't belong here."

"But, I do live here," Belle repeated.

"You live in the nice new house your daddy built for you," I said in a tone more much cruel and mocking than I intended to use. I took a deep breath, but I didn't apologize.

"No. He and my mom live there and this is where I stay when I come back to visit," Belle insisted. That could explain the amount of furniture and pots and pans in the house when I moved in.

"Why stay here?"

"Because I don't have to live with my parents anymore. I am twenty one and I can do as I please."

"Almost on both those counts," I said to bring her back to reality. I turned to address Bradley. "So, where do you live?"

"I have an apartment in New Orleans. I gave Belle a ride from the airport in Lafayette."

"I'm going to call my father!" Belle abruptly announced. The exasperation was back in her tone. I had obviously ruined her pool party, and any other plans she had for Saint Patrick's Day.

"Go ahead and try that," I said, believing I was calling her bluff. She pulled her cellphone out of her purse and dialed Kirk's number. I could hear it ringing repeatedly. She disconnected the call when it went to voice mail. "Kirk is not home, or he isn't answering."

"Both of those statements are entirely true," I informed her. "Would you mind telling me where you have been since abruptly leaving your classes at Tulane?"

"It's not like I dropped out," she defended herself against an accusation I certainly had not made. "I had a fight with my parents so I went to our place in Aspen. I just got home this morning. Both of my parents know where I have been."

"And you haven't been in touch with anyone else while you have been gone? Neither of these two?" I was beginning to dread what was coming.

"No. I went there to finish a research paper so Kirk could read it before I turn it in. It was the deal we made before I went to Colorado. He isn't going to be happy when he reads what I came back with, but I don't care." It seemed to do her some good to have a place to vent the displeasure she knew better than to direct at me.

"And you two have spent the entire afternoon with Belle and not said a word about her parents?" I was surprised and upset with her companions.

"I didn't want to ruin her homecoming," Bradley lamely tried to excuse himself. Jennifer said nothing.

"What's going on?" Belle demanded.

"You father is dead and your mother is missing. We found enough blood in the trunk of her car to be worried about her safety. I have been here for nearly two weeks looking for all three of you. So far I have only found your father." There was no easy way to phrase anything about finding her father's body.

"So, Kirk is dead?" This was all she wanted me to confirm. Not a single question about her mother. No interest in how, when, or where her father died, or if I had a suspect. Just an oddly casual request for confirmation that he was no longer in her life. It did far less to eliminate her as a suspect in his murder than her alibi.

"Yes, he is." I watched her go a little blank. I could tell she was thinking about the ways this might affect her, and I was taken aback by the realization that she was looking for a way to turn this to her advantage. I wanted to pour some cold water on her to see if that might affect her. "I assume someone can verify your presence in Colorado?"

"I can give you the name of the jet service our family uses. They are in Lafayette. I don't think I have the number of our housekeeper out there in my phone," Belle offered. Her voice sounded distracted and her eyes didn't seem focused on the room. Both of her companions kept their eyes on the highly varnished inlaid tabletop.

"We'll get to that." I had no reason to doubt her story. "Let's get down to basics. I understand you came home the day before your father died to argue with him about the research paper. Is that accurate?"

"Yes. He said he didn't send me to Tulane to dig up dirt on my own family, and that he sent me to Tulane so I could get into law school. I never planned to do what he wanted. I want to be journalist," Belle made no effort to hide the level of anger and frustration she must have shown her father when they crossed swords. I didn't see it as being strong enough to kill someone. "I think what Kirk does is disgusting."

"Where did things stand when you last spoke with your father?" She seemed a bit surprised that I did not ask her any questions about her father's line of work or why it upset it her so much.

"He told me to take a couple of weeks in Colorado to think about my future and to be ready to give him my decision when I came back. I didn't need that much time to come to the same conclusion I had when I left here. I wasn't going to drop what I found out, and I was never going to be part of what he does."

"Has anyone else read the paper?" I hadn't thought to ask that until just then.

"I helped her write it. We're in the same class," Jennifer spoke up.

I was at a loss for what to say or ask. It made sense she would have trusted someone she probably knew for much of her life to help with the troubling paper.

"Have you read it?" I asked Bradley. I was growing curious enough to want to read the paper myself.

"Belle made me swear I wouldn't talk about it with anyone." Bradley replied. I made a mental note that the kid could keep a promise. It meant he could keep a secret as well.

"And your mother? What did she have to say about what you found?" This time I was trying to lead Belle into disclosing something of what her father was so adamant about keeping hidden.

"She warned me that my dad would disown me if I persisted. I would have to drop out of Tulane if Kirk cut me off. I hope he didn't change his will." I could have easily taken that last sentence entirely wrong, but I was young once and knew she was worried about her finances and didn't mean to implicate herself in his murder.

"And you," I turned my attention to my cousin. She may have believed I had either forgotten about her or thought she was blameless. "Did you know Belle was in Colorado and chose not to say anything?"

"No, she didn't tell anybody where she was." The two girls looked at one another as though combining their fake sincerity would make it ring true.

A loud banging at the front door brought the girls a reprieve. Roux barked once and then marched into the entryway to await further instructions. The insistent knocking came to an end at the sound of Roux's bark, as though our guest might have chosen to reconsider their visit.

"Stay here." It didn't look like any them were about to make a run for it, but I needed to keep acting like the grownup in the room.

I spotted Chief Theriot's cruiser in the driveway even before I opened the door to find the burly lawman filling the door frame. Roux didn't slow him.

"What's going on here?" the Chief Theriot demanded and tried to take a second step into the house. This one was met by my outstretched arm and Roux taking a much more offensive stance beside me.

"Nothing that involves you." I didn't need this as a distraction in what was left of my day.

"I just got a phone call that you had a break in," Chief Theriot persisted. I lowered my arm, but continued to block any further passage.

"Belle was having a pool party when I got home. She failed to let me know in advance, so there was a little bit of confusion. That is cleared up and everyone is free to leave," I said to calm whatever was roiling the chief.

"When did Belle get home?" Chief Theriot asked. He appeared to be as surprised to learn the young woman was alive and well as I was. Her presence was enough to bring him back to business. "I need to speak with her."

"No, you don't. She's staying here and will call you if she needs anything from you," I informed him. His learning about Belle's return saved me from having to be the one to notify everyone with an interest in Belle's whereabouts.

"You're really becoming a pain," He snarled and turned to leave. He stopped after a couple of steps and turned towards me as if to say something, but he reconsidered whatever it was.

"Okay, we don't have a lot of time," I told the two girls after I watched Chief Theriot drive away.

"What do you mean?" Jennifer wondered, but could not have been entirely ignorant of the nature of her father's business.

"Your father will be here in about an hour. He will definitely drag you out of here, but he is also going to tell Belle's grandfather she is back in town." I was explaining what I considered to be entirely obvious while my mind was running dozens of war-game scenarios to find a way to protect Belle. "She can't be here when the senator comes looking for her."

"Why? I can take care of myself." Belle asked, with the same naïve tone as Jennifer. "We can tell him I have to stay because you are protecting me."

"Well I cannot protect you here. The first thing the senator is going to do is destroy every copy of your paper he can lay his hands on. Besides that, I am not about to be compromised by spending even one night alone with you in this house." A plan was forming in my head. I knew it was probably the right one because nobody but me was going to like it. I turned my attention to Jennifer and Bradley. "You two, do me a favor and drive straight home. Jenn, tell Uncle Felix that I placed Belle in protective custody. Anyone that wants to talk to her needs to contact me."

I ushered Jennifer and Bradley out the front door and immediately turned my attention back to Belle. "Grab your things. We need to leave."

Belle didn't need to be told twice. I did not figure for an instant that she was ready to surrender her privilege to test me on everything I did to keep her safe. She still had only the faintest idea of how much danger she might be in. For that matter, I didn't know the extent of the danger she was in, either, but I did know that Uncle Felix posed a danger to both of us.

Thirty-Six

My plan was simple, at least to me. I needed to place Belle where any attempts to physically remove her could be easily countered. It needed to be a place that would make sense to Captain Hammond, and be where Senator Donovan's legal reach was at its weakest. The location seemed obvious, but there were still a few things that could interfere with what I had in mind.

The first problem was going to be convincing Belle that the situation was as serious as I believed it was so she would follow my instructions whether I was with her or not. The second consideration was whether I could trust her not to burn the place down, and that might only last until she figured out how to get what she wanted from being a material witness. The final, but most crucial, hurdle was having enough charm and persuasive arguments to convince people I liked far more than Belle to babysit her for a week or two.

"Okay, Belle, here's the deal. I need to be sure you are safe and that nobody tries to use you to stop my investigation into what has happened to your parents," I began explaining to my still not entirely willing passenger. She was not going to argue with me with Roux staring up at her from between her knees, but our departure from Donovan must have seemed very sudden. "I am going to put you in an apartment in New Orleans for a few days."

"Do I have to stay there all the time?" Belle didn't reject the idea, but she was testing my limits on her freedom to roam. "Can I go to class if I want?"

"I could say yes, but frankly I don't believe that is the only place you would go if you left the apartment. You have to understand that, at this moment, neither of us knows why your father was killed, nor what has become of your mother. You might be alive only because you were out of town when whatever happened to both of them occurred."

"Do you think that might really be true?" Belle wasn't acting like she did, and that was a problem in itself.

"It only matters for now that it is one possibility," I steered clear of any discussion that might make me tell her she was also still my best suspect. What I didn't want her to know was that this move was my way to keep Senator Donovan or Uncle Felix from being able to take her from my custody with their combined stable of expensive attorneys. I still only had one witness to work with, and unfortunately she was it.

"Then fine. Make me your prisoner," Belle sighed in what I was coming to learn was her signature sound.

"It will be okay. The prison food is pretty good," I assured her and called Tony at Strada Ammazarre.

"I am coming back into town, but I cannot stay very long," I informed the chef after Jason had a server summon him to the bar phone. I knew dinner service was about to start, but I wanted Tony somewhere he could not throw sharp or burning objects when I asked for this favor. "I am going to put a material witness in my place and I need you to be sure she stays there until I come back for her. Can you do that?"

"I could try," my business partner barely offered. "Is she in any danger?"

"I don't know if anyone might try to kill her. Her dad was murdered and her mom has disappeared, so there is no reason to believe she would not be on a list if her parents were both killed." I doubted that Gwen Donovan was dead, but I was trying to convince a man used to handling genuine life and death situations to babysit. "At the very least some bad men may try to drag her back here and you can handle them as you see fit."

"Then I will do this for you," Tony agreed. I really did hope nothing came to pass, if only for the sake of anyone who tried to get past my human pit-bull.

I didn't expect the next sales call to be nearly as easy to close. Katie Reilly and I had not been dating for nearly enough time to ask her to babysit Belle. Tony could keep her in my apartment during the day, but someone needed to physically be with her every evening.

"Good evening, my love" I said as soon as Katie answered her cellphone.

"What do you need?"

"I can't call you up because I miss you and invite you to dinner?" I was taken aback by how swiftly she went on the defensive.

"You can, but that's not why you are calling," Katie said, only this time she laughed. "Do I need to tell you where I am standing right now?"

The background noise I had initially ignored told me she must have been close enough to listen to Tony's conversation with me. I had lost the element of surprise before I dialed her number.

"I really do want to have dinner with you, if you haven't eaten. I also need to talk you into sleeping at my place for a week or so. Belle Donovan magically appeared this afternoon and I want to keep her away from anyone I don't know, and quite a few of the people I do know in Donovan."

"I can do that. If I can't, I will talk your sister into it. She's at Tony's most nights as it is," Katie agreed, but not without making me pay a price.

"I did not need to know that."

"While the cat's away," she laughed and hung up.

Thirty-Seven

Belle was no less surprised to discover that her temporary accommodations were above Strada Ammazarre than I was to learn from her that the bistro is Judge Rogers' favorite place to eat in New Orleans that doesn't serve a truly great steak. The excellence of New Orleans' old-line steak houses is such that I took no offense.

Belle remained largely silent while she ate her way through the meal Tony brought to the chef's table. Belle, Tulip, and Katie were plainly trying to size one another up over dinner. The trio were talking and laughing on my sofa, and drinking my liquor, when Roux and I headed back to Donovan just after ten o'clock.

I alerted Judge Rogers that his granddaughter was alive and well. I told him I had her in a safe house in Orleans Parish, but not where, so he could be on the watch for any attempts by Uncle Felix or the senator's lawyers to find a judge in New Orleans willing to force me to surrender Belle. None of the judges in Saint Xavier Parish were going to be able to compel me to do so, and their authority did not extend to the front door of the bistro. Even so, I was working against an imaginary clock before Belle lost whatever value she might hold in solving her father's murder and her mother's disappearance. She was privy to their last conversations and movements, but her direct knowledge stopped when she left town. I didn't imagine she was likely to provide many fresh clues, but I didn't need many to get back on track.

My route back to Judge Rogers' house involved a drive on two-lane roads all the way to Lafayette before backtracking to Donovan on US 90. I hoped the poor subterfuge of arriving back in town from the west might temporarily convince Sheriff Mazant and Chief Theriot that I hid Belle somewhere closer to Lake Charles, or maybe Lafayette, than New Orleans. What should have been an hour's drive took until nearly two in the morning, but it was going to be worth it if Belle was inaccessible to Senator Donovan until I had a better idea about what had happened that fateful Friday. There was going to be an immediate and intensive campaign by the senator and Uncle Felix to create a narrative protecting the Donovan name against anything ugly that Belle's version of the truth might hold.

Thirty-Eight

I made extra coffee while I started cooking breakfast upon my return to Donovan because I expected at least one if not two visitors. I waited to scramble eggs until Uncle Felix's Lexus sedan was in Judge Rogers' driveway. He arrived on my doorstep just before seven o'clock, which meant seeing me was either an early start to his day or the last thing he needed to do before his night was over. I shooed Roux into his kennel before I answered the door.

"Shall we skip the part where I act like I don't know why you are here?" I suggested. "Have you had breakfast yet? I was just about to scramble some eggs. There's coffee and toast right now, but give me a few minutes and you can have bacon and eggs."

I was talking as I led him to the kitchen. He kept his silence until he was seated at the table in the nook overlooking the swimming pool. He glanced at Roux, but they didn't exchange greetings. I like to put Roux in his kennel, or tighten my hold on his leash, whenever he is near my uncle. It is meant to make Uncle Felix wonder about his safety around my pit bull companion. He makes his living being the most dangerous creature in any given room, so I use Roux to remind him he isn't nearly that powerful in any room the three of us share.

"Senator Donovan wants his niece released from your custody. Today would be satisfactory," he said without the affected charm of the Southern accent he uses for issuing his best threats.

"Yeah," I began cracking eggs into a large skillet skimmed with bacon grease. "That isn't happening."

"He'll go to court." It is the standard empty threat of any lout with an attorney on retainer. Tulip or Katie will tell you that going to court and winning in court are seldom the same thing.

"His money could be better spent." I flopped the eggs onto a platter and piled a pound of not-too crisp thick-cut bacon beside it. The toast was still warm from being held in the oven. I set everything on the table and went back for the percolator of coffee.

"Well he wants to see her," my uncle sensed I was not going to be any easier to intimidate working this case than any other he had expressed an interest in.

"I will work something out, but not today. It isn't likely to be anytime soon, I can tell you that. Belle needs to feel safe, and that may take a while, what with her father apparently murdered and her mother missing in a particularly messy fashion. If I were you, I would be more concerned about the senator's safety right now than Belle's."

"What makes you say that?" Uncle Felix is not prone to asking questions he doesn't know the answer to, or have a plan to handle if the answer is negative.

"If someone targeted Kirk over his legal work, it seems reasonable that they might hold his father equally responsible for their grievance since Kirk took over his father's law practice. With Kirk dead, doesn't it seem reasonable that, if they kidnapped Gwen, they might contact the senator about a ransom?"

"I try not to spin too many conspiracy theories like that if I can help it." Uncle Felix chuckled as he tried to counter my admittedly feeble arguments for why I didn't want to let the senator see his niece.

"Then take this reason back to the senator. I began worrying about Belle's safety and security when I found out she was about to air the family's dirty laundry, and what her father's reaction was to that news."

"We know she is supposedly writing about Duncan Donovan. The senator is already in contact with her instructor about passing her without her having to submit the assignment," Uncle Felix once again tried to be dismissive of what I saw as a reason to leave Belle in peace.

"I should have expected as much," I said around a bite of bacon.

"Can you at least tell me where she is?" he asked in a slightly exasperated tone of voice. His tones, sighs, and body language are like a set of golf clubs that he will choose from to make the perfect shot.

"I absolutely can," I assured him. "But I also most certainly won't. If I tell you where I have her, you will send some lackey attorney to get a judge in that district to issue a writ of habeas corpus. So, no, I won't play your game today."

"You're picking up far too much from that Irish girl," he hid his growing displeasure behind his coffee cup.

"I will be sure to let Katie know of your displeasure," I laughed. "I am giving Belle a day or two to wrap her head around the possibility of being an orphan and being a murder suspect along with her mother. After that, I will sit down with her and see what she can tell me about the last time she and her parents spoke. I suspect that she knows more than she thinks she does."

"Such as?" He needed something to take back to the senator to show he could get me to cooperate. There was a distinct possibility that his connection to me was why the senator had not already deployed the heavy guns at his disposal. He could lean on the state police commander to get me to do his bidding in much the same way he was pressuring Belle's college professor to waive his assignment. Felix and the senator both had attorneys and loyal judges at their beck and call. In the end, the senator also had Sheriff Mazant and the local chief of police to see to it that I got roughed up as much as it took to make me fall in line.

"Belle claims that the last conversation they had was about what she had found in the family records. Kirk told her to drop it, and then sent her to Colorado to write the paper when she wouldn't, which she said was his way of telling her he would cut her off if she came back and wouldn't do what he told her to do. Gwen took her side, but not where Kirk could hear her. I don't what she found, but what would Shakespeare have written about if it weren't for young love and screwed up families?"

"And someone put you in charge of this," Uncle Felix gave a genuine sigh of resignation and set his coffee cup down. He hates when I make jokes that he doesn't get. "What should I tell the senator?"

"Tell him I will arrange for Belle to have some time with him this weekend. I will set the place and time, but they won't be left alone. That's the best offer he is going to get, and I don't have to do that much." My uncle dropping by, even as anticipated as it was, told me that promising to allow the senator to speak with his niece was the only way I would keep the man at bay. I simply wasn't prepared to fight on more than one front at a time.

Thirty-Nine

Sheriff Mazant and Detective Chance did their best to give the impression that Belle's arrival in Donovan didn't change a thing. The two of them were in Sheriff Mazant's office when I arrived just after eight o'clock to brief Sheriff Mazant on the latest development in the case. I had ample reason to believe Belle had been the topic of discussion when I interrupted their meeting.

"Good morning, gentlemen," I greeted them as I took a seat in front of Sheriff Mazant's desk. Detective Chance straightened his posture in his own seat as I settled in. Sheriff Mazant gritted his teeth at the familiarity I displayed in sitting down without his inviting me, but he held his tongue.

"By now you have heard that Belle Donovan appeared in Judge Rogers' pool yesterday afternoon. I took her into custody as a material witness and will be questioning her in the next day or so. She needs time to adjust to the news of her parents' situations."

"We will want to question her as well," Sheriff Mazant informed me.

"I don't know why," I calmly stated.

"What do you mean? Of course we want to speak with her," Detective Chance took up the challenge to their local authority.

"About what? Is there a criminal charge against her that the two of you failed to mention?" My breakfast with Uncle Felix was making me playful. I only wished that this pair were sharper adversaries.

"No, but we have questions. Where has she been? What does she know about her parents?" Sheriff Mazant finally offered sample questions, as I knew he eventually would feel compelled to do.

"Those are questions that pertain to the homicide and missing person case we all agreed I would be the one to handle. I will keep you informed of anything I believe is pertinent, or that your department might be able to help confirm or deny," I could feel the air rush from the room and a very deep chill settle in.

"This is not the level of cooperation I believe we agreed upon,"

Sheriff Mazant snarled.

"Things developed rapidly and my responsibility was to place Miss Donovan in a safe place at the first opportunity," I lied through my teeth. I only meant to remind him that any cooperation at all was an act of courtesy, and nothing more than an act, at that. "I am telling you she is safe and healthy so your office is properly informed in case you get inquiries."

We glared at one another to silently acknowledge we both knew who would be making inquiries about Belle. I was certain the senator had already chewed on Sheriff Mazant that morning, or the night before.

"All the same, I would like an opportunity to have Detective Chance question Belle at some point. The sooner the better," Sheriff Mazant persisted.

"I will see what can be arranged as soon as Detective Chance explains his line of questioning." I had no intention of granting either of these men any audience with Belle without my being present.

"There are local matters at play here. Her grandfather would like to speak with her about family matters that do not pertain to your investigation," Sheriff Mazant gently pressed.

"I am sure he would," I did not try to contain my chortle. "Donovan family matters are on hold until my investigation is done. The senator need not worry about Belle doing anything rash while she is in my protective custody. There will plenty of time once I find out what happened to her parents to decide the poor girl's future. We'd be smart to all take a step back and let Belle and her grandfather be the ones to decide what is best for their family going forward."

"How is the case coming? Detective Chance here claims you haven't spoken with him in a couple of days," Sheriff Mazant was trying to regroup on solid ground. He was right that I had consciously avoided speaking with my liaison to his office.

"One of those days was a holiday," I pointed out. "I have interviewed a couple of people, but neither of them advanced the case so I chose not to bore your man with the results of those interviews. I am still waiting for him to tell me about his search for the boat."

"I haven't found it." His report was as useless as mine was to them.

He gave no sign of being ready to elaborate on the matter, so I moved on. I had only asked him to look for the boat as a way to occupy his time.

"We all seem to agree that both investigations remain at a standstill. I am personally not convinced that the person, or persons, who drowned Kirk are connected to Gwen's disappearance, but I am going to go back to the file and start again. Detective Chance is welcome to join me, or you can re-assign him as you see fit," I said and stood up.

I didn't want to give Sheriff Mazant too many things to remember when he called the senator. Solving the pair of cases was the only way I was going to leave, and that my leaving was the only way Belle was coming home was all I needed everyone to understand.

"Go with him," Sheriff Mazant said and waved the two of us from his office.

Forty

"Where do you want to start?" Detective Chance asked once the door to Sheriff Mazant's office was closed behind us.

"Like I said, we need to start over from the beginning. That means we find the boat captain who reported the Mercedes as being left on the boat ramp for three days." I was talking aloud, but my mind was still lining up the order in which I thought it best to interview everyone. We were back to looking for obvious inconsistencies and those stray things that people didn't think were important enough to mention the first time they were questioned.

Detective Chance glanced at his watch before he responded to my suggestion. "Captain Haskins ought to be down at the marina. The charter boats don't get much work during the week."

"You know his schedule?"

"I get to do a little fishing now and then. I know some of the other captains, and I have seen him around." It wasn't really an answer to my question, but it did tell me a little bit more about my partner.

We passed the Donovan Ship Building Works on our way to the marina. It was difficult to see exactly what was going on because everything was done inside one of three massive metal buildings. Chance said he wasn't sure what they built. He only knew that Billy Donovan, the senator's youngest brother, was in charge of the operation and that he had heard quite a bit of grumbling about most of the workers not being from Saint Xavier Parish.

This five minute explanation was the longest we had spoken in the twenty minutes it took to get to the parish's commercial marina. It was located less than a mile from the Gulf of Mexico, protected as best it could be from hurricanes by being tucked around the last bend in Bayou Beausejour. A small knot of raised camps nearby gave locals a place to escape the hustle and bustle of Donovan. They lacked a view of the Gulf, instead looking out over the diminishing wetlands to either side of the low levees flanking the bayou. There was a combination convenience store and gas station floating on a retired barge, and two bars, one built over the water and the other on stilts, providing bags of ice and cold beer to the boats and anyone else there for the weekend. Only a couple of the raised camps had cars parked beneath them, and their presence didn't lead me to believe anyone lived here full time. I took a deep breath of the salted air, ripe with the scent of the dead fish floating under the dock and the diesel fumes from the idling shrimp boats, and remembered how little I had enjoyed fishing trips with my father.

Captain Haskins' boat, a forty-five foot Graves, was docked amongst a dozen other sport fishing boats. His wasn't the newest, but it was one of the largest. I counted a half dozen shrimp boats docked on the opposite side of the bayou, with more berths open on that side of the water than where we stood. I took my partner at his word when he said nobody charters boats on Wednesday.

Chance proved to be correct about Captain Haskins being aboard his boat. The captain was a fifty year-old guy with a broad chest and well-tanned legs he had on full display in the shorts he was wearing. His T-shirt was smeared with almost as much grease as his hands and strong arms. Haskins explained that he could only do major repairs when the boat was idle during the week. He was supervising the installation of a new starboard motor and didn't seem real pleased to be asked to repeat his statement rather than do something he felt was obviously far more important.

"I didn't think anything about that car when I saw it there on Friday, but I was curious about why it was still there on Sunday. When I saw it hadn't moved on Monday I called Sheriff Mazant. I don't know what else I can tell you," he explained. This was actually much less than he told the dispatcher when he called it in. Captain Haskins thought we were done.

"You told the dispatcher you thought it might be one of the Donovan family's cars. How could you tell?" Chance started with the obvious question from the captain's initial statement.

"There aren't many Mercedes in town. I had seen it before, and I remembered seeing Kirk Donovan's wife getting in and out of it."

I decided to take a more roundabout route with my questioning.

"My dad owned a Graves before Katrina. We have a place out in the Rigolets and Katrina's storm surge carried the boat off as it went through. His was about ten foot shorter. He bought it new in about 1985."

"They are good charter boats. I can sleep four guests if need be," Haskins said. "Come on, I'll show you inside."

The boat was a larger version of what I grew up with. Its built-in seating could fold flat and the Sailor Barbie-sized kitchen was sufficient to cook a light meal for his charter guests. I had never thought there was anything for the captain to hide about his boat, but his statements about the charter left me with quite a few questions.

"You've got fuel and ice available here. What did you need in Donovan that you had to be all the way up there three nights in a row?" This wasn't the hardest question I was going to ask. I couldn't miss the deep breath the captain took before he answered. It was too early to decide whether he was about to lie to us or if being questioned at all unnerved him.

"My charter was staying in town and wanted door to door service. It happens, and I am not going to lose a charter just because someone thinks they are special," he grumbled, but also chuckled about it.

"Fair enough. Do we know who his charter was?" I asked Chance this rather than Haskins. My partner digging through his notes was meant to make the captain wonder exactly what we knew, and what we might have learned since he signed his statement.

"I've got the guy's name and number if you don't have it in your stuff. I can't remember if I gave it to Sheriff Mazant or not." Captain Haskins was certainly acting like the world's most cooperative witness. "It's a pretty easy name to remember. The guy's name was Duncan Hines." He spelled the last name, which only confirmed to me that it was an unimaginative alias.

"That didn't strike you as a bit fishy, as it were?" I thought the name was entirely unlikely to check out. "How did Mr. Cake Mix pay for this charter?"

"Cash, just the way I like it," Captain Haskins said and made no apologies for not making his clients use real names, or even credible aliases. "It takes about four hours to get from Donovan to the Gulf. His party sacked out just as soon as they came aboard. I like to leave here at the ass crack of dawn anyway so they can get in a full day of fishing."

"Your charter wouldn't drive down to meet you at dawn, but he was willing to be up at midnight for you to pick him up in town? That seems even more inconvenient than the drive." Chance pressed our line of questioning. "Where did you pick him up in town?"

"Bailey's Shipyard. The detective here can show you where it is. They'll confirm my story," Captain Haskins said, and his expression changed to let me know he knew I wasn't entirely convinced he was telling the truth.

"We can check that out next," Chance suggested. I think he caught on that I was trying to squeeze the captain just to see what might pop out.

"Anything else?" the captain asked and headed back to what he was doing. I guessed he was paying the repair guys by the hour.

"What sort of binoculars do you carry on board?" The captain and Chance both stopped in their tracks to turn and give me a quizzical look. It did sound like a question from way out in left field.

"I've got twenty power and fifty power Nikons. Why do you ask?" The captain couldn't get ahead of this sort of question. He seemed nervous about that.

"I was curious but what you had an infrared scope of some sort." I let my explanation hang for a long and uncomfortable moment. "I couldn't see the bayou when I came to the scene that night, so I have to assume you couldn't see the car from there. I checked the weather reports and there was heavy fog on the bayou for nearly two weeks, and especially dense night-time fog during the entire weekend you kept seeing the silver Mercedes through a silvery fog."

"What are you saying?" he challenged me.

"You know exactly what I am saying. I don't think you saw that car at all. Not on Friday night when it probably got dropped off, not on Saturday night, not on Sunday night, and sure as heck not on the Monday night you called to say it had been there for three days." I stopped walking. The captain took another couple of steps before he came to a stop, while Chance moved to place himself between the captain and the dock.

"I used my searchlight," he tried to explain.

"Searchlights would have made visibility worse." Telling the captain that my father owned a similar fishing boat had been a warning about trying to lie to me with anything related to running his own boat.

"So, how did you know the car was there?" I could tell this was a clue he did not see until I brought it up.

"I want an attorney," the captain declared and crossed his arms across his greasy T-shirt.

"You're going to need one," I assured him as I made my own way to the dock. "Bring him to Sheriff Mazant's department at ten tomorrow. I will send the state police to find you at ten thirty. I'll also let the harbor master know to report your boat to the Coast Guard if you try to leave here before we speak again."

"I'll be there," Captain Haskins promised. He was boxed in, but I think he believed his role in whatever he was mixed up in was so small he wasn't in much trouble.

Forty-One

We conducted our second and third interviews at once, as much to save time as because doing so made it difficult for either party to shift suspicion or blame to the other. The dispatcher who took the call about the Mercedes and the deputy who responded to the call both seemed nervous about sitting down with a pair of detectives investigating what could still prove to be a double homicide. Sheriff Mazant was not very happy about being shut out of the conference room where we conducted the interview. He strongly recommended we use one of the interrogation rooms, but doing so would have let him listen in and watch through the mirror.

"Do we need lawyers or anything?" the deputy was quick to ask.

"You have that right, but neither of us think you did anything wrong. We just want to go back over the night the Mercedes was reported," I said as casually as I could. It occurred to me that our investigation could potentially bring about the full employment of the parish's criminal attorneys by the end of the day.

"I'll let you know if that changes and you can get one then, how's that?" Detective Chance offer was much less friendly than it sounded. Either of the deputies perjuring themselves was going to cause a mess. Our two subjects looked to one another for support and then both nodded that this agreement seemed fine.

"Okay," I said and placed both hands on the heavy wooden table between us. "Why don't we walk through the entire process from the beginning? You took a call about the car being abandoned, right?"

The dispatcher nodded her head and then realized she needed to say something as well when I tapped on the tape recorder between us.

"Yes, that's right."

"What time was that?" I had this in the notes that Detective Chance and I shared between us. I wanted to see how good her recollection was of the major points before we delved into the finer points.

"Shortly after eleven o'clock," she was off by about half an hour on what she had reported that night.

"Where were you parked when you got the call?" I abruptly shifted the questioning to the deputy.

"I was on traffic duty. I was parked in the median up on the interstate," the deputy recalled.

"Using radar or just tailing anyone you wanted to stop?" Detective Chance cut in. I guess he had issues with the department's speed trap policies.

"Neither one. The fog was so thick cars passed me before I even saw them. I had my lights on and tried to act like a deterrent." It was a roundabout way of admitting he had been asleep behind the wheel when the call came in.

I was relieved to hear Sheriff Mazant's deputy confirm the fog was thick on the night in question because I had lied about checking with the weather service when we interviewed the boat captain.

"What did the captain say when he reported the car as being abandoned?" I was back to asking the dispatcher for the next building block. I did not want to keep up this pattern because in time they would anticipate the next question I was going to ask each of them by the question I asked the other.

"Just that we should send someone to check out a car on the boat dock that he had seen parked there for the last three nights."

"Did he specify the make or model of the car?" Detective Chance was playing hunches of his own. We had not worked out a strategy in advance, but peppering the duo with odd questions from two angles seemed to be working for the moment.

"No, he didn't." There was a pause as she played things back in her mind. Chance and I probably should have taken the time to replay the dispatch tape before we sat down to conduct these interviews.

"And how did he contact you?" Chance asked her, even though it was my turn to ask a question.

"By phone. We have a ship-to-shore radio, but he called it in by phone.'

"Is that unusual?" I asked. She made it sound like she may have thought it strange at the time.

"Not really, we have the ability to do either one," she still seemed unsettled by the question.

"And how long did it take you to get to the boat dock?" I asked the deputy.

"Maybe ten minutes. I used my lights but not my siren. Folks complain about the noise at night." Bless his heart. "There was only the one car there when I pulled onto the boat ramp. Nobody was around and I found the car keys inside when I opened the door."

"Couldn't you see the keys just by looking through the window?" I challenged him. Opening the door to the Mercedes introduced his fingerprints into the crime scene unnecessarily.

"I didn't think it was a crime scene," he lamely tried to excuse his lapse in judgement.

"It's always a crime scene when you arrive. It's why you get dispatched," Chance dryly coached him.

"What made you open the trunk?" I pressed ahead.

"I was looking for anything that might explain why the car was left there for so long."

"So you anticipated finding a body?" I tried to make this sound like an accusation.

"I thought it might be a possibility."

"How long have you worked for Sheriff Mazant?" I was less cordial in this new line of questioning.

"Six years."

"How many reports about abandoned cars have you responded to in that time?"

The deputy saw where this was headed. "I don't know an exact number. I has been more than a few."

"And you popped the trunk each and every time."

"No, of course not," the deputy shook his head. He looked like he was getting ready to say "attorney" so I smiled and gave a light-hearted laugh as though we were joking.

"Then why this time?" Chance jumped on him. "Did someone order you to do so?"

"No," the deputy denied the suggestion. "It stunk something fierce."

"The trunk did?" I helped him clarify himself.

"Yeah. You know what a dead animal smells like, right?" the deputy was growing a bit more confident, at least enough to try to defend his actions.

"I also know what a human body smells like after a few days in the heat," I reassured him, and let him know his nose didn't have any advantage over mine just because he grew up living in the country. I have encountered considerably more dead bodies than road-kill raccoons or deer in the course of my life.

"Well that's what I thought I smelled, so I opened the trunk."

"If you were so certain there was a body in the trunk, then why didn't you call Sheriff Mazant before you opened the trunk? Isn't that the proper procedure?" I pressed him again. The deputy had tainted a crime scene and I wanted him to at least admit to that.

"I didn't know that we have a procedure for dead bodies in cars," the deputy responded. His deadpan expression and delivery nearly knocked me out of my seat with laughter, but I choked it down and took a sip of water to get past the urge.

"Yet you knew to ask for him when you saw the blood," Detective Chance was quick to point out.

"Well, yeah. It was a trunk full of blood. Of course he would want to know about something like that," the deputy looked at us like we were amateurs.

"Okay, you found a trunk full of blood. What did you tell the dispatcher?" Chance wondered.

He and I were both skimming the transcript of the calls between the deputy and the dispatcher as we alternated questioning them. I was beginning to get the same sense of something being slightly off kilter. I had felt the same thing about the point in our questioning when the boat captain said he wanted to have an attorney present.

"Only that I wanted Sheriff Mazant to come to the scene. I didn't want anyone listening on a scanner to know what I found. It would have been spread all over town." This sounded fairly professional and logical, except that it was the thought process of a cop who didn't even know whether his own department had procedures for handling the discovery of dead bodies.

"How did you learn about what he found?" I asked the dispatcher.

"He told me when he came back to the station. All I knew was that Sheriff Mazant called me on his cellphone as soon as he arrived on the scene and told me to have the state police to meet him," the dispatcher sounded confident of the chain of events.

"Are police scanners a big thing around these parts? This department seems to expend a lot of effort on not using its radios to convey information." I directed this to Detective Chance rather than the lower ranked pair. I had not sensed their reluctance to communicate about specifics with one another when I listened to the tape the first few times or when I read the transcript, but sitting here listening to their explanation made me curious.

"There are people who like to start rumors, and there are people we try not to let get too involved," was all he offered by way of explanation. My thoughts went straight to Senator Donovan. I formed a mental image of the old man sitting in bed with his scanner and a glass of bourbon.

"What else did Sheriff Mazant tell you?" I went back to questioning the deputy. I had something in mind.

"He told me to secure the scene until he got there," the deputy said and shrugged.

"Who told you to walk out and leave your car?" I reminded him of his own actions.

"I must have thought to do that on my own," he said after a brief delay, but with a straight face.

"At the time you said it was Sheriff Mazant," I pointed out and dropped a finger on the transcript of the call.

"Then that was why I did it," he declared.

"Not because someone else wanted to be sure the tire tracks weren't disturbed?" I squeezed a bit harder.

"Nobody else even knew I was there," the deputy cleverly argued.

"So you say, deputy. So you say," I said and gave him one of my coldest stares until he averted his eyes and began fidgeting. "I think we're done, don't you?"

I addressed this to Detective Chance and he gave the pair a silent wave of dismissal. They couldn't get out of the room fast enough. The detective and I sat in our chairs and silently considered what we had just heard. I did not come into this interview believing we were doing anything that went beyond routine. We should have been able to confirm both of their stories, each of which should have been very small pieces in a big puzzle, and moved on.

Instead I was left wondering who played the role of Big Brother in Saint Xavier Parish and made the local police afraid to use their own radios. Who could the department be afraid of upsetting late at night other than Senator Donovan? Even the boat captain seems to have avoided using the radio to call in his dubious story about discovering the car.

"Who's got your department spooked about using their radios?"

"It's a long story," Chance grumbled.

"I'm not paid by the hour. What gives?" I was not going to let this go unanswered.

"Crystal Franks uses a scanner so she can be one of the first people to any crime scene. It is more than annoying and the sheriff makes sure all of his deputies use their phones for anything like this." I was not entirely disappointed that my guess about the senator riding herd on the parish proved to be wrong. I was now intrigued by the determination of the local editor to insinuate herself into any juicy cases.

"Okay, I can see that. But, why would the deputy assume Crystal was going to take any interest in another abandoned car, and why did Captain Haskins report spotting this one on a phone line rather than his shortwave radio?" Detective Chance's answer to my question only brought new questions to mind.

"Why do you suppose?" Chance wanted to hear me say it aloud.

"My first thought is that they assumed she was waiting for the car to be found."

"Do you think that sounds crazy?" Chance wondered.

"Not after these interviews. What are the odds of Crystal telling us what she knew about the car being there if we asked real nice?"

"I think it's pretty damn unlikely," Chance said and explained why. "She will print an article about how we infringed on her paper's First

Amendment rights. Plus, we have nothing to tie her to what happened to Gwendolyn Rogers even if she admitted to knowing the Mercedes had been left there."

"Good points." I sighed and stood up. "Then I guess we have to figure out how much Haskins knew about what happened in advance, and how much of it didn't go as planned, before we try to corner him."

"That's a much better idea than a frontal charge on the newspaper editor," Detective Chance laughed and breathed a big sigh of relief. I must have had the detective worried that our next destination was the newspaper office, followed by the front page.

Forty-Two

With the newspaper editor presently considered to be off limits and Captain Haskins not due to have to face us again until the next morning, we found our investigation at yet another stand-still.

"Where to next?" Detective Chance asked as we gathered our notes and files.

"We need see if we can confirm the captain's story about where he picked up his passengers," I said. I caught myself before I mentioned the only other interview that came to mind, deciding at the last second to conduct that one on my own. I was beginning to trust Detective Chance, and a part of my brain told me that was a good reason not to trust him. I needed to keep in mind that anything we learned together was going to be reported to Sheriff Mazant just as soon as my liaison and I parted ways for the day. I was certain that Senator Donovan was the second person on that phone tree.

Bailey Marine proved to be a bustling operation located on the Intercoastal Waterway, barely out of sight of Judge Rogers' house. They sold new and used boats and the parts to keep them running, in addition to running a fuel flat. There was a commercial towboat tied up to the flat-topped barge holding the massive fuel tanks of this part of their operation when we arrived. I wondered, not that it likely made any difference, whether Captain Haskins got his fuel here or at the fuel dock in the marina. He used enough fuel each charter that even the difference of a dime a gallon would add up to serious money.

"Detectives, how may I help you?" a portly dark haired man asked as soon as we stepped onto the curb in front of the business. I had to wonder but what we were expected.

"We need to confirm Captain Haskins's story about picking up a charter here the weekend before Gwen Donovan's car was discovered," Detective Chance said. I noticed he didn't use Gwendolyn's full name. I rather doubted that the locals were on such a casual basis with the senator's daughter-in-law.

"That was, what, two weekends back?" the man asked. He seemed to be talking to himself more than us, and still had not identified himself. His blue work shirt had the name Bud embroidered on it, but I had my doubts this was his birth name and it gave me no last name to link him to anyone else we'd met.

"Yes. He claims he had a charter that wanted him to pick them up in town, and that they went out the entire weekend and then again on Monday," Chance kept doing the talking. I paid enough attention to the conversation to catch whether or not my partner was telling the guy what to say, but I was also scanning the operation for anything that seemed unusual. The pair of Graves boats in the line of deep sea fishing boats for sale brought a couple of questions to mind I didn't think anyone might have prepped this guy to answer.

"Yeah, that sounds right," Bud said with a shrug.

This wasn't technically a confirmation as far as I was concerned. "Sounds right" and being a verified fact very seldom prove to be the same thing.

"Is there a log book or something we could check to be sure?" I pressed.

"We don't keep anything like that. There isn't any reason to, not usually anyway," Bud explained. He had a valid point, but I didn't mind making him think it was suspicious to a state police detective.

"Then how can you be so certain about the story Captain Haskins is feeding us?" I pressed a bit harder.

"I've known Jack my whole life. He isn't a liar. You can ask our night watchman if you won't take my word for it. He'll be here at nine," Bud grumbled. He didn't much like the idea that his honesty, much less his captain friend's word, were being doubted.

"Okay, we might do that," I said and left him with Detective Chance. He still had a rapport with Bud and could get answers to our questions about who it was that chartered Captain Haskins's boat for those three nights of offshore fishing.

I walked down the line of boats for sale. I was killing time, and I found the way Bud's eyes followed me rather than remaining in contact with Detective Chance while he was being questioned interesting. I stopped to admire the pair of Graves boats. Both were equipped with every bell and whistle I could imagine: flying bridges, deck-mounted high-backed chairs to strap into for extended fights with marlin or tuna, and auxiliary fuel and water tanks to be able to stay out for at least a day longer. They both carried the mid-six figure price tag I expected a boat their size and fittings would command. My father bought his used and still paid nearly what he did to build the house he docked it next to in the Rigolets.

"Unrelated to all of this, what's a new engine run for a 1987 Graves?" " I casually began to lie.

"New or rebuilt?" Bud had no trouble shifting gears from answering our questions to making a sale.

"I just inherited my dad's forty-two foot Graves and I cannot decide whether to have the engines overhauled or replaced." I was trying to build on my story, and distance the conversation from the obvious intent for my question.

"You ought to have someone rebuild the motors on a boat that old. New ones will run you nearly ten grand apiece," Bud said. "We can take a look at it for you and get you an estimate. How old are the radar and electronics?" I could practically feel my wallet shrinking in my pocket at the thought of what this man would try to sell me for a nearly twenty five year old boat. I was suddenly glad Katrina saved me from having this conversation for real.

"Like I said, I inherited the thing. I am sure that everything is out of date. I guess my dad was right, that a boat is just a hole in the water where you toss away good money," I tried to jest in order to keep Bud from considering whether I was serious or doing a little fishing of my own.

"They are also the only expensive mistress your wife can enjoy as well," Bud countered. He must have been one heck of a salesman. He handed me a business card and Detective Chance thanked him for his time and cooperation.

"What was all that about, getting them to take a look at your dad's boat?" Chance asked as soon as we were in the privacy of his patrol car.

"Oh, I don't own a boat," I laughed. "I needed to find what that new motor we saw going into Captain Haskins' boat set him back. What are the odds of the captain being able to afford an expensive engine swap at the end of the winter charter season before some guy named Duncan Hines hired him for three nights the same weekend Kirk Donovan's entire family disappeared?"

Chance held up both hands and tilted them back and forth as he answered the question.

"I'd say there was slim, and there was none."

"It looks like I will need to come back to the shipyard tonight. Hopefully the night watchman can describe what this mysterious Mister Hines looked like," I said and sighed. It was a performance to make Chance believe I held little hope of coming away with anything useful from interviewing the watchman, and that his presence was not required at the interview. I was doing all of this because I didn't want him anywhere near me once the sun went down.

"I'm not busy tonight if you'd rather I come back and talk to the night watchman," he offered. I was glad he was only making a faint hearted offer rather than sounding genuinely interested in doing so. He must not have felt I was likely to learn anything useful for the effort or he would have stayed attached at my hip.

"I'm a night owl anyway," I waved him away. "Get a good night's sleep so at least one of us is ready to fight with Haskins' attorney in the morning."

Forty-Three

I had begun to sense a guiding hand as Detective Chance and I conducted our interviews with Sheriff Mazant's deputies. Nobody we approached ever flatly refused to speak with us, but I found that everybody's replies seemed to raise new questions. I was beginning to wonder but what somebody had already coached them on what to say. The only time anyone's memory seemed to fail them entirely was if we had documents or statements we asked them to corroborate. Amazingly little seemed to get written down in Donovan, other than who borrowed the local tow truck.

The interview I wanted to conduct without Sheriff Mazant's knowledge was with the operator of the lift on the highway bridge south of town. Lift bridges and swing bridges became part of the Louisiana landscape when railroads and highways began to be built across the water where ferries had previously done the work. It was much cheaper to build a bridge that could be moved aside to allow boat and ship traffic to pass than it was to engineer one those same boats could cruise beneath. They are so common that I held a glimmer of hope that whoever was controlling the narrative of my investigation forgot to coach the bridge tender working the nights Captain Haskins supposedly passed by.

I waited until dark before I drove to the bridge. I parked on the shoulder and left Roux in the coupe to guard against anyone tampering with it. I walked the last few yards to the bridge tender's control room and knocked on the door's grimy glass pane to get his attention. The bridge tender was a guy named Bob. He was about my age, but shorter and leaner. He stubbed out the cigarette he was smoking and turned off the TV he was watching before he stood up and came to answer the door.

"Yes?" he asked through the glass. I held my gold shield against the glass in response. "Alrighty, then."

Bob quickly moved through the tight space to place his desk between us before I had barely entered the control room. The technology had not changed since the day the bridge was built, and little besides the girlie calendar on the wall seemed to have changed either. It was time for at least a new coat of paint.

"I am hoping you keep some sort of log book of who you open the bridge for," I said to explain my late night visit.

"We do," he said, but then made no effort to show it to me. "What are you looking for?"

I started to say something needlessly sarcastic. It was difficult to believe he was completely uninformed about the disappearance of Gwendolyn Donovan from the boat ramp that was barely a mile down the bayou, or that her car was reported abandoned by a local boat captain who must have asked for the bridge to be lifted that night.

"Routine verification of something we were told," I said to make my visit sound as unthreatening and boring as possible. "I was just hoping you might be the guy who was on duty the weekend before last."

"Sorry, I have enough seniority I only work during the day. Normally I am here from six to four Tuesday through Friday." Bob didn't sound the least bit sorry about his cushy schedule. "I'm filling in for Harry for the next couple of weeks. He started his vacation last Monday."

"That means you weren't here the night that the call was made about Gwendolyn Donovan's car."

"Harry was. We talked about it when I came to work the next afternoon," he was quick to declare. This made Harry's vacation timing very interesting.

"Can you confirm what time a given boat came by here?" I asked and watched his facial expression for any change that might mean he was lying to me.

"We record every time we open the bridge in the logbook. Harry wrote down that Captain Haskins' boat came through northbound just after nine, and then headed back south just after midnight. I am pretty sure that's right."

"Could you please check to be sure?" I pressed the issue and took a step closer to the desk. I did not want this to sound like a suggestion. I also wanted to get a look at the logbook's other entries.

Bob paused for just a moment and then reached for a large ledger. He very quietly thumbed through the pages until he found the entry he was looking for and swung the book to face me. His scrawny finger stayed in place to point out the entry marking when Captain Haskins passed the bridge going south.

The entries were understandably limited in scope. This wasn't a customs station or immigration check. I found the time of day, in military time, whether the boat was recreational or commercial, and the boat's registration number. Nothing about the number of people on board, cargoes, or even a note about anything the bridge tender discussed with the captain or pilot, or that the bridge tender found to be suspicious. He was only required to show a good reason for moving the bridge and interrupting the flow of vehicle traffic on the county road. Larger bridges over larger bodies of water or on larger highways may have required more documentation.

I tried not to seem as interested as I was in the entries showing that Captain Haskins passed this way on four consecutive nights. I casually thumbed through the previous two weeks as well, and the week following the discovery of the car on the boat ramp. Captain Haskins had made one trip this far north in the entire month prior to that weekend. He had not made another trip past the bridge since the night he called in about the Mercedes. It made me all the more curious about the mystery man that necessitated passing the boat ramp for so many nights because he insisted on being picked up in town.

I looked forward to Captain Haskins' explanation for why he needed two hours longer to make the round trip from the marina to Bailey Marine on the same night he called Sheriff Mazant about a car he had seen the two previous nights. I also wanted to know what he was doing in town the Thursday before his paid charter began.

"Thank you."

"Is there anything else I can help you with?" Bob asked in a helpful tone of voice. He sounded like he had something in mind, but couldn't volunteer it.

"I don't know," I admitted. 'Is there anything you would like to help me with that I don't know to ask?"

Bob closed the logbook before he answered.

"You might ask whether any other boats came through at the same time." His hand was still on the logbook. I realized he was trying to help me, but couldn't say anything unless he was asked. I thought I might have found the only honest man in town.

"Well, gee, were there any other boats traveling with Captain Haskins' boat on any of those nights?" I asked the bridge tender.

"Just one, on Monday night," he said and opened the book once again. I realized he had concealed the second boat from me when he pointed out the entry for Captain Haskins' boat that Monday night as it headed south. It was recorded simply as 'small boat.'

"Whose boat was that?" I asked. This was going to take forever if I had to play this game for each clue.

"That is a very good question, Detective," the bridge tender said and once again closed the book. He made sure to look me in the eye when he told me the rest of what was still bothering him. "The boat was running without any lights, and it was running almost starboard to port with Captain Haskins. Harry said it was a good sized boat running on outboard motors. He wouldn't have noticed it at all if the guy on that boat hadn't run his outboard so hard. They drowned out Haskins' boat."

"Harry didn't ask them for a license number or see the name on the stern?" It struck me as odd that this incident was not noted in the logbook. I needed to have the registration number or the boat's name to find out who owned the cabin cruiser.

"He tried to." Bob sounded a bit offended by the question, as if he thought I might be questioning his co-worker's integrity. "Harry tried twice to get them to answer on the radio, but they never acknowledged his calls."

"And he couldn't read the name on the stern?"

"Not in the fog we had that night. All he could tell was that there were two boats and they were way too close together," the bridge tender said and gave me a look that seemed to ask me to not make Harry tell me the story for the record. Someone didn't want it told, someone powerful enough for these two to fear.

"Keep that book safe, okay?" I requested. This had my hands tied for the moment. Bob could not hand me the logbook for purely legal reasons besides needing it to do his job. I couldn't use what Harry told Bob about that night without betraying where I learned about the second boat, and I couldn't get a warrant to seize the logbook without betraying that I knew something was amiss with Captain Haskins' story.

Forty-Four

I called Belle while I sat at the counter in Jean E's waiting for Nannci to bring the burger and fries I had ordered despite the risk to my health. Belle said she was bored, but that she enjoyed the time she was getting to spend with Tulip and Katie. It didn't take a lot of psychology training to read into this how much she missed her mother, or how much closer she was to her than to her late father. She had yet to ask a single question about his death or even whether or not she had missed his funeral. I noted she wasn't asking to see her paternal grandfather, either.

"I'm glad to hear you aren't climbing the walls just yet," I said to keep the mood light before I delved into why I was really calling. "I was hoping you might shed some light on a small thing for me."

"I can try. I don't know that much about Kirk's work if that is what you need to know. He always tried to keep it from me when I was a kid, and then when I got old enough to understand he was helping old men marry girls my age I stopped wanting to know about it."

"How old were you when you figured it out?" This wasn't why I called, but I was going to follow up on anything she seemed prepared to discuss.

"When I had just turned thirteen. One of the girls in my class came to school and said it was her last week in school because she was getting married to some guy her father knew in Arkansas." She sounded no less confused or upset than she must have been at the time.

"Did she say why she was getting married?"

"You mean, was she pregnant?" Belle was much more aware of her father's work than she had led me to believe.

"Well, yes, but I am curious about how these kiddie marriages got put together. Apparently your friend never even met the guy she was being married to."

"No, she didn't know him," Belle said, before adding a clue she may or may not have recognized as being one. "But the week after she left town her folks were driving a brand new truck. I thought it was funny at the time, because it looked like her parents got it as a wedding present."

"It sure does. That's not what I was calling about, though," I quickly shifted gears. I already knew I was going to be dwelling on what became of that girl for the rest of the day. "I just needed to know what sort of boat your father owned. We found a boat trailer at the back of your property but no boat. It would help a lot to know what we are looking for."

"It was a Boston Whaler Conquest. He bought it because he liked the name of the model. He called his the On Top, and I always had a real icky feeling about why he called it that. My mother accused him of using it to have his affairs on, and he was never very good at denying it. I think he enjoyed flaunting the fact he was cheating on her."

"So, your dad had a lot of affairs?" This had yet to come up in anyone's interview, even casually.

"I don't know how many he had, but I heard once he hit on some girls from the high school." Her voice conveyed the embarrassment that rumor had caused her. The nature of the arguments her parents had over the years was coming into sharper focus. I wanted to know whether Gwen also had affairs, but it might be better if Katie asked her.

I had what I needed to know, and more than I had thought to ask. The missing boat was a match for the sort of boat that slipped past the bridge with Captain Haskins the night he reported the Mercedes. Did someone take the boat because they knew its owner no longer had any use for it? Did they take it because they thought they could get away with it under the cover of so much fog? Was the boat perhaps payment for some service they had performed? These were all great questions to ask if Chance or I ever figured out who had stolen Kirk's Boston Whaler.

I had also learned another good reason for someone to kill Kirk Donovan. Lovers' quarrels and jealousy are the first thing a good detective looks for in any juicy murder. I was somewhat relieved that there might be a lot more women than his wife who no longer wanted to share the planet with Kirk Donovan.

Nannci brought my burger and fries as I hung up the phone. The burger was unimpressive, a gray circle of what might be beef that had been cooked on a stainless steel griddle rather than a grill, set on a thin bun and camouflaged with limp dill pickle slices and a thin cut of red onion. The fries at least arrived hot and had been cooked in cleaner grease than I expected.

"You're a waitress. So, I assume you keep up on the latest gossip," I kept a smile on my face, as if I might be joking rather than questioning her.

"I do my best. You gotta be careful about putting your ear to the ground around here 'cause people will stomp your head," she joked back, but with a bit of a disclaimer and a warning as well.

"Kirk Donovan's love boat," I said and stopped.

"You're a pretty good detective," she whistled and stepped just a little closer so she wouldn't have to talk too loud. I let her be the one to look around to be sure we had some privacy. "Who told you?"

"I wouldn't be a very good detective if I told you that," I said, still trying to make this seem more playful than both of us knew the topic was in this particular parish. "You know anyone I might want to talk with about this?"

"I know a bunch of people, but they aren't going to want to talk to you at all. They gotta live here long after you leave, and Kirk's messing around is sort of our own town's own little secret," Nannci explained.

"Can you maybe help me narrow it down to any jilted woman or jealous boyfriend that might do him the sort of harm he came to?" I was wondering how far down this trail she might take me. We were at a fork, and this might be where we parted ways.

"Any of them, and none of them," she finally said and shrugged. "Lots of hot heads around here of both sexes, but nobody ever thought he was going to leave his wife for them and he always made sure he left people happy. They might get some cash, a new car, some help with a problem they might be having, like a bum boyfriend or a kid needing a doctor. I know a few waitresses here paid their legal fees for DUIs and other stupid stuff on that boat."

I bit my tongue, but she caught the unasked question.

"I was never asked, and I never needed to sleep with a married man to get what I have. I was too old for him, anyway." Nannci looked about ready for a cigarette break.

"How old was too old for Kirk?"

"Thirty was way too old, unless you maybe had a daughter to bring to the party. That's just what I heard, not what you can pass on," she pointed out.

"You have a way of making me lose my appetite," I said only in partial jest. This was two meals she had brought me that I did not finish eating.

Forty-Five

I waited until ten o'clock that night to return to Bailey Marine to speak with the night watchman. I wanted to be sure he was alone, and I assumed he was expecting a visit from the police. I was almost looking forward to seeing whether or not I was about to run into another instance of witness tampering. The security guard was a much better guy to question because he should have actually spoken to Captain Haskins' mysterious passengers.

"I'm Detective Holland, with the state police. Did your boss tell you I would be dropping by tonight?" I said in my best tough-cop voice as I walked towards the man in the guard shack by the gate. My usual approach is to try to sound embarrassed about needing to take up a witness' time just because they had phoned in a tip or signed a written statement meant to help me do my job. I try to make the subject feel like they are comforting me by repeating the story about what they saw or heard. I wanted this guard to worry more about what I might do to him than he did about protecting anyone else from me.

"Yes. They said you wanted to know the name of the guy Jack picked up." He was well informed, and on a first name basis with the captain. I might be in luck.

"Do you have an answer?" I wanted to be patient.

"It was some fraternity from New Orleans. I am not good with weird names like that, but the kid I knew said they all went to Tulane together."

"Oh, really. What kid did you recognize?" I only knew one young man that was attending Tulane with any connection to Donovan.

"Bradley Ladd," the guard said. He didn't sound like this was in the least bit unusual or should even pique my interest, but it most certainly did.

"Does he bring his pals fishing here a lot?"

"A few times a year. The tuna were running strong that weekend. I heard they came back with a big haul on Saturday." The security guard didn't sound like he was trying to hide anything or feed me a story. I could ask around about how the tuna fishing was that weekend, so it would have made for a stupid lie.

"What nights did they go out, again?" I didn't care if he thought this was some attempt to trip him up. I needed the story confirmed for my report.

"That would be Friday, Saturday, Sunday, and Monday," he said without checking anything.

"Not Thursday?"

"Must have been a school night," he chuckled. He seemed to have no reason to think anything about which nights those boys went fishing.

"Can you think of why they would ask to be picked up here, and not meet the boat down at the marina?" This was still a nagging question.

"Easy. All of them boys drove expensive cars, and you don't leave cars that nice down at that marina if you don't have to. Things tend to go missing, if you know what I mean." It made sense. Big city kids out in the bayou might not want to chance some local taking a liking to their car stereo or tires. Just like country boys worry about parking their trucks on the street in the French Quarter. Everyone wants to believe they have something worth stealing.

"You mentioned that all the boys drove nice cars. Does that include Bradley?"

"Yeah, he just bought hisself a new V-8 Mustang. Nice car. Not as nice as that Cadillac of yours, but a real nice car for a kid that age." There didn't seem to be any particular envy on his part about this, just an appreciation for good Detroit metal and horsepower.

"He buy it, or his folks? Do you know?" I was still making conversation, but the topic had taken an odd detour.

"Kid's got his own money from what I hear. Some sort of big inheritance," the watchman seemed to have no trouble with gossiping just a bit more.

The story now seemed to all fit together perfectly. A local rich kid charters a boat to take his fraternity brothers out for a weekend of tuna fishing and boat drinking, and their boat captain notices that the car belonging to Bradley's friend's mother looks abandoned on a boat dock they just happened to pass by four nights in a row. Nothing but fate or coincidence tied Bradley to both the abandoned Mercedes and the fishing trip. That, and my ever-growing suspicion that nothing fit quite right despite the way I was being handed the pieces.

The other pieces on the table were that there was too much fog to see the car from the bayou, the captain came to town a full day before his charter, but had not made the same trip for weeks before that or since. Now there was also the mysterious boat that passed alongside Haskins' boat on the last night Bradley and his frat brothers headed out. They called the sheriff about the car, but didn't call the Coast Guard about a boat that nearly sideswiped them. I was going to make Captain Haskins glad he brought a lawyer to our meeting the next day.

Forty-Six

Tulip called while I was eating breakfast to say she was driving out to speak with me. I took this to mean that Belle shared some things with her that I needed to know. I asked Tulip to meet me at Sheriff Mazant's department. Then I asked her if she might consider doing me a favor while she was in town. I explained that I needed to intimidate a charter boat captain, and that I thought giving him the impression I was the lesser of two evils might loosen his tongue.

"I'm not going to impersonate a cop or a Fed," Tulip was quick to balk.

"I am not asking you to say you're a Fed. I just need you to act like one. Come on, sis, it will be fun," I cajoled her.

"Alright, fine, what time does the curtain go up?" she sighed, but I could tell she was actually looking forward to being a small part of another one of my investigations. I told her what time Captain Haskins and his attorney were due and suggested she arrive a little earlier so we could plan some basic strategy. I was going to wait until she arrived to tell Detective Chance about my ruse.

Captain Haskins was on time for his interview. He had an attorney with him, who Chance let me know was the best criminal defense attorney in the parish. That recommendation meant very little to me. Saint Xavier Parish's courtrooms were stacked with Donovan-approved judges. There was every reason to believe justice was ill-served in this parish, and that money and connections were better to have on your side in these courts than an expensive lawyer.

Interrogation rooms are designed to offer a suspect absolutely no comfort and make them believe their future will never get any better than that room until they cooperate. I set a different tone by staging this interview in the room Sheriff Mazant usually reserved for interviewing hiring candidates and for training conferences. The decorating wasn't much more hospitable than the formal interrogation rooms, but it gave Haskins a sense of security I intended to pull out from under him to get him to talk.

I opened the meeting by reading Captain Haskins his Miranda rights. "Now that the formalities are out of the way, are you ready to get started? We didn't get to talk very much yesterday before you decided to answer our questions with an attorney present."

"I know my rights," Captain Haskins declared, with a sense of the dramatic which wasn't going to serve him well in this situation.

"Yes, we know that. But, thank you for repeating that you understood the rights I just read to you on the record," I indicated the video camera staring at him from the end of the table.

"I'm sorry, are we being recorded?" the attorney asked. My expression questioned why we would not be recording the interview. "I know sometimes Sheriff Mazant has done an initial interview off the record. It lets someone that he doesn't have a case against speak freely."

"We might consider doing so as well," I said and paused. "If we didn't have a case against your client."

"And just what do you suspect my client has done wrong?" This was news to Haskins' attorney.

"The word 'suspect' is such a fluid term, counselor," I gave him a thin smile. Detective Chance was patiently watching both of our performances, unsure about when or how to intrude. "Let's just say that charges have not yet been filed against your client. We know what can be proved in court, so there is not much left for us to suspect the captain of having done."

"Care to elaborate on that?" The attorney didn't want to formally accuse us of intimidating his client until he was positive I was bluffing. He was a sharp looking guy about my age, with a nice suit and an expensive briefcase. I tried to think of what sort of criminal clients he might have in a parish where shoplifters were routinely diverted. Federal offenses were tried elsewhere, and the Donovans clearly owned all of the judges who would preside over any cases that might involve their own dirty deeds.

"I will," I promised and glanced at my wrist watch and frowned.

"Are you expected elsewhere?" the attorney chose to begin displaying some of the defensive aggression his client was paying him to show.

"No, we are expecting another investigator." I did my best to sound apologetic before I leaned towards Detective Chance to whisper in his ear. I made to speak loud enough to be overheard. "There should be a tax auditor waiting for us in the lobby. Bring her in."

"That gal from the IRS?" he whispered, but made sure to also speak loud enough for the others to hear.

"All I know is that she has questions for the captain," I replied. Chance stood up and left the room while I let the captain and his attorney settle a bit deeper into the wooden chairs across from me.

"I thought we were only asked to come here to discuss my client's charter," Captain Haskins' attorney finally broke the uncomfortable silence caused by Tulip and Chance slow walking their return. The attorney was clearly uncertain about how to approach the sudden shift in the scope of our inquiries. Federal tax cases were apparently beyond his usual area of expertise. It was something I had counted on in creating the ruse.

"Oh, we still are. I was informed there might be another investigation involving your client and asked if we might combine our initial questions. It saves everyone some time, and your client a little money on your billable hours," I tried to make it sound like the bad joke it was, but also to make them both even more nervous. My linguistic gymnastics sailed right past Haskins' attorney. At no point did I ever state on the record that the IRS had sent an investigator to this meeting, but he and the captain were now convinced that this was about to happen based on our overheard whispers. A video record of the meeting suddenly posed a larger menace to Haskins.

Detective Chance returned with Tulip. She wore a smirk only I noticed as she entered the room and sat between Detective Chance and myself before she set her leather briefcase on the table. The sound of the latches being snapped open was as dramatic as a guillotine blade falling home. I pressed one hand over hers before she opened it.

"Ms. Price is a tax investigator." I was under no legal obligation to play fair. Using my sister's middle name was entirely legal. Her being an IRS agent remained nothing but a possibility Haskins' attorney never questioned. My description of her was technically accurate, because my sister litigates a lot of corporate tax fraud cases. "She has agreed to allow us to ask our questions before she conducts her own inquiries."

Tulip smiled and politely nodded at the flummoxed men across from her. Detective Chance and I had not yet asked the captain a single question, but he now obviously believed he was on his way to prison. His attorney no longer knew what he was defending his client against, and by now was asking himself what information Captain Haskins might have withheld from him.

It was the perfect time to start asking questions.

"Captain Haskins," I straightened my posture as I addressed the nervous captain. Everyone else reflexively did so as well. "Who chartered your boat on the nights of March fifth through the eighth?"

"A fraternity from Tulane University." It was an honest, though only partial, response.

"And what was the contact person's name?" I had a pen in my hand and hovered it over a brand new yellow legal-sized pad of paper. The few questions I wanted to ask were written on the pad in big bold letters. The letters were large enough to make any responses I wrote very small in comparison. It made the answers look wholly inadequate, which was the point. I like when suspects try to fill the space on my pad.

"Bradley Ladd," Captain Haskin said in a very quiet voice.

"That much we already know," I shrugged. I wanted him to know this was information I discovered on my own after his refusal to answer our questions. The series of questions on my legal pad were intended to make Haskins believe that he was being led into a legal trap. Believing Chance and I had more information than we did might not make him any more honest, but it made it feel more dangerous to lie.

"How long ahead of time did Bradley arrange the fishing trip?" This question came from Detective Chance. He apparently didn't want to sit like a bump on the log, and he clearly wanted to show me that he knew the right questions to ask.

"A little over a week. He said it was going to be their post-Mardi Gras celebration." Captain Haskins was nervous enough now that he was eager to share anything he believed we might not know.

"Because Saint Patrick's Day was too long to wait for a party?" my sister mumbled under her breath.

"You passed the lift bridge northbound at the same time on the first three nights, but you went past there a full two hours earlier on the ninth. That was the night the Mercedes was reported to Sheriff Mazant's office." I needed to lay the groundwork for the much harder questions I needed him to answer. "What else did you need to take care of in town that Monday night?"

"Nothing. It was their last day. They said they wanted to get an earlier start so they could have a longer day," Captain Haskins had his answer ready, but I thought it might be his first attempt to lie to me.

"Except you didn't get that early start. You didn't pass the lift bridge southbound until almost the exact same time as the previous nights," I pressed him. The captain's attorney frowned and glanced at his client, whose hands twitched on the tabletop. "I'll give you another chance at the question."

"One of the boys ran late, so we had to wait," Haskins said, but with none of the conviction one hears of truth.

"Which boy?"

"I don't remember every one of the boys' names." Again, he was probably being honest, but this was not an answer to the question he was asked.

"Can you describe the car the kid drove?" I rephrased the question in a much harder way to plead ignorance. He ought to remember the make of the car he wasted two hours waiting to arrive.

"They all parked in the front lot and walked back to the dock, so I don't have any idea what kind of car any of those boys drives," Haskins protested. It was a good deflection, but he could sense we all felt he was lying. I was hoping that by now he suspected I knew exactly what he was trying to cover up, and was just waiting to spring it on him at the right moment.

"Okay, let's walk through that night. You loaded the frat brothers onto your boat and headed out to the Gulf about the same time as the previous nights. We all agree that it was foggy, and the bridge tender confirmed he could barely make out your boat as you went past. Were there any incidents along the way?" I made a point of mentioning that I interviewed the bridge tender to give him an opportunity to mention the mystery boat on his own.

"Other than noticing the car still parked on the ramp?" Haskins mistakenly believed this was the trick question I set in his path.

"We have already established that the fog was too thick for you to have seen that car, even with your best binoculars and a searchlight. So, that story was a lie from the start," Detective Chance was quick to remind him. Haskins' attorney noted his client's first clear vulnerability to criminal charges.

"Right. Other than the Mercedes C-63 you didn't see," I reiterated, with considerably more sarcasm.

Captain Haskins' attorney leaned over and began whispering into his client's ear, initiating a couple of minute's worth of drama on that side of the table. My sister silently adjusted her blazer and fidgeted a bit just to refocus their attention on the unaddressed purpose behind her presence in the room.

"I think you have a specific incident in mind. It would be best if you simply asked my client about this in a direct question, rather than try to trap him in some sort of mis-statement," Captain Haskins' attorney insisted.

"We can come back to that," The matter of what the bridge tender told me was left hanging between us. Captain Haskins now knew I was waiting to pounce on him about the boat he encountered that night. I needed him to realize that the boat was not a well-kept secret any longer, and to worry about what I knew of the boat and his reason for not disclosing it to us. "We will yield the floor to Ms. Price. She has been patiently playing the part of the tiger in the room. Your client's statement about preferring to be paid in cash, and his purchase of a new motor for his boat so close on the heels of this particular charter, raised a fair number of questions. I asked Ms. Price for help in finding any possible financial issues with your client's charter business."

"Are you are threatening my client with an IRS audit unless he cooperates?" The attorney was sharper than I believe even Tulip anticipated that he might be when we all sat down.

"Threats are so double edged. We would look pretty bad for having done such a thing if your client proves to be clean," I poo-pooed the accusation. "On the other hand, the IRS is entirely capable of deciding on their own whether or not to pursue an investigation based on a simple tip. We have nothing to threaten your client with besides his own honesty, or lack of it, counselor."

The ugly prospect of being simultaneously investigated by the state police and audited by the IRS drained the color from Captain Haskins' face.

"I assume you have an accountant I can get your records from?" Tulip opened her own salvos as she thrust open her briefcase and removed a stack of manila folders, filled with sticky notes and different colors of paper. She must have grabbed fistfuls of old trial records on the way out of her office.

"Yes," Haskins said very meekly. It seemed likely he and his accountant were creative in his filings.

Tulip opened one of the files and read to herself for a painfully long moment before continuing her brilliant performance. "There are a couple of questions I need answers for before I can decide how far we need to pursue this. What is your daily rate, and how many days have you been chartered in the last ninety days?"

Haskins was forced to do mental calculations to answer the second part of the question. "I charge five hundred dollars a day, or two hundred dollars per head per day for parties of four or more. I've been out a couple of dozen times in the past three months, something like forty days including those three. I would need to check my records to give you an exact figure."

"And you report every day of service?"

"Absolutely," Haskins stated. There was no other answer to give to an IRS agent, but it would be very bad to give that one and have it prove to be a lie.

"Okay, that means you may have grossed around twenty thousand dollars. Is that about average for a quarter?" Tulip made a point of writing everything down as slowly as she could, as if she was studying the answer. "How much did you report in taxable income last year?"

"Don't you have that information?" the attorney asked, perhaps sensing something might be amiss.

"Of course, but I am interested in hearing what your client remembers reporting to us. The deadline for filing last year's tax return is less than a month away. He should remember what he told his accountant." Tulip is at her best when she gets to take someone apart. She went so far as to point to the wall calendar behind the attorney.

"I made about thirty five thousand dollars," Haskins told her. "It was a much better year than this one has been so far."

"Out of any given hundred dollars you take in, how much do you spend on operating the boat?"

"Is this really the reward my client deserves for having done his civic duty by reporting that car? This is outrageous," the attorney bellowed while his client was once again forced to do mental math.

"This is what your client deserves for lying to us," I stated in my flattest Joe Friday voice.

"Please answer the question." Tulip slid a page from a sales brochure that she must have printed out on her office computer across the table. "I have the specs on your particular boat here, and the company estimates it uses about fifteen dollars in diesel fuel an hour. A charter like the one you took the boys on lasted close to fifteen or sixteen hours all told. Every charter costs you that in fuel, plus your bait and any additional crew. That's on top of the costs for the boat's normal maintenance and insurance. Would it be accurate to estimate you take home about twenty five dollars of any hundred you take in?"

"That sounds reasonable," Captain Haskins made certain not to claim this was an absolutely correct figure. "What is your real question?"

"Was the new engine in your boat paid for with cash or on credit? A pair of them would cost close to what you claim to have taken home last year," Tulip sprang her own first trap.

"I've been saving for a while. You learn to do that if you are going to survive in this business," Haskins told her, but he made a mistake when he got cocky. He was becoming defensive in ways that were going to be unhelpful with Tulip.

"Then you can produce savings account records that support this transaction." My sister didn't bother to phrase this as a question. It was purely a challenge. Haskins blinked and turned to speak with his attorney. Tulip turned towards me with a look that expressed her impatience with the game. I asked her there to ask questions she knew would make any businessman nervous, but had not told her what it was that I needed to learn from the captain.

"My client will answer any questions you have after you have spoken with his accountant. This sort of IRS investigation seems like nothing but a fishing expedition, or maybe it's just an intimidation tactic by the detectives." The attorney was trying to get his client to relax. The captain looked ready to burst.

"Is your client feeling intimidated?" I inquired.

"You clearly blindsided him with all of this. His decision to retain legal counsel was obviously a very wise one. If you have nothing else than these charades, we are leaving." The attorney stood up.

"I can't speak for Detective Chance, but I know I can prove your client has already perjured himself at least once in the past half hour. That is enough to hold him while we consider hauling him before a judge tomorrow morning," I snarled and waved the man back into his hard wooden seat. "Your client has intentionally failed to disclose facts pertinent to our investigation. I imagine it would not be in his favor to be known in this parish as the man who kept the state police from identifying Kirk Donovan's killer."

"What facts are you referring to?" the attorney demanded, but with far more respect in his voice, and eased back into his seat.

"If I have to tell you, I will charge your client. I will give the captain one more shot at telling us what happened that Monday night." I ignored the attorney and stared directly at Captain Haskins. "I will give you a clue. It involves another boat."

The attorney conferred with the captain yet again while Tulip and Detective Chance tried not to reveal their ignorance of what I was talking about. She did a much more convincing job.

"Okay, there was another boat. It tried to pass us as we went past the lift bridge," Captain Haskins was still not prepared to admit to any wrongdoing on his own part.

"Tell us about the boat. It was close enough to you that you ought to have had a better look at it than you did of the Mercedes," I wasn't playing nice, and I was not going to leave him any wiggle room.

"It was a Boston Whaler. It looked to be maybe ten or fifteen feet shorter than my boat. It was being run from the main cabin because of the fog, same as my boat." This alone proved that his story about Gwen Donovan's sedan was probably a lie.

"Did you see who was running it?" Detective Chance interjected. I realized I was cutting him out of the questioning.

"No. I was more worried about it forcing me out of the channel. There isn't a lot of room right there, and they surprised me when they made a run past us just then. The bridge makes that a narrow spot." Captain Haskins finally told us something close to the truth. He sounded like he was trying to describe a memory and not to tell a story he had practiced or been coached to give us. It came in a broken strand of words as he recalled each tiny piece of something that was annoying, but trivial, at the time it happened. "I had heard someone behind us for a while, but they were running in our wake and they didn't turn their own lights on until they were well past us. They gunned it as we pulled even with the bridge, and then they shot by us so fast they sprayed the boys standing out on the deck."

This last recollection actually brought a small laugh to his voice and he didn't try to hide the smile that recalling a bunch of rich frat boys being soaked had brought him at the time.

"How do you know it was a Boston Whaler? You claimed you didn't see the boat because you were trying to avoid a collision." I objected.

"Not a lot of people around here can afford one. I thought I recognized it when I heard the outboards go by. Only a Boston Whaler uses those big Mercury outboards. Those motors cost nearly what one of my diesels cost." Haskins recognized and appreciated good boats, I had to give him that. It also made me believe him. I can identify the sound of a dozen small arms without having to look at what is being fired at me. You come to know the tools in your specific trade.

"Who do you know that owns one?" Detective Chance asked an obvious question, based on Haskins' having said he thought few locals could afford one.

"I've seen a dozen or so small ones come through the marina. Most of those folks don't live around here, though," Captain Haskins replied, but he was hedging.

"Who locally owns Boston Whalers the size that you claim nearly rammed you?" I didn't ask the question in a very patient tone of voice.

"Only the Donovans own boats about that size,"

"Are they all Boston Whalers?" Tulip hissed the words in her most piercing manner. She had other things to do with her day than to sit beside me while I pulled the wings off a fly.

"I know that Senator Donovan and Kirk do," Haskins answered Tulip's question so fast it sounded nearly reflexive. There was an unspoken 'please, don't hurt me' in it, as well.

"Well, we know Kirk Donovan wasn't headed out to sea in his boat that night," I narrowed the field. "Did you recognize the senator or any other member of the Donovan family on the other boat?"

"No, sir," Captain Haskins said. He had discovered a whole new set of manners in the past few seconds.

"Could you tell if whoever was at the wheel was a man or woman?" Detective Chance spoke up. He had to get some questions in so he looked like he was doing his job when Sheriff Mazant and the senator played their copy of the interview tape.

"No," Haskins said, and then realized the thin ice he had stepped onto. "Like I said, I was focused on moving aside. It had nothing to do with the fog."

"We'll get back to that," I waved a hand to dissuade him from protecting his original story. "I just want to know who was on that other boat. Could you tell if they were alone?"

The captain shook his head rather than speak his answer aloud, and we allowed that to be his answer.

"Then we are back to the report you made with the dispatcher on the night of March ninth," I said and took a moment to pour myself a glass of water and to offer one to Tulip. She declined, ready for this to be done with.

"Okay," Captain Haskins sighed. He held up both of his hands and then plopped them onto the table and leaned forward. "I myself did not see the car. You got me on that, but I never told the dispatcher I was the one who saw it. One of the frat boys came up and mentioned that he and his friends noticed the same car sitting on the bank every time we went by. I didn't ask how he spotted it that night, I only did what he asked and called for Sheriff Mazant to go take a look. It was easier to say I was the one who saw it than to drag one of those boys all the way back here to go through this."

"Now you're saying it was a frat boy with X-ray vision who peered through the fog to see the car?" I was unimpressed with Detective Chance's version of sarcasm.

"That is what my client just stated," the attorney did not like Chance's phrasing any more than I had.

"It's your client's voice we need on the record, not yours, counselor," Tulip diced up the attorney one last time.

"That's right. One of the boys suggested that I call Sheriff Mazant to send someone to check out the car. It didn't make sense for anyone to leave a Mercedes on that boat ramp for three days," Haskins stated for the record. He even looked at the camera to say it.

"Was it the boat ramp or was it the Mercedes that didn't fit?" Tulip asked. She was bored and would continue challenging Haskins' semantics until I ended this interview and gave her the chance to discuss what she was there to share with me.

"The boat ramp is a concrete slab poured into the muddy bank," I explained rather than make Haskins try to defend his entirely adequate statement. "The car was clearly out of place."

"If you say so," Tulip sighed audibly and began loading the mock files back into her briefcase.

"I imagine you can identify the boy who told you about the car. At least this one stood right in front of you," I wasn't going to let him get by with a story like he gave on which boy caused them to get a late start.

"His name was Jacob. He was the boy who ran late. I just remembered that," Haskins tried to slip in what he knew he could no longer hide from us.

"What did he say to you? Repeat what he said as exactly as possible," I pressed. The kid's story stunk as badly as the captain's did, and for the same reason.

"He said they had all noticed the same car sitting on the ramp every night. He wondered if someone abandoned it there."

"Okay, now it is all of them seeing through the fog." I was growing as impatient as Tulip. The captain's account of the events was becoming much too loose. Now it wasn't just one boy, but rather an undetermined number of them and Jacob was merely their spokesman.

"I swear I'm telling the truth," Captain Haskins assured us. The three of us gave him the exact same dismissive look. I sighed and glanced at my watch again before I turned to look at the camera.

"It's eleven fifteen. We are back where we began, so this initial interview is over," I declared. "Captain Haskins needs to be available for further questioning and to assist us by identifying anyone in the charter group we may ask him to in the future. As I stated during the interview, it is up to the IRS to make its own determination on whether or not they will investigate Captain Haskins' business and personal finances."

"So, we're free to go?" the attorney asked. He tried to sound triumphant, but he couldn't quite pull it off.

"The matter of your client's continued freedom is still on the table, but you both may leave the room." I grimly conceded.

Forty-Seven

"That proved interesting," I grumbled to my companions once Captain Hastings and his attorney were gone. "Does it strike anyone as curious that so many young men had the ability to see a silver sedan through fog so thick nobody was able to read the name on the back of a boat running alongside their own?"

"Curious isn't the word I would use," Detective Chance huffed. "But the word I have in mind should not be used in the presence of a lady."

"He doesn't know me, does he?" Tulip laughed out loud. We both knew the word he had in mind and the three of us were in complete agreement that the story we were being spoon fed was, shall we say, garbage.

"What do you want to do now?" Detective Chance leaned around my sister to ask.

"I'll drive into New Orleans this afternoon and see if I can track down the boys on the boat. Why don't you question some of the other captains as to whether they have seen what we assume is Kirk's Boston Whaler lately? My guess is that the boat has been stripped or sold, or both."

"Someone must have known Kirk wouldn't miss it, which means someone already knew he was dead by Monday night," Tulip added her two cents worth. I had deduced the same thing, and that likelihood made me even more suspicious of the captain's story.

"It was nice to meet you," Detective Chance said and touched Tulip's arm as he stood up to leave the room. She ignored his familiarity and smiled at him as he left the room. She waited until I had turned off the camera and retrieved the video cassette before she said anything more. "Your partner creeps me the hell out, big brother."

"You and apparently everyone else he comes in contact with around here. I won't be exchanging any Christmas or birthday cards with him when this is all over."

She laughed and stood up. She left her briefcase on the varnished table top for the moment, and then glanced at the windows to see if we were drawing any undue attention for remaining in the room.

"So what did you drive all the way out here to share with me? Is Belle talking to you and Katie?" I was in no hurry to be anywhere else and hoped this was why my sister asked for an audience. Whatever she came this far to tell me must have been important, or she would have waited to update me the next time I drove back to New Orleans.

"She wants to see her friends. She cares a lot less about seeing anyone in her family. Neither of us has seen her shed a tear over her father, and she does not seem very concerned about her mother's situation. I can't tell if it is shock or if she really does not care what happened to either of them. She understands she has to stay where she is until you know if she is in any danger."

"This is what you need to see." Tulip opened her briefcase again and removed a spiral bound report.

"Oh, that ought to be something to read," I grinned and looked at what she held in her hand. She did not take my hint to hand me the report.

"It is," she assured me, but in a far more serious tone of voice than I thought necessary. "What do you know of the relationship between the Donovan and Deveraux families?"

"Senator Donovan is one of Uncle Felix's best clients and Belle and Jennifer apparently are close friends. Belle must have found something else, maybe further back?" I reached for the report. It only made sense. Our own family's long history in Baton Rouge politics had to start somewhere.

"Do you know the term 'placage'?" My sister asked and took her seat once again. I took her cue and sat down as well. This was apparently going to take a while.

"I know its translation. I am guessing it has some larger meaning that involves one or both of our families."

"It used to be common practice for rich white men to create formal agreements to take care of their Black mistresses. They couldn't legally marry a slave, but they could file paperwork to create what amounted to a common law marriage that would let them leave property or cash for the mistress and any kids they had together. Many free men of color

were the progeny of these arrangements. It was how they received their freedom and why they had the money to go into business on their own."
I had never given that any thought, but it made perfect sense.

"How does this link the two families? Neither of them were Black, that's for sure."

"Apparently our mother's family made its early money dealing in slaves," Tulip began, and I noticed the way she distanced the two of us from the Deverauxs.

"A lot of people did." There is a limit to the guilt I carry for the sins of omission or commission of my ancestors. I just do my best not to repeat any of them.

"Well, by the time of the Louisiana Purchase, they specialized in placage arrangements. They would buy all of the youngest and lightest skinned women off the auction block and train them to be the consummate mistresses. They even held formal parties and balls where rich young men, and probably a lot of old ones, could sample the wares to find a mistress who would do the things their legal wives must not have done as well, or maybe at all," Tulip summarized the report. This piqued my interest enough. I would make time to read Belle's report as soon as I could.

"What's a good Catholic girl to do?" I tried to joke. Tulip frowned, but thankfully she did not remind me that my girlfriend was a good Catholic girl.

"Anyway," she sighed deeply and continued. "One man took a mistress and kept her on his plantation in Plaquemines Parish. He never married. I assume his friends and business partners knew better than to make comments or challenge his preference in women. The place transferred to the mistress and their children when he died. Well, she had no idea how to run a plantation, so she asked for help from the only white man she thought she could trust."

"The man who got her into all of this in the first place," I could find my ancestor's name later.

"Right. He wasn't any smarter about running a big plantation than she was, but he knew the son of Jasper Donovan."

"Duncan was also his youngest son," I said and noticed the way her head cocked slightly to show the bit of confusion she had over my knowing the Donovan family tree without having read the report. "I took a tour. Like Katie suggested. Go on with the story."

"As you know, youngest sons never got land. They usually got kicked to the curb or joined the clergy."

Our father's family had essentially banished him when he was old enough to fend for himself. He was the youngest son in his generation and, as poor as the Holland family was in everything but tradition, about the only thing he had to look forward to when his father died was working for his oldest brother for the rest of his life. Being a cop in New Orleans must have looked like a better alternative.

"Go on. You said that Duncan was hired to run the widow's plantation," I was beginning to lose the thread. Hooking Duncan up with a rich widow surely didn't fully explain the next hundred and fifty years of our two families' connection.

"Mother's great-great-great-grandfather hired a lawyer to find a way for Duncan to inherit the plantation when the widow died in a yellow fever epidemic. I may have too many greats in there," Tulip laughed and then continued. "He and Duncan saw an even better opportunity to improve both their lots when the Civil War came to town. The Donovans supposedly agreed to protect the assets and interests of other plantation owners who took off for England to avoid the war. The Deverauxs used their placage clout with the judges and politicians put in place after the war to help the Donovans screw these people out of the holdings and fortunes they were trusted to protect. It is how the Donovans acquired so much land in the parish. They had a lot more, but coastal erosion has chewed into it. It was also how the Deverauxs built their own power. The prospective mistresses our relative was training were used in a string of brothels that serviced both sides of the war at one time or another. This gave the Deveraux family a lot of connections they were able to exploit during Reconstruction."

"So our families are connected by whore mongering and fraud. Welcome to Louisiana, sis," I didn't see where this story, illustrative and interesting as it was, had a single thing to do with my investigation. I also didn't think this was the best time to mention that Uncle Felix's

Rolodex contained phone numbers for multiple escort services. The Deveraux family might not have changed much more than the Donovans over the years.

"Can you imagine this story getting out?"

"I am stunned that some version of it hasn't," I practically laughed. "What's your point?"

"Mother's family built its reputation for knowing the right people in Baton Rouge off the brothels they ran. Senator Donovan sits in the same seat his family has held ever since they bought it with money they stole from legitimate landholders." Tulip's sense of outrage is easily provoked. Something as ugly and unfair as what Belle's report set forth as the foundation for the state's most influential dynasties was more than she could be expected to tolerate quietly. "The Deverauxs wormed their way into power in Baton Rouge on the backs of the poor women they whored out to the men who ran things during the Civil War. It gave them something to use as blackmail."

"They probably continued to sell those same women to men running things after the war. They may not have even blackmailed anyone. They could have just been the guys who threw the best parties."

"You're disgusting," she hissed, but she didn't throw anything or storm out of the room. It meant she despised my capacity to see things from a pragmatic perspective, which is seldom as righteous or noble as her own vision of how the world should work. Her deep and abiding sense of right and wrong usually exceeds the limits of justice. My pragmatism does not impair my own desire to see justice prevail no matter the written law.

"It's taken me this far, sis," I goaded her. "I am sure neither family would want to see this on the front page of the newspaper, but are you really suggesting that keeping Belle from turning this in played a part in Belle's father's death? We still don't know what they were fighting over, but I don't buy that it was this."

"That is because you never bought into the family dynasty thing that mother's side of the family is so big on."

"Point taken," I conceded.

"You are probably right that the term paper was not going to create a reason for Belle to kill her dad or her mother. Her father or the senator probably could have found a way to get her credit for writing it without it being read by anyone outside of the family," Tulip realized.

"Senator Donovan could have gotten her credit for writing it without her ever lifting a pencil." The senator most assuredly would not want to see it turned in or released, any more than would Uncle Felix. This is the exact sort of thing Uncle Felix makes his living by making disappear. "Thank you for bringing it out to me, Tulip. I will absolutely read it, but I can't think of a single way it might pose a motive for either Kirk's death or Gwen's disappearance."

"You're probably right," she said and closed her briefcase once again.

"Come on, I'll race you back to New Orleans. Loser buys lunch," I suggested. She has as heavy of a foot as I do, but lacks the flashing lights and shiny badge that lets me get away with it. "I just need to stop by to pick up Roux."

"I'll race you anywhere you want to go, but we both know neither of us are paying for lunch where you plan to take me," Tulip cheered up and laughed at my wager. She was doubly protected from ever seeing a bill at the bistro now that she was dating the chef.

Forty-Eight

I locked Roux in my apartment above Strada Ammazarre and asked Belle to join Tulip and me at the chef's table for lunch. I had found her sitting at my kitchen counter with her laptop and a stack of notebooks, so I assumed she was in touch with her Tulane instructors and getting her assignments online. She wore a pair of baggy shorts and a T-shirt of mine Tulip or Katie must have told her was okay to take from my dresser. I find it sexy when Katie wears my clothes, but it made me uncomfortable to find Belle in one of my shirts.

I returned to the first floor and found Tulip land Miss J laughing at Tony and his young Black apprentices in the prep kitchen. Chef Tony had recently purchased the pizza place across the street with the intention of letting Ritchie Franklin try his hand at running a legitimate business. These new pizza cooks were the last members of Ritchie's former street gang that he was able to convince having a straight job held less risk to their lives and futures than being drug dealers. NOPD's Chief of Detectives does his best to bite his tongue about the chef and I doing this sort of social work.

Not one of the six young men made a sound when Tulip kissed Tony's right cheek after I suggested the two of us go eat. The boys had been working at the bistro long enough to know the chef dating my sister was a touchy subject, but they had yet to determine which of us they needed to worry the most about upsetting with some cute comment.

"I believe the object is to get more of the flour in the dough than on your clothes," I kidded the group.

"This isn't as easy as Chef makes it look," one of the younger boys complained as he struggled to mimic Tony's ability to keep a disc of dough in the air. I didn't have to wait long before the swirling would-be pizza crust fell to the floor.

"Nothing ever will be," I assured him.

"Y'all need to step up to the plate," Miss J opined before she went back to what she had been doing.

Tulip and I took a seat at the chef's table to wait for Belle. Ginger, the lead daytime waitress, hastily dropped off three menus and silverware before delivering an order to one of her tables in the dining room. I decided against ordering a bottle of wine, knowing I had a busy afternoon ahead of me and not wanting to ply Belle with booze while she was being questioned. I needed Tulip to be sober in case Belle decided she needed an attorney.

"When can I go home?" were the first words out of Belle's mouth after she sat down. She wasn't being petulant or making a scene. She just wanted to get on with her life. She was going to need a new definition for the word "home" when this was all over. I still clung to the dimming hope that she wasn't already an orphan. That all of the liquid in the trunk of Gwendolyn's car was not her blood did not prove she was still alive.

"As soon as I am sure you aren't in danger. Right now, I think this is the only safe place you can be. You also aren't going to get a bar tab anywhere else." I allowed her to order wine or cocktails as a way to make feeling trapped here easier to handle. Katie had expanded this to include Belle's presence at happy hour.

"Well, when can I talk to Bradley?"

"Again, the answer to that depends on how soon I can sort out what part either of you had in what has happened so far."

"Do you honestly think Bradley or I killed my father or helped my mother disappear?" I noted that Belle was not suggesting she believed her mother was dead, despite the considerable evidence pointing in that direction. I had not yet told her my own suspicions about the scene having been staged, and decided only just then against doing so.

"Your mother did not simply disappear, Belle. She may be hiding, but she also may be as dead as your father," I set her straight. "Your mother's car certainly looked like a murder scene. I am still trying to determine whether that is separate from your father's murder."

"Do you think I know where my mother is?"

"Somebody does, and it would be great if someone could tell me what happened on that boat ramp. You are the last member of your immediate family I know to be alive, and my job is to keep you secure until I know what has happened to both of your parents," I explained and opened my menu. Belle took the cue and opened hers as well. I caught the quick shake of my sister's head, letting me know I had not resolved this issue by any stretch of the imagination.

We settled on an appetizer of char-broiled oysters and crabmeat salads for Tulip and Belle. I ordered chicken Marsala because ordering the veal piccata that I wanted would initiate a long lecture on animal cruelty from my sister. I said nothing when Tulip ordered a glass of champagne, but gave Belle a look when she considered doing the same thing.

"Both of your grandfathers want to see you, so we need to figure out how to make that happen. I was thinking of inviting one to dinner tomorrow and the other to brunch on Sunday." I still had a short list of things to discuss with Belle, and chose the most complicated one as the starting point.

"Whatever. Can Chester be first, so we can get him out of the way?" Belle sighed.

"It doesn't sound like you have a particularly good relationship with the man," I said with every ounce of 'tell me more' I could pour into the comment.

"That's a good description. The Man. That's what Chester has always been in our house," Belle said and tossed her head to one side, as though this might fling away whatever bad juju the name held.

"You call your grandfather Chester?" Tulip interrupted. She gave me a look to ask why I didn't say anything.

"Yeah, that's his name," Belle pointed out. "He doesn't like being reminded he's getting older. He also dates women way younger than he is."

"How much younger?" This I did want to know.

"He hits on my friends from Tulane."

"Eww." Tulip couldn't hold her tongue.

"I know, right?" Belle laughed and I caught a bit of the bonding the two had done in my absence.

"I understand that he used to arrange underage marriages before your father joined his practice." This was the meat of what I needed her to explain, and I was afraid to pursue it as hard as I wanted. My biggest problem was that I still had no idea what I needed to know but didn't know to ask.

"So did his daddy before him. Our family has always been who you talk to if you want to marry a child bride."

"What did your mother think about that?" Tulip spoke up before I could ask my next question.

"Nothing nice," Belle opined. "It was why Kirk knocked her around so much."

"And now you just called your father by his first name as well," Tulip pointed out.

"Maybe I do it because I didn't want to be part of any family that did this to little girls." Belle seemed to be having an epiphany and we gave her a moment. She composed herself and went on. "I didn't know what Kirk did for a living until he arranged for one of my classmates to marry some old guy before we started junior high."

"Are you still in touch with your friend?" I was trying to keep the conversation going until I decided in which direction to take it next.

"She died," Belle said a bit too casually. "She took off a couple of times and her husband shot her. My father told me about it right before I started my junior year."

"How sad. Do you know where she was living?" I braced myself for the response.

"Houston, Texas."

"Did you know Bradley is from Houston?" I tried to ease the possible connection into the conversation.

"So are a lot of people," Belle laughed. She saw the connection I was trying to make and was not going to even consider it. "Crystal Franks is, too."

"How did you meet Bradley?" Tulip tried a different approach.

"He agreed to tutor me through freshman algebra at Tulane. It was a lot harder than I remembered it being in high school. He helped a lot of the dumb kids like me," Belle said and laughed. "All I know about Bradley is that he lived with his dad in Houston. I just figured his folks split up when he was still a kid. He said he enrolled at Tulane after his dad died, so I guess he must have left him some money. I know one of his dad's businesses is in our parish. That's why he is in Donovan so much."

"You two don't discuss your pasts?" Tulip pressed. It is not like twenty-somethings have extensive pasts to discuss. Katie and I grew up together, for the most part, so we spend very little time rehashing our own childhoods.

"Not really, no. He never wants to talk about his dad at all," she elaborated, and went back to her salad. I had no doubt that she took every opportunity to not discuss her own father's history of abusing her mother, nor his line of legal work.

Belle excused herself to take a nap after finishing her meal. Tulip waited until Belle was on the elevator to let me know that naps were my prisoner's way of killing time. I needed to find a way to end her boredom and the sense that the walls were closing in on her. I asked Tulip for yet another favor, after I let her see the size of the luncheon bill neither of us were paying. I needed to know everything she could find out about Bradley Ladd's adoptive father and his death.

Forty-Nine

Bradley agreed to bring his fishing buddies to meet with me at The Boot at three o'clock that afternoon. The other option was that I have state police officers bring them to Donovan one at a time for questioning. I chose a time that I figured business at The Boot would most likely be slow, but it is a college bar so there is never a time that it is completely empty. Bradley and his friends chose a table that nobody else was sitting near. They didn't want our conversation overheard any more than I did.

I felt there was more to be gained by initially questioning the boys as a group rather than individually. I needed to see their group dynamic to sort out which of them would lie no matter what, and which of them was the most likely to tell the truth if I applied a little pressure. I certainly wasn't expecting to come away from this meeting with an honest version of their trip. I was only mildly surprised to discover all of the young men at the table had attended Belle Donovan's recent pool party. I took a moment to get the names of the two boys I let walk away from that incident, and made a note of which of the boys in the pool was not present here, including Mitchell Ursin. He had told me he lived in Donovan, so maybe he wasn't enrolled at Tulane. It might be a lead worth pursuing after I determined how tight the connection between these other boys proved to be.

"I'm sorry if I pulled any of you out of class to meet with me," I said to open the conversation.

"Anything to help find Belle's mom," Bradley spoke up. His companions all nodded or mumbled some sort of platitude about doing the right thing.

"Let's start with some basics. I have been told that this was a fraternity outing. Which fraternity do all of you belong to?" This was meant to sound like a softball question. I intended to use the answer to make a threat about notifying the fraternity's headquarters and endangering their charter if need be. I did not expect an icy silence in response to the easy question.

"That was just something we told Captain Haskins." Duncan McGee spoke up. His Irish-red hair had caught my attention at the pool party.

"So, you aren't actually in a fraternity?"

"Some of us were, but the school shut us down last year." Duncan explained, trying to sound casual about something that wasn't in the least bit routine.

"You guys were the ones who hospitalized some of your pledges?" I could not remember the name of the fraternity, but I distinctly remembered what they did to lose their fraternity charter. Someone had the bright idea to throw boiling water on the blindfolded naked pledges. The result was predictable, but Tulane's reaction was not.

"None of us threw the hot water," Jacob was quick to point out. They were still present yet did nothing to stop it, but I wasn't here to discuss that and let it drop.

"Look, all I really need you to explain is how you were able to spot Gwendolyn Donovan's Mercedes on that boat ramp through so much fog." My discovering an obvious flaw in their good citizen story caused considerably more consternation among them than I thought it might. None of them were very good at hiding their concern that I did not believe the story they must have spent long hours concocting. Their ranks were going to crumble when each of them began weighing their solidarity against the very real possibility of going to jail for obstruction of justice.

"I'm not sure what you mean." Bradley didn't surprise me at all when he feigned innocence.

"The ramp was fogged in every night that weekend. There was no way you could have identified Gwendolyn Donovan's Mercedes through a couple of hundred feet of thick bayou fog." I had no reservations about sharing the specific problem I had with their story. It would let any of them who wanted to defend their lie dig themselves an even deeper hole.

"We only reported seeing a car sitting in the same spot all weekend. We never said it was a Mercedes," Bradley tried to counter.

"You seem to spend a lot of time in Donovan. Isn't that where you might assume someone would park if they used that boat ramp?" I unspooled more rope for him to hang himself with by suggesting this was nothing but an assumption on his part.

"I suppose. I have never owned a boat, so I would not know for sure," Bradley retreated, but also didn't take my bait to explain why he spent so much time in Donovan. I wanted to hear him confirm Belle's story that he owned a business there.

"Well, did any of you see a boat trailer? If someone put their boat in there they must have had a trailer on their car, right?" I specifically addressed this to the five other boys sitting at the table.

"I suppose," Duncan piped up. "But we wouldn't have seen it if it was behind the car. I only saw the front of the car."

"So you actually saw the car?" I challenged him.

"I did on Saturday. The fog didn't reach all the way down that night. I assumed it was the same car on Monday because it looked like it was in the same place." Duncan finally made a good argument, and it even sounded like he believed it.

"But wasn't the moonlight blacked out by the fog that night as well? I have been back to that boat ramp a couple of times and it was always dark as a coal mine because of the tree branches over the ramp. I imagine fog would have made it even darker." I had, in fact, not set foot on the boat ramp since the night I was assigned to the case. I was debating them just to see who would fight me. So far it was only Bradley and Duncan. The other boys became mute, and avoided eye contact with me as best they could. Fred Jackson and Jacob Hammel struggled to keep me from noticing that their hands were fidgeting to beat the band under the heavy wooden table.

"Okay, let's assume for a minute that what you are telling me is what actually happened. I am sure I can punch holes in your story because you will not all agree, since each of you stood in a different place on the boat," I said and leaned forward to rest my forearms flat on the table. This brought me closer to the boys who wanted to put as much distance between us as possible. "I would still like to know why you bothered to call the car in at all. I am sure you saw a lot of things that you were curious about between Donovan and the Gulf."

"Bradley was who said to call it in," Fred Jackson piped up. Bradley and the older boys did their best not to give him a dirty look, but their instinct to silence him was too strong.

"Sheriff Mazant and I both found it suspicious that the car bothered you so much," I shoved harder, and invented Sheriff Mazant's disbelief.

"Why?" Bradley challenged me.

"It was just a car sitting on a boat ramp. You all went fishing every night, maybe whoever owned that car went fishing as well. What was so suspicious to all of you?" I decided it was time to start squeezing Bradley. All of this discussion about the car was only meant to expose the fault lines in their dynamic before I switched to the topic of the mystery boat.

"I don't know. It just didn't feel right," Bradley half-mumbled. There was no good answer, and he realized his excuses failed to overcome my doubts about this version of reporting the car.

I let a heavy silence fall over the table. It was time to see who still felt comfortable being part of the group Bradley had put into the sights of the state police. I did my best to look like a detective who would soon be haunting their every move.

"Did anything else not feel right? Did anyone see or hear anything else that weekend that made you stop and wonder what was going on?" I began to set my trap. Even the dumbest kid at the table had to believe I was now aware of the Boston Whaler that passed by them moments before they called Sheriff Mazant's office about Gwen's Mercedes. The smartest among them would be asking themselves how I learned about that incident, and how much I had already figured out.

"Like what?" Duncan asked, still straining to sound as casual as he could. His voice cracked by the time he got the second word out of his mouth and he hastily hid his face behind the bottle of beer he had been twirling in his hand since I sat down.

"You tell me." I stared each boy down in turn. The almost oblivious expression on Bradley's face was impressive. He might have convinced most people that he had no idea what I was talking about, but he was likely going to abruptly recall the Boston Whaler passing them after I 'refreshed' his memory by telling him everything I knew.

"Nah, I am pretty sure at least one of you can recall something else that happened. Maybe on Sunday or Monday night?" I wasn't going to give them a specific point in time to remember. There might well be other incidents and conversations these amateurs would blurt out trying to guess which ones I already had my eye on.

"I was late getting to the boat on Monday," Jacob offered. This did at least confirm the captain's reason for not getting the early start he intended.

"Why was that?" I pursued the topic just to give the others time to find something of their own to contribute.

"I got lost."

"You got lost going to a place you had no trouble finding the previous three nights." I let this hang.

"I was coming from a different direction," Jacob was quick to explain. He must have believed that this was enough of a reason that I would lose interest.

"Which direction was that?" Not that I cared.

"I went the wrong way on Donovan Boulevard."

"You came over the bridge and turned left instead of right, after having made the same turn two nights in a row?"

"That wasn't it," Jacob started to explain before he winced just a bit and leaned back in his seat. I did not hear the kick I assumed someone gave him.

"Then where were you when you made the wrong turn?" Now I was very interested.

"I was driving around in town and got lost." I had a hard time believing college-boy Jacob decided to tour Donovan, Louisiana after midnight on a week night to kill time before he went fishing.

"I think you ran an errand and got lost. I'll drop this if you tell me what you were really doing," I said and gave him my best version of indifference.

"I dropped someone off," Jacob admitted. He would have been fine had he not added, "At their house."

"Where else would you have dropped anyone at that hour of the night?" I wondered aloud. Jacob just shrugged and fell silent. I pondered for a moment how long it would take to get Jacob Hammel to tell me exactly who his passenger was and what their destination had been. I decided it would take less time if I pulled him into an actual interrogation room, even with an attorney present. This was going to be the last time any of these young men sat down with me without one. I knew that much for certain.

"So, Fred, you've been rather quiet. Why don't you be the one to tell me what else happened that Monday night? Maybe before you reached the ramp?" There was nothing to gain or lose any longer by making the matter of the Boston Whaler passing them into a guessing game.

Fred Jackson quickly glanced around the table, lingering the longest as he passed Bradley, before he coughed and answered. He ran a hand past the left side of his head, straightening his hair as well as collecting his thoughts for a moment. He had to be wondering what bringing the boat up now was going to cost him after holding his silence for so long. I think he was doing the math of what being the first to confess might gain him in the long run. I was going to do nothing to let him know he was in no legal jeopardy whether he answered the question or not, unless he lied to me.

"A big white boat zoomed by us when we were going past the bridge," Fred said all in a rush. The seal was broken on the topic and I could feel a rush of nervous energy circle the table now that this was out in the open. It made me all the more curious about the boat, these young men, and that call to Sheriff Mazant.

"How close was it when it went by you?"

"It splashed water all over us," Duncan offered as a measure of distance.

"Close enough you could see who was driving the boat?" The distance must have been close enough they might have jumped from one boat to the other.

"We were too busy trying to stay dry," Bradley was quick to insert himself into our conversation. I watched the other boys begin to focus their attention on the table top rather than on the two of us.

"So, a couple of minutes later you called Sheriff Mazant about a car at the boat ramp, but you didn't bother filing a complaint about the boat that almost ran into you. Why is that?" I was beginning to develop a theory of what had transpired that night that was going to be hard to prove, but harder on any of these young men if my charges made it into court.

"The boat was long gone by then, and it was a Coast Guard matter anyway," Bradley waved off any sort of accusation I might be making. It was a credible explanation, but a lousy lie.

"That's about all I can think of," I declared after a long moment of silence meant to make them think I was considering more questions. "To be clear, what you are telling me is that Jacob got lost taking someone home and delayed Monday night's fishing trip, that a big white boat splashed you but not one of you thought to complain about it to Sheriff Mazant or the Coast Guard, and Bradley made sure someone besides himself was the one to call Sheriff Mazant about the car you all swear you saw sitting for three nights on the boat ramp."

I stared at each boy in turn, pausing long enough to give them an opportunity to correct or add detail to my version of their collective story I had just repeated for verification. Duncan and Bradley seemed much more defiant than Fred and Jacob. I had their story, which might prove to be an alibi for one or more of them in time. I also left the meeting knowing which of them might yield the most results being questioned alone.

Fifty

I called Detective Chance as soon as Roux and I returned to my apartment after our afternoon run. Roux needs all the exercise he can get, and he seemed to forgive being left alone for so long after a half hour of chasing a softball along the bank of the Mississippi River. His negative history with being kept in cages and kennels makes me be careful that doing so is never an act of punishment or anger. To be totally honest, I have come to appreciate his company more than that of a number of humans I know, Detective Chance among them.

"Have you found anything new?" I did my best not to sound like I expected a negative answer.

"Not a thing. I was wondering how long it would take you to share what you found out in New Orleans this afternoon." The local detective wasn't being very coy about letting me know my travels were being noted by Sheriff Mazant, which meant the senator was aware of them as well.

"I may have found Kirk's boat, or at least figured out who may know where it is. What do you know about a local kid named Mitchell Ursin?" I was reluctant to involve Chance in this before I had more to go on than a hunch. I plucked Mitchell's name out of the stack only because he was the only boy at Belle's swimming pool party who wasn't with Bradley and his disowned fraternity brothers at The Boot.

"Nothing comes to mind. I think his father used to work at that boat supply place we went to the other day, but I would have to ask around about what his kid does to make a living. What am I looking for?"

The detective didn't realize he had solidified my suspicions with his offhand comment about the boy's father being associated with the marine supply store. It did not take much imagination to believe Mitchell or his father might know a few people in the market for a good deal on a well-maintained used Boston Whaler. I was curious how far they might need to take one to sell it without anyone connecting it to a report of one just like it being stolen in Donovan. I was not so curious, however, that I was willing to waste my own time finding an answer to that question when I had Detective Chance at my disposal.

"Run by the Coast Guard station and ask them how hard it would be to sell Kirk Donovan's Boston Whaler and get away with it. I think someone saw a golden opportunity and took it. If I am right, we may finally have someone who is able to tell us something about Kirk Donovan's death," I instructed Chance. I had every reason to believe I was going to be the third or fourth person to learn whatever the Coast Guard told him, but I was the only one who knew where that missing piece of the puzzle likely fit.

The scenario I worked out in my head on the drive back to Donovan went like this: Jacob got lost on his way to the boatyard after he dropped Mitchell at Kirk Donovan's house. Mitchell or Bradley could easily have been aware that Belle and Kirk were both out of town, and might have heard people say they spotted Gwendolyn leaving town as well, so the family boat was ripe for the taking. Sheriff Mazant's department in Saint Xavier Parish was not so large that they were going to be able to respond to very many calls at the same time. Finding blood in Gwendolyn Donovan's car was going to put any hijinks between two boats on the bayou way down the list of things to investigate. I felt I was finally seeing a big enough picture to stop letting myself believe everything that happened that weekend was unrelated. I had the distinct impression that Bradley's choice of friends to invite on that fishing weekend trip was by no means random.

Being associated with the reckless fraternity brothers was a sign that he was comfortable being around people with a demonstrated propensity for poor judgement. Kirk Donovan's expensive Boston Whaler being stolen would have stirred a huge hornet's nest were Kirk not being sought as a murder suspect. How he was supposed to have escaped in both a boat and the Ford GT was apparently not the sort of detail to fuss over. Being tied to conspiracy and grand theft, and the likelihood of one of Senator Donovan's hand-picked judges determining their prison sentence, might make one or the other of the young men I had just interviewed willing to explain what they had known about Kirk and Gwen's situations the night their boat was stolen.

"Anything else?" Detective Chance asked. He didn't try to hide the implication that I was dumping work on him that I could just as easily do myself.

"Not that I can think of. We are going to have to get a little creative in building this case. It looks like figuring out who told the person who took the boat the coast was clear is our ticket to finding out what happened." I was sure of my facts, but less sure about how to proceed. I had a deep fear that suspects and witnesses were going to start being harder to find or question if I let Detective Chance and Sheriff Mazant know who I had in mind before I interviewed them.

"I have ideas of my own. We should talk about it when you get back in town." This was almost tantalizing enough to make me drive back right then, but the opportunity to spend the evening with Katie beat that temptation.

Fifty-One

Katie Reilly still lives in the house she and her first husband, a former NOPD patrolman named Ray, bought on Nashville Avenue in Uptown. It was built to the river side of Saint Charles Avenue in the 1930s for a family far larger than Katie and Ray ever made together. Their marriage had lasted barely two years, just long enough to leave her with a house with a small garage but no car and a bad taste in her mouth about the word marriage. Ray still had their BMW, but it was now parked on the street at his walk-up apartment on Julia Street. Neither of the pair found my comments about the Divorce of the Magi to be particularly funny. The home's back yard was fenced, which made it an ideal place for Roux to romp about while I walked to Langenstein's Market to buy a bottle of Beaujolais and ribeye steaks to grill when Katie came home from work.

Food fell to the bottom of our priority list as soon as she walked through the door. Her aversion to the idea of being married did not affect her capacity for displays of affection and intense passion in her bedroom. We had a lot of both of these to catch up on, even though I had been in Donovan barely two weeks. Roux played quietly until the sun set and the yard began to grow dark. He barked twice and I went downstairs to let him in. He bolted past me at the French doors to the dining room and sprinted up the stairs to leap on Katie's four poster bed, and begin giving her his own slobbery kisses. She laughed and gently fended him off while I regained my place beneath the sheets and ordered him to calm down. He grumbled a bit before he settled for a place on the floor at the foot of the queen sized bed.

"How are you boys doing out in the bayou?" Katie asked as she began to brush her thick auburn hair.

"I think we may be rounding a bend. I may have a lead on what became of Kirk's boat."

"What could a missing boat have to do with Gwen's disappearance? Are you sure this isn't another of your rabbit holes?" She didn't need to be remind me of the number of my cases that went from molehill to mountain.

"I think whoever took the boat knew Kirk was already dead. So, whoever took it ought to be able to tell me how they knew the coast was clear."

"Reasonable assumption," Katie relented. "But, that person could easily be Gwendolyn Donovan. That would be bad, right?"

"Very bad, indeed, but I don't think that is going to be the case. I have my eye on some of Belle's friends, and my theory is that she said something to one of them that led them to believe they could get away with it." I wrapped an arm around Katie and pulled her against me. She rested her head on my chest and moved her hand under the covers to remind me that she was going to waste very little of our time that evening by catching up on one another's cases.

"That would mean Belle knew her father was dead, even though her alibi puts her in Colorado on the day the coroner says he died. Do you believe she was part of a conspiracy to kill Kirk?" Katie was upset enough at the idea of Belle being involved that she sat up and looked me in the face to gauge my level of certainty. "That would make both Gwen and Belle the prime suspects in Kirk's death."

She didn't need to tell me how unacceptable that idea was to her. Her childhood friendship with Gwen was a thing of the past, but I could tell she had grown fond of Belle over the past couple of days of babysitting her. We had been dating for only a few months, but I had come to admire Katie's capacity to separate her compassion from her prosecutor persona.

"I don't know if I would call it a conspiracy. I am just saying that Belle may have been acting when she tried to reach her father by telephone when I busted her in the judge's pool. It's also possible that people she thinks of as friends may be using their relationship for their own profit. I am only certain that someone murdered Kirk, and I am convinced that Gwendolyn was never dead in the trunk of her car. It is time for me to get serious about finding answers to just what happened to Belle's parents."

"You think?" Katie laughed and climbed atop me, wrapping the covers around us to avoid embarrassing our watchdog. Roux sensed what we were about to do and beat a hasty retreat to the living room sofa after giving one of his disapproving snorts.

Fifty-Two

I called the telephone number I had for Senator Donovan just after eight o'clock the next morning. It was Saturday and I had no idea if he was still at the state capitol or in town, not that it mattered one way or the other. His secretary answered and put me on hold while she transferred the call to his cellular number. Birds chirping in the background gave me the impression I was interrupting the senator's morning round of golf, but he might have just been having breakfast on his patio.

"Belle is available for dinner at seven o'clock this evening." I did not want to open any negotiations over this matter.

"We'll meet at the country club." He was not in the mood for negotiations either. I picked the time so he believed he could choose the location.

"Seven o'clock in the lobby of the Monteleone Hotel. We can walk to dinner from there," I countered. There was no need to tell him where the hotel was located, it is a Louisiana landmark. My plan was to put him in a car and bring him to the bistro, after leaving whatever team of lawyers or muscle he may have intended to bring along at the hotel. I could not trust him not to pull some sort of legal maneuver or to attempt to abduct Belle once she was located. Let me correct that. I knew Uncle Felix was willing to do so on his behalf.

"Fine," the senator snarled and hung up.

To say this brief conversation still colored my mood as I entered the sheriff's office an hour later would be an understatement. Detective Chance was at his desk, back to wearing the black poplin uniform Sheriff Mazant favored. I didn't ask if this was a sign that he had been demoted or fallen out of favor for failing to keep me in check. I avoided the subject altogether because I didn't want to strike up another nasty conversation with anyone before lunch.

"Okay, what was it that you couldn't tell me over the phone last night?" I asked as I sat down in the chair beside his heavy desk. The squad room was empty but for two deputies, and they seemed to be intent upon ignoring us from across the room.

"Not here. Let's go for a ride." Chance replied and stood up. I shrugged and followed him out of the building. He headed for my XLR coupe and I used the fob to hastily unlock the doors before he embarrassed himself by having to wait until I caught up with him. I followed his lead and buckled myself into my seat, still waiting for him to explain his cryptic message. He pointed directly ahead. "Head north."

I pulled out of the parking lot and drove towards the interstate. The only secluded place to talk that came to mind was the stretch of county road where Kirk Donovan practiced with his expensive Ford sports car. It was a nice day, and testing my own skills would relax me.

"My car isn't bugged and I am not wearing a wire. What the hell is it that you can't let anyone else hear you tell me?" I wasn't going to sit in silence the entire distance to the turnoff.

"Someone tried to kill Judge Aubuchon on Saint Patrick's Day."

"What makes you say that?" I had nothing to gain by arguing with him. As it so happened, I agreed with him that Aubuchon's allergic reaction made no sense as an accident.

"Because someone has been picking off everyone involved in arranging child marriages and adoptions."

"That's a lot to take in." This was just a simple statement of fact. "Explain this murder conspiracy."

"I think poor families have been selling their kids off to rich pedophiles, and the Donovans and Judge Aubuchon have profited from making the transactions into legal marriages and adoptions," he explained. I was torn between laughing at how absurd this sounded and asking to hear more.

"Do you believe someone is out for revenge, or are they trying to cut in on the operation?" I slowed the car to make the turn onto Highway H, Kirk's private race track, and began to accelerate sharply. Chance took a look at the climbing speedometer needle, but he stayed calm and answered my question.

"There were some weird deaths before I came to town, and a few more since I have been here. I believe someone is targeting anyone who had anything to do with exploiting the kids or arranging the marriages."

"Give me an example." I was going to have to be the one to focus this overly broad narrative.

"There was a family named Fulton that died in a suspicious house fire. They were court-appointed foster parents and most of the kids in their care were married off or adopted by some pretty sketchy characters. I think somebody set the fire to shut them up before they could talk."

"Talk to who? Was anybody asking questions about the marriages at the time?" I was going to lose interest if he kept bouncing between revenge killings and witness tampering. I did not want my mind to start spinning at the same speed as the tires on the XLR. I was keeping an eye on Chance to see whether he would get nervous about my rounding unbanked turns with no shoulder at eighty miles an hour.

"The FBI came to town with a warrant for the Fultons' computer a month or so before they died in that fire. The story is that Sheriff Dardenne called to tell them to get rid of the computer. He was the sheriff before Mazant." The detective sounded like he was about to begin to unravel a conspiracy theory I had no reason to believe. I was still prepared to ask the questions that he brought me here to answer just to kill time. "And what do you believe was on the computer the FBI wanted?'

"Supposedly, it was a lot of kiddie porn. The Fultons may have been making films to show that the kids in their care would do anything that an adult wanted them to do." The Fultons were lucky to be dead. It meant I would never get a chance to question them as I would have liked.

"Why would Sheriff Dardenne have tipped them off?" I had already formed a poor opinion of the local law enforcement, but this was a new low.

"Someone told him to. That someone had to be in a position to make him do it, unless he was already part of what was going on. He was also the sheriff who taught Mazant to ignore anything that happened between Kirk and Gwen Donovan."

"Okay, let me get this straight," I sighed. I hate convoluted theories. Most situations involving human nature can be summed up in three or four sentences. Conspiracies invariably give people too much credit for being able to think ahead. "You believe that the Fultons made kiddie porn to market children Senator Donovan and Judge Aubuchon intended to marry off or to put up for adoption, and you believe Sheriff Dardenne kept the Fultons from being arrested by the FBI to protect the senator. Is that about it?"

"That doesn't sound plausible?"

"I am a huge fan of coincidence, but my father used to say that not everything in a small town is as connected as it seems to be." I only meant to suggest he reconsider the sort of connections he was making. The accusations he had made so far were going to be very hard to prove without a confession.

"Tell me this, do you believe Senator Donovan is willing to have people killed to protect himself from a scandal?" Chance challenged me.

"Would he have people killed? Maybe. He definitely would not do so himself," I allowed. I know first-hand that we are all capable of doing some very bad things to protect our family or our own interests.

"Well, five people have died in weird ways in the last few years, including Kirk Donovan." Chance had the strength of conviction on his side. I realized I was here as a devil's advocate and not just an audience.

"Okay, I'll play along. Who were they?"

"Two counselors from a summer camp for poor kids the senator and some of his cronies used to own drowned when their cars ran into Bayou Beausejour. That happens less often than you would think, and almost always to anyone connected to that summer camp. Like Kirk." Chance began counting off his list of suspicious deaths. "The judge who used to have Aubuchon's job fell down the stairs in his house after having some sort of seizure. The local coroner wrote it off as a heart attack because the guy had just had one a week or so earlier."

"That does happen, you know. What did the autopsy show?"

"That was the autopsy. The coroner knew he had heart problems and wrote it off as a heart attack. The law says he had to do an autopsy, but it doesn't say it has to be a good one." Unexplained deaths are far less common than poorly investigated ones. I felt relieved to know that Kirk was in the hands of the state medical examiner.

"The deputy who investigated the death of the Fultons had an allergic reaction to a pasta dish he ate. Someone used walnuts to make a pesto sauce and didn't tell him."

"That could just be an accident." It was an obvious case of criminal abuse of a classic recipe, but that isn't an actual crime.

"True enough," Chance conceded. "But, his death left Sheriff Dardenne in position to finish writing the report that was released the next week. Do you think there might have been a few edits involved?"

"Point taken."

"The last one to die before Kirk was the district attorney Gabouri replaced." Chance began to wrap up his dissertation. This particular death seemed implausible as a homicide.

"The guy choked on a sandwich!"

"And what did each of the other four deaths have in common? Suffocation. The first two guys drowned. The judge's wife said he complained that he couldn't breathe just before he grabbed at his heart. The DA was alone in his office when he needed to have someone give him the Heimlich maneuver. Sure, they could have all died in accidents or from natural causes, but what are the odds of so many people all dying from some form of suffocation?" Chance finally made a compelling point.

"Assuming you are correct about a serial killer being on the loose, why do you think it is Senator Donovan?" I was open to suggestion.

"He has the most to lose if anyone begins poking into the number of underage marriages he arranged. Times are changing, and people have begun to think differently about older men getting married to much younger girls. The marriages are bad, but imagine having to defend arranging one for a profit." Chance made yet another compelling point.

"That would explain why he told Sheriff Dardenne to tip off the Fultons," I said. I caught myself being pulled into his theory. "And you're sure that the computer had child pornography on it?"

"That is supposedly what the warrant the FBI showed to Sheriff Dardenne claimed. It was why he knew bad things would happen if they were caught with it," Chance pressed his argument. "The child pornography is the key to all of this. What do you think molesters do with kids when they start to grow up? A two year old doesn't know right from wrong, but a ten year old victim will start asking questions and might even start fighting back."

"I'd like to think so," I muttered. Very bad images were forming in my mind. I wanted this conversation to end soon.

"When a girl hits puberty abusers have to be more careful about what they do with her. Getting rid of her might be the best solution." I realized his long-winded explanation about the mysterious deaths was leading to something larger he still wasn't sure he wanted to share.

"So, how do you get rid of a pubescent girl?" There were other questions about young girls I wanted to ask him, questions like, 'Why would you sleep with another man's underage wife?'

"Or a young boy," Chance added. This was a wrinkle I had not even considered. Of course there were abused boys, as well.

"It's legal to marry a girl under the age of sixteen if the parents and a judge agree to it, but young boys can be adopted at any age. Imagine a town where you could pick out a child who was already broken in to your sick tastes." Chance's picture of quaint little Donovan, Louisiana was becoming very dark.

"Or a town where exploiting child abuse was a family business?" I offered. Ugly as this was, the pieces to his theory were beginning to fit together.

"How about one run by a powerful state senator with a law practice specializing in marrying off young girls and putting sexually abused young boys up for adoption? Chester Donovan controls the laws and judges necessary to keep child marriages legal. Every sheriff in the parish is hand-picked and told to keep an eye out for children to exploit. Imagine if someone could make a deal for a kid where the parents only had to admit to Sheriff Mazant that they were not fit to be parents. Sheriff Mazant could put their kids into the care of the same court that helps to marry them off. A few weeks later the parents might be spending a lot of cash." Chance finally laid out the essence of his theory. It made sense, and it pulled all of the levers of corruption at the senator's disposal. It also fit the exact scenario of what happened to Belle's friend.

"I could see where the Donovans and their judges would want to protect such a lucrative business."

"I think Senator Donovan realized he had dodged a bullet when the FBI left empty handed. Those guys never give up, and sooner or later they were going to find somebody to implicate the senator and his son to save their own skin. Senator Donovan can't afford to have anyone in a position to blackmail or testify against him." Chance's voice held a sharp edge. "So, is this finally beginning to sound plausible to you?"

"This might also explain Kirk's fake racing trophies. I just ran this highway about as fast I dared, and it would not have prepared him for any actual race course. Kirk might have taken over the marketing if his father decided not to replace the Fultons. Maybe they decided to make it more of a family business. Kirk could have been taking the kiddie porn around to market kids to his prospective clients whenever he claimed to be at a race. This would also explain why his house was scrubbed down before we got there." I hated how well the evidence supported Chance's theory. "But now you are suggesting that Senator Donovan has decided to shut things down, and want me to believe he killed those counselors, burned up the Fultons, killed a judge and a district attorney, drowned his only son, and then tried to kill Judge Aubuchon. It's a big reach."

"But you know I am right, don't you?" Chance was a true believer in his own religion. "And, like I said, it doesn't have to be the senator doing it. He could have hired someone to take care of all this for him."

"When did you start to work on this theory of yours?" I began to look for any places to punch holes in his narrative. The detective had only been in Saint Xavier Parish for the past four or five years to the best of my knowledge.

"I heard Chief Theriot mumble something at the funeral for District Attorney Lepanto. He said Raziel probably killed him."

"And you thought he was naming the person who he believed killed the guy." I could see why.

"Well, yeah. Then I figured out he was actually saying Lepanto was the victim of a serial killer."

"Because someone told you that Raziel was the name of the angel responsible for keeping secrets?" It was the first time in over a decade that I had used any of the intense religious indoctrination from my time in a high school run by Jesuit priests.

"Well, no. I had to look up the name," Chance sheepishly admitted.

"How did you put together the theory you just told me? A lot of that happened before you got here."

"I had some help. Actually, it was more of a guiding hand," he said, but seemed to be keeping his source secret.

"Let me guess," I said and looked at his face to see if he gave away the identity when I hit the name. "It could have been Sheriff Mazant or Police Chief Theriot. Maybe they didn't want to have to keep covering up murders."

He didn't react to either of these names. I did not believe they were conflicted about any role they played anyway. A new name came to me.

"Crystal Franks. She seems to know everything that is going on in town. Tell me is wasn't her."

"Okay, I'll tell you it wasn't," Chance agreed, but his smile only confirmed my worst fears. "Crystal had some suspicions of her own and she offered to help me use the newspaper's archives to piece everything together. She found obituaries for people who might be connected, and I went through the old police files. Things don't get investigated right around here, let me just leave it at that. Crystal also made me aware of the number of kids who change hands. She helped me go through the local newspaper archives to make a list of all of the kids who appeared in any of the photographs or articles about the camp. We compared every announcement of an underage marriage or adoption to the names of the kids in those pictures. All but a handful of the kids who changed hands were at that camp."

"That's a lot of coincidence for any one parish," I was now willing to think his findings were credible because of how he went about his research. It was how I might have done the same thing, but this was only circumstantial. It also happened to be compelling. "Who is still alive that is on your list of people left to kill?"

"Besides Senator Donovan?" he asked. I just nodded my head. "Well, thanks to you, Judge Aubuchon is still alive. That leaves Sheriff Dardenne and Judge Rogers from the summer camp days, and Kirk's legal secretary if you believe the senator is really going to scorch the earth to hide what he did." Chance rattled these names off so quickly that it took me a moment to catch Judge Rogers was on his list of suspected local child abusers.

"Judge Rogers? The man who asked me to look for his daughter?" I had to be sure we were speaking of the same man.

"Yeah, he owned the piece of land where the summer camp was located."

"He built his house where that camp used to be?" I didn't want to validate the accusation.

"No," Chance shook his head. "The camp used to be where those rental cabins are that we passed back there."

I had not paid much attention to the sign for the cabins, but I would give it a lot more attention on our next pass.

"Where is Sheriff Dardenne these days?" I wanted to get back to the big picture and away from its specific details.

"Weldon is in the old folks' home east of town. He is damn near blind and deaf, and he supposedly has dementia. That isn't near enough of a living hell for a man who did what he did to those kids." Detective Chance was clearly upset that the retired sheriff was not already roasting in the fire of some concentric ring of Dante's Inferno.

"Crystal couldn't have known the extent of the child abuse that happened before she, or you, arrived here. It seems to have been a very well-kept secret among the locals. What made her suspicious?" Surely a lot of other locals died as well in the span of time this handful of notable locals passed away.

"She had pieced together a big part of this after she started reading the newspaper's archives. She said she started out wanting to have a better idea who everyone in town is, but then she started reading the wedding announcements and noticed how many young girls were getting married to older men from all over the country. Chief Theriot's comment made me start to think that Lepanto choking on his lunch was no accident, and she showed me what she had found when I went to look up anything about the DA's past that might point me to who might have killed him. Crystal said she had followed things as far as she could, but that it was going to take someone with access to the sheriff's records to confirm everything. I started looking at the old case files on the weekend, when almost nobody is around. It seemed pretty obvious that a serial killer was at work, but the only one who has a reason to want all these people dead is the senator, if he is trying to cover his tracks."

"Do you really think Senator Donovan is prepared to get his hands this dirty just to protect his reputation?" This was the weakest part of his hypothesis as far as I could tell.

"It doesn't have to be him, Maybe it is someone who works for him," Chance dismissed my own dismissal.

"You work for him." This was not an idle observation.

"So does your uncle. In fact, cleaning up messes like this is what someone like Felix Deveraux supposedly does the best, right? Do you think it is too farfetched to believe your uncle hired a couple of hitmen to work down a list of people that the senator handed him?"

"I'm going to say yes because he is my uncle." I had never considered the reasons behind my Uncle Felix's interest in what he calls my 'special training.' He was very intense about recruiting me after I left the Special Forces, but he was even more so following my disavowal by the intelligence community and my abrupt return to New Orleans. I have met men in his employ that I believe are entirely capable of staging a homicide to look like a natural death or an accident. I had never really considered just how far beyond blackmail and back room negotiations my Uncle Felix was willing to go to meet the demands of a client like Senator Donovan. I decided to turn our conversation back to what was keeping me in Donovan, a place I was now all the more determined to leave as soon as possible.

"And where does Gwendolyn Donovan fit into your theory? Do you think she is dead or alive, and do you think she may have had anything to do with Kirk's death?"

"I think she killed him, probably in an argument, maybe by accident, and ran. I don't know where she would have gotten enough of her own blood to make that mess in the trunk of her car, but that proves she meant to throw us off." The detective must have been working on building a case separate from my own from the beginning. All of these disclosures about the town and its past would have eluded me entirely as they were not the focus of my attention, but now I had to consider what part the town's horrid past played in why I was here. Judge Rogers' own involvement in this might be why I was the detective chosen to look for his daughter. "What do you think?"

"I think I need some time to digest everything you just told me. Overall, it makes a little too much sense and answers a lot of questions I would never have thought to ask. Lend me your notes when we get back to town and I will give you a better assessment in a day or two." I wasn't about to tell him where I planned to take the file, or whose opinion I would seek.

We both fell silent as we gathered our own thoughts when I turned back onto the main highway and headed into Donovan. It seemed much more like an omen than perfect timing when it began to rain the instant we entered the city limits.

Fifty-Three

The head of the FBI's office in New Orleans, Special Agent in Charge Michael Conroy, and I have a troubled professional relationship on the best of days. He is convinced that I murdered a rogue FBI agent after discovering the man shot my father and left his body to rot in a swamp. I have never answered the accusation, but have also been very careful not to brag about having had a hand in the agent's fiery one-car accident close to where my father's bones allegedly remain to this day. I have also provided information to Conroy anonymously that has helped his career, and I admit that each of the tips served my own purposes, as well.

Wild conspiracy theories about Louisiana's most powerful political family operating a child sex trafficking ring, and the possibility of a state senator being a serial killer was the very sort of thing SAC Conroy has come to expect from me when I appear on his doorstep. The man works seven days a week, and I knew he would be in his office when I arrived there unannounced just after two o'clock Saturday afternoon. I was sure he was aware that I was trying to find Gwendolyn Rogers, and that he was also aware Gwen had gone from being a missing person to a suspect in her husband's murder because of my unique way of making a mess of things.

"What are you selling today, Holland?" Conroy shouted from the safety of his office even before I opened my mouth to ask his secretary for a moment of his time. His eyes were laser focused on the thick binder in my hand. Detective Chance had compiled a very impressive 'murder book' to support his theory.

"Not encyclopedias. How about some help closing one of your own cold cases?" I smiled at the sly grin his weekend assistant flashed me as I headed into SAC Conroy's inner sanctum.

"You came here to offer to solve a case for us? I think that gets a hard pass, Detective Holland." He laughed as he said it. I was catching him on a good day. This made me all the more worried about being the one who ruined it for him.

"Donovan, Louisiana. Ring a bell?"

"A lot of bells, none very pleasant. Have a seat, I guess. This is probably going to be one of your long ones," Conroy waved me towards the table and chairs beside the window in his office. His view down Poydras towards the river was enviable. I don't even have an office to call my own.

"I need to swap what I know for what you have on your raid of the Fultons from Donovan, and anything you might have on a sheriff's detective out there named David Chance. He came there from Houston's police department a couple of years ago and the local sheriff has stuck me with him as my liaison." I set the binder on the tabletop.

"I'll have to ask around about the detective, not everyone's reputation precedes them as yours does. The Fulton situation happened before I took over this office. The agents who worked that case are still here, and they use that warrant as a warning to our new agents about trusting their sources. I'll have to get back to you." I didn't press him to explain what he believed the agents thought they had learned. I just trusted that he would, indeed, tell me what happened. I knew I was asking him to relive the sort of failure the FBI is loath to share with outsiders. His eyes fell back upon the unmarked binder I carried under one arm. Its neatly divided sections had caught his attention and he suspected I was about to peel the scab off one of his agency's wounds.

"Now, it's your turn. What do you think you have that is worth my sharing anything?" It wasn't his best pitch, but it was a Saturday, and he hadn't expected to even be sitting down with me when he came to work.

"For one thing, I already knew about the last sheriff's role in what happened in Donovan. I have no idea how much the FBI wound up paying for ruining their suspects' stellar reputations, but I may have proof that Sheriff Dardenne was not the only one who needed to make sure you came up empty."

"I am still curious about your interest in Detective Chance. Is he hindering your investigation?"

"I wish it were that simple," I had to admit. "Today he spun a tale that made enough sense I am bringing it to you to get your opinion. I was sort of hoping you might know, or can find, something to impeach his credibility."

"What is this theory?"

"He wants me to believe that a seventy-year old state senator plans to kill everyone else involved in running a child exploitation ring." I stared at his face the entire time I spoke. I watched for the involuntary blink or shift in expression which would betray he was already aware of any part of what I came here to discuss.

Conroy maintained a neutral expression. "You are suggesting that there are both pedophiles and a serial killer on the loose in Donovan, Louisiana. It's a mighty small place to have so much big-time criminal activity, don't you think?"

"I think the Donovans and my Uncle Felix aren't going to be limited by things like time or space. Chance says that this has been going on for quite a while, but that your warrant for the Fultons' computer likely forced Senator Donovan to make changes in the operation. His theory is based on the senator and some other high profile people using a summer camp to single out children to exploit, and that individuals involved in running the camp later died from causes involving some form of suffocation. There have been too many accidental deaths among these people to be a coincidence. Two people died in car wrecks that put their cars into the bayou, smoke inhalation killed the Fultons, the parish's last DA choked on a po-boy, and Kirk Donovan drowned in his car. That's just a few of the incidents." I moved my hand and began sliding the binder towards SAC Conroy. It was all he could do not to grab it from my hands, but he tried to act as casual about its contents as he could. "The reason I ask about David Chance is that this is his binder. I heard his ideas about the trafficking and the serial killer for the first time this morning, and I can't punch enough holes in either theory to sink his conclusions. I was hoping the FBI considers him to be a pathological liar based on something he did in Houston."

"Well, I'm sorry to say that I can't do that." This was an unusually brusque answer even for Conroy. I stopped pushing the binder, and went so far as to rest my arm across it.

"Tell me what you can." I didn't care if I sounded like I was pleading.

"Captain Hammond inquired about Detective Chance a week or so ago. I called our field office in Houston to see if they knew anything. They claimed Chance tried to drag them into a homicide case that his own department had told him to leave alone. He was convinced a kid named Bradley Ladd got away with killing his own father, and that he might have killed another man as well. The second victim had claimed self-defense when he killed his teenaged wife. Chance believed Bradley may have been having affair with the dead wife. The Houston PD dropped their investigation because Chance's persistence compromised the evidence and witnesses so badly. The department agreed to fire him to settle a harassment lawsuit Bradley brought against them. I was unaware the detective had landed in Saint Xavier Parish. I don't know that there is much more to know, but I can dig a little deeper into it for you if that is what you need."

"Captain Hammond also suggested to me that Chance had an affair with the dead girl, and that his obsession with Bradley might stem from jealousy. I think Chance also might hold Bradley responsible for the girl being murdered by her jealous husband. I don't want to ask him about this directly without some idea of what the truth actually is." I was letting the FBI Special Agent get the better of me.

"Okay, like I said, I will ask around and get back to you. Can I take a look at the binder now?" Conroy tugged at it once more. This time I let him take it.

Conroy opened the binder. He ran his fingers over the divider labels and flipped his way through the binder, taking an agonizingly long twenty minutes to go through what Chance presented as evidence. Conroy took a yellow tablet from his desk at one point and began to make notes. I did my best to not interrupt him or betray my curiosity about the notes he was taking. I turned my back to him and watched an oil tanker as it waddled past the French Quarter and the Convention Center, probably taking its cargo to one of the big refineries in Norco. I didn't turn around until I heard him close the binder and his chair creak as he leaned back and gave one of his deepest sighs. Conroy's expression was not that of an FBI agent ready to dismiss a stupid idea.

"I need to stop letting you in here," he finally spoke.

"You buy it, too, don't you?" I was not sure how to feel about the top

FBI agent in Louisiana agreeing with a disgraced detective from Texas and a Louisiana State Patrol detective he loathes as much as he does me.

"I honestly do," he absently nodded his head. His thoughts were still elsewhere and having a conversation with him was going to require waiting until he finished internalizing what he had just read. Conroy eventually focused his attention on me and frowned. "What are you going to do with this? How can you even test his theory?"

"We'll have to wait and see whether or not the next person who suffocates is on Chance's list, I guess," I was not entirely kidding. I admired Judge Rogers enough that I hoped it wasn't him, but in general I hoped they all died slow, frightened deaths if Chance was correct about what the surviving names on the list had done.

"That's not funny," SAC Conroy snapped. I knew it was not something to joke about, but I also knew he felt the exact same way about pedophiles. There were pictures of his grandkids on his desk. "Seriously, what can you do to catch a senator? Taking on Senator Donovan will get you fired. Underage marriages are still legal, even if some sort of shenanigans are behind them, so trying to build a case against him for arranging any of those promises to be an uphill battle you would lose in the end. I still can't believe the state police gave you a badge, but I would hate to see you lose it over taking on someone you cannot possibly defeat."

"Chance has put a couple of years into this. I don't want to be stuck out there that long. My assignment is to locate Gwendolyn Donovan. I'll be honest, my inclination is to do nothing more than that and to leave Chance with this whole mess." I was not kidding.

"We could put together a task force if the state police ask for our help, but first the locals have to ask for yours. I don't like the idea of any serial killers getting a free pass from either of us." I had to admire Conroy's level of professionalism. He wasn't going to let vigilante justice stand, even if only a bunch of old child molesters were the victims.

"Sheriff Mazant is not about to ask for my help. I doubt he would agree with us about there being a killer on the loose. I believe he would just hire more deputies to protect the judge and the senator for as long as it took Chance to find the killer. Let it be their problem if he is right about Senator Donovan being a serial killer." I tugged the binder away from Conroy and stood up.

Apparently David Chance was going to remain an enigma for the time being. Conroy's few insights only added to the questions I had about my temporary partner. Conroy would be kept awake at night until something was done if Chance was right. It would gnaw at his gut until someone was caught, or until the killer made their way through the list in their sick head and confessed or committed suicide.

Personally, I would only be kept awake until I understood Judge Rogers's role in all of this. I was now very curious about why he left behind such a nice home, and a thriving law practice to support it, to start over in New Orleans. I could tell him, from my own bad experience, that there is no distance long enough to outrun one's past sins. There are also not enough good deeds he could ever do to balance the karma of the damage he may have inflicted upon the children of Saint Xavier Parish.

Fifty-Four

Here's the thing about the people around you. You don't really know anyone until you see them pushed to their breaking point. You will meet some people and form your opinion of them within minutes, and that vision of them might last your entire lifetime. You will meet other people and be so impressed that you will wallpaper over any flaws you discover later. Then there are those you immediately dislike, and nothing they say or do ever changes your mind, even when you realize you misjudged them. Everyone you know fits one of those categories, and it is why I trust so few people I haven't seen tested to their limits.

My negative opinion of David Chance as a person was not likely to change, but I found myself having to believe he was a far better detective than my initial impression indicated.

I absolutely believed Uncle Felix would do anything Chester Donovan asked of him, even if that was to have one or two people murdered. The cold stares the senator and I exchanged at his country club left no doubt that both of us were willing to eliminate any menace to our families. Too much blood stained my own hands not to recognize it on Senator Donovan's.

The question which confronted me as I left Conroy's office was how far Judge Rogers might go to protect himself or his family. He called on me to find Gwendolyn because he knew I could not be intimidated by the Donovans. Something made him leave his hometown after his youngest daughter married Kirk, and it may have been what kept him from protecting her from the physical and mental abuse which came with being the daughter-in-law of an influential politician. Perhaps using me to find incriminating evidence about the Donovans having orchestrated Gwen's disappearance was meant to be his absolution.

Not knowing his motive in having me assigned to the case made my phone call to inform him that Belle was in my protective custody trickier than that same call had been to Senator Donovan. For one thing, Belle would now be in Judge Rogers' jurisdiction if he wanted to play a legal wild card of his own to lay claim to her.

"Good morning, Detective. What, pray tell, made you call me on a Saturday afternoon?" I realized that justice and crime fighting kept different office hours. "You said we should only speak to each other through Gwen's attorney."

"That is true about anything involving Gwen. This is about Belle," I was surprised that he was not the one calling me about his granddaughter.

"Please, don't give me more bad news." His tone was that of a man ignorant of Belle's situation.

"I'm afraid it's a bit of both. Your granddaughter is alive and well, but I am limiting access to her until I sort out what became of her parents." I knew better than to refer to Belle as a murder suspect.

"Surely you don't think she played a role in Kirk's death or her mother's disappearance?" I noted that he no longer spoke of Gwen as being a homicide victim.

"I am concerned that whoever has harmed her parents may have Belle's name on their hit list, too."

"You believe someone targeted the entire family? Who would do that?"

"I would like to sit down and discuss that very subject tomorrow morning." I watched the second hand tick by on my watch. Five seconds is a long time to spend accepting a breakfast invitation. Ten seconds of silence was long enough to make me up the ante. "She would like for you to join us for brunch at ten o'clock tomorrow morning at Strada Ammazarre. I suggest bringing Dan Logan as well. He can represent Gwen's interests, and yours if you feel the need."

"Why would I need an attorney?" he asked. He seemed barely able to control his anger.

"I never know how anyone is going to react to a detective from the state police asking very personal questions, Your Honor. You are not a suspect, but I believe it's time you shared some things with me." No good was going to come from making him defensive before I could question him.

"I'll see the two of you tomorrow." Judge Rogers disconnected the call before I could say another word.

Fifty-Five

I took a seat at the Carousel Bar in the Monteleone Hotel just after three o'clock. I wanted to spot any advance security detail Senator Donovan or Uncle Felix put in place. Men who fit that profile entered the lobby at five o'clock to look for any advance security detail of my own. I paid my bar tab and slipped out of the hotel before anyone had the bright idea to check the bar. There was no way to leave the hotel unnoticed if teams were watching the hotel from the exterior. Parking near the hotel is a problem, which made it unlikely the security detail was positioned in parked vehicles. I quickly scanned the nearby doorways and headed back to my apartment.

I hired a limousine for an hour and asked the driver to meet me at Strada Ammazarre ten minutes before I was supposed to meet Senator Donovan at the hotel. The driver was still laughing about why he was hired as he tucked the extra fifty bucks into his pocket and followed my Cadillac station wagon to the hotel.

Senator Donovan and Uncle Felix stood in front of the hotel, surrounded by a slightly larger security detail than I counted entering the hotel earlier. I had waited at the bistro until the last minute to see if it occurred to anyone to send someone to watch me. I was very disappointed that an important state senator and my uncle were protected by bodyguards who did not see the threat posed by a man with my reputation for disruption.

"Get in. Your detail can ride in the limo. We don't want them to be part of what we need to discuss on the way," I said through the open window of my car. I used my thumb to point towards the Lincoln Town Car parked directly behind me. The senator and my uncle exchanged a couple of words, but ultimately did as I instructed. They seemed to believe that the chances of an attack were slim, and the odds of my abducting the two of them even less. All the same, I am sure the security detail were quick to threaten my hired driver with all sorts of horrible things when he drove straight ahead on Royal, with the doors locked, after I turned right at the next corner. I took a long route back to the bistro, leaving their men to try to track their phones to guess where we wound up.

"What the hell are you up to?" Uncle Felix bellowed as soon as he realized the Town Car was no longer on our rear bumper.

"I only invited the senator to dinner, but we can set another place for you," I watched their expressions in the rear view mirror. Uncle Felix figured out where we were headed when I turned on Dauphine. He assured the senator that they were not being kidnapped. I noted that he also did not call the detail to inform them where we could be found. I assumed this was their last day working for him.

Our maître d', Joaquin Guerra, waved us past the line at the host stand and had our waitress lead us to a private dining room on the mezzanine level. This room seated only eight guests, and I had asked Joaquin to schedule Belinda as our waitress. She has the very tightest lips about what she sees and hears, and this was going to be an evening that required all possible discretion. Uncle Felix grasped the situation when he entered the room and discovered Belle was flanked by Tulip and Katie. He tugged the senator's sleeve and whispered something, undoubtedly a warning of some sort, into his ear as I leaned over to kiss Katie on the cheek. I was very glad to see her, but I also wanted to further emphasize the forces I had arrayed against the senator and my uncle. They joined us at the table with the expressions of skilled tacticians who knew when they had been outflanked.

"It's nice to see you, Chester," Belle said and held out a hand towards her grandfather. He gave her a wan smile and squeezed her hand for just a moment.

"I see you brought your own backup." My uncle's tone was not as pleasant as the smile he forced upon his face.

"A girl's gotta eat," Tulip taunted. She and Katie were as much in their element as the older men were at a loss. I took a moment to introduce the senator to my sister and to Katie, including her job title, and then motioned to Belinda that she should begin filling everyone's glass with champagne. The three women had already helped themselves to the better part of a bottle before we arrived.

"A toast to families." I needed to break the mood. This sounded neutral but, in a room full of this much familial dysfunction, the toast was a joke.

"And the safe return of Belle," the senator added. I was unclear whether he had some darker meaning.

"I was only in Colorado," Belle's comment was funny enough to provide the much needed laugh.

Belinda passed menus to the senator and Uncle Felix. The women had all dined at the bistro enough to already know what they wanted. Belinda wrote down everyone's food order before she left us to the first round of what promised to be a long fight.

"When will you be coming home?" the senator asked Belle. His eyes were focused on me, however.

"I don't know. I am still waiting for permission to return to Tulane. Cooter seems to think someone is out to get me," Belle responded.

"Cooter?" the senator was genuinely confused.

"That's me." I held up my hand. "My father's sense of humor is a topic for another day. I think we can all agree that Belle's safety is our utmost concern. I have no way to know how much danger she faces until I learn the story behind her father's death and her mother's disappearance."

"I can protect her," Senator Donovan snapped, undoubtedly in part because he needed to reassert his sense of being in charge of the situation.

"Senator, with all due respect, I just outsmarted your security detail, and nobody at this table thinks I am particularly bright," I tried to soften this blow to his ego as best I could. I only wanted to make the point that he was not able to protect Belle. I wasn't going to say I was protecting her from him as much as I was from any unknown threats.

"True dat," Tulip and Katie said almost in unison. I did not need their help to make my point. Uncle Felix was quick to move his napkin to hide his grin.

"Well, the two of us have private family matters to discuss," the senator persisted.

"Such as her term paper?" I wasn't going to act like the room wasn't overcrowded with elephants. I saw any number of topics the two of them needed to discuss, and Belle would be smart to have Tulip at her side for most of them.

"What do you know of that?" the senator barked.

"We have all read the paper, Senator," Tulip once again took the lead. "There was no good way to own slaves, but the Deverauxs still managed to find the most reprehensible manner of exploiting them. The Donovans built their fortune as two-bit con men, but how our families made their fortunes and got their start in politics is of little more than historical interest. What harm can the actions of our ancestors do to us now?"

"Are you truly so naïve?" Uncle Felix snapped at her. The senator was even less pleased to discover such a dark family secret was a topic of casual conversation.

"That's true, but do either of you really believe anyone who knows anything about your families believes your ancestors were saints?" Katie spoke up. Luckily, Belinda timed her return with our appetizers perfectly.

"Well, you are not handing that paper over to any professor at Tulane University," Senator Donovan said, ignoring Belinda's presence.

"I have to if I am going to pass the course," Belle pointed out.

"I believe something can be worked out," Uncle Felix weighed in. Of course he believed that. Making those arrangements is how he makes a living.

"I have had an offer to publish it as a book." Belle dropped this bombshell on all of us. Tulip flashed me a bemused look. I assumed she had made a call to our father's former literary agent.

"Oh, no, that is definitely off the table," Senator Donovan roared and nearly levitated from his seat.

"I don't want to jinx this. I have not said yes to them yet," Belle's response sounded like she had a very good idea the senator would threaten to sue anyone who placed his family's dirty laundry on a bookshelf.

"The book deal is not why we are here." I saw nothing but acrimony and more threats coming if this topic was not immediately shelved. "You wanted to see that your granddaughter is alive and well. She needs to know that you care about her, and will be there for her if it turns out something has happened to her mother."

"Of course I am." Senator Donovan shifted gears more smoothly than his son ever did in his Ford GT. Belle also seemed to reconsider the wisdom of poking a bull the size of her grandfather.

"I just want to go home as soon as possible. I see your point that I may not be safe, so I trust you to tell me when I can go," Belle sighed and shifted her gaze from her simmering grandfather to me.

"And I want to come home as well. I am doing all I can to find your mother, and learn who killed your father. But, I am being slowed down by obstacles being thrown in my path."

"Such as?" Senator Donovan seemed pleased that he was going to finally be able to ask me questions, rather than hope Sheriff Mazant or Detective Chance brought him second-hand information.

"For one thing, I am only beginning to figure out who plays for what team. I realized Sheriff Mazant and Chief Theriot are in your pocket the day I got there. I only recently learned that the detective Sheriff Mazant saddled me with was hired at your personal request." My disclosure visibly rattled both of the men sitting across from me. It confirmed my suspicion that Uncle Felix played some role in David Chance moving to Donovan. "How am I to find out what happened when there is campaign to keep me from learning what I need to know?"

"What you need to know didn't happen until the night you were assigned to the case," the senator declared.

"Are you saying twenty years of spousal abuse and decades of covering up child abuse in the parish played no part in what happened to Belle's parents?" Katie kept a straight face as she nibbled at the appetizers.

"Nobody abused this young woman. Did they?" The senator pointed at Belle. His tone of voice was meant to indicate there was only one right answer to the question.

"Not physically." Belle spoke up. The short time she had spent with the women flanking her taught her about resolve. "But, I lived in a house full of abuse. My dad beat my mother almost every night. He also married my friends off to men at least twice their age when I was growing up. How is that not abuse?"

"Don't be silly," Senator Donovan scoffed. "Who is going to take care of a young girl who got herself pregnant or whose parents can't take care of her?"

"Nobody gets themselves pregnant," Tulip cut in. "That sort of patrimonial argument has always been a way for men to justify what they do before they leave the women they harm to clean up the mess."

"This isn't the time, Tulip." Uncle Felix held both hands up before his chest. He cut short the scathing response the senator was about to deliver for Tulip intruding upon his lecture to his granddaughter.

"Let's just say that I am at a point where it seems I am finding more and more people to question, and more and more reasons that someone could have wanted to do your son and daughter-in-law harm. I imagine one or two of them might consider targeting Belle or yourself if they have the opportunity."

"Who do you suspect?"

"Today?" I was not about to answer the question. "Today I would include anyone you or your son married off or arranged an adoption for. I would toss in any child who attended the summer camp you ran, and their parents and siblings."

"That's almost the entire parish," Uncle Felix needlessly did the math for all of us.

"Now you understand why I think Belle is safest anywhere *but* Saint Xavier Parish. I suggest you spend as much time possible in Baton Rouge, as well." I was not playing with the senator this time, and the way he stared at me for a long moment indicated he took my advice seriously.

"So, your theory is that someone is targeting my family over things my son and I did that are entirely legal?" He seemed to be grappling harder with the idea that he did anything wrong than he was that his life might be in danger. No politician wants to be challenged about their ethics, although they are usually the first thing they lose after taking office.

"Would you like to explain to the senator how it is that something legal may not seem to be fair or ethical to someone on the losing side?" I directed the rhetorical question to my sister. Far too many of her clients came to her as the likely loser in a fight against far more powerful opponents.

"We'll discuss this a little later," Uncle Felix said and gave me his devil-at-the-crossroads smile. "The senator is having some difficulty understanding why his son was targeted at the same point in time his wife went missing along with all of her possessions. Does it not seem plausible to believe this could simply be a much easier homicide case to solve than this mess you seem to imagine exists?"

"It is certainly to someone's advantage to get me to believe so. I have not ruled out the possibility that Gwendolyn played some role in her husband's death, but she could have easily stabbed or shot him in the midst of one of his beatings if she wanted him dead. She had no reason to ruin a perfectly good Mercedes to get rid of someone like Kirk."

"How dare you!" Senator Donovan was clearly at the end of his rope. He was outfoxed, outgunned, and well out of his element. His control over the situation and environment was lost so long as he stayed seated at this table. He had a very tough decision to make about whether to retreat or remain, because Belinda had just set a twelve ounce medium rare beef filet and a plate of fettuccine alfredo in front of him.

"Would you care for a glass of wine to go with that?" I taunted him one last time. "We offer a very nice Barbaresco."

Katie kicked me even before Uncle Felix waved his cutlery above his own plate of food to warn me to stop prodding the senator. It occurred to me that he would have some pointed questions of his own for his client during their drive back to Baton Rouge. My purpose here had been to make the senator aware that I was going to turn over rocks he felt were immovable, and that what lay hidden beneath the heaviest ones was going to see the light of day. His minions were incapable of delaying the inevitable, and he was beginning to see I was not the sort of state employee he could boss around. I was going to hear from Captain Hammond very soon, and I would have to assure him that I could behave myself. We would both know I was lying.

Fifty-Six

I hoped brunch with Judge Rogers would go better than our dinner with Senator Donovan. The only things that seemed to have been resolved by the end of the previous evening was that everyone left the table feeling threatened, and that nobody took anyone else's threats very seriously. Uncle Felix was not about to let the senator have me removed from a case he knew I would continue to pursue, but without the restraints imposed by my badge. Belle's threat of publishing the tell-all history of our families made a better bargaining chip than it did a book. I needed to focus on the parish's history of underage marriages. I was now convinced that this was the spark for the fire burning inside whoever was responsible for Kirk's death and Gwen's disappearance.

Ugly as the topic was, it was going to have to be a focus of my conversation with Judge Rogers. I saw no reason, however, to discuss his involvement in what happened in St. Xavier Parish while Belle was at the table.

"You've come alone." I noted the absence of his daughter's attorney as he approached the end of the bar.

"I'm all the attorney I need," he said and grinned. It was not particularly convincing bravado. I laughed all the same and pointed him towards the kitchen.

"I have never been here for brunch," the judge commented as we entered the bustling kitchen and took seats at the chef's table. Belle and Tulip were already seated and sipping mimosas. "I also never knew about this cozy set-up."

"It can get a little noisy in here during a weekend night, but it gives us some privacy as well as a floor show." I was doing my best to be a convivial host for as long as I could.

"How are you doing, young lady?" Judge Rogers asked Belle. He ignored Tulip's presence, but I was sure he understood why she was sitting beside Belle.

"As well as can be expected, Grandpa." I studied her face to see if this was her subtle way to slap back against being having been called a young lady. He seemed to take it as an endearment. "Detective Holland has convinced me I may be in enough danger that I am doing whatever he tells me to do."

"That is quite a feat," the judge congratulated me and broke into a wide grin.

"We'll see how long it lasts," I said to keep the mood light. Belle had been instructed not to inform either of her grandfathers that she was living in my apartment above the bistro. It was best to let them each assume that I brought her there because it was a place I felt was safe.

"Are you back at Tulane?" His question reminded me how far out of the loop I was keeping the judge.

"No. Tulip has arranged for me to receive my lessons online for the time being. I do miss being on campus, though," Belle explained. It wasn't hard to imagine the four walls of my place beginning to close in.

"How much longer do you anticipate holding my granddaughter in your custody?" The judge seemed to be trying to make a point with the way he phrased his inquiry. He makes his living by being precise in his wording, so any unspoken words were just as important as those he used. He made a point not to refer to our current arrangement as being protective custody. He was letting me know that he saw her as being my prisoner.

"Locating her mother will go a long way towards my allowing Belle to leave my custody. Right now I am divided between my duty to protect her from whoever harmed her parents and having to decide whether or not she had anything to do with their fates." Belle and I had this conversation enough times that she no longer took offense to the implication she may have played a role in her father's death or her mother's disappearance. The judge, however, was caught off guard.

"Surely you don't believe Belle had anything to do with any of that," he protested. It wasn't a loud protest, and it wasn't one that seemed intended to dismiss the possibility.

"What I believe isn't germane. It may even be counter-productive." I didn't explain myself, despite the expression on the judge's face.

"Children have killed their parents before, and the odds of Belle's parents being targeted by entirely separate sets of strangers on the very same day are barely lower than Belle being responsible. It's a mess, and I may only be getting started on sorting it out."

"What do you know so far?"

"I cannot discuss that with you," I didn't even try to act apologetic about this. He was a judge, and well aware of the legal problems that would come with my answering any questions about an open investigation involving his own family. "Here is what I can say, though. I believe this is somehow tied to the past, and that some dirty secret the entire town seems to be keeping might be proving too much for someone to handle."

"What sort of a secret are you suggesting?" the judge once again failed to sound properly dismissive of my suggestions. He could have easily said I was being melodramatic or getting off track if he had no idea of what it was I might have uncovered.

"I'm sorry, but this isn't the time or place to go into detail." I did not bother to act regretful, and the judge chose not to make a scene.

"I guess I am going to be here a lot longer then," Belle sighed with perfect teen angst. We all enjoyed a good laugh and I appreciated her trying to relieve the tension.

Ginger, our waitress once again, suggested we help ourselves to the brunch buffet rather than hand us menus. I saw how busy Tony was on the cooks' line and knew this was not a time to insist on preferential treatment. Tulip led the judge and Belle through the double doors leading into the packed dining room.

The dining room was louder than the kitchen. A hundred conversations were competing with the jazz combo playing just to the left of the host stand. The room was also filled with the odors from the array of food spread across the tables just outside the kitchen doors. The options included bacon, multiple kinds of sausage in link and patty form, grits and grillades, and our signature chicken and andouille hash. Shredded hash browns, Miss J's buttermilk biscuits, and cream gravy were the items the food runners had the hardest time keeping stocked. A punch bowl at the end of this first table was filled with a gingered fruit compote. There were additional stations offering three kinds of eggs, including the option of made-to-order omelets. A steam table next to the omelet station offered piping hot beignets, battered French toast made with day-old brioche, and warm calas pastries stuffed with boudin. The carving station held ham and fried chicken, smoked salmon, and a large beef roast. A steam table beside the array of meats offered four vegetables and mirliton dressing. Chef Tony loves the culinary challenge presented by this weekly feast.

Judge Rogers and Belle seemed to be at ease in one another's company in a way that she did not share with the senator. I imagined that these two saw one another rarely other than Thanksgiving and Christmas. I kept one ear open for them to slip up and mention times the two of them met while she was at Tulane. The other ear was tuned to Tony's verbal barrage upon his cooks as they struggled to keep the buffet line stocked. He and I locked eyes at one point and he smiled to let me know he was in his element and that his cooks were up to the task without his odd outbursts. His sharp tongue, even in a new language, was part of why I enjoyed listening to him. His wild malapropisms were why his cooks provoked him.

"Can you spare a minute or two?" I asked the judge as Belle and Tulip excused themselves from the table once the plates were cleared. Tulip and Belle planned to shop in the nearby French Market until I escorted Judge Rogers out of the building. It was the best way to keep him from suspecting his granddaughter was hiding out two floors above the bistro's kitchen.

"Of course I can." The judge sounded annoyed at the very idea that he was too busy to help with my investigation into his daughter's disappearance.

I led him to the far end of the bistro's L-shaped cypress bar. We could watch the weekend foot traffic on Decatur Street while we spoke, and Tulip could watch us through the large plate glass windows to know when the coast was clear to return Belle to her gilded cage. Jason set tall glasses of bloody Morgan before us. This is the bistro's popular brunch cocktail, replacing the vodka in a bloody Mary with spiced rum. The flavorful rum gives the usually acidic cocktail a mellow finish and subtle sweetness.

Jason is our only male bartender, and he brought a lot of regulars with him when we hired him. He had worked at a bar in Mid-City that didn't survive its own recovery from Hurricane Katrina. A distressing number of places which had been in business for decades failed to regain their footing in the first years after the storm, largely because the population that could not afford to return, or were afraid to return, were replaced with people wholly unfamiliar with the city's landmark bars and cafes. New Orleans seemed destined to become another place that lost its culture to new-comers intent upon rebuilding the city in the image of wherever it was they came from.

"I don't know if it is a lead, or how it fits into Gwendolyn's situation, but I need to know about the summer camp." This was going to be a touchy subject, so I decided to approach it slowly.

"Summer camp." He didn't phrase his response as a question, but I nodded my head to let him know he heard me right the first time. "I am not sure I know what summer camp you are referring to, Cooter."

Casually using my first name seemed like it might be his way to avoid turning my inquiries into formal questioning. I had no intention of reading him his rights, and I would be at a loss for how to proceed if he declared he wanted an attorney present to discuss events from so long ago. The statute of limitations was long expired on anything he might have done wrong unless he had killed someone. I could not imagine the parish would have the same level of indifference towards someone murdering children that they seemed to have about strangers sexually exploiting them.

"You owned the property where Senator Donovan built a summer camp for poor kids to go for a week or so at a time. This was at least twenty years ago, so you may have a little trouble remembering what all happened." I was willing to play along with jogging his memory, and I even acted like I had no idea of exactly when the camp was in operation or what might have caught my attention.

"I haven't thought about that place in years. If I remember right, we called it Camp Dumaine. Yeah, that's it. I can't believe I even remember the name, it's been so long." He didn't sound all that strained to pull such an obscure name out of his memory. I remembered this was the name of the camp on the shirt Kirk wore when he was pulled from the canal. It was curious that Kirk wore what looked like a new T-shirt from a long defunct summer camp. I could only assume it must have been a special place for him. This created a fresh question about why Detective Chance didn't comment on the shirt when he saw the crime scene photographs if the camp was ground zero for his conspiracy theory.

"Dumaine? How the heck did you come up with that name?" I only knew Dumaine as a street name in the French Quarter.

"It was the name of a packet steamer that used to run up and down the bayou. They carried as much weight in pecans as they did cotton." The judge's explanation made a lot more sense than any theory I might have developed. "Anyway, the boat ran aground near where the camp was built years later. We pretended to be pirates or captains on the wreck when I was growing up. Senator Donovan ordered it burned during our last summer. It had become too dangerous to play on."

"I am sure he just wanted to be sure the kids were kept safe." It was a purely offhand statement, but I could not ignore the way the judge's brow creased when I said it. I had struck a nerve, and realized then that he knew what I really wanted to talk about.

"You really are pretty clever," Judge Rogers said after a moment of silence passed between us. "I like how you have left it up to me to tell you what went on. Are you expecting some sort of confession?"

"Confessions apply to crimes one can prosecute. I would settle for an explanation at this point." It was important that he understood I wasn't trying to trick him into any sort of legal jeopardy. It occurred to me that this was going to be difficult enough without him trying to cover for his actions or blame anyone else.

"There is no good explanation for what happened to some of those children. That camp ruined many lives, and it still haunts me that I had any part in what went on." The judge gripped his glass with white knuckles and swallowed half the cocktail, daring me to pursue a subject he had just made clear would be personally painful to him.

"How did it ruin your life?" I could not forgive or forget any sins he chose not to share with me. I was offering him a chance to unburden himself.

"It cost me my home. It cost me my daughter, and it might have cost me my granddaughter if it were not for you. Thank you for finding her." Judge Rogers obviously had no idea about how I came to be Belle's protector. This was not the time for me to be modest. I reached beneath my blazer and acted as though I were scratching an itch, but in fact I turned on a micro-recorder. The tape would be inadmissible as evidence, but I needed to record what Judge Rogers was about to tell me to pluck out any possible leads.

"Let's break this down into smaller pieces, shall we?" I suggested with an even tone. Jason was bringing us a fresh round of drinks. I signaled him to hold back. "Tell me about starting the camp."

"I worked as an attorney in Lester Donovan's law practice after I graduated from Loyola. That was Chester's father. I filed a lot of the paperwork that led to children being placed in the care of the court. That was the first step in them being married or adopted. Anyway, Chester approached me about using a piece of land I owned to build a place where poor kids could spend part of their summer. He made it sound like we were going to run the sort of place our own kids got to go. He had the backing of everyone he and his father had put into office, and a number of other businessmen. It wasn't like I could say no, anyway. Staying employed meant not getting on the wrong side of the Donovans."

"The camp sounds like it was a noble idea," I said, without any sarcasm or back-handed sense of judgement. The idea as he presented it did sound very generous and positive for the community. I understood his dilemma with crossing the Donovan clan. "So, what went wrong?"

"Who said anything went wrong?" the judge was quick to demand. I hastily estimated the amount of alcohol he had consumed with his meal and took note of how white his knuckles were on the cocktail glass. A drunken confession was not what I was looking to pull from him, but it was clearly what I was about to get. He must have known this conversation was coming after I deflected his earlier question.

"You did, your Honor," I quietly reminded him. I pushed him back into the story before he lost his momentum. "Okay. You donated your land and they built Camp Dumaine. What happened that made you question the real purpose of the summer camp?"

"I recognized some of the names of the men who were coming to town to get married or adopt kids. They were all donors to the camp." I hated that I needed to interrupt him, especially once I saw where he was headed. I just needed to get every detail on tape as we went along.

"The summer camp was funded in part by people with no connection to Donovan?"

"Right, but they did all have some connection to the Donovan family. I was slow to recognize the nature of the connections." Judge Rogers was obviously still beating himself up over what he saw as a personal failure.

"What was the connection you missed?"

"The only purpose of the camp was to find young girls and boys who could be exploited." He said this as though it were obvious. "They used to get the boys and girls to swim naked and took pictures of them. We had them put on plays where they acted out scenes clearly meant for adults, with kissing and touching. It was so open that I never gave any of it a thought, and none of the kids ever objected. Later on I found out the camp counselors told all of them that they would be sent home, and that their brothers and sisters would never get to come to the camp, if they told any of the grown-ups no."

"No to what?" I realized I was questioning him in the tone of voice I used with a criminal suspect. He was responding as though he were in confession at St. Louis Cathedral just a few blocks away.

"Anything. The Donovans ran the camp. They hired the counselors, and some of them were already known around town for trying to have sex with underage girls. The Donovans also arranged the large donations from men who married or adopted kids the Donovans invited to the camp."

"Adopted?"

"Men adopt young boys. I only realized later that they might adopt them for the very same reason other men want to marry very young girls. Their tastes were a little different." We both found we needed a drink, as what his words made me imagine settled into my thoughts.

"Can you explain how a child went from summer camp to be married or adopted by strangers who did not even live in Donovan?" I had heard one version of this, but I still needed to hear it from an actual participant.

"Chester would send pictures and movies he took at the camp to anyone who donated money to the camp. A couple of months later Sheriff Dardenne would get an anonymous tip about one of these children being sexually abused by someone in their household. Sheriff Dardenne's investigations never resulted in any arrests. That was because the parents were often the source of the tip that led to their kid being hauled away. The kids I saw in court were usually surprised to find out what was about to happen, but they never tried to get out of it. Now I see that they were only afraid to say anything because the adults they should have been able to look to for help put them in the situation." Judge Rogers began to cry and he finished the rest of his drink in another single gulp. I signaled Jason that it was time to let the judge have a refill. Alcohol was the only sedation I had at my disposal.

"You helped set up a summer camp that was used to recruit young girls and boys for rich pedophiles. You worked for a powerful man who expected you to legalize the continued sexual abuse of these same children, and you did his bidding. It is not my place to forgive you for any of that, but it is obvious you have never forgiven yourself, either. What finally changed for you?" Judge Rogers did not argue my summation. Something must have made him see the light, and something else must have given him a window out of his situation.

"Lester Donovan died in his sleep when he was in his eighties. It left Chester in charge of their law practice, and the governor appointed him to his late father's Senate seat. That was in nineteen eighty-five. Chester wanted me to take over running the summer camp, but I said no, and I told him why. I should never have told him that." The judge smiled at Jason as the bartender set two fresh cocktails on the bar. I had barely touched my first one, but Jason replaced both to keep up the appearance that the judge and I were drinking at the same pace.

"I take it his reaction was pretty bad."

"Things got worse by the time I left town." The judge said. "Gwendolyn told us she was pregnant, and that Kirk Donovan was the father. Chester wasted no time calling her a liar, but the blood test and Kirk admitting to being the father ended that fight."

"That's why Gwendolyn married Kirk?" I needed him to say the words on tape.

"Yes. My wife was in favor of her having an abortion rather than ruin the rest of her life, but both of our families obeyed the Catholic Church. My wife divorced me the first time Kirk sent Gwen to the hospital and I did nothing about it."

"And why did you leave town?" I regretted making the interruption because it gave him time to think. I was letting myself get too hung up on getting every detail.

"I didn't fight to save Gwendolyn because I knew I would lose in any fight with the Donovans. I also would not have had any way to save her when I finally saw the chance. So, yes, I abandoned her. I turned the house you're staying in over Gwen and Kirk and moved to New Orleans. I won my seat on the bench here five years later, with Senator Donovan's endorsement." His way of closing out his long-winded, self-pitying confession struck me mostly as a vain attempt to try to distance himself from his role in what was still happening in Saint Xavier Parish.

"This is where I should tell you that you didn't do anything illegal." I took a sip from my drink instead.

"But?" Judge Rogers recoiled as the light in my eyes perceptibly dimmed. It is an involuntary physical manifestation of my capacity to internalize outrage. I developed it while serving as a shadow warrior sent to deal with villains my government considered to be beyond reason or the reach of the courts.

"Doing nothing illegal does not mean you did nothing wrong. I think you have punished yourself a great deal more than the system would have. That may not be near what Judgement Day holds for you. I cannot absolve you of your past, and I don't think I would anyway."

"What about my daughter?" Judge Rogers did not ignore what I had just said. He had more important things to worry about than my opinion of him, as did I.

"I'll bring her back to you." I didn't worry that this sounded like a promise. "And then we will have a conversation about using me to do your dirty work. I will not rain revenge down upon the Donovans for what they did to your family. I cannot absolve you of what you did to those children who needed the legal system to protect them. I will keep Belle safe, and I will find Gwen. After that, I will try to forget either of your families breathe the same air as my own."

"That's pretty harsh," Judge Rogers complained. I thought about slapping him to demonstrate exactly how harsh I could be.

"Whoever said the truth would set you free never heard the confessions of people like you." I knew this was not the reaction he had hoped to get from me after he made his carefully worded confession. He had portrayed himself as ignorant about, or unable to stop, what was happening. He was neither of those things. He was weak, and his explanation only showed me that he still feared losing his position of power more than he feared harming those who needed the protection of what power he held should have provided.

I no longer cared about the signal my sister was waiting to see before she brought Belle back to the bistro. I was finding it difficult to remain standing beside a man capable of living with what was done to those children, much less to his own family. I stormed out of the bistro, leaving him to consider what I had just said.

Fifty-Seven

I wanted to break something. I needed to break something. I was going to break something. I knew I was in a dangerous state of mind, so I walked to the corner and turned to follow Governor Nicholls Street across the French Quarter as far as Dumaine before I turned around to get my car and head Uptown. The pace of Sunday afternoon traffic was nearly enough to set me off again.

Jacob Hammel would bear the brunt of the anger and frustration I felt towards Judge Rogers. I had the sense not to take my frustrations from either emotion out on the judge, but members of any fraternity banned at Tulane was fair game as far as I was concerned. The last conversation I had with Jacob Hammel should have left him expecting at least one more visit from a detective. He was probably hoping it was going to be David Chance who called him.

He answered my call on only the third ring. I was sure Bradley's fishing companions had my phone number highlighted in their contacts. "Mister Hammel, this is Detective Holland. Where are you at this very minute?"

"I'm playing golf at Audubon Park," he said with barely a moment's hesitation. My question did not allow for much wiggle room.

"Meet me in the clubhouse in ten minutes. I have follow-up questions for you." I did not use a voice that invited challenge or question.

"Do I need an attorney?"

"You have that right. It's a golf course, you should have no trouble finding one. Just know that I will take it as a sign that you may not be answering my questions honestly." This line had made suspects over-think their options in the past. I was implying that having an attorney was the equivalent of lying to me. Jacob was not in a position to trust Tulane to overlook his running afoul of the law a second time, and most definitely not in a homicide case.

I scanned the course for any of Jacob's pals as I pulled off of Magazine Street to park at the clubhouse. Audubon Park's eighteen-hole, par sixty-two layout takes up most of the open ground. It came as no surprise that none of Jacob's fishing companions wanted me to see them with him. Any of Jacob's other friends would not want to be on a list of students I might want to question.

"I apologize for ruining your round," I said with as much sincerity as I could muster. It was nearly perfect weather for playing golf.

"I've been slicing all day. I should thank you for the excuse to stop embarrassing myself," Jacob said. He did not seem nervous to meet me, and he had not sought out an attorney to join us. "What do you want to discuss?"

"I just need to verify what I pieced together from your group's version of things. This is when suspects start to set one another up to take a fall. I don't want you to be anyone's sucker." Chance and I had not yet pieced together any version of the weekend. We were counting on one of Bradley's friends to implicate one or more of their fishing companions.

"You don't really think we would do that to one another, do you?"

"If the choice is between you and someone who did something worse going to Angola, how prepared are you to take the rap?" I had yet to sit across from anyone presented with that question who lacked justification to put their own welfare before that of their friends.

"Why are you asking me anything?" This was the sort of response I expected from him. I anticipated dealing with a boy used to getting away with things. Jacob was not among those charged or disciplined for the injuries to his fraternity's pledges, but he had done nothing to stop, nor to defend, those who were expelled.

"I like to give anyone who is only an accessory to a felony the first chance to make a deal. You know what went on, but your own role seems smaller than that of anyone worth prosecuting." This was true, but it was also bait in a second trap. Telling him this would get him to talk, and his efforts to keep his own role limited incentivized lying to me. He could skate on the crime and still face charges for lying to an investigator. "I'm going to read you your rights, but you are not under arrest. I just need to be able to use whatever you tell me against anyone else I may charge later."

"Will I have to testify against them?" The thought of that rattled him more than being arrested.

"Everyone on that fishing trip will be called to testify, so don't worry that anything you tell me put you on the stand." This was absolutely not true, but making his fate sound as if it were already sealed might squeeze more out of him. "Look, Jacob, we just need you to confirm Mitchell Ursin was at the wheel of the boat that passed by you at the bridge."

"How would I know that?"

"Spare me getting a warrant for your car's GPS. Let's start with you confirming that it was you who drove Mitchell to steal the boat."

"Yes, I dropped him off." The significance of the confession was lost on Jacob. It was the first break in my investigation since Kirk Donovan was pulled from the canal.

"What did Mitchell tell you he was going to do?" I wanted to hear Jacob's first attempt to distance himself from the crime.

"He said Bradley told him nobody was going to be home to stop him from taking the boat." Hearing his own words raised Jacob's eyebrows. "Does that mean they knew Belle's father was already dead?"

"What do you think?" It was hard not to draw that conclusion, but he knew the pair better than I did. I think he had come to realize how little he really knew either of the boys from Donovan.

"I don't know," he tried to claw back what he just said. "That sure makes it sound like they did."

"It also makes it sound like you didn't," I offered. The look in his eyes made me worry that he was on the verge of wanting an attorney. I needed to change the subject for a while. "What can you tell me about Bradley and Belle? I was told they are dating."

"That isn't happening," Jacob said and laughed at the idea.

"Who isn't whose type?"

"Bradley is too much of a player for her."

"Bradley thinks of himself as a ladies man?" Nothing changed based on this knowledge. "How do you know that?"

"I've seen him in action. He is a smooth talker, and he's rich." Jacob sensed he knew a few things I did not, which meant to him that he might still have some bargaining chips.

"How about any of the other guys in your group? What about Mitchell?" I wondered aloud.

"I don't think so. His dad works for the Donovans, and from what I hear they don't pay very much. Everyone knows Bradley has money, but he doesn't make a big deal about it. He picks up our bar tab most of the time, which means he gets first pick when we meet a bunch of chicks."

I miss the narcissistic logic of college boys.

"Bradley picks up your bar tabs? What else does he pay for?" I remembered now that Chance told me Bradley inherited a sizeable fortune when his father died. It had not occurred to me to ask exactly how much money we were talking about.

"He paid for the fishing trip." Jacob had a good sense of what bones to throw in my direction to keep my attention on someone else. "He called us up on Thursday and told us where to meet him on Friday."

"Does he do that a lot?"

"It's been a while. I think the last time he paid for a trip was just before last Thanksgiving. We all went duck hunting together."

"Where was that?" I wanted to keep him talking. I expressed interest in the duck hunt so that he might not notice when I returned to the subject of the boat theft.

"We always wind up out where he lives. He seems to know everyone, so we get away with a lot more than we might in some other place." Jacob knew a good thing when he saw one. "That time he rented a couple of cabins on the bayou and we just hung out. He showed us where some boat had hit a snag a hundred years ago, but it was burnt up. There were still a few pieces of wood poking out of the water. We drank more than we hunted. Bradley made a lot of liquor runs into town that time."

"Really. Do you remember where those cabins are?' Bells were suddenly ringing in my head.

"Only that they were north of town. We had to wait for a while to get there because some rich guy was using the road as his personal racetrack. Must be nice to be *that* rich, huh?" Jacob asked. "I could get directions from Bradley if you want."

"Don't bother. I was just curious," I waved off his offer. I did my best to make it seem irrelevant. I knew a call was going to be made as soon as my back was turned and did not want him to mention the cabins when he spoke with Bradley. "I only have one other question. Did Mitchell say where he was taking the boat?"

"No. He just said he was going to get a lot of money for it. I assumed he and Bradley had a buyer lined up, but I didn't want to get involved."

"Yet you drove Mitchell to steal the boat," I said to remind him that he remained an accessory.

"I meant other than that." Jacob's face contorted just enough to let me know he understood that he had just been dumb enough to confess to a felony.

My interest in pursuing charges against Jacob was waning by the time I steered the XLR out of the parking lot and into the mid-afternoon traffic from the zoo across the street from the golf course. My sights were set on Mitchell Ursin. He held all the answers to Bradley Ladd's role in my investigation.

Bradley knew about life under Kirk Donovan's roof. He apparently knew about Kirk planning to be out of town racing, and that Belle was also leaving town, but I had no idea what he might know about Gwen's strange disappearance. She may have said something to Belle that got passed along. I still could not prove Bradley knew Kirk was dead at the time he helped Mitchell Ursin steal the boat. He only said he knew Kirk would not be around. I was curious how long he and Mitchell thought they could keep their part in the boat's theft a secret. I still didn't know anywhere near enough to name a suspect in Kirk's homicide, but I was finally sorting out who I needed to question and what to ask.

Not bad for the thirteenth day of an investigation that grew in complexity with each new day. The old maxim my dad taught me that the first forty eight hours provide the best chances of finding a killer was proving to be useless. I was using a lesser bit of his wisdom, that my gut can have better sense than my brain.

Fifty-Eight

Roux and I were only an hour's drive from Donovan, but I was certain to be running behind any warning call Jacob made to Mitchell Ursin or Bradley Ladd so I placed a call to Detective Chance.

"Pick up Mitchell Ursin and toss him in a cell. I have someone who can testify he played a part in the theft of Kirk Donovan's boat." I wasn't comfortable with sharing Jacob's name.

"So, do you want me to arrest him?"

"No. I want to hold him for a day or two before we even question him. Just let him know we have a witness willing to testify against him. Don't even let him know what we are going to charge him with," I directed.

"You want to see what else he might confess to." I had to give Chance some credit for understanding the point of the detention.

"It will be interesting to see what all he wants to deny taking part in. We know he took the boat. Now I want to know why he thought he would get away with it."

"You think Mitchell knew Kirk was dead?"

"Somebody did. Kirk was gone a lot of weekends and nobody ever took his boat. Why did they steal it the same weekend that Kirk and Gwen both went missing?" This was not a conversation I had meant to have over the phone. I only wanted him to gather up Mitchell Ursin before he tried to outrun us. We could hold Mitchell until Tuesday before the DA would have to charge him or release him. I might be able to convince DA Milquetoast to let me call Mitchell a material witness just to keep him in my custody. I could not paint Mitchell as being a flight risk before any of Senator Donovan's judges to keep him locked up if he was arraigned. Then again, the boy might understand that there was no safe place to await trial after stealing from a Donovan.

"I'm on it," Chance said. "See you tonight?"

"In the morning. Make sure he misses supper." The call had lasted all of a minute. I hung up and started making a list of things I needed to do in the next two days. The first thing on that list was to find what had become of Kirk Donovan's boat.

Fifty-Nine

"We locked Mitchell Ursin up just before six o'clock last night. The deputy who brought him in said Mitchell acted as though he had expected to be arrested," Detective Chance reported as I finished cooking our breakfast just after eight o'clock the next morning. We decided to begin meeting at the house rather than the sheriff's office to keep a tighter lid on our investigation. Chance said he was prepared to make sure Sheriff Mazant remained a day or two behind. I had little choice but to accept this, but saw no reason to trust that he would keep his word. Roux's distrust of him was evident as Roux paced about his kennel while we ate breakfast.

"What has your boss had to say about holding Mitchell without charge?"

"That the state police are on the hook if he wants to sue anyone." Chance chuckled. "I'm sure Sheriff Mazant will make sure Mitchell's attorney knows who to blame."

"Mitchell already has an attorney?" I thought it would take at least half a day to find one.

"Apparently the family keeps a pair on retainer. I guess that's what you do if you need one as often as they do. Usually it's the old man who gets in trouble." Chance stopped talking long enough to take a bite of the omelet I set in front of him. It was stuffed with chorizo and some of the salsa I had brought from New Orleans the night before.

"Then the clock is ticking," I mumbled mostly to myself. "We need to find the boat before we sit down with Mitchell."

"It might be easier than we thought. Boston Whaler has stopped making boats like Kirk's."

"How does that make anything easier?" I asked with my mouth full. I washed down the bite of food with a gulp of stout chicory coffee.

"There is a big market for them. I looked at online boat dealers and located three of them within a hundred miles of here. There are two others within the next hundred miles, but I am sure that whoever he sold it to was nearby," Chance suggested.

"Why do you think the boat is even for sale? I think it makes a lot more sense for Mitchell to have sold it to someone who planned to piece it out."

"A boat like that is worth more intact. You would have a hard time registering a stolen boat on your own, but a dealer has an easier time cleaning the title. It's not that much different than stealing a car." Chance grabbed both empty plates and rinsed them before setting them in the dishwasher. I stayed at the table to finish my coffee. It was promising to be a very long day.

"So we're spending the day in a car," I sighed.

"Maybe not the whole day. I know a guy in CGIS, the Coast Guard's police. He told me only one of the names on my list has been cited for selling stolen boats in the past. It's near Port Arthur. That sounds like the best place to start." I was tempted to ask how he knew the agent, but there was already too much I didn't know about Chance to add this to the list.

"That's in Texas. My jurisdiction doesn't stretch that far, and I know yours sure as heck doesn't." It was an observation, not an objection.

"I thought we were trying to find the boat. Doing that doesn't mean we have to arrest anyone," Chance pointed out. "Can't we just go ask some questions?"

"Let me change clothes and we can take my car." I was dressed in khakis and a polo shirt. It was going to take a necktie to look properly intimidating. It would take a special kind of numbskull to confess a crime to a pair of out of state cops, but the world I live in is full of them.

Sixty

Deep Channel Marina was located across Sabine Lake from Port Arthur. We arrived just past eleven o'clock and there was already a good deal of activity among the boats despite it being a weekday.

I had brought Roux along, with the notion of implying we might check a boat or two for narcotics. We had no warrant to do so, but a dishonest man doesn't usually expect the police to be any more honest than himself.

The business took up about a third of the marina where it was located. There were a number of live-aboard boats docked in the marina, which would have posed a problem for anyone trying to sell Kirk Donovan's Boston Whaler. His boat was twenty-three feet long and powered by a pair of two hundred horsepower Mercury outboard engines. It would have needed nearly half a day to get to the marina from Donovan. The thief and fence may have loaded to it onto trailer between the two points. Either way, the thieves would have likely arrived at the marina during the light of day, and that put them at considerable risk of being seen.

Chance and I split up to inspect Deep Channel's inventory. I was walking past the office as one of the salesmen came out to greet us. I bit my tongue about our purpose and kept my jacket over my badge as I shook his hand. There was no percentage in playing either good cop or bad cop when we had no authority to even be there.

"Huey Carlyle at your service. How may I help you this morning?" Huey looked like he spent as much time on a boat as he did selling them. He was in his fifties and his skin had been tanned to leather from constant exposure to the sun. He was soft around the waist, but had the upper body of a sailor. His hand was calloused and his handshake was meant to test my own. He glanced down at Roux, who was still sizing him up. "Does your dog bite?"

"Only if I tell him to. Want to hear his bark first?"

"I'll pass," Huey stepped away from us.

"My friend and I heard you had some used Boston Whalers for sale. I'm in the market for a Conquest model. I understand they are being discontinued, so I want to get one before they get priced as collector's items." I had exhausted most of what I knew about the boats, and most of that was thanks to Detective Chance.

"Smart move. They will definitely be sought after in the next couple of years," Huey said and gave me a solid pat on the back. I felt his arm trail down and press across my shoulder blades. He was feeling for a wire or a shoulder holster. I stepped to his right to get out of his reach before he felt the pistol tucked into the small of my back. I had shifted it from my hip in an effort to conceal its bulge under my sport coat. Apparently I was a little too well dressed to be a genuine prospect. "Is that your friend on the dock? Where are you two from? I don't remember seeing either of you around here."

"New Orleans. We get out on Lake Ponchartrain as often as we can, but we have been using David's brother's boat. It's time I had my own." Chance and I had worked up a story that we would use for as long as possible before admitting we were a pair of nosy cops from Louisiana.

"Then a Boston Whaler might be more boat than you need," Huey said as he shook Chance's hand.

"I want to enter the tarpon rodeo down in Grand Isle, so we need a good salt water boat," Chance lied to keep the conversation going. We made sure that we introduced ourselves using our real names.

"Then a Whaler is exactly the boat you need to own," Huey assured us. "You mentioned the Conquest series. That would be the two on the far end."

I started to walk that way but then saw the look on Chance's face and froze.

"Aren't those Ventures?" David objected. I turned in time to catch the salesman's expression. He knew we were not buying a boat, but he was struggling to figure out what our real purpose was in being there. I had to assume he was stalling us while his partners in the office did whatever it was that they did when trouble came knocking.

"Yes, they are. I meant to point to the other end," Huey immediately corrected himself, as though it were an honest mistake. We had already passed the collection of Conquests, which might have been what made him suspicious.

Detective Chance and I closely inspected each of the Conquest hulls. We were looking for any sign that the numbers on the boats had been changed. The cheap stick-on numbers most boaters use leave a ghost from sun fading and grunge build-up behind when they are removed. Each of these boats had what looked like their original numbers attached, which meant none of them belonged to Kirk Donovan. It took a moment to realize that only one of the boats was registered in Texas. The others were all registered in Louisiana, Oklahoma, or Alabama.

"Tell me, Huey, what are the odds that the only people with Boston Whalers to sell you came from hundreds of miles away? Why are you are selling so many boats with out of state registrations?" I asked the salesman, while shifting my position to block him from running past me in panic.

"We get most our boats at auction," he calmly, and rationally, explained.

"So you probably send a few boats to auction as well, right?" Chance squeezed a bit harder.

"A few. We always try to keep a fresh inventory," Huey continued to defend himself. This was not the sort of conversation real customers had with him. "Is there a specific Boston Whaler you are looking for?"

"How about a 2008 Boston Whaler Conquest with the registration number PA1246BD?" Chance recited the registration number from memory.

"I'd have to look at our records, but that number doesn't sound familiar." Huey sounded very nervous.

"Does the name Ursin sound any more familiar?" I asked. I tried to sound as menacing as possible. "You might have taken a call from him between the second and the fifth of the month. Does that jog your memory?"

"Who are you two?" Huey wondered aloud. His tone lacked any sign that he was prepared to defend himself if we turned violent. Huey knew he must have made a serious miscalculation about making a deal for Kirk's boat. Chance and I silently decided to wait to identify ourselves until Huey stopped acting so guilty. This was a guy who would want to call his attorney before he answered a cop's questions.

"We're the guys the Donovans sent to find their boat," I snarled. Doing so cued Roux to snarl as well. Huey was understandably afraid I was about to set Roux upon him.

"Why do you think we would have it?" Huey tried to reason with us, but his eyes never left Roux.

"Because your first question wasn't 'Who are the Donovans,' you dumbass," Chance chuckled. I acted as though I was about to unclip Roux's leash. That proved to be Huey's breaking point.

"I didn't know who it belonged to until I checked the registration. I already had a buyer and couldn't back out of the deal." Huey had no future in being a serious criminal. Knowing who bought the boat was just a question away, but frankly I didn't care who had it and I was in no hurry to do the Donovans any favors. Getting the boat back would be a problem for Detective Chance's pal at the Coast Guard, but only if Chance cared more about getting the boat back than I did.

"We want the name of who brought you the boat," I said and reached inside my jacket as though I might be reaching for a weapon. I came out with my cellphone and set it to video record his answer.

"A kid named Mitchell Ursin sold us the boat. We paid him fifteen thousand dollars for it," Huey readily confessed to my camera. "Please don't kill me."

I would need to edit that last piece out before I let Ursin's attorney see the video.

"We aren't the ones you need to worry about," Chance told him and opened his own jacket to show he wasn't armed. "But you should expect another visitor."

It was a cruel thing to say, and we both had a hard time keeping straight faces. We left Huey shaking on the dock and waved at the curious faces in the office window as we walked past on the way to my car.

Scaring Huey was easy, and enjoyable in the way that making criminals projecting toughness confront their weakness can be. It also gave both my partner and me an indication of how little either of us cared about being the sort of cops who won't step over lines. Neither of us broke character while sweating Huey for answers. Neither of us voiced any concern about how we handled questioning the man. This raised more concern about working with Detective Chance. I now had no any idea what limits the detective might have when it came to proving his conspiracy theory.

Sixty-One

Mitchell Ursin was well stewed in his own anxieties by the time we sat him down in an interrogation room later that afternoon. Nearly twenty hours in a cell with half a dozen local lowlifes he wouldn't have wanted to know on the street, plus a series of barely edible meals served on a metal tray with nothing but tepid water to wash them down with helped us educate the young man on what a career in crime held in store. His hair was dirty, and he looked like he had not slept. I hoped he was prepared to cooperate in order to improve his situation.

"Good afternoon, Mitch," I said as Detective Chance and I took our seats across from him at the table. I turned on my portable tape recorder and set it on the empty table between us. "It is seventeen thirty on March twenty-second of two thousand and ten. Saint Xavier Parish Detective David Chance and state police Detective Cooter Holland will be interviewing Mitchell Scott Ursin. Mitchell, you have the right to remain silent. Anything you say can and will be used against you in a court of law. You have the right to have an attorney present during this interrogation. If you cannot afford one, one will be provided at no cost. If you choose to remain silent, this interview will end. If you ask for an attorney, this interview will end until they are present. Do you understand these rights?"

"I do," he said loud enough to be recorded, but in a monotone that I took as being resignation.

"Then the ball is in your court. Do you want to let us ask you a few questions before you decide on the matter, or do you want to have an attorney present from the beginning?"

"What sort of questions? I have no idea why I am even here," Mitchell tried to question us.

"I am going to stop you before you dig too deep of a hole, Mitch," I said and held up my hand to let him know to stop talking. "You are about to tell us a lie that is an entirely separate, but serious, charge from why you are here. Don't be that kind of fool, okay?"

Mitchell had no response, but he took this to mean exactly what it did. We had enough evidence to arrest and convict him of something for which he apparently thought he had covered his tracks. He leaned back in his chair and considered his options.

"We know you stole Kirk Donovan's Boston Whaler. We know who you sold it to. That's grand theft and interstate traffic of stolen goods right there. Stealing from a Donovan may carry a penalty all its own around here. The fact that Kirk Donovan turned up dead a week later makes you our best suspect for his homicide, as well." This was the shoe Mitchell had been waiting to hear fall all along. He pressed his elbows onto the table and buried his forehead in his hands. He began to hyperventilate, and then to sob.

"Look, Mitch, this is when smart guys shut up and ask for an attorney," I seemed to be advising him. Detective Chance gave me an alarmed look. "But you aren't a particularly smart guy or you wouldn't be here, and we only have one more question for you. Take my advice and answer this one easy question honestly. It will give your attorney something to work with when we walk this over to the DA."

Mitchell looked up. His brown eyes were rimmed with red and tears were flowing.

"What's the question?" he sighed.

"Who told you it was okay to take the boat?" I had hopes of a celebratory dinner and a good night's sleep if he coughed up a name.

Mitchell blinked and rubbed his eyes. He stared at me for a moment, glanced at Detective Chance, and then refocused on me. He took a deep breath and fell back in his chair.

"Bradley Ladd." He said this in something of a croak and I had to have him repeat it clearly for the tape recorder.

"How did Bradley know it was okay to take the boat?" Detective Chance leaped into the conversation.

"I have no idea. He called me Monday morning and said I could probably get away with it because nobody was going to be home for a while. I figured he knew the family's plans because of how close he is with Belle."

"Have you two pulled other heists like this?" Chance pressed.

"You mean taking dead men's boats? No." Mitchell shook his head. "I think I need that attorney."

"Yes, you do," I agreed. I picked up the recorder and began speaking into the attached microphone. "This interview with Mitchell Scott Ursin has ended. It is now eighteen hundred hours on March twenty-second of two thousand and ten."

I unlocked Mitchell's hands from the cuffs on the table while Detective Chance knocked on the door to bring the jail deputy to take Mitchell back to his cell.

"So, I am under arrest?" Mitchell asked.

"You will be arraigned in the morning. Detective Chance will notify your parents."

"Call my dad and tell him what's going on. He knows a couple of attorneys." Mitchell requested of Chance.

"That's what I hear," I shrugged. "You might be better off going to jail than going home."

Mitchell turned back to look at me, but he had no comeback for my jab. I believe he agreed with me.

Sixty-Two

"So, you two don't even want to see Mitchell arraigned for stealing Kirk Donovan's boat?" Gabouri snorted after an hour of listening to Detective Chance and I lay out our case on the theft of Kirk Donovan's Boston Whaler, and our intent to use Mitchell Ursin's testimony to leverage Bradley Ladd for what he knew about the murder of Kirk Donovan. Bradley may not have committed the murder, but he had said things that led us to believe he knew Kirk was dead a week before his body was found.

"Not particularly, no. What tipped you off?" I readily admitted.

"First off, Mitchell's confession to having stolen and sold Kirk Donovan's boat is inadmissible. What you brought me is a tape of him not fighting you when you put words in his mouth. All he has told us so far is that Bradley Ladd told him he could get away with stealing the boat if he wanted. You have a witness who can put Mitchell at Kirk Donovan's house that Monday night, but he did not see him actually steal the boat, and you can't establish when the boat first went missing."

"The guy in Texas said Mitchell sold him the boat." Detective Chance was not going to give up on having a case against Mitchell Ursin.

"Yes, a boat dealer in another state, that you did not identify yourself as police officers to before questioning, was illegally recorded saying he bought Kirk Donovan's boat from Mitchell and sold it to a buyer you did not ask him to identify. Good luck getting a prosecutor in Texas, where he illegally sold the boat, to take the case with this evidence."

"We could turn what we have over to the Texas Rangers and encourage them to interview the boat dealer," I suggested.

"You would be better advised to give them an anonymous tip from a payphone. They aren't going to be able to build a case off the tape you have, because you never identified yourselves. The man you want them to question can be heard pleading for his life. Cooter, were you really going to have your dog attack him if he didn't confess?" Gabouri asked and sat back in his chair, throwing his arms wide and taking a deep breath as he continued shaking his head. I felt bad enough about being so soundly rebuffed by a man as ill-suited to his job as Gabouri without having to bear these theatrics.

"Tell me this," Detective Chance said, clearly disappointed. "Are we wrong?"

"About what?" Gabouri stood up and offered to pour from his very recently refilled bourbon decanter. It was only ten-thirty in the morning, which meant the closest happy hour was still somewhere in Europe. That should have been a clear sign it was too early to get drunk, but I was too much of a Southern gentleman to allow the district attorney drink expensive bourbon alone.

"About Bradley Ladd knowing something about Kirk Donovan's murder." I took up our cause.

"I don't see any reason to disagree with your conclusion," Gabouri said and returned to his seat on the sofa. "But, you are further from taking that accusation to a grand jury than you are that of Mitchell. I doubt we could get an indictment against Bradley with what you have. Bradley Ladd owns a business here, and he pays better than the Donovans."

"What's the business?" I had neglected to ask this question the first time someone had brought it up.

"It's a metal recycling place, mostly junk metal from the oil rigs and shipyards. Lots of folks sell him cans they pick out of the trash to make a few extra bucks," Gabouri filled me in. "Folks have to live with these people, and charging either of these boys with a felony, and not coming away with either a plea deal or a conviction, would create a bad situation. Neither of you have lived in small towns, have you?"

"My father grew up in one. He would see the argument you are making." I sighed and set my drink on the table between the chairs Detective Chance and I were sitting in. "We're going to have to cut Mitchell loose today, and he is going to make a bee line for Bradley to tell him what we know. That is only going to make it harder to get anything on either of them going forward."

"Any suggestions?" Chance asked Gabouri.

"Actually, I have a question." Gabouri frowned as he straightened his posture and leaned towards us. "You two are much better detectives than such sloppy work on the boat would indicate. You said you are on a fishing expedition to find out how Bradley Ladd knew the coast was clear to steal the Donovans' boat. I think there is more to this that you aren't telling me about."

I waited for Detective Chance to speak up. I used the tumbler of bourbon to block my face as I glanced towards him to see what he planned to do. He seemed unusually hesitant to share his conspiracy theory, so that job fell to me.

"Detective Chance has nearly convinced me that you have a serial killer in your midst. There have been a number of deaths that he believes were staged to look like accidents."

"Give me a name or two." Gabouri stood up to pour a fresh round, and set a glass for Chance next to my own refilled glass.

I was kicking myself for not having thought to bring Chance's evidence binder with us. "Your predecessor was one of the people we suspect was murdered."

"Lepanto choked on a sandwich. Are you trying to tell me someone made him choke on his lunch?" Gabouri shook his head again and seemed to be ready to end the conversation.

"His secretary claimed he always ate lunch by himself. She was not in the office when this happened. Maybe someone did force food down his throat," Chance recalled. "By the way, she is still your secretary."

Gabouri raised an eyebrow at this. He took a long pull from his tumbler and leaned back on the sofa, once again spreading his arms.

"There is a common denominator in the way all of the victims died. It was always some form of asphyxiation, be it a bite of food stuck in their throat, or drowning like Kirk Donovan." I used a sip of the bourbon to wet my dry throat.

"Interesting. And nobody else has picked up on this? Not Sheriff Mazant, not Chief Theriot, not the FBI, or the state police?" Gabouri was just arguing to draw out our own arguments. He seemed to be considering the theory Detective Chance had invested so much of time building.

"Why would they? The chief and sheriff had jurisdiction unless they called us in, and I doubt Senator Donovan was going to let them pursue it. Chance has a suspicion that the senator might be the one orchestrating all of this anyway." I knew I had shared too much with that last bit, but now that accusation was up for debate.

"Why would Senator Donovan want to get rid of these people? He owned Lepanto, and he likely had something on anyone else you can name." Gabouri and I shared that reason for dismissing the senator from suspicion.

"They all had the same thing on him that he had on them. Every victim played a role in what happened to the kids who went to that summer camp. Senator Donovan's law practice handled dozens of the marriages and adoptions, and it was still the primary business after Kirk took over the practice. The senator also hand-picked the judges who rubber stamped the approvals Kirk needed. I think everything hit the fan after the FBI took an interest in what was happening to kids from here. That was when someone began eliminating anyone the senator could not trust to stay quiet," Chance argued. His throat must have been drier than mine because he downed about half of the bourbon in his own glass. "I don't know that he did the killings, but I do know he had the ability to get them done. His fixer has a nasty reputation."

"Isn't that your uncle?" Gabouri turned to me and waited for me to defend Uncle Felix from this hideous insinuation.

"He is. I also believe he knows the people to call to make something like this happen. I do not think he did so, but that he could have is reason enough for me to believe David," I said.

"What made you interested in this in the first place?" Gabouri asked Chance.

"I was part of the investigation into a pair of murders Bradley may have been in involved back in Texas. His father was murdered and his alibi was that he was celebrating his eighteenth birthday with some friends at the time. Bradley's birthday made him old enough to inherit his father's estate."

"How large was the estate?" Gabouri asked in a tone that didn't show a lot of interest in the response.

"All told, about twenty five million dollars in cash and property. He still draws a few hundred thousand dollars a year from that recycling place. It was probably where his adoptive father met Senator Donovan." This was far more than Gabouri expected, and it was more than Chance had shared with me up to this point. I had a suspicion that he had held back information about Bradley he planned to use against him after I left town. "I believe he may have personally shot the husband of a friend of his. She used to run to his place to get away from her husband, until he shot her. The husband was shot in an armed robbery just a couple of weeks later."

This was all a lot for Gabouri to take in. Detective Chance and I had come to his office intent on making a case for charging Mitchell with stealing Kirk Donovan's fishing boat. We wound up unrolling a serial murder conspiracy and some nasty accusations against a local business owner at Gabouri's feet, all while giving him a reason to fear his own secretary.

"Okay, here's what I can do to help you. I will question Mitchell again. I'll do it by myself, with or without his attorney present. I will not be able to make a better case against him than you unless he confesses outright. But everyone in town will know he talked to me for an hour or so before I decided not to have him arraigned. I don't imagine anyone will believe Mitchell was able to convince me of his innocence. There will almost certainly be an assumption that a deal was struck, and the only thing Mitchell has to offer would be to testify against Bradley."

"So your big plan is to set the dogs upon each other?" I started to believe Katie was a little too quick about dismissing Gabouri's capacities. He might be lousy in a courtroom, but he had a solid grasp on how to wring some sort of victory from an unwinnable case.

"If Detective Chance's theories about the senator and Bradley Ladd are correct, one of them won't want to leave a potential witness alive. If either of them makes a move to harm Mitchell, it will take much less to get a local jury to believe they might have killed someone else." Gabouri expanded on his thoughts.

"Do any of us really think Bradley killed Kirk?" I know I still wasn't convinced.

"I do." Chance answered immediately, but he was always going to rely on his own history with Bradley to make that assumption.

"I don't think I do, but I do believe he knows who did the deed. I seriously doubt he or Mitchell are willing to go to prison to protect anyone else. I believe that whoever killed Kirk will eventually start eliminating everyone who knows they killed the man. Making Bradley into a target should make it easier for the two of you to find your serial killer, unless he's the killer." Gabouri seemed eager to have a serial killer case on his docket. Such a high profile prosecution could be his ticket out of Saint Xavier Parish. His prospects brightened all the more if the conspiracy theory about Senator Donovan's involvement was right. Someone was going to have to fill the senator's seat if he was sent to prison, and I could tell Gabouri saw his name high on the list of prospects.

"We just need see if Bradley tries to kill Mitchell or if someone tries to kill Bradley. Piece of cake, right?" I was suddenly very glad that I had not presented this case to Katie. Not only would there have been no bourbon served, she would never have concocted such a rickety scheme to find out whether Detective Chance's serial killer was real or imaginary.

Sixty-Three

I returned to New Orleans to begin surveillance on Bradley Ladd, while Detective Chance tried to figure out a way to watch Mitchell without being obvious. It was going to be hard in a town the size of Donovan, and I had no advice to give him. We had nowhere near the evidence a judge would require for anything more than sitting in a car and watching our suspects. I missed my days of access to satellite and drone tracking, hacking a suspect's cellphone, and an unlimited budget to pay informants. Those were still available, but only if I convinced the FBI one of our suspects was a terrorist and agreed to hand the case over to Conroy.

The SAC did not sound at all interested in taking my case away when I returned the call he made while I was en route to New Orleans. He told me to be alone when we spoke, but being alone while driving seventy miles an hour was not what he had in mind.

"Okay, I am stationary and alone," I tried to at least start on a humorous note when I reached Conroy in his office an hour later. I was not entirely alone, just at the far end of the bar at Strada Ammazarre with a drink in my hand.

"Okay, let me start with the warrant you asked about. According to the agents who were part of that investigation, the evidence used to get the warrant turned out to be deeply flawed. They had what sounded like a solid tip, and they had verified that the IP address of the computer they were looking for repeatedly accessed the internet to download child pornography in the house they raided. The problems began when they discovered the couple who lived there didn't own a computer, and the agents say they certainly didn't seem to know how to operate a computer. The couple claimed they were being framed, and that does seem like what happened. Also, that couple were never foster parents, at least not according to Family Services. There might have been some hinky sort of arrangement, but that seems doubtful."

"Well that punches some holes in Chance's theory. But only small ones." I was not sure if I was relieved or concerned. Chance was heavily invested in his conspiracy theory, and it was going to take a lot more than this setback to persuade him to re-evaluate his position.

"I also have pretty much all there is to know about what led to David Chance's being terminated," Conroy sighed aloud and paused. I imagined him reaching for one of his yellow pads. "A girl named Amorel Hickman seems to be at the heart of all of this. She was sixteen, and she had been married to Clive Hickman for four years when she died. It should be no surprise to you that the couple's wedding took place in Judge Aubuchon's courtroom and the parents' attorney was Chester, now Senator, Donovan. Amorel tried to file for divorce almost as soon as she landed in Houston, but apparently the law believes girls who are old enough to be married as children are not old enough to get a divorce until they turn eighteen, because minors cannot enter into a contract. Detective David Chance entered the picture when Amorel called the cops after Clive broke her nose. He ran the husband in and put her in a woman's shelter. The charges against the husband were dropped, but she stayed at the shelter for another couple of months, until she went back to her husband. There was an unsubstantiated complaint that Chance slept with the girl, but he denied it and she was never questioned. Amorel went to stay with that Bradley Ladd kid the next time, or should I say times, she left her husband. Nobody seems to know how the two of them knew one another, but the husband would always ask that Detective Chance be the officer to bring Amorel home."

"I had already heard about that," I half-mumbled into the phone. I decided against dashing the FBI agent's sense of accomplishment in learning these details by telling him exactly how much of the story I already knew. I appreciated having his verification.

"There was apparently a fight between the girl and Hickman before she attempted to take off the last time. Hickman asked Chance to come to his house. When the detective arrived at the residence he found the husband had shot the girl. He claimed she came at him with a butcher knife, and Chance was the first one on the scene so he bagged a kitchen knife and the husband's handgun as evidence. Houston's police chief was less than pleased about how involved Chance was deeply involved in all of this, so their police chief put a different set of detectives on the case and told Chance to stay out of it. The grand jury bought the husband's version and that should have been the end of the story." Conroy carefully enunciated each bullet point. He obviously didn't want to have to tell the story twice.

"Should have." I repeated. Those words alone were a bad sign of what was to come next.

"Hickman died in a mugging outside of a bar a week after he was cleared. No video, no witnesses, no weapon recovered, and nothing taken from the victim. It doesn't sound like any mugging I have heard about. How about you?"

"Clean getaway with nothing to show for it? That is very suspicious." I could not recall a single similar mugging in New Orleans. I did not think this was a sign that we had the better muggers.

"Detective Chance wasted no time pointing a finger at Bradley Ladd. He tried to paint him as Amorel's vengeful boyfriend," Conroy was beginning to enjoy recapping the trashy details.

"But, nobody bought his story, right?"

"Oh, no. Houston PD was fully on board with the idea, until Bradley Ladd's alibi held up. A half dozen witnesses placed him miles away at the time of the killing. Chance did himself no good by trying to sell a Houdini story for how Bradley happened to be out of town and surrounded by witnesses when both his father and the husband of his murdered girlfriend met very violent ends. He just seems to be a lucky guy." Conroy did not sound like he believed any more in luck than had Detective Chance.

"After Detective Chance destroyed his career trying to prove Bradley Ladd had something to do with killing the two men, Bradley headed to Tulane University to meet the daughter of a man who also died while he had a great alibi. People need to stay the hell away from Bradley Ladd." I wasn't entirely joking. I realized we were both stuck in the awkward position of believing Detective Chance was correct in his suspicions about the young man. I, for one, did not like knowing none of us was able to break Bradley Ladd's alibi in any of the deaths. The best chance of catching Bradley was to anticipate who was going to be the next to die and do our best to tie him to that murder. It was meant as a joke when I mentioned it before; now it seemed like our only option.

"You need to stay away from him," Conroy advised me. "The common denominator in this is that any man who crosses him ends up dead or out of a job. You could be his next victim either way."

He had a point.

"I will keep that in mind. Are you sure you don't want to step in and take this over?"

"Positive. But, feel free to let me know how things turn out." Conroy seemed relieved that he was not going to get sucked into this.

"One last favor," I said before he could hang up. The idea had just then come to me.

"Which is?"

"See what you can dig up on the newspaper editor in Donovan. Her name is Crystal Franks."

"She must be a real hot number," Conroy almost immediately laughed. "Being named after a pair of hot sauces."

"You tell me," I repeated the request and hung up on him. I was not comfortable that two people I had crossed paths with in Donovan both used the grocery store to come up with aliases. It was a strange enough thing to do that I had a hard time imagining two people each thinking of it on their own.

Sixty-Four

I hung up the phone after my conversation with SAC Conroy and turned my attention to the best way to keep Bradley Ladd under surveillance. It occurred to me that he was especially protective of Belle. He had hidden that he may have known her whereabouts until I found them together in the swimming pool, and even then he had placed himself between the two of us. It also occurred to me that I was the wrong person to watch Bradley.

Belle was sitting at the kitchen counter when Roux and I walked into my apartment. She was finishing an online chat with one of her instructors so I did my best to stay out of the camera frame and to keep Roux from jumping on her until she signed off. It was nearly three in the afternoon and she was still wearing the loose sweatpants and T-shirt she used as pajamas. There was a to-go box with the last bites of a po-boy she had ordered from downstairs sitting beside the sink.

"You're bored," I observed.

"Did they teach you to sense things like that at the police academy?" she joked. She was restless after having spent barely a week under what amounted to house arrest.

"Why don't you invite Bradley to come to happy hour? You two can have dinner here and then go to Frenchman Street. You cannot go anywhere else and are to be back here by sunrise." I tried to sound like the idea had just come to me, but Belle's expression showed she was looking for my purpose behind such a generous offer.

"What if I want to hang out with someone else?"

"I trust Bradley more than I do any of your friends I haven't met. I still think you might be in danger."

"You must not trust my other friends at all then," Belle laughed and stood up.

"Not true. There are only a couple of them that I do not trust." I shook my head and took a seat in one of the heavy Stickley chairs facing the leather sofa in my living room. Roux was quick to claim the other one, and the leather on it showed how often he sat there. Belle came over and sat on the sofa. "Mitchell Ursin has admitted to taking your dad's boat, and he claims Bradley told him he could get away with it. But I'm supposed to be looking for your mother, not your dad's boat. Nobody is pressing any charges unless your mother decides to report the boat as having been stolen."

"Do you really think my mother is still alive?"

"I do," I declared. "I still don't know everything you might know about her disappearance or where she could be hiding. Right now, she is safer than if I found her."

"Well, I don't know anything about why she took off and I wouldn't know where to begin to look for her that you haven't probably already looked," Belle claimed. "My only question is why she didn't take off before now. I am sure you have heard how bad my parents' marriage was."

"That's what I have heard from everyone who would discuss it," I said and tried to make it sound like a joke. "And the timing is one of the first things I will ask about when I find her. It was unfortunate that she took off the same weekend your father was murdered."

"She didn't do it," Belle immediately spoke up in her mother's defense. "I mean, she would have before now if she was going to, right?"

"That's the theory I have been working with as well," I reassured her. "But not knowing who really did kill your father is why I still need to protect you."

"Well, why are you suggesting I hang out with Bradley then? You seem to be sure that he stole from my family. Why don't you think he would hurt me?" Belle had managed to bring the conversation full circle.

I scratched Roux behind the ear until his hind leg began to move involuntarily and he gave me a look of utter joy. Belle sat waiting for an answer and I decided to be straight with her. The worst that might happen would be that she would tell Bradley what I said, but that might scare him enough to make some sort of mistake or to change whatever plan he had.

"I want you to get close to Bradley because it will make it easier for me to keep tabs on him. I still have your phone in the tracking app on my own phone, so as long as you are with him I know where he is and what he is doing," I explained. "Detective Chance thinks Bradley may have killed two men in Texas, and that he might have played a part in a few murders in Donovan since he came to town."

"That's stupid," Belle scoffed.

"I thought so, too, at first." I was not going to elaborate on why Detective Chance and I felt her friend was a viable suspect. I only wanted to use her to let Bradley know Detective Chance was still on his tail, and that he now had some help. I knew Belle would ask him about what happened in Texas if I gave her this teaser. "Whether he has anything to do with any of the deaths or not, there is good reason to believe there is a serial killer running loose in Donovan. They are who almost certainly killed your father and, until we know what their motivation is, I have to assume they might come after you, as well."

"If your partner thinks Bradley is a killer, then why are you asking me to hang out with him? Am I some sort of bait?" Belle was taking me seriously at last, and her question deserved a better answer than I was going to provide.

"Like I said, I don't think Bradley intends to do you any harm. I cannot say for sure what he has in mind for anyone else. That he was certain enough about getting away with taking your dad's boat just tells me that he had some sort of knowledge about what was going on with your parents that weekend. Did you tell him anything before you left for Colorado?"

"No. Kirk told me not tell anyone where I was going, so I didn't," Belle said.

"Had Kirk ever told you not to tell anyone about your travel plans before?" This was a detail about her most recent trip it just occurred to me to ask.

"Never. It seemed strange, but you did what Kirk told you to do. Period," she said and smacked a fist into her open palm.

"Then nobody but your parents knew where you were the entire time you were in Colorado? No phone calls, no emails to anyone?"

"I called my professors, but I never told them where I was. They probably thought I had the flu or something." Roux hopped off his chair and went to lay his head in Belle's lap. She idly petted him, not grasping that he was signaling to me that she was hiding her distress.

"Now that you think about it, does it worry you that your father apparently wanted you to go into hiding?"

"A lot. Maybe he told my mother to leave town after I did. Do you think that's why she is still hiding out?" Belle's mind was now full of a lot more questions than either of us could answer. I was beginning to regret bringing up the subject.

"I might use that as my new starting point. Maybe your father knew he was in danger and wanted to make sure the two of you were safe." This could explain why so much effort went into faking her mother's death, but I was then confronted with the question of how Kirk might have known about some sort of danger facing his family. I was back to treading water.

"And Detective Chance thinks Bradley may know something about all of this?" Belle asked. I had told her as much earlier, but that was before she believed me. She still might not share our suspicions about her friend, but she seemed to be considering them more seriously.

"I would appreciate it if you didn't make any of this a topic of conversation tonight," I said as I leaned towards her. "You need to have a night out of here, and you need to enjoy yourself. I get paid to worry about this stuff, so let me ruin my night and you go have fun. Okay?"

"Okay," she sighed and rubbed Roux's belly one last time before she stood up and headed to her room. Roux looked to me and I nodded. He quietly slipped off the sofa and followed Belle. I was never going to fully understand that dog's mind, but I was resigned to the fact that he had decided the women in my life were more fun to hang out with than me.

Sixty-Five

Katie and I were headed home from a late dinner at Jacques-Imo's Café when my cellphone rang. She picked it up and showed me the caller ID before I nodded for her to answer it and put it on speaker.

"I hope I am disturbing something," Detective Chance said with a noticeable lack of sarcasm or humor.

"You are, but that isn't why you called," I said and just shook my head when Katie gave me a questioning look.

"Do you know exactly where Bradley Ladd is at this moment?"

"I can tell you if you give me a second." I pulled my coupe over and went to the phone tracking app. It took a moment for the cursor to home in on Belle's location, but it eventually gave me the exact building where her phone was located. "He is at the Spotted Cat. What's up?"

"Judge Aubuchon is dead," Chance said and waited for me to respond.

"Do we know how he died?"

"The judge's Oldsmobile reportedly veered into the path of truck. He died on impact. He was headed to the country club to have dinner with Senator Donovan and your uncle," Chance explained. The way he gave me the guest list for the dinner seemed to imply he had a theory about the judge's death.

"Senator Donovan and Bradley Ladd both have great alibis if the judge didn't just have an accident," I said. Katie sat back in her seat, quietly prepping her own questions for when I hung up.

"That's right."

"Is there any reason to believe the judge was murdered? Is there any sign of foul play?" I hated having to rely on someone else to give me information like this.

"He was alone in the car. One of Theriot's deputies just happened to be following him. He claims the judge began driving erratically and hit the truck after he swerved too wide making a turn," Chance elaborated.

"Well, be sure to ask the coroner to do a toxicology screen." I had every reason to believe Detective Chance would think to do so, but I said it so I was on record as wanting one done.

"I'll do what I can. The accident happened inside the city limits and Chief Theriot claimed jurisdiction. I heard him tell the coroner that it was obviously a heart attack. Sheriff Mazant seems to be happy that Theriot is insisting on taking a suspicious death on his own plate," Chance informed me.

"I'll call my captain see if we can find a reason for the state police to take over. There is every reason to believe Aubuchon's death could be connected to Kirk's, especially considering they both died behind the wheel."

"I guess I'll see you in the morning?" Chance wondered aloud.

"There isn't much reason to keep watching Bradley. There's no way he was involved, and I may have given him the perfect alibi." I was ready to kick my own ass about this.

"Perfect how?"

"I'll explain tomorrow," I promised him and immediately hung up. I didn't want to hear any criticism of my decision in stereo.

"Start talking, mister," Katie demanded as soon as I set the phone down.

"The judge somebody tried to kill on Saint Patrick's Day died in a car wreck this evening. Detective Chance has a credible theory that either Senator Donovan or Bradley Ladd made a list of people they want to kill off, and the judge's name was probably on that list," I was trying to hit only the high spots, figuring to fill in any blanks she couldn't work out on her own after we got to her house. She wasn't going to prosecute any case I was able to make against anyone in Donovan, but she had a professional curiosity about what was keeping us apart for so long.

"Okay, that's your problem to deal with. What is this about Bradley Ladd having such a perfect alibi? This is the first time you have ever described anyone's alibi as being perfect."

"I gave it to him." I sighed and pulled the car back into traffic so I wouldn't have to face her. "I used Belle to keep him busy while we went out for dinner. I am tracking her phone on mine. She would have called me if he ditched her."

"You used Belle to do your job so we could have dinner together?" Katie was not impressed by the lengths I had gone to make our romantic dinner possible. She obviously was seeing our evening together in an entirely different light.

"Uh, yeah." I admitted.

"I don't know whether to smack you for being a schoolboy romantic or a lazy cop," she said sharply and turned away from me.

"I missed you," I lamely offered.

"You'll be around a whole lot more if you lose your job. What were you thinking?" She sounded less angry, but I knew she wasn't making a joke about my being suspended or fired.

"I think we both have to agree that you give me too much credit for thinking," I suggested.

Katie let me stew for a couple of blocks before she reached over and took my hand. We rode in silence the rest of the way to her house, which was close enough to not make the silence awkward and far enough to let her calm down a bit more.

"So, you aren't going back tonight?" Katie asked as I held out my hand to help her out of the low-slung Cadillac.

"The judge's condition isn't likely to change. Detective Chance sounds like he is handling things as best he can to avoid Theriot muscling in on the case. I want to speak with Belle about her date before I head back." I tried to list as many reasons for her to let me spend the night as I could.

"Come on in, then." She kissed my cheek before she took my hand and led me inside.

Sixty-Six

Detective Chance's use of the word 'collision' grossly understated the full force of the impact. The judge had driven the 1971 Oldsmobile Riviera he maintained in near showroom condition into the path of a four-door Dodge Ram 2500 diesel-powered work truck with a lift kit. This had raised the height of the front bumper to nearly door handle height on the judge's car. It was the judge's double misfortune to have bought his car before the introduction of side air bags and to cross the path of such a massive truck while it was traveling over twice the posted speed limit.

The judge's body was in worse condition than his vehicle by the look of the crash scene photos Detective Chance handed me when I took a seat on the corner of his desk the next morning. The grille of the truck struck the Oldsmobile almost dead center on the driver's side door and pushed sheet metal, interior seats and trim, and the two hundred and fifty pound judge about two feet deeper into the vehicle. The seatbelt strap crushed the judge's ribcage and the whiplash from the freight train-like impact snapped his neck and nearly decapitated him. It was doubtful he would have survived the accident had the pickup been traveling at the posted thirty-five mile an hour speed limit, but the force of the impact guaranteed the judge didn't live long enough to see his beloved car destroyed.

"Where is the judge's body now?" I asked. I was hoping the local coroner had possession.

"The funeral home already has him," Chance informed me and waited for my reaction. "Chief Theriot had the coroner rule it was an accident at the scene last night. FYI, the funeral home director is our coroner."

"How the hell could the coroner decide that on the spot?" I barely avoided shouting.

"His deputy described the way the judge was acting when he lost control and the coroner said it sounded enough like a heart attack to satisfy him. The judge had survived two previous heart attacks, so he must have based his decision on that." He no more believed that was acceptable than I did, but Chance had a much better grasp on local flexibility with laws and procedures. There was no good going to come of finding the judge had been poisoned or drugged by a third party, and the senator likely told the police chief that he didn't want his friend cut up any more than the accident had already done.

"Where's the police chief this time of day?" I asked. We needed to work fast before I completely lost my temper.

"He is likely at home," Chance said and stood up. He knew we were headed to fight the chief of police on his home turf, but he held his tongue because I would be the one who led the charge.

The city's contract with the chief of police gave him use of a 1940s-era bungalow near downtown. It served as a home for the chief and his family as well as an office. He did not need a jail as his authority primarily involved misdemeanor and civil offenses. I imagined he would ask Sheriff Mazant to hold anyone he saw fit to detain. Chance further explained that Sheriff Mazant provided four of his own retired cruisers to the police chief and his deputies to use as their patrol cars. I had a feeling that Sheriff Mazant retired those cruisers just ahead of their heaviest maintenance cycles.

I let Detective Chance knock. I knew I would have pounded on the heavy oak door as though I were intent upon knocking it down. Chief Theriot opened the door after only the second knock. He was obviously expecting confrontation with one or both of us and pointed towards his office, which was nothing much more than an enclosed porch.

I glanced at the living room and dining room as we made our way through the house. All of the original wood trim and features were still intact, and the floors shone as though brand new. The furniture matched the lifestyle of the chief and his family, not the era or style of the home itself. There wasn't a good argument to be made for worrying about that when the family lived only one election away from being back on the street looking for a place to live.

"I know what you're going to say, and frankly I don't care to hear it," Chief Theriot summarily dispensed with any niceties or formalities.

"This happened within the city limits and Senator Donovan approved my taking care of it."

"Let's start with what you are not taking care of," I suggested. "My partner here tells me that you ordered the coroner to make a determination about the cause of death at the scene of the crash. State law requires he do an autopsy of any violent or suspicious death."

"There isn't much more violent way to meet your maker than having a big old pickup truck T-bone you, but a car wreck like this isn't the sort of violent death the coroner or I take that law to mean. My deputy claims he saw the judge let loose of the wheel and move like he was having some sort of problem. The senator agreed that the gestures the deputy showed him were consistent with a heart attack, and the judge had a history of those. I don't know what other explanation you two might be fishing for, but Senator Donovan and I are satisfied that an old man died a tragic death in a real straightforward way." Chief Theriot clearly anticipated my next few objections. His explanation did not erase those objections, but it did illustrate how a serial killer could operate so effortlessly.

"I truly respect your Andy of Mayberry way of policing your town, Chief Theriot. The thing is, neither you nor the senator are trained medical professionals capable of determining the cause of death. Furthermore, nothing in either of your authorities lets you tell a coroner what to do." I said to get the ball rolling on the fight that was about to erupt. "Here's your real problem. The collision happened on a state highway, and the state police are extremely interested in whether or not Judge Aubuchon was incapacitated prior to his death. I will be the one investigating this accident investigation starting now. I will give you until noon to deliver any evidence you have gathered and your witness statements to me at Judge Rogers' house. You do remember where that is, right?"

"And if I refuse to cooperate?" he challenged.

I reached into my pocket and removed the subpoena Captain Hammond was able to get for me earlier that morning. I tossed it on his desk.

"Then you might not be the chief of police come supper time." I said and stared him down. I caught the brief smirk Detective Chance fought to contain when I surprised both of them with the court order to cooperate. "You best get cracking. It's ten-thirty now."

There were probably many things Chief Theriot wanted to scream in my face, but he remained mute and scowling as Detective Chance and I walked out of his office.

"What do you think he's going to do?" Chance asked as I backed out of the driveway.

"First he's going to call Senator Donovan to ask his advice. Then he's going to cherry pick what he hands us to fit the decision he made last night. Which way to the funeral home?"

Detective Chance pointed to my right and I headed towards our second stop of the morning with my coupe's blue lights flashing and siren blaring. It was just for show, and meant only to remind the Chief of Police, who we could see staring at us through his office window, how limited his authority was.

I knew Theriot was going to want to find a way to save face, and I was aware of his past history of putting State Patrol officers in the hospital. The way his muscles flexed under his shirt when I pulled the rug out from under him was a sign that the two of us were going to go another round or two before I was able to leave town.

Sixty-Seven

Joffre Funeral Home was five blocks from the home of the chief of police. I felt silly for making such a big production of leaving Chief Theriot's residence to drive this short distance. I parked in the circular driveway of the modern-looking building and followed Chance inside the funeral home.

I was wearing my usual khaki pants, polo shirt, and work boots, so I felt under-dressed for visiting a funeral home. I decided to let the local detective do the talking.

"Robert Joffre." The owner introduced himself as he stepped out of the office just inside the tall double doors. He handed us each a business card.

"Detective Chance with Sheriff Mazant's Office, and this is Detective Holland from the state police," Chance said as we showed the man our badges.

"I have been hearing stories about you," the grinning middle-aged man said to me. "I guess you know by now that the Reaper always wins in the end. You saved Judge Aubuchon from death, but you only bought him a few more days among us. How tragic."

"Interesting choice of words, sir," I said to broach the potentially delicate subject of the way he determined the late judge's cause of death. "We are here to determine whether the judge's death was tragic or whether it was possibly intentional."

"How so?" The owner was understandably taken aback that we were only there to question his judgement and not to pay our respects to the dead.

"Detective Chance tells me that you are the coroner as well as the local funeral director," I said and started walking further into the business. My intent was to draw him away from his office. He followed me as Detective Chance silently blocked his path of retreat. "I would like to see the judge's body if you don't mind."

"That's not possible," Joffre declared.

"Why is that?" I pressed. Finding a judge to sign a court order was going to be a lot harder than finding a way to get this man to cooperate.

"His body has been sent for cremation."

"Before you did an autopsy?" I was no longer concerned with my personal appearance and Chance was being very slow to ask questions.

"I did a blood test for drugs and alcohol and found neither," Joffre hastened to give us an explanation. "I took tissue samples and sent those and a second blood sample to your own lab in Baton Rouge in case something else may have contributed to the accident. I just don't see what that might be."

"You still seem in quite a rush to dispose of the victim's body." I made a mental note to call Captain Hammond as soon as we left to have him lean on our lab to expedite the results. I was still waiting for Kirk Donovan's toxicology results. My patience with being in Saint Xavier Parish was nearing its breaking point now that I seemed to be finding a range of things other than Gwen's disappearance begging to be resolved.

Joffre wanted to assure me that he was not making these decisions on his own. "His final instructions were to donate his organs and cremate what remained as soon as possible. His exact words to me, when we made his funeral arrangements some years ago, were 'There's no reason to avoid the heat if I am going to Hell,' and I took him at his word.

"That didn't strike you as odd?" Chance finally joined the conversation.

"Not if you knew the judge, no. The judge made a lot of comments about being unfit to judge others. I think it's why he shifted to the civil law court. I only wish I had been able to do as he requested." Joffre elaborated. I knew neither Chance nor I were privy to the judge's past, both being outsiders and only having recently landed in the parish. The comments about the judge's mental condition did nothing to make me any more comfortable with how rapidly his last wishes were being carried out.

"What part of his final wishes were you unable to fulfill?" Chance pursued the matter.

"That damn Theriot kept the poor man's body at the scene for four hours after the accident. I had to send the organ recovery people away empty handed. Chief Theriot let that woman from the newspaper stand out there taking photographs from every damn direction, and he did sobriety tests on the other driver and every witness to the accident. The man has no idea what he is doing!" Joffre obviously needed to vent. All I took from his rant was that the police chief and newspaper editor were close enough friends that he called upon her to document the scene of his brief investigation.

"Well, I am in charge now, so hopefully things will go a little more smoothly. Did you see anything suspicious when you worked on the judge's body? Chief Theriot claims one of his deputies was following him and thought he saw him having a heart attack." I have problems with letting sheriff's deputies make medical diagnoses on the fly.

The funeral director seemed relieved that I had taken over the investigation. He shared my inclination to laugh at the deputy's opinion, and chuckled at my own scorn.

"I saw nothing to support any such opinion. In fact, I hoped to see his heart transplanted last night." The man seemed genuinely saddened at his inability to share any organs. "The judge believed that donating his organs was a path to immortality."

"Immortality seems preferable to the damnation you said he saw in his future just a moment ago." I pointed out. Joffre shrugged.

"I suppose you are right about that. Anyway, I called the organ bank and they had a team here an hour or so after he died to collect what they could. They were not pleased to have to stand there and watch the organs go to waste," Joffre continued.

"What now?" Detective Chance asked. Joffre and I both turned towards him to see which of us his question was directed towards.

"There will be the usual visitation tomorrow evening. We'll provide a stand-in casket, and then we will bury his ashes on Saturday," Joffre explained the business end of things. "If something turns up in what I sent to your crime lab, which I do not expect will occur, I will be in touch with you."

Chance and I looked at one another in a mix of frustration and anger. Clues were being taken from us, or being delayed indefinitely by bureaucracy and procedures beyond our control.

"Thank you for your time," I sighed and shook the funeral director's hand. Chance did the same and we fell in step behind him as he went back to work. "Oh, come to think of it, who is the executor of the judge's estate?"

"Senator Donovan. They were lifelong friends. Please join us for the visitation. I know the judge was well respected, but I also know he has no family, and I don't think he had many close friends." Joffre closed the glass office door behind him. We glanced at one another, but were at something of a loss for what to do next. Getting into a state senator's face about how he interfered with the investigation into his supposed friend's death seemed profoundly unwise. So unwise, in fact, that I immediately abandoned the idea.

Sixty-Eight

I found myself stuck for the moment. I had overcome my initial temptation to let Detective Chance know that I had been informed there was a hole in his still credible big-picture-of-things by the time I returned to Donovan.

Advising him that I had consulted with the FBI and that they believed his information on the Fultons was faulty only promised to create a wall between us going forward. There was absolutely nothing to be gained by altering him that FBI agents were busy investigating his background, either.

I drove back to Judge Rogers' house to wait for Chief Theriot. I had no idea how I was going to enforce the subpoena if he did not hand over what I demanded from him. The idea of arresting the local police chief had a bit of a thrill to it, but I grasped that it would make me a pariah in town. Any cooperation I might hope for from the locals would be gone, and his own stature elevated. I counted on Senator Donovan having second thoughts when the chief called him. Surely he wasn't interested in waging a fight with the state police that used Chief Theriot as his proxy. Hopefully the senator would be satisfied that he had thrown a wrench or two into the investigation.

I phoned Captain Hammond to notify him that he needed to send another wrecker to George's Automotive.

"You need to stop collecting dead people's cars," he only partially joked.

"To be fair, I believe only one of the two of them is dead. I still consider Gwen to be a missing person," I tried to counter.

"I'll believe that when you march her into my office." Hammond apparently still favored the dumped body theory to explain Gwen's fate. I realized I was behind on sending him the progress reports that showed how I came up with my own theory. The last time we had spoken about the case in depth was the day he handed me the early autopsy report on Kirk Donovan.

"I will have a much easier time doing that as soon as I have Kirk's final autopsy report. I still hope there is something in the toxicology report that explains how he drowned." I was glad I had called now. I had not been sure how to apply pressure on the state's medical examiner to get Kirk's final results any faster. Maybe my captain had that ability.

"Don't count on that," Hammond advised. "I understand there wasn't a lot to work with since he was in the water for so long. The crabs ate a lot of the evidence, as you can imagine."

"All the same, can you see how that is going? I don't want to be left hanging out in this place waiting on not one, but now two autopsy reports." I didn't mind that I sounded like I was pleading with him.

"I'll make a call and see what can be done."

I waited for him to be the one to end the call and then tossed my phone on the kitchen table.

"Trouble in paradise?" Chance asked and grinned. He had only heard my half of the call, and he knew nothing of the dynamic between my captain and myself.

"Always. My biggest hope right now is that there is something in the toxicology reports that will link Kirk's drowning to Judge Aubuchon's accident. That would solidify your own theory about how certain people are dying around here."

"So, you still believe me?" Chance must have had some reason of his own to suspect I had begun to doubt his research. Maybe he had tried to convince Sheriff Mazant before I came to town. That could not have gone well at all.

"Your theory is as good as any I have. Sooner or later things will fall into place or fall apart. That's when we figure out what the heck is going on around here." I stood up and went to the refrigerator for a cold drink, and offered one to Detective Chance. I caught the expression on his face and wondered if he was still trying to figure out whether my last comment was meant to encourage or to warn him.

Sixty-Nine

Chief Theriot arrived at the front door with a minute or two to spare. He carried a single cardboard file box in both hands and set it just to the left side of the front door. He rang the doorbell and turned to walk away.

I let him pout and leave without a word. It was not a good time to try to discuss the case with him, and I wanted to comb through what he left us before I began peppering him with the questions I had every reason to believe his shoddy police work were going to leave.

I began laying out the dozens of color photos Crystal Franks took. We figured that the best ones had been duplicated or culled for the next edition of the paper. We were already racing against the clock with the witnesses either of us wanted to question further. People would read her article and then begin to imagine her news account were their own memories.

Chance used the kitchen table to separate the witness statements from the files of photographs, and then began to separate the statements even further based upon the distance the witness stood from the accident. He combed through each statement to find anyone who actually watched the impact. He dismissed anyone who turned around after hearing the collision, or had been a block or more away from the scene, at least for the time being.

I began arranging the color photographs in a circle on the dining room table, trying to imitate walking around the car at the scene. It must have been a loud and horrible crash. Pieces of the judge's car and the truck's massive grille were recovered nearly a block away. Death had to have been instantaneous, but the judge was fully aware his car was crossing in front of the truck. I know the sinking feeling of inevitability in one's stomach all too well. I felt it as I saw the fiery arc of the RPG that tore apart a vehicle I was riding in the first time I died. To be a bit more precise, I should have died, but did not. I was resuscitated twice on a civilian hospital operating table while Tony held a gun on the doctors. *That* was a story I was not about to share with Detective Chance.

I was trained to analyze photographs by the best people in the intelligence business when I began to work for one of our shadowy three-letter agencies after leaving the Special Forces. Human nature is to look for what is familiar, but the things I learned to seek out are what I learned about in grade school. I began to seek anything that didn't belong, that was out of place, or that looked like it might have been added just for the photograph.

What immediately struck me was the expression on Judge Aubuchon's lifeless face. I expected to find some expression between terror and sad acceptance of his fate. Widened eyes, an open mouth, a very strong grip on the steering wheel are all of the things normally found in photographs of the victims at such crash scenes. All of that was present, but so were a couple of other small details I was sure that the police chief and the senator ignored. I was not convinced the coroner would have paid any attention to the one thing that stood out to me in the photographs. In fact, Joffre's comments had already confirmed he had missed them.

"What did you find?" Detective Chance shouted when I crossed the kitchen in a hurry. I ignored the question as I grabbed a file from the box of evidence related to Kirk Donovan's homicide. I removed all of the photos taken of Kirk's body when his Ford GT was recovered from the canal. The same thing had stood out to me when I saw those photos, but I had dismissed the possibility at the time. I accepted that prolonged immersion or the recovery angle when the car was pulled from the water would have affected Kirk's corpse. Seeing the same facial contortions twice was unlikely to be a coincidence.

I pulled one photo from my circular arrangement of Judge Aubuchon's accident photos and placed it on the kitchen counter next to the one I pulled from Kirk Donovan's folder. Detective Chance laid down the witness statement he was reading and came to stand next to me.

"Do you see it?" I asked. I knew I was going to have to explain what I saw in the photos.

"Neither of them looks like they died a very pleasant death," he lamely offered.

"Neither of them died a natural one, either," I said and moved my index finger towards the points that I wanted to show him. "Both of them had substantial rigor. Look at the way their shoulders are hunched slightly forward and upwards, and their faces have that weird contortion? It looks like they ate a bite of something sour, but they are actually having trouble breathing."

I gave him a moment to see what I was pointing out before I continued. I placed my index finger on one of the photos from the judge's accident. "And that is not how your body hits your shoulder strap in a car wreck. Your inclination is to try to duck as low as you can at the last instant. You want to avoid hitting the windshield. These days that puts your face in the path of the air bag. You are better off hitting the windshield."

"Okay, so both bodies went the wrong direction at the moment of impact, and they both had trouble breathing. What does that mean?" Chance was intrigued, but he also seemed to hate appearing clueless.

"There is a poison that causes shortness of breath and that sort of muscle spasm. A very low dose will make your muscles contract until you think you are about to lose your mind. The level in your blood stream is so low a toxicologist might ignore it. Your urine and kidney would carry a bit higher concentration, and there might be more than enough left in a kidney to kill anyone who got it in a transplant." The importance of this last piece of information was clear to Chance. There might have been more than incompetence to explain Theriot's being so slow to release Judge Aubuchon's body to the coroner. Maybe whoever wanted Aubuchon dead did not carry enough anger to intentionally endanger unknown organ recipients so they slowed his already botched investigation.

"And how do you know so much about this particular poison?" Chance wondered. It was a perfectly normal question, and it was one that ordinarily would have deserved an honest answer.

"I read a lot," I lied. The truth was that my own experience with using strychnine in small doses involved what could generously be called a war crime, but was far worse. I had allowed prisoners to be injected with doses meant to cause a level of anxiety and pain waterboarding never achieved. Knowing a man is capable of inflicting such a thing upon another human being was a large part of why I was not in favor of Chef Tony Venzo, as he calls himself now, courting my sister. "Someone absolutely wanted these men to suffer before they died."

Detective Chance stared down at the open mouthed and clearly pained expressions on the faces of the two men. There was every reason to believe they were both terrified of the inevitable death they saw no way to avoid, that they suffered a great deal in their final moments, and that neither of them had successfully bargained with death to repent the sins that brought this upon them in their final moments.

I walked over to the table and picked up my phone. I re-dialed the last number and watched Detective Chance pick up each photo in turn to study the contortions he now could not un-see.

"Detective Holland, it's been so long. How may I be of assistance?" Captain Hammond laughed into the phone.

"It's been just long enough to figure out what the lab needs to look for," I said in as serious a tone as he had ever heard me use.

"Which is what?" He came back to business as well.

"Have them check both men's kidney tissues for trace amounts of strychnine."

"Rat poison? You think someone killed them with rat poison? What's that all about?"

"It's about making sure they couldn't save themselves from a death they both would have seen coming." I was positive about the poison, and equally positive of the killer's motive in using this particular poison.

"I'll have them check when I hang up. Stay close to your phone. Does this tell you who is responsible?" Captain Hammond sounded a bit too optimistic.

"No, but revenge is a sloppy motive for murder. I just hope this points me to some other mistakes," I offered and hung upon him.

Seventy

I wouldn't call it an epiphany. The memory that came to mind when Roux nudged me in the dark to alert me to Chief Theriot's latest morning vigil was the result of wiggling a loose tooth in my conversation with Judge Rogers over eggs and mimosas.

Buried in his admission to lousy parenting was a choice of words that seemed to suggest a deeper meaning. Judge Rogers rationalized that giving his daughter's hand in what proved to be a bad marriage was part of some plan in which he would eventually come to her rescue. His exact words, which it took me a few minutes to find on the tape recording I had made during the meal, were "I also would not have had any way to save her when I saw the chance."

Had Judge Rogers seen a chance to finally get his daughter out of that marriage? I was not prepared to imagine he was the one who killed Kirk. For one thing, the modus operandi was the same as used to kill Judge Aubuchon, and I was confident that Judge Rogers was still in New Orleans when his old friend was murdered. What opportunity did the judge see to help his daughter escape? Questioning the judge was not the best way to find out.

He was the one who had me assigned to the case and created a scene to proclaim that it was Kirk who had killed her. I also didn't see Judge Rogers as being a man who went to extremes to protect anyone. As for his abused daughter, there were far too many past incidents that warranted killing Kirk, and too many easy opportunities for him to have done so in an easier way.

I knew I was not going back to sleep with this puzzle moving its pieces about in my head. I made a pot of coffee and watched Theriot sit in my driveway while I built and rejected a variety of scenarios to fit what Judge Rogers had said at brunch.

I rejected every scenario I came up with, but could not dismiss the piece which kept falling into place in the majority of the puzzles. I had to believe Judge Rogers knew where Gwen was the entire time I had been looking for her. The troubling question was what he meant by 'help her when the time came.' Did the two of them load trash bags filled with her belongings into his Lincoln Navigator and drive her to a place they both felt she would be safe? Belle was away at college and they may have seen this as her perfect opportunity for Gwen to leave Kirk, and his abuse, behind. Maybe Gwen meant to divorce him, which was further proof she was not the one who poisoned him. Having some sort of legal recourse to reclaim her life made it nearly impossible to imagine her killing Kirk to escape the hell he made of their marriage.

Seventy-One

The sun was barely rising when I left Donovan for New Orleans. Belle was still asleep when Roux and I came into my spare bedroom and turned on the overhead light. I had taken three deep breaths before I opened the door, but the four hours I had been awake and thinking about her mother's disappearance made me increasingly anxious to test a couple of theories, and to ask questions Belle and Judge Rogers were unlikely to want to answer.

"What the...?" Belle groaned at the burst of light and Roux's grinning face suddenly appearing inches from her own.

"I need some answers," I said and sat on the foot of her bed.

"Right now? You need to ask me questions right now?" She was still trying to wake up. I was counting on her being a bit confused to keep her from lying to me, or at least lying poorly.

"Do you know where your mother is?"

"What?" Her tone was one of confusion. "No. Why would I? Aren't you the one supposed to be looking for her?"

"This is what me looking for your mother looks like," I informed her and held my next few questions until she finished sitting up in bed. I took a moment to be thankful she slept fully clothed.

"What's this all about?" Tulip demanded as she came through the doorway. I was glad she was present. She could give Belle legal counsel while I questioned her client.

"I need to find Gwen. Today. I believe either Belle or Judge Rogers helped her leave town the same day Kirk died," I finally explained the wild interruption to both of them.

"That's a nasty accusation to make against either of them. You really want to be sure of your facts before you get in the judge's face," Tulip warned me. "And why is today more important than any other day? You have had three weeks to get this excited about tracking her down."

"Because I think someone plans to kill her, Judge Rogers, and Senator Donovan. I haven't figured out why, but I know that your mother and grandfather have bullseyes on their backs for sure," I said to Belle and tried to explain myself as best I could to the still groggy women.

"I take it you have had a break in the case," my sister sighed and leaned against the doorframe. She was wearing one of Tony's cashmere pullover sweaters as a nightgown. I was not about to ask how that came to be.

"Captain Hammond is having our lab confirm that both Kirk and Judge Aubuchon were given doses of strychnine to incapacitate them long enough to arrange their murders to look like accidents. I believe this all has something to do with Camp Dumaine."

"What is Camp Dumaine?" Tulip asked. She gave me the expression she reserves for when someone's story has jumped its tracks.

"My grandfathers ran a summer camp for poor kids years ago. I don't know why they quit," Belle told her.

"Finding out why may explain why so many people are dying now," I said. "You went to Colorado to write your paper. Do you have any idea where your mother might have gone to hide out?"

I was counting on Belle knowing her mother well enough to know the woman's happy place.

"Not really."

"Any friends or family she could count on to give her a place to hide?" I was already debating the idea of approaching Captain Hammond about a search warrant for Judge Rogers' house in New Orleans. Surely the judge was smarter than to hide the daughter he asked me to locate in his own house.

"All of her friends live in Donovan," Belle said. "Her best friend is that lady that owns the newspaper. You might ask her."

"I might," I said without betraying the buzz piece of information sent down my spine.

"I know she used to talk to my grandmother every week. She might have a better idea," Belle continued to try to help. She was considerably more awake, and better able to comprehend the urgency I placed on locating her mother in the next few hours.

"I need your grandmother's phone number and address." I decided to pursue that lead rather than bang on her grandfather's door. He needed to be the last person I accused of harboring his daughter.

"I'll get it for you," Belle mumbled and left the room.

"I haven't seen you this worked up in a while. What's really going on?" Tulip pressed as soon as Belle was out of the room.

"I am a step behind a serial killer who is working their way down a list of everyone who had anything to do with that summer camp. They have killed a half dozen people so far, and Senator Donovan and Judge Rogers are two of the last names I believe are likely targets," I said in a voice loud enough that only Tulip heard what I had to say. "Her pal Bradley is mixed up in this as well, which puts him on the wrong side of the law."

"Oh, dear." Tulip glanced out the doorway and down the hall. Dear wasn't the actual word she used, which was only part of the reason she checked to see if Belle heard her.

"Stay with her until you hear from me. Don't let her use her phone at all. No incoming or outgoing calls, emails, or texts. I have no idea how you will enforce that, but she needs to understand her mother and grandfather are at risk."

"I'll take care of her. You know Tony will, as well," my sister assured me. I took comfort in knowing Tony would defend her. I might not get past him myself.

"Here's my grandmother's address and phone number," Belle said and handed me a piece of paper.

"Thank you. Now do what your attorney tells you. I need to go change clothes." I gave her an unexpected hug and she silently watched Tulip give my cheek a kiss as Roux and I headed out the door.

Seventy-Two

I put Detective Chance on my car's speaker phone as I drove Uptown from the French Quarter. He was already at Sheriff Mazant's department and wondering when I would be there.

"Go see Gabouri and have him get a warrant for Judge Aubuchon's house so you can search for anything with strychnine as an ingredient, no matter how little. Be sure to check out his medicine cabinet."

"His medicine cabinet?" Chance scoffed.

"Yes. Strychnine has been used in homeopathic drugs for years. Maybe the judge didn't realize it and took too much of something that contains it. Be sure to wear gloves and not to drink or eat anything you find there." This last was a needlessly condescending warning. Of course he would not be eating or drinking the dead man's food or booze. "That includes using any of his glasses to drink from."

"Got it," Chance said a bit testily. "We don't know how he was poisoned. Someone may have dusted his food or dishware. Anything else you want to lecture me on?"

"I'll be sure to call you back if I think of anything. Just be careful, okay?" I tried to make my rudeness seem like it was more of a joke than it was. One careless move in the late judge's house could lead to another funeral.

"What are you up to right now? It sounds like you are driving."

"I am. I am chasing down something that is probably nothing. Let's get together later this afternoon. I will call you when I get back in town."

"I'll let you know what I find at the judge's place. We can compare notes." What he meant was that he expected me to tell him about the lead I was after in exchange for what he found in the search. Sheriff Mazant was going to be upset by his being shut out of what I was up to yet again, so he needed to have something to offer his boss.

The address Belle gave me was to a stately home on Audubon Street, one block from Audubon Park and within easy walking distance from

Belle's house. The home I parked in front of spoke to me of a childhood far different than that of even the Donovan children from Saint Xavier Parish. This was the sort of old money and manners I knew from my mother's family, and I intended to act accordingly.

I chose to knock on the front door rather than to try to contact the family by telephone, although I had considered calling first and waiting to see if anyone tried to flee the house. My decision was based on understanding that Gwen was protected by more than just her mother's obvious social position. There were very likely one or two good lawyers on speed dial as well. I had decided to change clothes when I saw the address Belle handed me in her bedroom. I was now wearing one of my better blue suits and a pressed dress shirt and red necktie. I needed to project as much authority as possible.

"May I help you, sir?" a Black woman of about fifty, in a maid's uniform complete with apron, cracked the door just enough to ask the question. Her expression did not change upon seeing the badge I held in my hand.

"I need to speak with Gwendolyn Rogers, if she is here." I said this as politely as I could, even though it implied legal peril for the occupants of the home.

"Please excuse me. I will fetch Missus Bellerive," she said and closed the leaded-glass door. I swore I heard her latch it as well.

A slender woman about my mother's age was the next person to open the door. I managed to count to fifteen between when the door closed and when the door opened the second time. In my experience this meant my presence was known before I stepped foot on the porch. Someone may have noticed when I parked the XLR coupe at the curb, or they had been tipped off that I was on my way. The latter meant the chances of finding Gwen here were now a lot less than I had hoped.

"What is it that you need?" the woman asked. Her tone and rigid posture reminded me of my mother. This woman's clothes and hair cost far more than what my own mother shelled out to look immaculate. I should also add that my mother never wears nearly as much expensive jewelry before noon on a weekday.

I waved my golden badge at her, but took no steps forward. "I am

Detective Holland from the Louisiana state police. I am currently investigating your daughter's disappearance from Saint Xavier Parish. I believe she may be here."

'Why would you assume any such thing, Detective?" the woman dismissed my hunch with a thin smile.

"Because, frankly," I said and looked her in the eye. "I do not believe she has anywhere else to hide."

Mrs. Bellerive blinked at my rather stark response and then let her lips drop into a slight frown.

"So, you have come here to arrest my daughter for the murder of her late husband."

"I am here to do nothing of the sort. No warrant has been issued for her arrest, so we both know I don't have the legal authority to tell you to step aside." I was trying to be my most disarming self. We also both knew I could produce a warrant, a street full of NOPD officers, and half a dozen news crews with a phone call. Neither of us were excited at the prospect of being on the evening news.

"If my daughter is not a fugitive, then what interest do you have in her whereabouts?" The woman remained firmly rooted in the doorway.

"She can answer questions I hope will lead me to her husband's killer. I do not believe she played any part in murdering Kirk, but I believe she knows the identity of the person who poisoned her husband and left him to drown." There was no point in holding any details back from this woman. If my hunch was correct, she was going to hear all of this after I spoke with Gwendolyn, anyway.

"Would that not place her in great danger?" Gwen's mother was no fool. "Would her being here not place this family in danger? I cannot believe you think my daughter would endanger her own family."

"Who better to protect her?" I countered, and then stepped inside. I glanced into the rooms opening onto the foyer. "Madam, as my father used to say, if we are going to dance then I get to lead. Yes or no, is Gwen here?"

"She is not," a younger woman spoke from the top of the stairs. She wore nothing but a dressing gown.

"Good morning. May we speak in private?"

"We can speak, but I am not who you are looking for." She turned and disappeared down the second floor hallway. I assumed she was on her way to change clothes or to call her attorney, or both.

"May I offer you a cup of coffee while we wait?" Mrs. Bellerive asked as though I were an old family friend and waved me towards the living room. The maid was already setting a tray with china cups and saucers and a silver coffeepot on the sideboard which usually served as a bar. I yearned for a splash of their Irish whiskey in my coffee.

The blonde poured herself a cup of coffee and took a seat beside her mother before she introduced herself as Magdalena, Gwendolyn's older sister. She shared her mother's refined taste and wardrobe budget.

"I am not going to read you your rights. Neither of you are considered to be a suspect nor do I want you to answer me as though you believe you are one. I am here strictly to learn background information on your sister's marriage and her late husband's law practice. I am trying to better understand what happened the day Gwendolyn left town. I have no intention of taking her back to Donovan if you divulge her location. In fact, I suggest she remains in hiding until I notify you that it is safe for her to come home. Belle is presently in protective custody, in case you have been worried about that." I wanted to ease any fears of a trap being laid by my questioning. I very firmly believed one or both of them knew where Gwen was hiding, but would go to jail before they divulged her whereabouts. "Okay?"

"What would you like to know?" Magdalena asked and leaned towards me. She and her mother occupied the sofa while I flanked them in one of the matching upholstered rolled-arm chairs. My coffee was getting cold on the small table between the chairs.

I removed my tape recorder from my pocket and showed it to the women before I turned it on and placed it atop a stack of magazines on the coffee table.

"Whatever you can share with me. I find it curious that Gwendolyn did not leave Kirk before now. I base my assertion that she did not kill him on the fact she has had ample opportunity to kill him in self-defense, if she were so inclined. He was a lousy husband, engaged in a fairly odious line of legal work, and was raised by wolves. I understand

Gwendolyn married Kirk because she was carrying his child and your family was opposed to her terminating the pregnancy."

"Not the entire family," Mrs. Bellerive declared. "I had absolutely no issue with doing so, if it meant sparing our daughter a lifetime under a Donovan roof. There was nothing to be gained by destroying the lives of two teenagers to protect one unborn child. I think you would agree that marriage ought not to carry a life sentence. Have you ever been married, Detective?"

"My father said something very similar when he advised me to avoid marriage for as long as possible," I shared for no particular reason. "I imagine the situation brought considerable stress to your household."

"Can we stop pussy-footing about here, Detective?" Mrs. Bellerive sighed and set down her own coffee cup. "I divorced Cyrus because he insisted our daughter marry that dreadful man-child and give the Donovans yet another heir to corrupt. It meant Gwendolyn had to leave high school in her sophomore year and to be stuck in that miserable town for the rest of her life. She toughed it out to make sure that Belle fared better than she did. She has mentioned the idea of divorcing Kirk once Belle finished college, but I never imagined she might leave him now."

"Why would she have done so that particular day, in your opinion?" I probed as gently as possible.

"I imagine she must have felt her life was in danger from someone other than Kirk," Mrs. Bellerive said and furtively glanced toward her older daughter.

"She mentioned to me that she believed Kirk was having an affair with a woman who intended to be his next wife, at any cost," Magdalena put forth. This was a new avenue to pursue, and entirely credible from what I now knew of Kirk's infidelities.

"Did she mention any names?" I nearly pleaded.

"Names? I like your sense of humor, Detective," the older woman chuckled. "My daughter mentions that one woman had designs on her husband and you immediately leapt to the idea of their being a veritable stable of possible women."

"Since we're being so honest, we all know that there was. I was just curious if Gwendolyn mentioned any one of them in particular. Perhaps your daughter ran because she couldn't look over more than one shoulder at a time." This was becoming a parlor game and I was about ready to stop playing along.

"I'm sorry, but no, she did not mention any names," Magdalena apologized without sounding apologetic.

"Is there anything else you can tell me? Perhaps you could point me in a direction to find your daughter." I suggested rather firmly as I stood up. This had not been a waste of time, but it was certainly not as productive as I had hoped it would be.

"I'm sorry, but there simply isn't anything I can tell you," Mrs. Bellerive also failed to really apologize as she stood up. She took my hand in hers and then gave me a very curious look. "I do believe you look more like your mother than your father."

"That should be difficult to determine. I needed reconstructive surgery a few years ago and my sister chose this face from a magazine," I said, as much to confound the woman as to invite an explanation for her last statement. "How do you know my parents?"

"Well, I wouldn't say I truly knew your father. Your mother and I have been in the same PEO chapter for years, but then how would you know that? You were absent from New Orleans for quite some time. You really should stop to see her before you head back to Donovan."

"I will be certain to do just that," I assured her. It was going to be my very next stop, in fact. Maybe my mother had more answers to give me, along with her own advice or more wry words of wisdom from the internet swami she insists on paying to speak to her in the sort of aphorisms my father drove her nuts with for years.

"Do give her my regards," Mrs. Bellerive said and dropped my hand. I was a bit dazed as I followed the silent maid to the door and headed straight to my car.

Seventy-Three

Roger met me at the front door of my mother's house in the Rigolets, the narrow space of marshy ground between Lake Borgne and Lake Ponchartrain, even before I knocked on the heavy cypress door. He wore a bemused smile as he silently swung the door wide and used his left index finger to point me towards the patio. I could see my mother and another woman enjoying the brunch being served by my mother's Vietnamese housekeeper. The Black housekeeper I grew up with could not afford to return to New Orleans after the storm, and my mother was delighted to find someone willing to work at the pre-storm wages she wanted to pay. It had occurred to me more than once that the new housekeeper might be stealing our family's silver to supplement her paltry paycheck, but I didn't really care.

The two women briefly turned at the sound of my sliding the door between the living room and expansive patio open. I immediately recognized Gwendolyn Donovan from the photographs in her new home. I also recognized the triumphant smirk on my mother's face, her prideful way of letting me know she believes she is always going to be smarter than I am. I will concede that she is certainly always going to be more devious.

"I should have known," I said as I shook my head. "You came to the bistro to let me know you were going to find a way to get into this. Was Gwen already staying here when you and Roger dropped by?"

"Of course. She has been here since the day she left her dreadful husband," my mother laughed and offered me a mimosa. I refused, but only because I was going to want a stronger cocktail very soon.

"And you probably recommended me to Judge Rogers after she called her mother and he called you." I had little trouble piecing this particular puzzle together. "What I want to know is why you thought it important to have me in place at all. The only person who knew Kirk was dead the night I met your father was whoever killed him. Hiding out does not make Gwen look innocent of having a part in that murder."

"I needed help after I received a phone call telling me Kirk was dead. The caller told me that my brilliant plan to make it look like Kirk had killed me was going to make it look like I killed him," Gwendolyn explained how she had inadvertently put herself in this mess.

"Who called you?" I asked. I had a very brief hope that I was about to discover the identity of Saint Xavier Parish's serial killer.

"I didn't recognize the voice. It was a young man who sounded like he was in his twenties. That is all I can tell you." Gwendolyn apologized.

"Could it have been Bradley Ladd?" I suggested.

"Bradley? Why in the world would you even suggest such a thing? He and Kirk got along fine, and he is one of my daughter's closest friends." Gwendolyn seemed truly incensed at the idea.

"What do you know about Bradley Ladd?"

"He was Belle's math tutor at Tulane. She found out he lives in Donovan, as well, and used to invite him to use the pool at my father's house. Bradley told us his father had died and he moved to Donovan to learn the ropes of the family business. Kirk gave him legal advice from time to time." I watched Gwendolyn struggle to make sense of what part Bradley may have played in her predicament.

"There is a lot about him that you don't know and should."

"I still can't see Bradley killing my husband." She had made up her mind and I would only waste time trying to make her change it.

"Walk me through your leaving town. What time did you leave the house and how did you get here?" These were the obvious questions, and the ones I knew she would have the most practiced answers to give me.

"Kirk left the house about eleven o'clock. He always claimed he was going to make some test laps before leaving for his races, but what he was really doing was meeting his mistress in one of the rental cabins at the old summer camp our fathers used to run." Gwen delivered this new tidbit with no emotion. She either didn't care he was cheating on her then, or she was past caring about it now that he was dead.

"The cabins that used to be Camp Dumaine," I interjected to let her know I was familiar with the camp's history.

"That's right," she said and paused to take a sip of her mimosa. I wished I knew how many she had already been served.

"Your husband seemed to have an affinity for the place. He was wearing a T-shirt with the camp's name on it when we found him."

"Really?" she asked and paused. "He never owned a shirt like that that I can recall."

"It did look new," I added. She just shook her head. "I began packing everything that I wanted to take with me into trash bags the minute he left the house. I took all of my clothes, and a couple of photographs of Belle and myself," Gwen began. I hated to interrupt her again, but I needed to do so.

"And that is all you took with you? The house was nearly empty of photographs. Your husband's desk was cleaned out. We found his laptop in his car when we pulled it from the canal."

"He always had that thing with him," Gwen said in what sounded a lot like a hiss. "He had a lot of video files on it from the annual pageant. I would find him sitting in his office watching them at night."

"Uh, huh," I mumbled. I was hoping there was more to that part of her story. She snapped out of whatever memory had been triggered and gave me a look I couldn't interpret.

"You used to run that pageant, correct?" I merely meant to let her know I was aware of her supposed role in organizing the event.

"What I did was to try to keep it from being obscene," she said with surprising anger. "What my husband and his father wanted was something along the lines of stripper tryouts. They insisted on a bathing suit competition involving ten year old girls doing not much more than parading around the stage for twenty minutes. The talent segments were a joke, largely because none of the girls had any talents. The local schools don't have music or theatre departments to speak of. More money goes into home economics than women's sports at the high school. The swim suit part of the older girls' routine was what drew the crowd every year. It took me a long time to realize this was all just a means for the senator and Kirk to show off very young girls to men who might be interested in marrying them." Gwen avoided looking at my mother's facial expression.

"How many of the girls would you say wound up married after the show?"

"Oh, no, it was never that obvious. It might be a year or two before the girls were married off. I would say Kirk handled two or three under-age marriages every month. There were also a few boys he and Judge Aubuchon put up for adoption," Gwen calculated. She could see my mother's growing revulsion and straightened her posture before she tried to explain what she believed we were missing. "It is not like there was an assembly line. The culture in Saint Xavier Parish is that females are put on this planet to serve the men. A young girl is said to get herself pregnant, as though the father played no part in it whatsoever. The only acceptable solution to unplanned pregnancies is to marry the girl off to a man willing to raise her child as their own. It means fourteen year old girls are being seduced and then finding out the price of their mistake is to wake up next to some stranger her dad's age for the rest of her life. There is no such thing as rape out there, either. If a young man forces himself on someone then the court is willing to drop the charges if he marries her. It was how Kirk got away with raping me."

"Where are the parents in all of this?" I asked. I could tell that this was perhaps the first time my mother had heard any of these stories. She was visibly distraught.

"Most of them cannot afford to raise their daughter *and* her child. The Donovans only pay a bit more than minimum wage to anyone that isn't an illegal immigrant they can pay even less. It makes everyone so afraid of losing their job that they do whatever the senator and his brothers tell them to do. Kirk kept tabs on every family in town and was always ready to help them get rid of a kid or two, and he had a waiting list of people looking for children. I know for a fact that at least one or two of the men he helped had histories of sexually abusing children. Kirk would handle the legal work and a couple of weeks later the parents would suddenly have cash to burn. It was obvious what was going on, and it made selling your children a little too tempting for some people." This confirmed the worst things I suspected her late husband of having done.

"Supposedly the pageant raised money for the Donovan Foundation. What did the Foundation do?"

"There is no Foundation. That is just a story Kirk and Chester tell everyone to get them to take part. I think any contributions they get are funneled into Chester's re-election campaigns." Gwendolyn snorted at the idea of either man being benevolent.

"How much of this had to do with the abuse you endured for so long?"

"A lot." Gwen was finally able to smile. "I gave Kirk an earful every time he and one of the senator's judges sent another child into hell. I didn't care how hard he beat me. I wanted him to know what a piece of..."

Gwen stopped and took a deep breath. My mother and I remained mute as she gathered her emotions and checked her anger enough to get back to our conversation.

"Let's just work on that Friday," I suggested. "Were you aware of Belle's travel plans?"

"Yes. Belle going to Colorado was my suggestion. I didn't want her to be there when Kirk came home and found out I had left him."

"So, what, the plan was to hide out here and file for divorce?" I was beginning to see the ways her grand plan had gone off the rails.

"I planned to come here until it was all taken care of. Belle was away at school, and she had already made it clear that she was never going to live under Kirk's roof again. She gave me the strength to get away from him myself."

"How did your car wind up with a trunk full of blood?" She had not mentioned this part of her plan.

"That was not part of my idea," Gwen said and sighed. "That was Crystal's way of making things hard for Kirk and the senator."

"Who is Crystal?" my mother asked. It occurred to me that the two of them had not yet had this conversation. My mother apparently allowed her friend's daughter to hide at her home without once asking why, or probably for how long. I remembered that she never asked me about Tony's taking up residence in the former boat house for nearly a year while he was getting Strada Ammazarre up and running.

"She is the local newspaper editor. Belle interned for her last summer and we became friends. I don't have very many of my own friends, so it was nice," Gwen explained.

"Back up a bit. Why were you trying to make things so hard for Senator Donovan?" To me he seemed slightly removed from her issues with her husband.

"The senator is blocking a bill that would change the child-marriage laws in the state. He is in charge of the committee that is supposed to debate it and send it to the floor for a vote. He refuses to even let it be brought up. Our idea was to give him something more important to think about. It was going to look pretty bad for him if his son was the prime suspect in my murder."

"That it would," I immediately agreed. I saw a bit of genius in the plan. Uncle Felix would have been envious of its simplicity. "So, you came up with this plan all on your own?"

"No. Crystal Franks was the one who suggested I fake my death to make Kirk squirm for a while. She helped me recruit my father to collect the blood to fake my death. He is all in favor of crippling Senator Donovan's stature in the capital, and he has his own reasons to hate the Donovans. I would make a trip to see him every couple of weeks and he began storing my blood."

"He told me he served as a medic with the Marines in Vietnam," I shared this for no real reason except that his picture came back to me when she said he took her blood.

"Right," Gwen was obviously quite surprised that I knew this about her father. "The goal was four pints of blood, enough that it would look like I had to be dead."

"Our lab estimates you only used half that much," I interrupted again.

"That's probably about right. Kirk banishing Belle to Colorado gave us the perfect opportunity. Everyone but Kirk would have an alibi. I made a point to get in a couple of arguments with him at the country club. Crystal planned to start some gossip that Kirk might have wanted me out of the way to marry his mistress. Anyway, I read that they use corn syrup and dye to imitate blood in the movies. I used real blood instead of the dye, but I was still worried corn syrup might ruin the DNA sample."

"It might. We matched the blood type to see if it was yours, but still don't have your DNA results." I informed her. "It took the lab a few days to sort out what you mixed the blood with. You left behind a very convincing crime scene. Which brings me to your father's stellar performance the night he insisted I be assigned to the case."

"I never told him where I was going to hide," Gwen started to explain.

"I told him to ask for your help after Gwen received the phone call about being framed for Kirk's murder," my mother interrupted for a second time. I think she was just rubbing my nose in the fact she had helped to put this together. "You never would have heard about this if that call didn't happen. Senator Donovan insisted that the local police could find her. They would have allowed him to become a lot more involved in trying to prove his son was innocent. Gwendolyn was going to reappear and divorce Kirk after the bill was sent to the Senate floor and voted on. It would surely pass."

"Best laid plans of mice and women," I grumbled. The two women were right. Senator Donovan would have insisted that Sheriff Mazant conclude that his son did not dump his wife's body in the bayou.

"I made sure I filled up my car at a station with good surveillance cameras, and I made a few appointments to do things I was never going to have done, just to make it seem like I had plans to be around. I went home and Crystal heled me cram everything that I could into my car and drove me to meet my father at the boat dock. Crystal and my father poured the blood and syrup into the trunk of my car and he dropped me off at a gas station where my sister was waiting for me. My sister drove me here so nobody else in my family would know where I was hiding but the two of us. We figured Kirk and Chester would beat the bushes pretty hard to find me. Honestly, my plan was just to let Kirk be a suspect for a couple of weeks and then hit him with the divorce."

"You must have freaked out when you heard Kirk was dead." This put the largest possible fly in the ointment.

"To say the least. I was going to be the prime suspect, and my father would be an accessory. I not only lost my alibi, but I became the most obvious suspect in his death. All of our fights, the fact I had cleared out all of my stuff, the fake evidence in the trunk of my car. My father and I were framed perfectly." She sounded as if she admired the person who went to so much work to thwart her.

"Who do you think set you up?" I had an idea or two.

"I have no idea. The only person who knew about the whole plan was Crystal. I doubt she double crossed me." I was a lot less sure, but she knew Crystal better than I did. I would not have trusted Crystal to tie my shoes. "I told your mother about the call and the mess I got my family into. She told me not to worry, that she had an idea for how to fix things."

"I guess I was supposed to be that big idea?" I asked my mother.

"It's worked so far," she laughed said poured herself a fresh mimosa. I assumed the maid had been given the rest of the day off to get her out of earshot of all of this. "So tell us what you are going to do now."

"I wish I knew," I admitted. "There were two attempts on Judge Aubuchon's life while I have been in Donovan. The last one worked. I think I know how he and Kirk were killed, but it is a much harder job to prove something than it is to believe it."

"I understand. Do you think you can prove I did not kill Kirk?" Gwendolyn was almost pleading.

"I will need to figure out who made that phone call to you. I think it takes more than one person to pull off the homicides I have been able to isolate as being their handiwork. Maybe one of them drunk dialed you, or they just wanted to make you sweat."

"You have to find them. What if they go after Belle to get to me?" Gwen insisted.

"You are both are safe, for now," I assured her. I had some other questions I still wanted to ask. "There are some other things I need to know about you and Kirk. I believe all of this is tied to something that happened years ago. You said you didn't believe Kirk owned a T-shirt from that summer camp. Do you agree that whatever sparked this killing spree might have begun there?"

"That's such a long time ago," Gwen balked.

"Revenge is a dish best served cold, right? What can you remember from the summer camp that might have ruined anyone else's life?" I asked. "It probably has nothing to do with the sort of exploitation that seems to have happened every day."

I still had a hard time imagining that anyone considered the things the camp expected of those children to be just 'kid fun' or normal. Gwen's description of the place confirmed my worst fears that the camp was used to teach children to accept being used and that he kids were screened for vulnerabilities.

"I have the best reason for revenge, but I swear I did not kill my husband," Gwendolyn said and paused. "It was where Kirk raped me. We were both counselors one summer, and everyone used to party at the wreck of the old riverboat after lights out. I did not usually go, but this one night I went to tell Kirk that the girl he had invited had twisted her ankle and was not going to be there. She didn't want him to think she stood him up. He insisted that I hang out, and a couple of the other counselors talked me into staying. I got a little too high and drunk and Kirk offered to walk me back to my cabin. He got me alone on the old boat and then he pushed me down and raped me. I tried to remind him that the girl who was supposed to be there still wanted to be with him, but he said he didn't care about either one of us. He told me we were put on the planet to keep him happy, and he made himself a lot happier than he did me. It stayed that way until the day I packed up and left. I still don't see what that has to do with anything. You need to focus on protecting my family."

"That is made easier by knowing everything about your family." I was not going to tell her that her story only made her seem like an even better suspect in Kirk's death. Only the additional killings and the caller's intent to drag her father into the matter made me question her guilt.

"Your father tipped his hand when he told me he always tried to be in position to help you when he could. He waited an awfully long time to come get you."

"It took us twenty-two years, but we hoped that my leaving Kirk might hurt the Donovans as much as they hurt our family. Kirk cheated on me from the beginning and Chester Donovan never treated Belle like he did any of his other grandchildren or nieces and nephews. Chester is livid about the research paper Belle has written about the Donovans. He threatened to disown Kirk if he didn't find a way to make her stop."

"She says she has a book deal," I tossed in.

"Good!" Gwendolyn cheered her daughter on. "That would be perfect. Let the old man try to explain away the truth about his family's history. His reputation is built on a house of cards. They try to act like they are owed everything just because their family supposedly helped build the state. Wait until everyone finds out how they stole everything they have from the very people he counts on to vote for him."

"It could get very interesting," I quietly agreed. My mother and Uncle Felix were not likely to be any happier with the book being published than the senator.

"What are you going to do now?" Mother asked. "Surely you aren't going to drag this dear girl back to Donovan with you."

"No, that was never going to happen," I shook my head and then turned to face Gwendolyn directly. "To be clear, you do not need to fear any charges for anything that happened after you left, but I will need to find a way to expose the killer so I can clear you. I still have Senator Donovan and your father to use as bait. Hopefully they will go after Chester first."

"That's hardly a plan," my mother protested as I stood up to leave.

"When has anything I ever done worked the way I planned?" I joked. I used to be very good at planning things, but lately I was having considerably more luck with making things up as I went along. "Just do both of us a favor, alright? Don't let anyone know I have tracked you down. I'll call if I need either of you to help any further, or when the coast is clear."

Gwen nodded her agreement. My mother raised her right hand into the air, directing me to kiss her on the cheek. I was scowling in direct proportion to how much she was smiling as I made my way across the patio towards my car.

Seventy-Four

I stopped for lunch at The Joint, a barbecue place just a couple of blocks from the river levee on Poland Street. It was one of the first places to eat in the neighborhood after the post-storm flooding subsided. I was unwilling to pass up the opportunity for good barbecue just because I was wearing a necktie. I washed my plate of sliced brisket down with an Abita Turbodog. The beer was about as dark as my mood, but my spirits improved the longer I sat at the outdoor table enjoying the day's unseasonable warmth and the satisfaction of discovering Gwendolyn's whereabouts.

My phone rang just as I was standing up to leave. I looked at the caller ID and sat back down before I took the call.

"Hey, Captain, please say you have something good." My captain owed me a stack of things that promised to provide at least a few more clues to pursue.

"I have quite a bit, actually. I was going to drive down this afternoon and give it to you." This meant he had something he felt was unusually sensitive to share with me. He doesn't usually mind using patrol officers or an email to send me routine paperwork, but he always hand-delivers evidence when he wants to be sure to see my reaction.

"I'm on the interstate now. Why don't I come by your office in a couple of hours? I have something to tell you as well." I wanted to share Gwendolyn's explanation for having left Kirk with him just to see his reaction.

"Good, Lord," Captain Hammond said and rubbed his eyes when I stepped into his office. "I believe I am seeing things. Is this really you in a suit?"

"I own a couple of them," I drily responded. I wore a tuxedo to the crime scene of my first homicide case, but that was because Chief Avery and I had to leave a dinner party to be there. "Do we draw straws for who goes first?"

"No. You are going to tell me what you know and then I am going to send you away with a lot more things to do," Hammond said with uncharacteristic humor before he sat down behind his desk. He had a small stack of file folders in front of him. They were very neatly bound with a pair of rubber bands and a Post-it note with my name on it.

"Gwendolyn Donovan is hiding out at my mother's house in the Rigolets."

Hammond's face tightened just a bit and his grin collapsed into a tight-lipped scowl as he digested the information. "You didn't take her into custody?"

"I don't think she did anything wrong," I said and held up a hand to ward off the stern lecture I saw coming about trying my own cases. "She claims Crystal Franks and her father helped her fake her death. She wanted to leave her husband, but wanted to do it in a way that would also distract Senator Donovan. There is some piece of legislation stuck in his committee that the two women didn't want him to think about as much as he would have about Kirk being arrested for killing her. Gwendolyn claims she knew nothing about any plot to kill Kirk, and that she only learned about that when someone called to let her know she had framed herself. She says that it was a male in their twenties, but she didn't recognize the caller's voice. I gave her a name, and she says it was not them, so I don't have much to work with there."

"I might have something to steer you in a new direction." Hammond pulled the bands from the stack of files and removed the third one down. He opened it and tossed a mugshot across the desk.

"Say hello to Pamela Fulton. She is the daughter–in-law of Jack and Bernice Fulton, and the widow of their son Hank." I picked up the photograph and studied the face of a much younger looking Crystal Franks. It took a moment to recognize her. Her hair was lighter and her breast size and nose had been surgically improved. The coldness in her eyes was not something time or surgery would ever remove.

"The same Fultons who died in a house fire?" The connection was obvious, and it threw another wrench into Chance's conspiracy theory. Now the question was why she would have steered his research to that fatal fire in the first place.

338

"The couple were probably murdered before the house caught fire. The local fire chief wrote it off as a space heater fire, but there is a report in here from the state fire marshal that claims an accelerant was used. The couple's bodies were so badly burned we couldn't do much of an autopsy. The coroner could not tell they had not died from smoke inhalation."

"Why did anyone even consider that they were murdered?" I felt like I was starting my investigation over.

"Because Pamela publicly threatened the couple. It is safe to say the woman you know as Crystal has anger issues," Hammond smiled and slid me the top file. "She married Hank when she was seventeen. He was nineteen. They had two children by the time she was nineteen, as well as a miscarriage. Her crack addiction probably had something to do with the miscarriage. Hank divorced her after that and went to live with his parents. Pamela began supporting her drug habit by pimping her children out to anyone who would pay for her crack. Hank found out and petitioned the court to take the children from her. She threatened to kill Hank and his parents during the hearing, and wound up stabbing Hank in an argument not long after. She had a couple of bruises and the district attorney decided not to press charges against her because he wasn't sure he could get a conviction. Hank's parents got stuck with raising the kids. The children had literally been raised by wolves and Hank's parents were way too old to control them. They asked Senator Donovan for help and wound up letting him put both kids up for adoption. The boy was adopted by a single guy from Houston. That man's cousin married the daughter, who was all of twelve, rather than adopt her. I have a fairly sick idea of why he chose that option. The grandparents received what I will politely call a finder's fee, which they offered to use to pay for Pamela to go into rehab. Losing her kids must have sent her further around the bend. The fire happened a week after her daughter's wedding."

"Nothing incriminating in that timing at all." I shared his skepticism.

"You'll love this. Pamela was still the beneficiary on all three life insurance policies. She cashed in and skipped town."

"If she wasn't arrested for killing the Fultons, where did this come from?" I asked and held up the mugshot.

"That is the only chink in Pamela Fulton's grand plan to reinvent herself. She was arrested for drunk driving in Houston, Texas five years ago. They took the fingerprints of someone calling herself Crystal Franks and ran them through the system, which spat out a drug arrest in Saint Xavier Parish of a woman named Pamela Fulton. Try to guess where her left thumbprint turned up next." Captain Hammond took a deep breath and gave me a moment to absorb the contents of this first file. I understood why he insisted on personally giving me all of this.

"You got me," I threw up my hands in mock surrender. I was impatient to get the files in my hand.

"Inside Gwendolyn Donovan's Mercedes."

"Gwendolyn said Crystal Franks came up with the idea of staging a fake death to mess with Kirk and his father. It was a convoluted idea, and it backfired when someone used it to cover for their own killing of Kirk Donovan."

"Backfired indeed," Captain Hammond nearly burst into laughter at my understatement.

"Can you agree that Gwendolyn was framed for Kirk's murder?" I needed him on board, especially since I had just told him where to arrest Gwen and exposed my mother to a charge for harboring a fugitive.

"I am willing to give you a little more rope to hang yourself with if you're wrong. The fingerprint only shows the two of them were in the car together. That could have happened at any point in time. We didn't find either of their fingerprints on the Ford GT, and Gwendolyn's were the only ones found in her house." Hammond opened the second file in the stack. "The coroner's report says minute traces of strychnine were found in the kidneys of both Kirk Donovan and Michael Aubuchon. He also says neither of them ingested anywhere close to a lethal dose. They might not even have eaten enough to make them sick."

"It was probably only enough to paralyze them to make it easier to kill them." I suggested.

Hammond gave me a quizzical look. "I was about to tell you the coroner said that exact same thing. How did you know?"

"A lesson from a different time and place," I looked up for an instant, and then buried my face the file on Pamela Fulton. Hammond immediately grasped that I was speaking of something from the large black hole in my resume and dropped the matter. "She wrote for a weekly paper in Houston, one of those suburban editions. That was where she came up with the name Crystal Franks. It was her pen name.""

"Right. That is probably how she learned everything she needed to know about how to run a small town newspaper," Hammond suggested. "Here's your next tasty tidbit of information. Guess who owns the newspaper."

"Senator Donovan." It was the first name that came to mind.

"Um, no," he said, but then nodded his head that my off-hand guess was no longer too outlandish to consider. "It is a company called Steersman Metal Recycling. They paid cash and made her the new publisher, editor, and lone reporter. Look at the paperwork and tell me what you think."

I am not Tulip when it comes to picking apart legal papers or seeing who controls what in a contract. I still had no trouble noting that Steersman Metal Recycling was based out of Houston, Texas, or that the company's owner was Bradley Ladd.

"That's interesting. What is their connection?" I doubted whether or not Captain Hammond knew the answer.

"Maybe something in here will tell you," Hammond sighed. He closed the autopsy file he was looking at and replaced the rubber bands. I slid the file on Pamela Fulton into the stack and leaned back in my chair. I realized I had been holding my breath through most of our short conversation. In the span of barely eight hours I had gone from having a hunch about where Gwendolyn took refuge to having admissible evidence of two recent murders which might have some connection to a woman credibly responsible for previous homicides.

I realized I could not arrest Pamela with what I had in hand. Questioning her at this point would let her know to destroy any evidence against her that might be left to uncover. I was baffled about how to even approach her. My biggest fear was that any plan she came up with to escape justice probably risked endangering more people, myself included.

Seventy-Five

"I can't believe I trusted her. This chick is messed up," Detective Chance realized as he read through the state police file on Pamela Fulton that I handed him. We were sitting at the kitchen table in Judge Rogers' house once again. I was not about to allow any of the files to fall into the hands of Sheriff Mazant. His detective was free to take notes and report anything interesting second-hand.

"To say the least." I was distracted by the details in the autopsy reports spread before me. I was comparing them line for line to find any other consistencies than the use of an all too common poison against the two men. I noted that Judge Aubuchon had eaten a piece of key lime pie very shortly before his accident. There was not enough left of Kirk's stomach to analyze the contents. "It sinks your grand conspiracy theory. You worked so hard on it, too. Even the FBI was impressed when I showed it to them."

"You shared what I gave you with the FBI?" he did not sound pleased to learn about this.

"Don't worry. They want no part of it. Conroy was very quick to let us handle finding your serial killer. I don't know that he would be any more interested in swooping in to take credit for finding one now that we have a name to work with. I guess their chasing the bogus laptop was embarrassing enough."

"I was just thinking about that. What if Pamela tried to frame the Fultons? All she needed to do was use their phone to connect to the internet and upload those porn files to make them the target. I don't know where she would have found pictures like that, but that seems to be consistent with how she operates," Chance said. "She gets someone to do her dirty work for her and then sets them up to take the fall. The Fultons took her kids so she may have tried to make them look worse than she was so she could get them back."

"And that is her weak spot," I realized. "She has her own vision for how the world works and makes her plans according to that. She set up the Fultons to look like the sort of child molesters she was hanging out with, thinking the court would hand the kids back to her. The court decided to send her children to foster parents and strip her of any rights at all. That is why she was set on killing the district attorney and the judges. They all blocked her plans."

"She's the sort of crazy that doesn't just happen overnight. She is determined to take down anyone who has ever crossed her. I worry that saving Judge Aubuchon from her first attempt earned you a place on her list," Chance summed up the woman and her sick plot that seemed to be unfolding before us.

"Pamela may have helped you build the theory you brought to me to discredit you. She manipulated you into compromising that homicide investigation in Houston. If she could get you to falsely accuse Senator Donovan of being a serial killer, nobody would believe anything you said after that; not about Bradley, not about her, not about any plot to kill half of the parish." I was beginning to fully envision her plan. I had to check myself at every turn because I was a little afraid that I might be taking a fresh trail of breadcrumbs meant to lead me down a path as wrong as the one Chance took.

"Okay, let's try rearranging the pieces in the puzzle," Chance challenged me. "None of these facts are wrong, but we have been looking at them wrong."

"Start with the summer camp. She put Kirk in a T-shirt she had made to leave as a clue only the locals would understand when we found his body." I took up the nearest dry erase marker and wrote 'Summer Camp' on the plate glass window for lack of a white board. I moved to the middle of the pane of glass and wrote 'Kirk Murdered.' We had to fit every piece of evidence we could between those two points.

"Maybe it was meant as a warning and not there to taunt us. Neither of us knew a thing about the summer camp when we found Kirk in that T-shirt, but it wasn't meant for us," Chance said and I was inclined to agree. "We need to find anyone who remembers that camp. It is pretty obvious now that something that happened there is what started all of this."

"The only thing I know that happened there is that Kirk Donovan raped Gwendolyn on the old riverboat. I think that also explains why the senator had it burned that same summer. Gwen being pregnant is the only reason why she and Kirk got married." I wasn't inclined to share any more of that story with Chance than this. "I will call Gwendolyn to see if she knows anything about Pamela Fulton's being at the camp at about the same time."

"You know where Gwendolyn is?" Chance's eyes lit up and he was visibly excited to learn she had been found.

"We have spoken, and I have a number to contact her. You'd have to agree that bringing her in right now only makes her a target as well." I needed him to get on board with keeping this development between the two of us. "I need you to promise you will keep this a secret from your boss for now."

"No problem," Chance assured me. We locked eyes for a moment while I tried to judge the likelihood of his sitting on the information. "I understand your point. Go ahead and call her right now."

I couldn't tell if he was testing me, or if he was as anxious to know what Gwendolyn remembered of Pamela as I was. I picked up my phone and dialed my mother's phone number. I was going to have to be sure Chance did not get hold of my phone until I erased the call from its log.

"Good morning. You are on speaker phone," I wanted to warn my mother to be careful with what she said. "My partner from the sheriff's office and I have a question for Gwendolyn. Is she close by?"

"I'm here, Detective," Gwendolyn spoke up. Her voice betrayed how nervous she was to speak to me with any of Sheriff Mazant's men so close at hand.

"One simple question. Do you remember a girl by the name of Pamela Fulton being at the summer camp about the same time you were?"

"Her name wasn't Fulton then. It was Dardenne. She was the sheriff's daughter."

Chance and I were both surprised to learn this. It was a good way to explain how she seemed to be a step ahead of us until now. She understood what investigators would be looking for, and knew what blind alleys we might race down. Gwendolyn had added another piece to the puzzle.

"Do you remember when I said I went to the party to tell Kirk the girl he was expecting wasn't coming? That is who I meant. What does this have to do with anything?"

"Hopefully nothing," I told her to keep from alarming her. Telling her that Pamela grew up to be Crystal Franks was not something to drop in her lap. "Thank you, and I will be in touch."

"Well, now," Chance said and leaned back in his chair.

"Pamela married Hank Fulton not that long after Gwen and Kirk got married. He must have looked like a consolation prize to her. I think it is obvious that she always intended to be a very young housewife, but she planned on being a richer one than it turned out. Her get-married-for-money plan didn't work out like she wanted, so she began getting high to fill the void." The puzzle was forming on the windowpane in a way that fit the available evidence better. We needed more of Pamela's background to develop a solid profile.

"Her drug habit killed the marriage," Chance offered.

"I think the miscarriage is what did that. It is unlikely she was doing crack all by herself. I think Hank was into it as well, but losing the third kid sobered him up at the same time that it made her worse." We were out on some thin ice since neither of us had ever been drug addicts or had lost an unborn child. I have no idea how I might react to either of those situations, much less to both at the same time.

Detective Chance was right about Pamela Fulton not working up the hatred necessary to do what we imagined she was doing overnight. It struck me that she was trapped in that point in time when everything went wrong for her. She was unable to process those disappointments and the things she may have done in the moment, so that now every slight or setback remained unresolved. Her largely self-inflicted wounds had been festering, until she now posed level of menace to society I had never seen before.

"Whose kid was it?" Chance thought to ask about the miscarriage.

"Let's put a question mark next to that for now," I suggested and added a question mark beside the word 'miscarriage.' Chance's expression showed how much he wanted to pursue it. "That's a rabbit hole we need to avoid. Maybe we find the father later, but looking for him in what we have now will only distract us. We don't have that kind of time."

"Fine. This puts us at her losing her kids," he said and waved towards the growing mass of ink on the window.

"No, this brings us to when she began selling her kids to support her drug habit. That could be how she knew where to find the kiddie porn to frame the grandparents who had her kids."

"Maybe the kiddie porn was of her own kids. That would have really put the FBI on the Fultons. They had the kids and here was a lot of nasty stuff with them in it on their computer." I liked his idea. "Pamela would come to see her kids and hook up the computer to the Fulton's phone to make it look like they were the ones uploading the porn."

"And it would have worked if the FBI did not contact Sheriff Dardenne about their warrant. He knew the Fultons, and he knew this wasn't who they were. I also don't doubt that he suspected his own daughter was capable of being that devious. He probably told them to find the computer and get rid of it so the FBI would not haul them off to prison." I felt I had come to understand Donovan well enough to understand why the local sheriff would put himself in danger with the FBI to save two nice people trying to help their son and the sheriff's grand-kids. He also may have felt guilty about his daughter's behavior.

"Then she kills them all. The bruises she had when she stabbed Hank could have come from anyone. Maybe she paid someone to smack her around a bit before he showed up. She was going to have the money to pay them off when she collected on those three insurance policies. Hank's parents weren't going to give the kids back just because their custodial parent died. Especially not when he died at the hands of the woman who was trying to get them back, and who was probably known to have sexually exploited both of them. The court didn't see things her way so she killed the parents and put the name of the judge on a little list she was going to come back to when things died down." Chance didn't seem to mind at all that his conspiracy theory was in the trash.

"Jump to your side of the border. The kids both get put into new homes. I think Senator Donovan knew at least as many pedophiles as

Pamela. What do you want to bet that he sold her son and daughter to a pair of cousins in the market for kids who were already pre-disposed to being abused? That put Chester's name on her hit list, as if forcing her to marry his son to keep him from being a rapist weren't reason enough already. It also neatly explains the connection between Bradley and the woman we know as Crystal." I was going to risk a serious disagreement with Chance in the next few minutes. He was still unaware that I knew he might have had an affair with Amorel Hickman, but that would need to be addressed.

"I knew the daughter," Chance volunteered this without my having to say a thing. "Her name was Amorel. She was a really cute girl, and she was married to a monster. She said he used to wager having sex with her in poker games. He bet lengths of time someone could have her. She took off a couple of times and he beat her with a belt every time she was brought back."

"And at least one of the times she ran away you put her into a battered women's shelter." I needed to ease into letting him know what SAC Conroy and Captain Hammond dug up on him.

"Twice. I took her there twice and she went back to him both times." Chance sounded defensive and we were not even to the worst of what I knew about him.

"And you tried to hide her at your house one time? Did something like that really happen?" I had to know how they wound up together.

"Only once. She showed up at the station. She wanted to thank me for trying to help. I bought her lunch and sent her home. I got a text message with a picture of the two of us together. Amorel said she was going to send the video to my captain and tell him we were sleeping together unless I helped her leave her husband for good." Chance's version sounded notably self-serving. "I met her again, just to tell her that blackmailing me wasn't a good idea. Sleeping with her when she talked me into hiding her the next time she left her husband was an even worse idea."

"Quite a bit worse," I said without any sympathy for his lapse. You don't sleep with another man's teen-age wife purely by accident. Calling it a lapse in judgement was an understatement. "I guess your fetish for younger women was your own weak spot."

"What?" Chance demanded.

"Asking the women you sleep with to call you 'daddy' is not a role play exercise most men ask their girlfriends to entertain," I pushed ahead.

"You've been talking to Nannci."

"And you aren't going to do a thing about it," I said with every ounce of menace I had at my immediate disposal. "I needed to know who I was dealing with when Mazant put you on my back. She said many nice things about you, as well. She is not part of this."

"Screw you," Chance snarled and stood up. I expected him to walk out of the house, but he went no further than the refrigerator and came back with two beers.

"Moving on," I suggested and opened mine.

"Amorel started hiding at Bradley Ladd's house instead. Being brother and sister finally explains how those two knew one another. She never mentioned to me that he was her brother. I tried to warn her husband about abusing her, and he told me to stay out of his marriage. He suspected I had a thing for her, so anytime she left he would tell my captain to have me bring her back to him. I wasn't in a position to tell my boss why the guy used me as his personal cop, but I could tell he was not pleased that I was in the middle of their soap opera." This was almost certainly the beginning of the end of his career in Houston.

"I just made that connection myself. Bradley and Amorel must have been the kids Pamela lost in court. That probably explains why she took a job in Houston. Did your paths ever cross?" I was curious to see what role she played in any of what happened then or later.

"No," Chance replied. I waited a moment for him to continue, but he seemed to be trying to phrase a fuller response. "But she wrote about both of the shootings. In fact, she even wrote an article that implicated Bradley in the killing of Amorel's husband. She painted it as a lover's triangle, but I guess it was just a big brother trying to protect his kid sister."

"All she really wanted you to do was muddy the investigation and maybe get you fired for messing with her daughter when that came out."

I said. I was beginning to run out of room on my diagram. I had taken to making long arrows to the time line and writing lower and lower on the window.

"My captain did everything he could to keep me away from that homicide," Chance offered. "He reassigned me from Missing Persons to Auto Theft to try to keep me out of the loop."

"Your captain thought your previous involvement with the girl would come back to bite both of you," I suggested. Chance nodded and hid behind his beer, hoping I would move on.

"But I was positive that Bradley was who killed Amorel's husband," he persisted. "I still am, because it made perfect sense, even without the articles Pamela wrote as Crystal Franks. It still does. Bradley always had the best motive."

"Second best motive," I argued. "Amorel's mother had a better motive. Anyone as narcissistic as she is would have one. Pamela killed Amorel's husband, and making you obsess about Bradley being the shooter ruined your career. Bradley's harassment lawsuit made him untouchable."

"That does fit better." Chance admitted.

"Explain to me why Pamela thought Bradley's adoptive father had to die." I challenged him.

"He was rich, for one thing," Chance gave me the only obvious clue either of us saw.

"How rich was Amorel's husband?" I asked out of not entirely idle curiosity.

"He was a big time defense attorney, which is why the detectives handling the case only focused on his clients. They lived in one of the richer subdivisions."

"Okay, consider the combined fortunes Pamela's children would have had if both of them had outlived the men they went to live with." I knew I had turned over a big rock when I saw the look on his face.

"Pamela planned to kill both of those men all along." Chance was no less chilled by this idea than I was. It was a very long con to pull off, and the only thing that had not worked so far was that her daughter had died before they could collect on her husband. "She found out her kids were both in Houston, so she moved there to be close to them. She found out how rich the men who had them were and the greedy wheels in her head started turning."

"Can you find out who inherited Amorel's husband's estate?" I had a suspicion that some of it found its way to his cousin.

"I think so. I like what you're suggesting."

"I don't. I believe Pamela Fulton could beat Boris Spassky at chess. She is always twelve moves ahead of anyone she goes up against." My confidence in building a prosecutable case against her dropped with each piece of the puzzle we put in place. The two of us were having trouble piecing this together, which meant explaining it to a grand jury full of people who didn't deal with psychopaths like this on a fairly regular basis would only cause brain freeze among the jurors.

"She used her son's money to buy the local paper and move back here. She had been gone long enough, and had enough plastic surgery, that nobody recognized who she was. She came to town under her pen name and slid right into the shadows. Nobody wonders why a reporter shows up at a crime scene, why they ask questions, or how they spend their spare time. She still looks good, and she may have had no trouble catching Kirk's wandering eye." I used 'Bought Newspaper' to fill in what little space remained before the terminus I established as being Kirk's murder on the window's transparent timeline.

There were still a lot of things that needed to be filled in. Most of the finer details were missing, but I was positive that we were right with where we placed each piece in our revised puzzle.

"Okay, what now?' Chance asked. "We think we know who, what, when, where, and how. Whatever happened at the summer camp explains the why. Can we sell this to the district attorney?"

"Not this one. I am afraid she has compromised his little head, so we cannot trust his big one" I speculated. It took Chance a moment to understand what I was implying. "Her confession would not be enough evidence for him to charge a woman he has been sleeping with. He can't be expected to recuse himself from the case because he was stupid enough to sleep with an accused serial killer. That is career ending in a way that beats your firing in Houston all to hell."

"Okay then, what do we do next?" Detective Chance suddenly seemed to no longer have an issue with me spearheading the case.

"We need to find as many people as we can to testify against either her or Bradley. She might cut a deal to save her son, but I doubt it. We will need quite a few people to agree to testify, because she might start killing everyone on our witness list before we can arrest her." It was just a fact we needed to not shy away from.

"Who knows enough to testify against her? Bradley is not going to turn on his mother, and I don't want to see anyone make a deal with him, anyway." Chance still sought some vengeance of his own.

"Mitchell Ursin." The name popped into my head.

"The kid who stole the boat."

"Think of the bigger picture," I suggested and began rummaging through the file on Kirk's crime scene. "Why would Bradley tell him that it was okay to take Kirk Donovan's boat? Mitchell would never intentionally cross the Donovans and expect to get away with it."

"Okay. Tell me why you think he took the boat." Chance saw nothing to argue.

"Because he already knew he could get away with taking the boat. That was probably why Mitchell got cute with his pals when he passed them at the bridge. He was screwing the most powerful family in town and was going to get away with it." I would have.

"But how do you think Mitchell knew Kirk was dead?"

"A Ford GT weighs almost two tons fully loaded down with gasoline and a driver. Its manual transmission was in neutral when it was pulled from the canal. I think Kirk was poisoned to make him develop muscle spasms that made it impossible for him to drive the car. It would take a couple of fairly strong bodies to push the car from the driveway all the way to the boat ramp and into the water. Pamela does not have the strength to do it, even with her son helping. Bradley and Mitchell, and maybe one or two other pals of theirs, must have pushed it. Maybe the boat was Pamela's way of paying Mitchell off for his help."

"That all fits," Chance initially concurred. "But, let's say for a moment that we are wrong about Pamela. What if she and Bradley just came back to their hometown to show everyone they survived, and even triumphed?"

"They would have announced it by now. They have both been here for a few years and haven't told anyone their real names. They have even kept their connection to each other a secret." I was entirely satisfied that we had identified the right suspects.

"Stop and think for just a moment. Maybe they didn't tell anyone because people still believe she killed her husband and his parents. If she and Bradley didn't actually kill any of these people, who else would benefit from their deaths?" Chance abruptly balked.

I was satisfied with our current working hypothesis, but I had to agree that we needed to make sure we weren't fooling ourselves. I have suffered the unintended consequences of a plan gone wrong. It would be foolish not to accept that this theory might be as wrong as the one I took to the FBI. My partner had already been fooled twice by Pamela Fulton and didn't want to be tricked again.

"Senator Donovan." Chance and I reached the exact same conclusion and spoke his name simultaneously.

"The senator is supposedly blocking legislation that would change the child marriage laws. What if someone has threatened to expose that he trafficked children if he doesn't let the bill come up for a vote, or if he keeps blocking it? He wouldn't want a scandal to derail his career."

"I am sure he doesn't, and he has better resources to get this done. Pamela and Bradley may have done what we think in Houston, but just to get back here. Maybe the senator recognized her and has been setting her up to take the fall all this time." I said.

"Well, great. I thought we had this solved," Chance said. He was smiling, but neither of us found this very funny. Only one version could prove true in the end. Chasing the wrong person meant an end to one or both of our law enforcement careers. You cannot apologize for falsely accusing a state senator or a newspaper editor of being a serial killer and think all will be forgiven.

"We do," I shrugged. "It's just that we only have one bullet, so we need to be damn sure we shoot the right bad guy."

"Well, I vote proving that Pamela and Bradley are the ones doing this. How about we keep chasing them until we find anything that says they couldn't have done it and the senator could."

"Let the chase begin," I sighed and tossed the marker atop the stack of reports and photographs covering the kitchen table. "Now tell me what you found at Judge Aubuchon's place."

"Nothing. No rat poison, no home remedies, nothing with strychnine in it at all," Chance reported. I was okay with this summation. I was not all that interested in anything he might have found. "I am curious about one thing now, though."

"What's that?"

He picked up the judge's autopsy report. "It says here he had undigested key lime pie in his stomach. I didn't find any key lime pie in his house. I did not find a dirty plate in his sink or dishwasher, either. What if our killer took him the pie and then came back and cleaned up before I got my warrant?"

"Not like we haven't seen that happen before." I liked his suggestion more than I did the prospect of our chasing a neat freak serial killer with no remorse.

Seventy-Six

I asked Detective Chance to drive to Mitchell Ursin's home. I wanted the neighborhood to see a car with Sheriff Mazant's emblem parked in the family's driveway. While it occurred to me that this was nothing new, based on what I had learned of the family's frequent brushes with the law, I still needed to feed the rumor grapevine. It was important that Crystal and Bradley suspect we had questioned Mitchell about Kirk's death.

"You can't speak to my boy until his lawyer gets here," Mitchell's father declared. He was in the driveway by the time we even opened our car doors. The man was as tall and hard as an oak log. I was counting on his not being as dense as one. We planned to offer him a good bargain.

"It's your choice whether we talk to Mitchell about homicide charges or we talk to you about something that happened twenty years ago," I told him and kept walking towards his house. Chance followed in my footsteps. He was not feeling good about how this was going to go, and appeared to want to use me as a shield, as well as to be in some position to back me up if need be.

"Then I guess I need a lawyer," he grumbled and took a couple of steps backwards.

"We can't arrest you for anything you tell us. We are looking into things that happened so long ago that the statute of limitations protects you from prosecution." I informed him. We were now barely two feet apart and standing face to face. "You can invite us in, or we can talk about this where the whole world can hear."

"Come on," he decided. He led us into the two-car garage beside the bungalow. His wife was scowling at us through the kitchen window. A new Jeep Grand Cherokee and an immaculate Bullitt-edition 1968 Mustang fastback sat side by side in the garage. Together they were worth more than the man's home. "What's your question?"

"Tell us what you know about a woman named Pamela Fulton." I said and watched his reaction.

"Damn." The word was accompanied with a sad and rather pained look. "What's that bitch got to do with me or my son now? I haven't seen her since about 1988."

"She's around," was the most I was prepared to let him know. I could easily imagine his charging into the newspaper and breaking things.

"We are interested to hear why Pamela might hold a grudge against you. It could be over something very small, but we think it has to do with Camp Dumaine and Gwendolyn Donovan."

"Did she tell you that Kirk raped her best friend? He always bragged about popping Gwen's cherry." It took every bit of self-control I had not to break his nose just then.

"We're here to find out how you crossed Pamela." Chance watched my hand clench and looked for a way to inject himself into the conversation. The man calmly turned from me to look at Chance as he tried to decide on an answer. He showed no sign of being concerned that either of us might beat the answer out of him.

"You're talking to the wrong person about that. Pamela only had a red ass for Kirk's wife. Pam used to get all worked up when she was high about how Gwen stole her life out from under her. All I ever did was sell her dope back in the Eighties. It started with cocaine and then went to crack. She was pretty good looking back then and I didn't always need her to pay in cash." I was surprised, and repulsed, by his candor. "I stopped selling her anything after she put that knife into Hank. She had a look in her eye that just flashed 'Crazy Bitch' and everyone began to back off from having anything to do with her. The whole town gave a big sigh of relief when she vanished after the fire that killed Hank's folks. Everyone knew she did it, and we all knew she was going to get away with it, just like she did when she killed Hank."

"She does seem to have a talent for that," I said mostly to myself, but loud enough for him to catch what I said. "Do you have any idea what Pamela meant about Gwen stealing her life?"

"Not at all. I just let her ramble whenever she brought it up. What's any of this got to do with Mitchell?" he asked.

"We think Pamela might be back in town and working down a list of everyone she thinks crossed her in any way. We believe she killed Kirk

Donovan and Judge Aubuchon. Mitchell may have got himself caught up in helping her kill Kirk. That's why he thought he could get away with taking Kirk's boat." I did my best to make this seem like a casual conversation and not that we were trying to trick him into saying anything about his son's crime.

"How so?" Chance and I both noted that he did not argue that his son was innocent. Mitchell must have told him some version of the story we were here to learn.

"He may have helped roll Kirk's car into the canal. Pamela and Bradley either offered him the boat as a way to buy him off, or he was set up to be blackmailed by them after they said he could get away with taking it," Chance laid out our arguments.

"She probably wanted to set him up to take a fall. That may have been how she intended to punish you for whatever she believes you did wrong to her. I'll bet Mitchell doesn't have any proof that they killed Kirk, but we have witnesses in Texas who are ready to testify that your son sold Kirk Donovan's boat after we can prove Kirk was already dead," I moved the narrative a bit further forward.

"What do you want from me or my boy?" he asked. His tone was a lot less confrontational.

"I haven't asked Gwendolyn whether she cares one way of the other about Kirk's boat. It might only be of interest to the cops in Texas if your son sold something that wasn't his," I said to lay the groundwork for the deal I was going to offer. "I would rather talk to Mitchell about what he did here than report what he did to any cops over there. Doing that just starts a lot of paperwork and travelling to and from court that Chance and I don't really want to do."

"I'll be right back," he said and left us alone in the garage. There was the possibility he left to tell Mitchell to make a run for it, or to pick up a gun and kill the two of us in his garage. I felt we stood a decent chance of his taking the trade.

"My dad says you'll drop the charges if I tell you Bradley and his mom killed Kirk," Mitchell said when he and his father returned a couple of minutes later. Neither of them seem cheered by the prospect of taking our deal.

"No. What we said was we would rather talk to you about what you know about Kirk than to tell the cops in Texas where to find you and the Donovans' stolen boat. Don't make up some wild story to get us to forget what you did," I was quick to warn him. "We know enough that all you need to do is tell us your version so we can see if it matches ours."

Mitchell looked at his father, whose parental disappointment was palpable, and then back at us. The silence was getting thick, and we had one more stop to make whether Mitchell did the smart thing or not.

"Bradley called and asked me to help him with something. I went to his apartment and he said we needed to meet Crystal Franks at Kirk Donovan's house. She was in his house when we got there. He was throwing up in his bathtub and had the shakes real bad. I thought we were going to take him to the hospital." Mitchell's story meshed with what we knew from the autopsy report, so I nodded for him to keep going. I noticed he stopped talking before he admitted to doing anything illegal. "She told us to get him into a shirt and to carry him downstairs. It was some stupid T-shirt she handed Bradley. It was hard to get him into it, mostly because he was having those convulsions. He had this wild look in his eyes but he couldn't say anything. We picked him up and carried him to the kitchen, but she told us to get him back into race his car and to buckle him in. She yelled at Bradley for putting Kirk in the passenger seat. We moved him over and then she pointed to the canal and told Bradley to 'finish it.' I told them I wasn't going to help them kill Kirk, and then she pulled a gun on me and said to help him or I would take the ride with him. She said my fingerprints were all over the inside of the house and the cops were going to blame me whether I helped or not. She and Bradley had been wearing gloves the whole time. So I helped Bradley push the car into the canal and we all stood there until it sank. I don't think any of the neighbors saw anything. They were all at work."

"Thanks. I know you think you're in a pretty tight spot right now," I smiled and put a hand on his shoulder. His muscles were tight.

"You mean I'm not?" Mitchell was confused by the way we were treating him. He had just confessed to the murder of a state senator's son.

"Oh, no, you are most definitely still in a lot of trouble," Chance was quick to assure him. "Just less so with us. Now, tell us about the boat."

"I was convinced they were going to set me up to look like I killed Kirk all by myself. Crystal told us to leave while she cleaned up the house, but the more I thought about it, the more I suspected she was planting more evidence against me. I called Bradley and he said we were all good, that Crystal made sure it would look like an accident or maybe suicide. I told him I didn't believe either of them and wanted twenty thousand dollars so I could hide if need be. He said to keep it together and he would call his mom, and that paying me wasn't going to be a problem. He said he would give me the money if she wouldn't. He called me the next day and said his mom said it would look suspicious if they gave me any cash, that the cops could track any money they moved around to pay me to stay quiet. Their idea was to steal Kirk's boat. I could keep the money from selling it. Crystal knew a guy in Port Arthur who had been in trouble for selling hot boats before, and she said she would call him to see if he could help me. I got thirty-three thousand dollars for it, and then Crystal met with me and said she would turn me in for stealing the boat if I ever told anyone about how Kirk died. I feel pretty stupid for ever getting involved."

"Well remember that feeling. It is what you were," Chance suggested rather unkindly.

"Okay. He told you what he knows. We have a deal, right?" his father asked. He must have realized he may have done something really stupid by having his son confess.

"They have built quite a body count so far, so we don't have to focus on their killing Kirk. I just needed your son to confirm what we believed." I explained, without absolving Mitchell for his crimes. "If we can get them for something else, then it is up to Gwen about the boat. Like we said, Texas might have more interest than we do, but we'd have to tell them about what your son did to make them interested."

"What do we do in the meantime?" his dad asked. He sounded like he felt he had been double-crossed and left exposed.

"Keep your heads down and don't go anywhere near those two. You are still a liability to them."

Mitchell's father stopped, looked at Mitchell, then at us, and back to his son again before he asked, "Who is going to explain to me how Pam Fulton turned into Crystal Franks and how Bradley Ladd is her son?"

"Just take our word for it," I suggested. "The devil is truly in the details."

Mitchell and his father quietly walked inside their house. Chance and I headed towards the funeral home. We looked both ways as Chance pulled onto the street to see who might be watching before we both realized we had no idea what Pamela drove. We shared a brief, hollow, laugh.

"What's Mitchell's old man do for a living?" I asked.

"He works for the Donovans, like everyone else around here," Chance said.

"Specifically."

"He works on one of those boats that takes stuff out to the oil rigs. They do crew changes and haul groceries and supplies. Why?" Chance was still just making conversation.

"Do you think he makes enough money doing that to own those cars?" I was developing a notion that Mitchell's father might not have changed his spots.

"No, I do not," Chance smiled once the same thought crossed his own mind. "Maybe he only stopped selling dope to Pamela."

Seventy-Seven

There was an impressive crowd waiting in line at Joffre Funeral Home to pay their respects to Judge Aubuchon. The well-dressed queue extended out the front door and into the parking lot when we arrived. The mood was not as somber outside as it was inside, where one needed to at least try to give the appearance that the occasion was solemn and not merely social.

Detective Chance and I hung our respective badges from the breast pockets of our suits and strode into the gathering as though we came with some purpose. I knew we were only beginning to put together a viable case against Pamela and Bradley. The pieces to our new puzzle might hold together better because Pamela's alter ego Crystal was not the one feeding them to us.

I scanned the judge's visitation for familiar faces. Chief Theriot greeted us at the door, along with one of his uniformed deputies. I assumed the two of them were acting as de facto security.

"Thanks for leaving your dog at home," Chief Theriot jabbed.

"I brought Mazant's lapdog instead," I retorted. I was surprised that Chance smirked rather than frowned. I especially enjoyed the flummoxed look on Theriot's face.

Senator Donovan and Uncle Felix were standing with a group of men about their same age. Four grim looking men in their early thirties flanked the senator. They intentionally did not interact with anyone they encountered, but their hands were constantly brushing against anyone wearing a jacket or glancing into open purses. They were either there as Senator Donovan's new security detail or worked for Uncle Felix. They took immediate note of Detective Chance and myself, and the shiny badges we wore. One of them nodded to me when he realized his attempt to blend in had failed. I had to wonder but what they were only meant to serve as scarecrows. Donovan is a small enough town that the locals would never have mistaken any of them for being anybody's long lost son or a distant relative of the judge.

"Having new bodyguard try-outs?" I tried to mock the senator and my uncle about the show of muscle.

"What do you mean?" Senator Donovan asked in a less than amused voice.

"If the security guys aren't yours then who is paying them?" I pointed out the four men in question, and then stopped to consider whether there might be one or two women actively working the room.

"The senator always travels with security," my uncle dismissed my inquiry. "You should know that."

"Oh, I do," I said and then took a step closer to keep what I said next between us. "I also know you feel like you need extra men right now."

"What does that mean?" The senator's questions were beginning to echo.

"Judge Aubuchon was murdered, as was Kirk. What is news to me is that this isn't news to either of you." This was a fishing expedition, but Senator Donovan had better security than Huey Long.

"Are you implying that the senator has withheld information relevant to your investigation?" Uncle Felix moved to stand between the senator and me.

"If you are asking whether or not the senator is obstructing justice, the answer is no. I do, though, believe that the senator is actively trying to avoid justice that has nothing to do with common law or the courts." I lobbed what I considered to be a bomb into their midst and waited to see who knew to run for cover.

"That's a ridiculous thing to say," Senator Donovan huffed. Uncle Felix was a lot slower to take the bait.

"It might be ridiculous, but that doesn't mean it isn't happening, gentlemen. You have a vigilante killer on at least one of your tails and I think you have known about the threat longer than I have been in Donovan," I was pushing harder because the color had drained from both of their faces and they now stood like marble statues.

"What do you think you know?" Uncle Felix snarled and grabbed my arm. He was equally quick to release it when he saw my expression as I looked from the arm to his face.

"I think I know that one or both of you have things to tell me. I know that people close to you have been murdered and that Chester here is probably meant to be the last target. Or maybe he just intends to be the last one standing." I stepped forward until the senator and I stood nose to nose.

Senator Donovan stood to benefit as much from the deaths in the parish as anyone. He could nominate a younger judge to fill Aubuchon's bench, one who would carry out the senator's agenda after he retired or passed away. The senator no longer needed to rely on his son to quash Belle's research paper, and my uncle was likely already hard at work looking for a way to block her book deal. The death of anyone in the senator's inner circle with connections to the summer camp was one less mouth to contradict the history of the place as he told it. Pamela Fulton might very well have him in her own sights, but so far her rampage was helping her supposed target more than she was scaring him.

Detective Chance coughed into his hand, no doubt to alert me to the danger I might be in. I took a step back and made sure my hands were in plain sight to the men in suits eyeing our conversation while the senator and Uncle Felix considered their options.

The two of them began whispering back and forth while I scanned the room again. Pamela and Bradley were noticeably absent. The boy might get away with not being here, but the newspaper editor ought to be seen as caring enough to show up. She needed to make an appearance, or have a good excuse for not covering the largest visitation in recent memory for her paper.

"Can we talk in private?" Uncle Felix asked and shot a glance at the Detective Chance.

"We can talk anywhere you want," I assured him. Whatever was said to me in confidence was going to be shared with Chance. I certainly no longer needed to concern myself about what we discussed getting back to the senator.

Senator Donovan led the way to the space usually reserved for the family of the deceased to grieve in private, or to begin the argument over dividing up the estate. I motioned Chance to guard the doorway, as much to keep any of the private security men from getting past him and into the room with us as to watch for Crystal Franks.

"I am pretty sure we are both targets of a serial killer, Senator, and I am equally sure that you have known about the killings long before I arrived. I also believe they are connected to an incident at Camp Dumaine during the last summer it was open. Did you have anything to do with the summer camp, Uncle Felix?"

"Not a thing. I only handle matters that have to do with his work in Baton Rouge. He never asks for help with anything at home."

"Then you might survive," I said and turned my attention back to the senator. "I think it is very likely linked to your son assaulting Gwendolyn Rogers."

"That's insane," Senator Donovan exclaimed in disbelief.

"Tell that to your son, or to the empty casket out there. The idea certainly does sounds crazy. Just keep in mind that, while the person who came up with it may be certifiably insane, they are quite determined to kill you, sir," I tossed the last word in to soften the tone of my response to his non-denial. "Now it's your turn to tell me what you know."

"I received a letter about couple of years ago. It was just a piece of paper left in the mailbox of my house here. I have no idea how long it sat there before I came back from Baton Rouge and found it mixed into my other mail. I almost put it with the junk mail by accident."

"I take it you don't suspect the mail carrier."

"Do you want to hear this or not?" Senator Donovan snapped. "They used words cut from a newspaper."

I bit my tongue.

He continued. "The note said I was going to have to pay for the sin of opening Camp Dumaine. The letter said I would lose my friends, then my son and his family, and then my power. They wanted me to believe that I was the one responsible each time someone I knew died."

"Why didn't you tell anyone?" I pressed.

"I believed I could handle this quietly. We had no idea what the killer believed Chester had done that was so bad, but we knew there were a number of things which went on at the camp that would not be good to have judged by today's standards. We wanted to avoid a possible public relations debacle, and nobody died for a while after he received the letter," Uncle Felix spoke up. It was his mess, so he needed to be the one to try to rationalize making it.

"Then people did start dying, but they never seemed to be murdered. How long did it take you to realize what was happening?" I continued questioning the senator.

"I received a copy of the obituary of anyone they tried to take credit for killing," Senator Donovan admitted.

"It took a couple times before we understood the idea was to make this a personal thing between the killer and Senator Donovan. He would know they were working their way towards him, but nobody else would," Uncle Felix continued finishing the senator's answers.

"So, whose idea was it to bring Chance into the mix?" I asked.

"Chester remembered Bradley Ladd when he arrived to run his late father's business. Chester handled the boy's adoption. He knew Detective Chance was convinced the boy killed his adoptive father, so we had the sheriff hire the detective to keep an eye on him. One killer running loose in town was enough," Uncle Felix fielded the question.

"Do you think Bradley knows the killer you are after?" I asked. I was not going to share what I knew no matter what the answer proved to be.

"I doubt it. The boy has never done anything to make me suspect him. He seems nice enough. He even used the money he inherited to attend college." Senator Donovan seemed indifferent to Bradley.

"But, that was when he became friends with your granddaughter, Belle," I pointed out.

"I have never given much thought to what that girl does," the senator shrugged. "I will always think of her as being what ruined my son's future. He could have filled my seat one day, if he had not had his way with that Rogers girl. I could never trust her to keep her mouth shut, and having her announce my son assaulted her when they were children would not play well in Baton Rouge," Senator Donovan grumbled. He seemed to still hold Gwendolyn responsible for the fallout from his son's actions. "Belle would not be hawking her trashy tale if she were a real Donovan."

I found myself at a crossroads. I could continue a useless argument with the senator about his attitude or I could get the answers I needed to perhaps save his life.

"I think they may have killed the district attorney who was in office before Gabouri," I said and paused as a new thought tumbled into the puzzle pieces.

"I received his obituary. It was how we realized their plan was cover their tracks so only the senator would know who they killed," Uncle Felix confirmed.

"Okay, back to the killer," I said with a faint sigh. "Now Gwen has disappeared, Kirk is dead, and Judge Aubuchon was just poisoned. Whoever is after you seems to be keeping their word."

"Disappeared, hell. That woman was behind every one of these killings. She hated her husband and she blamed me and her father for making the two of them get married. She is using her father's love for her to get you to build an alibi for her." Senator Donovan began ranting. "That idiot DA of ours will certainly never build a case against her."

"You suspect Gwendolyn of all these murders." I mumbled this rather than phrase it as a question. I saw his argument, but was also certain he was wrong. "Speaking of DA Gabouri, who recommended him to the Attorney General? There doesn't seem to be anything about him that would have attracted anyone's attention that high up."

"I think it was that new woman, the one who bought the local paper. She was real interested in who was going to replace Robert. She made a big stink about how the Donovans always have a hand in every election. I think she got the attorney general's ear and gave him the name of someone she thinks hates my family."

"Does he?" I felt it needed asked.

"I have no idea. I have had no issues with him. He certainly has not distinguished himself since he took the job. Maybe he can make a name for himself prosecuting whoever you catch," Senator Donovan suggested. He seemed profoundly indifferent to that possibility.

"Oh, so you're going to let the court handle your son and friends having been murdered by someone who is clearly insane?" I challenged my uncle on this more than I did the senator. "I don't buy that for a second. I think you two have been trying to use me as a bird dog ever since I came to town."

"Now, Cooter," Uncle Felix sighed. I shot him a look to silence him before he lied to me.

"I believe whoever started this wants you to kill them. I think they have everything planned out to where you are ruined no matter what you do. There is some sort of insurance policy out there that you need to worry about a lot more than the person holding it. What aren't you telling me?" A lot of what I had just told them came to me as I was saying it. I could tell by their expressions that it led them to believe I knew more than I was telling them. Other than what I knew of Pamela, I was just as ignorant of her plan as they were. I had talked my way into believing the door to Senator Donovan's closet full of skeletons was about to open and spill the contents out into the open for all to see.

"There are a lot of things that are nobody's business but my own," was the best I was going to get from the senator or my uncle. I gave them both a withering stare, in hopes something more might fall loose. It didn't, and that left me in a not much better position than I began. I only came away knowing Senator Donovan was not surprised by his son's death, or even the death of his friend we were there to mourn. Detective Chance and I left with one other certainty as well. Neither Senator Donovan nor Uncle Felix knew Crystal Franks' true identity. They had stopped looking for the killer the minute Gwendolyn disappeared and they began looking for a way to pin everything on her.

Seventy-Eight

Roux met me at the front door when I returned from the funeral home. This was not where I had left him, and he had a dangerously frantic look on his face. I pulled the Glock from its holster and began clearing the ground floor of the house room by room. I listened for any sound coming from the second floor and sensed Roux was keeping two paces behind me as Roger had trained him unless I ordered him to scout ahead of me. I began running through a mental checklist of ways the home might have been breached or things which might have spooked Roux into leaving the lightweight travel kennel he was trained to stay in when I was not at home. The front door was locked when I arrived and every window was closed, but I silently checked each lock to be sure this was not how anyone got into the house.

I took an extra moment when I reached my bedroom to check and inventory the arsenal stored under the bed. I accounted for every rifle and handgun, counted the stun grenades and boxes of ammunition, and eliminated this as a routine burglary. Those would have been the first things taken in a typical snatch-and-go break in.

Roux's wire mesh kennel was lying on its side when I reached the kitchen. There were droplets of blood on the kitchen floor that I ascertained after I checked him for wounds were not Roux's. Roux had freed himself from the flimsy wire cage by pushing the solid metal on the bottom loose from the thin wire of its sides. He then made the home invader suffer for their intrusion. Dog bites from teeth the size of Roux's were not something to be left untreated. The intruder was a lot luckier than they realized. Roux has killed a man.

Nothing was missing, but the files Detective Chance and I had gone through were disturbed. I noted that the autopsy reports seemed to have been the intruder's primary interest. I looked at the writing on the window and realized that whoever came through here in my absence left well informed about our investigation.

Uncle Felix hires professionals who are capable of ransacking a place without leaving any sign of their presence, so this was not done out of any frustration he and the senator felt about being out of the loop. Sheriff Mazant was not the sort of cop who would be this sloppy, either.

I called Detective Chance to let him know. He said he would alert the area hospitals and clinics to be on the lookout for anyone with a dog bite. We discussed the files that were disturbed and the fact someone was now aware of our way of looking at the case. We both felt like idiots for having left the diagram on the window.

The break-in could have yielded some valuable information to whomever made the effort, but only someone local would recognize any of the names and locations the timeline divulged.

I gave Roux a handful of his favorite dog treats and took a shower. I warmed up a plate of Chef Tony's braised short ribs for supper before I sat down to watch the video record of the break-in. The lone burglar had anticipated being caught on camera. They had walked out of the property's rear tree line and gained access to the house through the garage. One of the doors still required manual lifting to open and didn't have a working lock on the handle. The door from the garage had an old style button lock anyone could pick with a credit card. I imagined that whoever broke in knew the home fairly well. The lone burglar wore loose clothes and a full head covering to disguise their physical size and face. I could not discern whether it was Bradley or Mitchell, but it certainly was not Pamela. That was a good thing as neither of the boys was likely to have made much sense of the murder board on the window. They may not even have read the files they pulled from the cardboard box.

Maybe all this burglar wanted to do was to show me they could get into the judge's house, and if they could do so while I was away, then they could do so while I was asleep. There would no longer be any kennel separating Roux from the intruder if they were stupid enough to repeat the stunt. I was too tired to be afraid. I poured a tumbler of bourbon and headed to bed. I phoned Katie and told her about finding Gwendolyn at my mother's, which elicited a hearty laugh. I also explained Chance's and my thoughts about the possible connection between Kirk's decades-old sexual assault on Gwendolyn and my current investigation.

Katie assured me she was waiting patiently for my return to New Orleans, and I knew her average case load meant she likely appreciated not having me around as a distraction for a while.

I hung up and turned out the light on the nightstand. I placed my Glock under my pillow and positioned a Kriss .45 caliber carbine equipped with a green laser sight on the far side of my bed. Roux took up a defensive position in the hallway and we both tried to get what rest we could.

Seventy-Nine

I ate breakfast alone and chewed my cinnamon toast while I re-read my handwriting on the plate glass window. Every piece still fit as well as it had when I wrote it. The timeline was still reasonable and the evidence, what evidence we had, fit what we believed and didn't require us to ignore any part of it. The coroner's files were in hand to extend the story past Kirk's death to that of Judge Aubuchon, and statements from people like Mitchell's misogynistic father shed a bit more light on the vindictive woman we were certain was the mastermind of a series of murders, if not the actual killer.

A comment Mitchell attributed to Pamela caused a ripple upon the smooth pond of our theory. Supposedly Pamela made Gwendolyn into the prime suspect in Kirk's murder because Gwendolyn ruined some twenty year-old plan Pamela had for marrying Kirk. The only thing I had heard in the past few days that connected all three of them was Camp Dumaine.

Going to so much work to get Kirk into a T-shirt printed with the defunct camp's name was a glaring clue that something had occurred at the camp that sparked this long delayed campaign of death and destruction. Gwen's rape certainly changed her life, but it seemed to have had some sort of butterfly effect on Pamela's life as well. I was not keen on subjecting Gwendolyn to any more stress by re-hashing the night she was raped by Kirk. I wondered if her father might be able to answer some of the questions that were coming to mind.

I reached Judge Rogers by phone just as he walked into his chambers at the courthouse in New Orleans.

"Do you have a break in the case?" he immediately wanted to know. We had not spoken since I left him standing at the bar on Sunday.

"I have had a few breaks recently, none of which I can discuss with you. I am calling about something that I hope might explain what is happening out here. There seems to be a good chance that someone with a very old grudge went to a lot of work to make your daughter the prime suspect in Kirk's murder."

"What in the world are you talking about?" he asked in a tone which sounded like genuine bewilderment.

"I need to know everything you can remember about Gwen's rape at the summer camp." I surprised myself at being able to say the words without sounding like I was in any way unapologetic for bringing up the subject.

"Who told you about that?"

"You wanted me on the case because I dig deep. This is what I found, and I wouldn't bring it up if I did not think it played some part in what is going on. Every detail you can remember will be helpful." I needed to get answers to my questions before I responded to any of his.

"It was the last summer the camp was open. What was that, nineteen eighty six or seven? It happened during the summer before Belle was born. It was also why we closed the camp." Judge Rogers' memory seemed as strained as his voice. "Kirk assaulted her after they left a party with some of the other camp counselors."

"I understand she didn't plan to go to the party. My source told me she was only there to relay a message to Kirk." I needed to be careful not to reveal so much that he would realize I had spoken with either his ex-wife or directly with Gwendolyn.

"That's what Gwendolyn told us when she let us know she was pregnant with Kirk Donovan's child," Judge Rogers confirmed.

"And I understand that the girl who sent the message eventually married Hank Fulton." I didn't say her name in order to see if he might. I also wanted to test whether he had a source out here to feed him information on the investigation.

"I think her name was Pat, or Pam. She left town under a cloud after Hank and his folks died. I think a lot of people thought she had a hand in Frank's parents' deaths, but it might have been a coincidence. I really don't see how any of this has anything to do with your current investigation. I think you are running down blind alleys." He sounded very disappointed in my dredging up old memories and poking at old wounds.

"It's more important that I can tell you, Your Honor," I apologized.

"Well, okay. I just hope you find Gwendolyn safe and sound," he sighed.

"One more thing, Judge," I said before I let him go. I wanted it to sound like an afterthought. "I was wondering if you planned to attend the graveside service for Judge Aubuchon tomorrow."

"Of course I will be there. He was a very close friend once upon a time."

"I realize he was an important man in the town. How would you feel about hosting the post-funeral repast at your house here in Donovan? I can have Chef Tony come out and handle the food service. I'll figure out some way to get the state to foot the bill." Asking his permission was the polite thing to do, but I needed to do this whether or not he gave his blessing.

"That would be fine." His response showed no particular enthusiasm for the idea.

"Thank you. I will see you tomorrow. There might be more to share with you by then.

"That would be good. I need to get to work now, though," he said and allowed me to be the one to hang up.

My next call was to Gwendolyn. It promised to be a bit trickier, because I intended to ask her to place herself at risk. I did not advise Judge Rogers about the risk that attending Judge Aubuchon's funeral would expose him to because I didn't want him to back out of attending. I had an idea for how to build a trap for Pamela, and I needed to set it with as much live bait as I could.

"I need you to come home," I told her. "There is a funeral service for Judge Aubuchon tomorrow morning at eleven. Your father just gave me permission to open his house out here after the funeral for everyone to come and do the hugs and tears thing."

"Why do you want me to be there? I imagine my just showing up in the middle of something like that would be a huge disruption. It would be disrespectful to the judge and his family."

"I'm told he doesn't have any family. The truth is, I am hoping you do cause a disruption. Having you show up unannounced might be enough to puts the brakes on whatever the killer is planning to do next. If you are the real target of their anger, they will have no choice to but to deal with you first.'

"That sounds dangerous," Gwen protested.

"I won't lie. It will be dangerous, but there will be a lot of cops and security around. I need to knock whoever it is off their game and force them to make a mistake that we can use to trick them into confessing." I didn't offer any details beyond this because I didn't have any details to give her just then. All I knew was that Crystal Franks would not be expecting to be exposed as Pamela Fulton in a house full of people who had not forgotten why she left town.

"Okay. What time? Wait a second, hold on." She placed her hand over the receiver to say something to my mother. A sharp, and very loud, shriek of disapproval made its way through the phone to my ear. I was really glad to have chosen not to handle this in person. I waited to continue until it sounded like her hand was removed from the receiver.

"Just come straight to the house, say about eleven o'clock. I will have someone here to tell you what we need you to do until it is time for you to re-appear. You will be safe under this roof," I promised.

My third call of the morning was to Tony at the restaurant. He was already hard at work supervising the line prep for lunch by the sounds in the background.

"I need you for a catering job out here tomorrow," I said and paused while he walked to the quiet of his office next to the elevator to our apartments.

"That is only a Saturday. So nice of you to choose a quiet day to ask this of me," he chided me. There was no way he was going to refuse to help, but it was going to cause some problems for the restaurant.

"Just bring food for about fifty people to munch on after a funeral. Anti-pasto and a couple of pans of Miss J's jambalaya or something like that would be fine. I need you, and your new cooks, on hand.

"New cooks?" Tony was obviously thinking of the bistro's three newest line cooks, two of whom were female, whom he had hired while I was gone. They were not at all who I meant.

"The pizza boys. I hope they still know how to shoot a gun," I clarified both who I meant and why I was asking him to cater an event on such short notice. There was no other way to explain so many Black boys attending the repast for an old dead white judge they didn't know.

"How many?' Tony immediately began forming a team in his mind.

"Five plus you should cover what I'll need you to do. There are half a dozen Tasers in my gun locker. Don't bring anyone looking for a shoot-out. I just need to be able to control what happens when things start to get crazy. Having the Ford Raptor on hand might make a difference if we needed to block the driveway or ram someone's car.

"Tell me when and where." I could tell he had already planned his menu, picked his men, and began to run every scenario imaginable through his head.

"People will start showing up at Judge Rogers' place about noon. I need to leave the house about ten o'clock. There will be a blonde haired woman come through about eleven that you need to hide and protect. Her name is Gwendolyn. She is Belle's mother.""

"That is who you went to look for, yes?" Tony asked.

"Right. Do me another favor and bring Belle as well. I may as well overload the trap." I didn't expect my partner to understand what I meant by that, and he didn't need to in order to do what I asked of him.

"I will see you tomorrow," Tony said. He was the first person I had spoken with all morning who was genuinely happy about the impromptu repast. Then again, nobody else I spoke with hoped to get to hurt someone.

There was a knock at the front door. I hung up and approached the front of the house with my Glock in one hand and Roux once again following close behind.

"Something up?" Detective Chance asked when he saw the pistol in my hand.

"I had a visitor while we were out and about last night," I said and pointed him towards the kitchen. I don't know what he thought when I continued to carry the handgun rather than holster it.

"What did they take?"

"Maybe everything we know about Pamela Fulton. I don't know that they actually tried to figure it out. The video I have of them in here seems to indicate they just wanted me to know they could get in," I said and pointed to the ruffled files and scrawls on the window.

"That can't be good. Do you think it was Pamela, and that seeing what we know caused her to run?" Chance touched the side of the coffee pot to confirm I had made a fresh pot. He quietly poured himself a cup and sat down at the table while I continued to pace the room. Roux found a place to lie down under the table. I could tell he missed having his kennel.

"No. I think she is out there somewhere planning one last frontal attack. The last names on the list of people we think she wants to kill will all be attending Judge Aubuchon's funeral tomorrow morning. I don't think we need to worry about a car bomb or her trying to pick anyone off with a rifle. Her pattern has been to get others to do her dirty work while she focuses on destroying reputations and relationships. We need eyes on Bradley and Mitchell from now until the funeral is over. I plan to open this place to the funeral guests after the graveside service. I hope it is that this opportunity is too tempting a way to finish what she started for Pamela to resist. I have no idea what she might pull, but it is our best shot at putting an end to all of this."

"I look forward to finding out what all of 'this' even is," Chance said and grinned behind his coffee cup. He had a good point. "What's the next move?"

"I'm going to go to the newspaper with a press release saying the coroner determined Kirk was a suicide and the judge died in an accident." I liked the way his eyebrows shot up at this. I imagined Pamela was going to have an even more pronounced reaction to the lack of interest the state police seemed to have in either death.

"When did you hear that?'

"Oh, it's a lie. I may have to write it myself, but the point is to pull the rug out from under her. She can't blackmail Mitchell or frame Gwen for murdering Kirk if the medical examiner declares his death was a suicide." Captain Hammond was almost certain to refuse to push the envelope this far, but I had stationary with the state police letterhead to write the release myself if he refused my request.

"I'm glad I am on your side," Chance mumbled and stood up to refill his coffee cup. We shared a laugh before I dialed Captain Hammond's number.

Eighty

Captain Hammond surprised me by agreeing to have the state police compose and email the requested press release directly to Crystal Franks at the newspaper office. The official-looking statement would declare that the state police's 'extensive investigation' into the death of Kirk Donovan was completed. The statement would close both cases by saying the state's medical examiner determined Kirk Donovan's cause of death was a suicide over his dismay about his wife planning to file for divorce, and that Judge Aubuchon died from the blunt force trauma suffered in his collision.

"Did I not properly explain what I am doing?" I all but stammered the question.

"You are planting a story to see what the reaction is. I am on board with you trying to determine whether or not a serial killer is operating in the community, but there is something else you need to understand," Hammond told me. He paused for a brief moment before he dropped the other shoe on me. "Senator Donovan has been pressing the Commandant for a resolution to his son's death ever since the preliminary autopsy report was released. He is anxious to focus his attention on other matters."

"His son's death is a distraction?" I saw no other way to interpret his words.

"I don't think he believes his daughter-in-law is in any way responsible for Kirk's death. I also get the impression he would appreciate it if your homicide investigation did not turn into a circus trial. He seems to believe your investigation is drawing too much attention to his family, which invites scrutiny on other family matters as well." Hammond was undoubtedly giving me a carefully worded version of what must have been a series of heated phone calls to himself and the Commandant.

"Am I hearing that the state police are open to closing both cases this way?"

"The state police would be satisfied to see both cases closed with as little fanfare as possible. Whether you can let them go is another matter. Are you prepared to drop any further investigation into either death?" Hammond sounded as though he began to hold his breath.

"You know better," I admitted.

"I assumed that was going to be your position. Feel free to give whatever you are up to a chance to succeed, but don't be surprised if that press release you asked for is distributed to everyone and not just your target there." Hammond lacked much in the way of diplomatic skills. He likes results and he likes order. He has begrudgingly learned to appreciate that the disorder I bring to an investigation results in both justice and a return to surface normality.

"In other words, I have this weekend to wrap this up," I stated as much as asked.

"That is probably about right," he agreed.

"Then I need to get busy," I said and hung upon him. I didn't mean to cut him off, and he didn't call me back.

Eighty-One

Pamela was working on the layout for the next week's edition of the paper when I arrived at the newspaper office just after lunch. Her computer screen was filled with the mock-up of an interior page on which she was arranging the display advertising before filling the blank space with what passed for news in a small town full of gossips. I understood enough about the newspaper business to know that the ads paid the bills, not news.

"I hate to do this to you," I said as I tossed the press release onto the high countertop blocking access to the back office.

"Do what?" she asked, but I saw her eyes dart to the handcuffs on my belt and the pistol on the opposite hip. I made sure both were within sight. I carried my badge on its lanyard around my neck.

"The state police have declared that Kirk Donovan committed suicide and Judge Aubuchon died from blunt force trauma in his car accident. You should be getting an official statement by email shortly. Here's a copy I just printed." I said and used my fingertips to push the paper forward. I watched her expression, and she gave me the flushed color and quick blink that let me know this was not the story she wanted to print.

"But what about Gwendolyn Donovan? Isn't she still missing?" she pressed. "What if it turns out that she killed Kirk and staged her own death?"

"I haven't anything to support that idea," I lied. I was surprised Pamela didn't challenge me on what she must have known was a blatant lie since she had helped plant the fake blood evidence. "Gwen is likely hiding out on a sunny beach somewhere just waiting for the coast to clear. I think she faked her death to run away from Kirk and found herself trapped in the lie when he turned up dead. She'll probably come home as soon as we release the news on Monday. I just wanted you to have the scoop. You are the hometown newspaper, after all," I smiled as she read the one page announcement.

"You're also saying Judge Aubuchon's wreck was an accident," she numbly repeated what I had just told her. The disappointment in her voice was such that anyone might have questioned why she felt so strongly about a tragic motor vehicle crash.

"There is no reason to believe he intentionally steered into the truck's path. Theriot's deputy made a good case for it being a heart attack, even though there was no sign of it in the autopsy. I guess you could read this to say that whatever he ate might have disagreed with him." I couldn't resist the bad pun.

"Can I see the autopsy reports? If the cases are closed, there is no reason to seal them. I could file a Freedom of Information Act request, or you could just let me take a look and save everyone a lot of time."

"It's not my time you'd be saving," I pointed out. "It's always best to do things legally. I'm sure you agree."

The look she gave me was classic. It was a blend of a burning anger, lingering disappointment, and curiosity as to whether all of this was just a way to torment her. I left her with the press release and the rest of the day to make her own decision about that.

Her request to look at the autopsy reports interested me in a number of ways. For one thing, I knew of no sort of medical training in her background that made a review of the records worthwhile. Both cases were closed, so there was really nothing to see but the usual horror movie slide show of internal organs and a wide open human body. The pictures she took at both scenes were likely of a better quality than those taken by crime scene techs focused on detail rather than perspective. She may have been testing me to see if I was pliable about the rules, may have been intent on 'discovering' something trained experts had missed, or she may have just wanted a last, lingering look at her handiwork. Mostly, her request confirmed that she was not the one who broke into Judge Rogers' home the night before. I was narrowing down the short list of suspects, and Chief Theriot was beginning to look like the person I needed to confront about it.

Senator Donovan received the press release only a bit better when I called on him at home. I made sure to change clothes from the jeans and pullover I wore to see Pamela to a pair of creased slacks and a sport coat before I rang his doorbell.

A member of his imposing security detail answered the door and patted me down. They reached for my handgun and received humiliation for the effort. I could have said no, but intentionally chose to twist the man to a kneeling position before I released his wrist and allowed him to escort me to the senator's office.

"What brings you out this afternoon, Detective?" the senator asked from his seat on the sofa in front of the fireplace. It was not very cold out, but the smell of burning wood and the cozy atmosphere it created was worth the bother. Uncle Felix and two young men were hovered over stacks of paper on Senator Donovan's massive desk.

"I wanted to personally let you know pressuring my boss has finally paid off." I didn't care whether or not he took offense to my tone or implication. This was one of the last times I intended to see the man or hear his name, and I was sure he would reciprocate in the future. "There will be a press conference in Baton Rouge on Monday morning to announce your son died of an apparent suicide and Judge Aubuchon's death was the result of his traffic accident."

"I don't believe that for an instant. We both know Gwendolyn murdered my son, but apparently you are incapable of proving that. I'm sorry you went to so much work digging around in my family business instead of doing your job," Senator Donovan said to return the nastiness of my opening comment.

"Yeah, it's been fun."

"What can you tell us about Gwendolyn? She is still missing the last we heard. Are you planning to question her as a suspect in Kirk's death when you do finally track her down?" Uncle Felix inquired. Senator Donovan turned his back and left my uncle to be the one to deal with me going forward.

"We are aware of her whereabouts. She will be home in a few days and can begin settling her husband's affairs. At least anything that doesn't involve his other affairs." I saw no reason to show Kirk any more respect than he deserved.

"She can stay where she is if she wants, as far as I am concerned. I am the executor of my son's estate," Senator Donovan informed me. "I can tie that process up indefinitely."

"No doubt." I didn't spare my uncle the look of mild disgust I felt towards his powerful client. "Your family has been nothing but caring and giving towards Gwendolyn from day one."

"Watch your tone, Detective. You can find yourself without a job very easily," Senator Donovan turned and snapped at me.

"That's two of us, Senator," I calmly pointed out. "We both need to remain popular, don't we?'

"Meaning what?" Uncle Felix asked. He needed to find a way to separate us and he could tell I was intentionally goading the senator.

"Imagine the things people will say about this family when Belle's book is published."

"I'm not worried," Senator Donovan assured me. His voice said otherwise.

"I'm not either. It sounds like a very interesting book to me. I'll have to get an autographed copy for my mother for her birthday." I fired this line directly at my uncle. He knew there was going to be as much repercussion for the Deveraux family name if the book was published.

"Funny." He wasn't smiling.

"Maybe we should sit down with Belle and her mother after the funeral tomorrow. They both seem reasonable," I suggested. I intended to give the pair a clear indication that Gwendolyn and I had spoken since her disappearance.

"We'll have to see." Uncle Felix made a hand motion that led to the security guy's hand on my own shoulder just a moment later. "Until tomorrow."

There was no reason to say goodbye when I was being forcibly removed from their presence. I left them with a lot to talk about, and a lot to think about myself in the time I believed I had left.

The security guard I humbled was no longer guarding the front door. A much stouter bald-headed member of the team was standing there to be sure I left the house with no further incident. I stood on the senator's front porch and studied the front driveway and grounds. I had counted four armed men inside the house. I had seen another three through the

French doors of the senator's study, and counted an additional four on full display to passerby on the street. I rounded their numbers up to twelve and began working on a plan for the counter-measures Tony and I might need to use the next day.

I glanced at my watch. It was barely three o'clock and my to-do list for the day was complete. The state police ended my investigation rather than leave a potential can of worms open, Pamela Fulton needed to come up with a new way to destroy the last targets on her list, and I had managed to rile the senator and assess his security detail's capacities.

Eighty-Two

Saturday brought rain. I had anticipated the day would be miserable without this added element. I hoped the next few hours would bring the case to a close, and to ending Pamela Fulton's murderous rampage. I looked forward to curling up in my own bed later that evening, and to not waking up next to Roux for a change.

I was not looking forward to confronting someone as cunning and dangerous as Pamela Fulton. I was impressed that she had managed to concoct a unique name, which nobody in town seemed to question, from a pair of local hot sauce brands. It was fitting for Louisiana that someone would think to add hot sauce to revenge, the dish famously best served cold.

A fierce banging began against the front door just as I finished dressing. I slid my Glock into its holster and motioned for Roux to walk behind me as I went to see what the commotion was all about. It was much too early for breakfast with Detective Chance, or for Tony and his catering crew to need into the house.

I looked through the sidelight and spotted Chief Theriot and two of his deputies on the front porch. The deputies were standing on the stairs while their boss put his weight behind each blow made upon the heavy wooden door. I timed opening the door to knock Theriot off balance when his next blow hit thin air. He nearly fell into the entryway.

"It's six in the morning, Chief," I complained as I assessed the situation he had brought to my doorstep. The deputies looked more embarrassed than determined to back up their boss. I could smell liquor on the big man's breath, and assumed it was also amplifying the anger that fueled his assault on the door at that hour. "We don't open for business for another couple of hours."

"You'll be gone in another couple of hours," Chief Theriot bellowed. He was drunk, but that only added to the danger he posed to both of us. The snap was off on his revolver, but I knew I could have my gun drawn and fired before he cleared his holster in this condition. We were standing close enough I could just punch him if he went for the pistol or the baton on his belt. "You have failed to find your suspect. It's time you got the hell out of my town."

"If only things worked that way, Chief," I said and took a single step forward. I wanted whatever happened between us to occur where nothing of any value to Judge Rogers was likely to be damaged. The house would be full of mourners in a few hours and I didn't want them to walk into a crime scene. "I don't believe you are the one who gets to determine anything I do. In fact, I know you are not."

"I am through with you. You and that dog," Chief Theriot persisted. He pointed his finger towards Roux and I chose not to give Roux a command that would have cost Theriot the use of that hand for a few weeks.

"Tell me again who broke the news about closing the case," I casually asked. I assumed Pamela Fulton had put a bug in his ear because she, and everyone else in town, knew by now that the man was looking for a reason to fight me. There was also a chance Senator Donovan had fed the police chief a story about my case being resolved and suggested that I be sent packing. That would leave his own security team to handle Gwendolyn when she arrived in Donovan. He surely realized that he had shown me his cards at the funeral home. Now I was in the way more than ever.

"I don't reveal my sources," he laughed. He took two steps back and made a slight wince when his left foot came down on the bricks. I knew then who had broken into the house in my absence.

"Fellas, if you take your boss home right now I will forget this ever happened. It's either that or I arrest him for burglary and interfering with my investigation," I said to the deputies. They were almost certain to be aware of both offenses, and neither of them seemed inclined to take part.

"Not until I have beat your face into a pulp," Chief Theriot roared and pulled himself erect. He had reached a dangerous point of intoxication, where he felt strong as an ox, but was dumb as a fence post.

"That isn't going to happen, Chief. Go home," I said, but also stepped further onto the porch and took a defensive posture to his left, which seemed to be his weak side. This also placed Roux in the doorway behind him if he moved to engage me.

"Let's go," Chief Theriot yelled and threw his first punch. It was a good right hook, but he swung short of my face and committed too much of his weight to the punch. I threw a punch of my own that landed just below his right armpit and knocked much of the wind out of him.

"Chief, I have to apologize up front," I said as I kept moving to avoid his next punches rather than to engage him further. "I was never trained to fight."

"What?" he asked and paused to process what I told him. "You're supposed to be some kind of Special Forces bad ass."

"That's what I am saying," I elaborated, but also prepared my own attack as I spoke. "I have only been trained to kill, not to fight."

This warning surprised and confounded him long enough for me to close the distance between us. I threw a sharp left jab straight into his windpipe. This caused him to gag and double over with both hands at his throat. My second strike drove my right knee into Theriot's skull, breaking his nose with a distinct sound of crushed cartilage. He tried to stand erect, but my left elbow caught him at the base of his skull. He was unconscious before he realized he was struck. I made no move to keep the chief from dropping face first on the rain-slicked bricks. There was blood running freely from Chief Theriot's nose and forehead when his deputies rushed to his aid and picked up his considerable inert weight.

"Take him home and keep him there," I instructed them. They silently nodded acknowledgement of my order. I could not make out what they were saying to one another as they struggled to carry their boss to his car, but it certainly did not sound like either deputy was advocating a call for reinforcements.

Roux walked over and gave a quick lick to the back of my hand to let me know he was there. I looked down and swore he was laughing. His eyes were unusually bright and his spotted tongue was lolling about in his perpetual grin. He may have been thanking me for avenging the scare the big man tried to give him, but I think he was just letting me know that he was glad this was done. I knew the chief and I were going to have this fight the first time we met, and I had practiced those three

offensive moves every morning until they were muscle memory.
It was how I was trained.

Eighty-Three

The morning's cool temperature and steady rainfall diminished the number of mourners at Judge Aubuchon's graveside. A color guard from the local American Legion served as pall bearers and buried him with full military honors. It is very difficult not to cry when you hear taps played on a bugle in the distance and three bursts of seven rounds each are fired in a final tribute.

Judge Rogers' house was a welcome change from the chill of the cemetery. The house was warm and filled with the fragrance of the food Chef Tony and his crew set out on the dining room table to accompany the casseroles and desserts many of the locals brought to the repast. Leaves were added to the table in order to accommodate this growing spread. Ritchie Franklin stood to one side of the sideboard in order to coordinate the food runners moving back and forth between the dining room and the kitchen. It also gave him an excellent view of the front sidewalk and the entryway in addition to the dining room.

The catering help I had asked Tony to bring were dressed in their new chef coats. The heavy cotton jackets were black, with the logo of Tony's recently acquired pizzeria embroidered over the pocket. Six months ago, these boys had belonged to a street gang selling Mexican heroin and waging a constant battle for turf against rival gangs. Today I was counting on them to not lose their cool heads under fire and to counter the senator's security detail if need be. Tony kept the team moving through the crowd, picking up empty plates and cups while they kept a minimal distance between themselves and Senator Donovan's armed guards. I was absolutely clueless what the senator's reaction to Gwendolyn showing up here was going to be, but spiriting her away was not going to happen. I needed Gwendolyn to be the bait in the trap Chance and I had set. Our goal was to force Pamela Fulton into publicly dropping her disguise. Too much was riding on the success of our plan to allow Senator Donovan to mess things up with any wild ideas of his own.

Tony confirmed that Roux was keeping Gwen safe in Belle's bedroom on the second floor before I began working my way through the dining room and living room. I wanted to know where everyone was at all times. Senator Donovan and Judge Rogers took control of the sunroom, as it was somewhat isolated from the rest of the house and afforded them the most privacy. I watched locals come and go from the room to pay their respects to the two men, or maybe to swear fealty. Uncle Felix stationed himself beside the French doors, screening who gained access to the room. He tried to appear to be in casual conversation with two of the security guards.

"I am going to have to go on a diet," Belle mused when I caught her coming out of the dining room with a plate piled high with meat and cheese. "Tony spoiled me."

"You are welcome at the bistro anytime." I was not about to say she did look as though she had gained weight. Belle just smiled and moved towards the doors opened to the patio. I continued on to the sunroom to take a head count there.

"This all looks and tastes wonderful. Thank the chef for doing this on such short notice," Judge Rogers said when I passed through the sunroom.

"Oh, Tony loves days like this," I said and laughed at my private joke.

"I see you're still in town," Senator Donovan hissed as I stepped close enough to him that our conversation was not going to be overheard. "I was hoping you might allow the local detective to close the case on his own."

"I like to finish my own cases. It was nice of you to send someone to politely suggest I leave town, though," I said with a thin smile. I had no idea if anyone had told him of the altercation between myself and Chief Theriot, but the fact was that I was here and that his attempt to muscle me out of town had failed.

I remained on the prowl for Pamela Fulton. I had not seen her at the funeral, but I refused to believe she would miss the repast. Detective Chance and I were, in fact, counting on her showing up. Literally everyone she still likely wanted to kill would be in this house at the same time.

I found Bradley and Mitchell Ursin smoking on the back patio. Belle had made her way there and was sharing her haul from the buffet. I was very disappointed Mitchell was ignoring the warning Detective Chance and I had hoped he had the sense to take.

"I thought we had this conversation," I whispered in Mitchell's ear as I approached the trio from behind. He shrugged uncomfortably in response when he saw it was me who was speaking to him. I turned to Bradley as though I had no issues with him. "Nice of you to pay your respects."

"Respects, hell," Bradley nearly spat the words out at me. "I just wanted to be sure that the man who ruined my life was really dead. Aubuchon was the judge who signed my adoption papers."

"From what I understand, you needed a better home than the one you were living in," I said. My purpose was to add fuel to whatever fire was burning inside of Bradley. I suspected his mother needed him to have a clear head when she called upon him to help exact her revenge.

"The man who adopted me was a child molester. He abused me every day of my life until I was old enough to stand up to him. I wasn't his little plaything by then anyway. He liked real young boys, if you get what I mean."

"I'd say you've made yourself clear. Didn't one of his cousins adopt your sister a few years later?" This wasn't idle conversation. I had a destination in mind for this line of questioning.

"He was even worse," Bradley growled. This was not a topic he wanted to discuss among his friends.

"I heard she used to hide out at your house when she would run away from him," I casually tossed in, trying to make it sound like common knowledge.

"And that bastard you are working with kept dragging her back until he got her killed." This time Bradley came at me and jabbed his right index finger in my chest. "Everyone pays in the end. You just remember that, Detective."

"Noted," I said and tossed up my hands before I took a step back. I had learned what I needed to from him. Belle and Mitchell could be the ones to calm him down. Bradley's comment seemed to confirm that

Detective Chance and I were on Pamela's list of people to kill or destroy.

One of the food runners was just coming from the kitchen with a key lime pie when I returned to the dining room. Bells began clanging in my head and I intercepted the food runner before he could set the pie on the table. I gave a hand motion for him to turn around and return to the kitchen and followed him through the door.

"Where did this come from?" I demanded as I grabbed the pie from the bewildered boy's hands.

"Some lady dropped off three of them. She was a fox," one of the other boys explained. He was not the first to be enthralled by Pamela's good looks.

"Nobody touch the pies. Not a bite," I said loud enough for everyone milling about the kitchen to hear me, including Tony. He made his way over to me and looked at the pie.

"What's wrong?"

"The woman who handed this to you used pies key lime pies to hide the flavor of the strychnine she used to kill at least two men. Maybe we shouldn't help her kill any more people." I grabbed a roll of plastic wrap and covered the pie with four layers of the clear wrap. It would be a few hours before I could get it to the crime lab in Baton Rouge to confirm its poisonous ingredient.

"When did this get dropped off?" I heard my tone of voice and tried to calm down.

"Just now," the young man who had taken it from Pamela informed me. "I'm sorry, boss."

"It's all good. You didn't know," I reassured him. I moved the wrapped evidence away from the rest of the food. Tony brought me the two uncut pies and we wrapped them, as well. This was a close call, but it was the first thing I could say had gone right for me so far.

I imagined that Pamela Fulton was sitting close enough to see the judge's house, but to still be out of sight. Bradley could text or call her with updates or any news of interest, such as my probing his adoption. I imagined that she was waiting for the strychnine in the pies to take effect before she moved ahead with her plan. A random handful of people having convulsions and vomiting at the same time would cause ample disruption and confusion to the gathering. She might slip in and out of the house without being noticed. It would be a bonus if Senator Donovan or Detective Chance ate any of the pie. I was sure she had some other means in mind of dealing with both of them. I was still unclear whether she meant to kill them or to stage something in public that would end their careers.

I spent the next twenty minutes trailing Bradley and Mitchell as they roamed the rooms. They never went into the sunroom, but it was obvious Bradley made sure he knew the senator's whereabouts at all times.

I watched him check his wristwatch and then make a slow pass of the desserts set out on the sideboard under Ritchie's constant attention. He came out of the dining room with a noticeable frown on his face. He pulled his cellphone from his pants pocket and began texting. I believed his texts were to alert his mother that the pies were never served.

Pamela would only make an appearance at the repast on her own terms. I doubted that she meant for her arrival to be of interest to anyone in the room. She might try to enter the home with someone who might draw more attention than herself.

I motioned to Detective Chance after he entered the house and paused in the entryway. He preceded me into the kitchen, and I timed my own entry to make it less apparent that the two of us were about to confer. I wanted Tony to be part of what I discussed with Detective Chance.

"Did you happen to see Pamela on your way here? I am sure she is nearby," I asked Chance.

"No, but I drove by her house on the way over and she is not there," Chance informed me. I didn't immediately know what to think of this. I could only hope she did not drop off the pies and then skip town.

"Then I guess we need to see if we can make her break cover," I sighed. This was roughly Plan D. "Tony, this is the local detective I have been working with. David, this is my partner and the chef of the restaurant we own in New Orleans. I have armed his cooks with Tasers to take out any of Senator Donovan's men who get in our way."

"Really," Detective Chance said and looked about the room. "Are you sure they are up to it?"

Tony snorted and walked away with a smile on his face. I simply nodded.

"I am going to have Gwendolyn make her big debut. I think it might be the only way to get Pamela to make her move," I told Chance. "Find a corner of the living room to hide in. I will have her meet me in the sunroom. Feel free to come on in if it sounds like things have gotten out of control. You know the senator is going to have something to say."

"To say the least," Chance said. "Don't be surprised if he tries to kill her with his bare hands. You told me last night that he still believes it was Gwendolyn who killed his son."

"I just hope that Crystal, I mean Pamela, takes the bait. It is going to take a lot to convince the senator that Gwen did not kill Kirk. I would say we are counting on Crystal to prove Gwen is innocent, wouldn't you?"

"Yes," Chance agreed. "And I am counting on you to keep Pamela from killing anyone when she finds all of you together. Don't forget you are as much of a target as the two of them."

"Just be sure to keep tab of Bradley." I placed a hand on his shoulder and looked him in the eye. "Be careful. I do not know if his piece of this is to back her up or to use whatever she does as a distraction to get to you."

Detective Chance sighed and took a very deep breath. He released it slowly and cast his eyes on my own.

"Is this how you close all your cases?" he asked. I didn't take it as a criticism.

"Yes, he does," Tony spoke up from close by. He was obviously listening to our review of the loose idea we had for how to ensnare Pamela.

"Ignore the cook," I said and waved away Tony's statement. Nothing good was going to come of Chance beginning to doubt the wisdom of what I had talked him into doing.

Detective Chance and I walked out of the kitchen together. I waved my right index finger in a circular motion as I passed Ritchie, to let him know we were ready for him to begin positioning his team. Chance began to make his way to the far corner of the living room as I walked upstairs. He placed his back to the wall in a position to watch the doors to the patio, the front door, and the doors to the sunroom. He could move in whichever direction he believed would advance the public exposure and capture of Pamela.

I knocked on the door to the Belle's bedroom. I heard shuffling and then a single warning bark from Roux, advising me against opening the door.

"Zitten," I instructed him through the closed door. I waited a couple of seconds and then opened the door to find Roux sitting as instructed. He remained at the ready to defend Gwendolyn, but relaxed when I was the person to enter the room.

"What's going on?" Gwendolyn asked. I could only imagine the anxiety she felt while sitting here alone and listening to familiar voices downstairs.

"It looks like we are going to have to smoke her out. I think we thwarted her attempt to disrupt things, so now we will have to give her a reason to go through with whatever else she had in mind." I could not bring myself to remind Gwendolyn that she was here as bait in a flimsy trap.

"So, it's time for my debut," Gwendolyn sighed and swung her feet off the bed. She was wearing a thigh-length dress, with her hair in a loose ponytail and just a touch of makeup. She stepped into the flats she had set by the bedside table and smoothed the dress while I silently waited for her to let me know she was ready.

"I'll see you downstairs in a few minutes," I said and gave her what I hoped was a reassuring smile. I patted Roux on the head as I passed him, but gave him another instruction in Dutch to keep him out of the coming fray. "Oponthud."

I thought better of relying on Roux's training to keep him in the room when he heard any commotion. I turned and motioned for Gwen to close him into the bedroom on her way downstairs. I left ahead of her and made my way towards the sunroom. I took up a position near Uncle Felix and waited for things to begin either falling into place or falling apart.

The reaction to Gwendolyn descending the stairs was immediate and spectacular. The entire house gradually fell silent as word of her presence spread to the rooms where mourners had not seen her walk down the stairs. The food runners and cooks emptied from the kitchen to begin to mingle among the distracted guests, each of them working towards a member of Senator Donovan's well-dressed security detail. They palmed the stun guns Tony had provided them and stood ready to incapacitate anyone who made a hostile move towards Gwen as she quietly walked through the crowd towards the sunroom to be reunited with her father.

She looked in control, of her own emotions and of the entire house, as people stepped out of her way to let her pass. She smiled at a few people, and most seemed to be genuinely glad she was alive and well, but nearly twice as many responded with shock and disbelief. I could only imagine how many people had lost money betting on her being dead, or how many needed to start working on the apologies they were going to have make for things they said when they believed that she was dead or her husband's murderer. I watched Bradley as he used his phone to record her stairway descent and then forward the video. There was almost certainly to be only one person with much interest in watching it.

It would take a few minutes for Pamela to barge into the gathering. I was sure she would make an entrance no less dramatic than Gwendolyn's. This left only a few moments for Gwen to have her moment somewhat alone with Senator Donovan.

"Good, Lord," Senator Donovan blurted when she stepped into the room and walked up to kiss her startled father's cheek and hug him. The senator glared at me, but his eyes were past where I stood. He was looking for Uncle Felix to do something. My uncle did all he could do, which was to close the sunroom doors and seal us into the space. There were still a handful of witnesses present to tell the story of whatever transpired.

"I am so sorry for your loss, Chester," Gwendolyn said with surprisingly convincing sympathy. "I know how much you loved Kirk."

"Don't you say his name," Senator Donovan snarled. "We both know you killed my son."

"That is not what the evidence shows," I reminded him.

"You set up this silly stunt," Senator Donovan roared at me. "You have disgraced Kirk's memory by inviting his murderer to come here. How dare you!"

"My daughter did not murder your son," Judge Rogers immediately entered the conversation. His argument was based far more on being her father than anything he knew would stand up in court. "You need to stop saying that she did."

"I don't care what poppycock you came up with to sweep this under the rug, but Gwendolyn will never see a dime of Kirk's money. That I can promise." I did not intend for this unhappy reunion to be quite such an airing of grievances. It was, however, the sort of circus I had hoped for. The pair of glass paned doors to the room were closed, but the senator's voice carried his accusations and protests throughout the house.

"She will get more than just his money if you insist on slandering her name in public, Senator," Judge Rogers said and went toe to toe with the man who sent him into self-imposed exile. He was far too protective of Gwen to realize that a change in roles had just taken place. It was Senator Donovan's turn to stand down and regroup.

"Senator, we have a suspect in your son's death. We have simply lacked a way to prove they are responsible for not only Kirk's death, but all of those people we discussed having been killed in the last few years." I was responsible for what led to this scene and needed to be the one who defused the situation before it became any more hostile.

"Explain yourself, Detective," Senator Donovan was quick to turn his anger upon me.

"Pamela Fulton. Does that name ring a bell? She was married to Hank Fulton until she stabbed him to death. She probably killed his parents after they allowed her children be married off or adopted. That is what this is all about, Senator. Old fashioned, straightforward, revenge." I tried to minimize what I actually disclosed because there were too many potential jurors in the room, and all of them would be anxious to share what they heard.

"Revenge for what?" he demanded. I was not sure if he did not remember the details from so long ago or if he simply didn't see that any of this warranted what came next, including his son's death.

"She holds everyone involved responsible for her pain, and for the continued abuse her children suffered in their new homes. You and Judge Aubuchon handled both the adoption of her son and the marriage of her twelve-year old daughter to pedophile cousins in Texas twenty years ago," I elaborated. The senator calmed down as he began to grapple with what I was telling him. I noticed Uncle Felix and the security detail were quietly herding anyone not involved in this out of the room before they heard any more juicy details.

"We arranged marriages for dozens of young girls from around here. How were we supposed to know some of their husbands were bad men?" he lamely argued.

"Maybe you could have at least checked," I suggested and did not care in the least what his reaction might be. "What reason does any thirty-five year old man have for driving this far to take a twelve-year old as his bride? They are looking for a live sex toy at best and someone they can exploit even further at worst."

"Most of the girls got themselves pregnant. They were all responsible for their own situations!" The senator had no intention of accepting any blame for things he may not have given the thought or attention he should have. He certainly refused to believe his son's life was the price for his own dereliction.

"No girl gets pregnant on her own," Gwendolyn shouted into his face. "I didn't hold myself down while your son raped me."

"Marrying you ruined his life," Senator Donovan blurted out. "He was never happy being married to you, but he gave you a good home, didn't he?"

"Your son beat me, as you damn well know. Kirk went to law school, but raising Belle meant I never even finished high school. I lost my entire future because Kirk *raped* me." she put a lot of emphasis on that word and finally made the senator flinch. "I was twenty before I got my GED, and I fought your son to get permission even to do that. I had dreams, too, and being forced to join your sick family killed every one of them, except for getting Belle free from Kirk. It is so ironic that Kirk allowing her take a journalism class is going to expose how corrupt and cruel your family has always been. I was the one who told her about your family's archives at the museum when she started writing her paper."

"That paper of hers will never be published as a book," Uncle Felix interrupted. He needed to do at least act like he was going to do something to earn the money the senator was paying him to avoid scenes like this.

"That doesn't mean it won't be read," Gwendolyn said and laughed. "It's going to be the two of you against the internet."

This should have been the point at which negotiations over Kirk's estate and not releasing the term paper began. What happened instead was a loud commotion in the living room. We heard screams and the sound of a hundred sets of feet trying to find the front door at the same time. The two security guards in the room immediately flanked the senator, pushing Judge Rogers and Gwendolyn away to fend for themselves if the room was breached. I rather wished that was on video for all the world to see.

I pulled my Glock and made my way to the sunroom doorway. I looked into the living room but could not see what caused the chaos. I looked towards the dining room and saw Ritchie doing what he could to usher guests out of the house through the kitchen. I opened the sunroom doors and stepped into the stampede with my handgun aimed at chest height. It likely added to the level of panic in the room, but I was more concerned with my own safety for the moment.

Detective Chance was lying on the floor with wounds to his abdomen. One of Tony's cooks had a towel over the wound and tried to shield him from further attack as best he could. I doubted that the young man had even seen who had stabbed Chance.

"Grab the bandages in my bag," I shouted to Tony and leaned down to see if Detective Chance could speak.

"What happened?"

"Bradley got the drop on me. He had Mitchell act like he was going to whisper something in my ear and then reached around him to stab me," Chance explained. His tone of voice sounded as though he was impressed by the ruse that might cost him his life. Chance was in shock, but it was that odd form of shock when everything seems to be absolutely fine to the victim when the exact opposite was true. He was losing a lot of blood and was going to pass out by the time an ambulance arrived.

"We're going to get you to the hospital now, okay?" I smiled and gripped his bloody hand. Tony knelt beside us and pulled a compression bandage from my bag. "Get him into a car. There's no time to wait for an ambulance."

"Go. I have this." Tony said as I stood up.

"Did anyone see what direction the boys ran?" I asked the handful of people who were either still frozen in place or had chosen to stay and tell me what they saw.

"There were two boys. They ran towards the patio," an older woman said and pointed to the open doors.

I was about to take the bait and chase after the two boys when I spotted the pair moving towards the sunroom close behind Pamela. They had likely circled the house and then joined her as she went against the flow of people dashing through the front door to slip into the house unnoticed. She and Bradley were both armed, but neither of them raised their guns towards me. Mitchell looked like he had been swept up in things he could not understand, and the pair had him bracketed between them to add to their numbers.

The trio surprised Uncle Felix and the pair of armed men flanking him. Bradley and Mitchell shoved ahead as the entire group made their way into the sunroom. I entered the room steps behind them and prevented Mitchell from closing the doors and creating a hostage situation, but creating an armed standoff was not necessarily a preferable alternative.

Pamela's unexpected arrival in the sunroom with Uncle Felix and the senator's armed guards ahead of her gave her a momentary advantage over the two men trying to protect the senator. Neither of them were prepared to take a bullet senselessly by trying to draw their weapons. They moved to place themselves in front of their client instead. I took a step back to put the door jamb between me and any shots Pamela or Bradley might fire in my direction.

"Get their guns, Mitch," Pamela shouted at her clearly stunned accomplice. She had a clean shot at the guards who had failed to protect Uncle Felix, and none of the security detail doubted she was prepared to shoot them where they stood. Bradley was holding the other two in his own sights. The trio counted on my reluctance to fire into the crowded room.

The bodyguards sullenly allowed Mitchell to take their side-arms. Pamela used the barrel of her weapon to motion for the men to leave the room. They each gave me an apologetic look as they passed. I waited for the last of them to clear the room before I motioned for the locals who were caught in the path of our potential crossfire to leave as well. I trusted that Pamela's anger was limited to the people I had invited to be here and that she would not randomly gun down any other guests or bodyguards.

It took less than a minute for the sunroom to be cleared of everyone but Senator Donovan, Uncle Felix, and Judge Rogers and his daughter and grand-daughter. I faced three armed assailants, but I was a far better and faster shot and held my Glock free of its holster. I could bring it to bear and fire three shots faster than any one of the others could get off a shot. The problem was that a ten millimeter round has a mind of its own. The fast moving hollow point was likely to flatten as it bored its way through the head of my targets and keep flying until it hit either someone else or a piece of something hard enough to stop it. Everyone was standing much too close to each other to risk killing someone I needed to protect by a needless show of shooting skill.

I slowly slid my heavy semi-automatic sideways into the holster on my hip. I then extended my empty hands slightly before me. I could draw and fire my weapon in two seconds and had already worked out the order in which I would need to shoot the three armed assailants.

"You get out of here, too," Crystal ordered.

"I can't do that, Pamela," I said as calmly as I could. I hoped using her real name would rattle her a bit. She must have been thinking everything was working well so far.

"You know my name, big deal," she huffed. It came as a surprise to almost everyone else in the room.

"You are Pamela Fulton?" Senator Donovan asked, but it was not a question directed at anyone in particular. "I don't understand. I thought you left town."

"She did," I answered the dangling question. "Now she is back."

"Shut up, both of you," she snapped, but didn't bother waving her gun at either of us. She seemed to be at a bit of a loss as to what to do next. It was not a hesitation based on confusion. She simply had too many targets to choose from. She had dreamed of this moment, but not about what to do next.

"Why don't you tell the senator why you're going to kill him?" I suggested. I wasn't trying to be helpful, just to stall her for a while.

"You aren't going to try to stop me?" Pamela asked. I shrugged and crossed my arms across my chest rather than rush her.

"I'm not going to take a bullet for him, that's for sure," I assured her. "He has done a lot of harm and ruined a lot of lives besides yours. I can't say that he should get a death sentence, but there ought to be a price for what all of these men have done."

"Excuse me?" Judge Rogers protested.

"You and the senator exploited the children at your summer camp. You have admitted as much. We don't have enough time to discuss everything my uncle here has done. Senator, you have been sitting on a bill that would save young girls from being forced into marriages like you and the judge sentenced your own children to." I really didn't care what anyone in the room thought of my speech. I was only trying to draw Pamela into the conversation. I wanted to hear her own justification for what she and her son had done since her return to town. She did not immediately pick up the thread so I pushed her again. "I am just curious what you blame Gwendolyn for. She did not take your kids from you. She didn't sell you dope like Mitchell's dad. She even tried to be your friend when you moved back to town. She probably would not have if she had known what a heartless bitch you are, but at least she was nice to you."

"Nice to me?" Pamela all but spat the words in Gwen's face as she began nervously pacing the room. I had thrown her off her game and she was struggling to regain control of the situation. "She destroyed my life!"

"How? How did I do that?" Gwendolyn risked adding fuel to the fire obviously burning inside Crystal.

"You stole Kirk from me," Pamela snapped and waved the pistol in Gwendolyn's face. She saw the fear in her face and smiled at the reaction. Pamela wanted the entire room to bow before her and beg for mercy she had no intention of granting. Bradley seemed to be on board with whatever her plan was, but Mitchell was clearly in over his head. "I was supposed to be with Kirk that night. I only asked you to give him a message, not to screw him."

"Pamela, Kirk raped me. You know that he raped me," Gwen tried to remind her former friend without arguing any more than necessary.

"Oh, that's your story. Kirk told everyone how much you liked it," Pamela persisted. "He said you could never get enough of him."

"I had enough of him that night for a lifetime," Gwen said. She may have figured she was going to die, but she was not prepared to pay this price for her husband's lie. "I never slept with him again. Not once."

This brought a moment of stunned silence to the room. I don't think anyone had ever given their sexual relations any consideration until she opened the topic.

"He wanted to divorce you and marry me. He told me that a bunch of times. We were having an affair, did you know that?" Pamela insisted. She was beginning to sound hysterical and the clock was running down on whatever end game she had in mind.

"He had a lot of them," Pamela calmly retorted. Judge Rogers tugged at her hand to tell her to stop pushing the crazy woman holding a gun. All of the men in the room kept glancing at me as though that might inspire me to get myself shot for their benefit. Everybody was going to wind up dead if I was the first one shot.

Pamela turned her anger upon the senator. "I am killing you last. I want you to stand there and know everyone else died because they did what you told them to do."

"You're crazy," the senator said with much less dignity than usual. It was difficult to tell if his words were a protest, a realization, or an insult. They were lousy last words, and his life was spared just then only by Pamela's contrary plans for his death. "I have only done what is best. I did not want my son to marry some local girl, and certainly not just because she was pregnant. Even so, I could not bring myself to approve of their love child being destroyed to avoid it. I needed to keep all of the pro-life voters behind me in the next election."

"Right, Senator. So much better to destroy the lives of two teenagers than an unborn child neither of them wished to have. You're such a humanitarian," I said. I did not intend to appear to agree with Pamela or to influence any other person's opinion on the subject. I just could no longer hold my tongue about what had loosed this spree in the first place. "Why don't you go ahead and tell our hostess here what you would have said if Kirk asked for permission to marry her instead."

"That doesn't matter. It never happened," Uncle Felix interjected. He was so used to helping his clients dodge such public relations bullets that he put himself in line to take a real one before he realized it.

"I was as good as this bitch," Pamela snapped at my humbled uncle. His eyes never left the gun she held in his direction. "My father was the Chief of Police. What were you, Judge, just another flunky lawyer?"

"Yes, I was just a flunky," Judge Rogers agreed. He was a sharp enough attorney to know an out when he saw one. He jumped on the chance to appear lower than Pamela considered herself to be.

Sirens sounded in the distance. Sheriff Mazant, and perhaps State Troopers, were moments away from being on the scene. There would be no way to leave this room once a perimeter was established. I could not imagine Pamela's plan was to kill everyone in the room, including herself and Bradley. I was very sure than her son did not come here to die for what other people may or may not have done to his mother before he was even born. Mitchell was beginning to understand her grace was not going to extend to him, that his father's supposed sins would doom him, as well.

"Clock's ticking, Pamela," I pressed her and raised a lone finger to my ear in response to the sound of the sirens. It also allowed me to move my hand and place it in a good position to drop and draw my pistol.

"Watch him," Pamela told Mitchell and then pointed at me. She stood next to Bradley and pointed towards Judge Rogers, Gwendolyn, and Belle. "You shoot them, the senator is mine."

"I'm not going to shoot Belle," Bradley whined. I was not encouraged by his apparent willingness to murder Belle's grandfather and mother.

"She doesn't deserve to live," Crystal insisted.

"No!" he repeated.

"Then move," Crystal snarled and raised her handgun to aim at Belle's tear streaked face.

"Stop it!" Bradley yelled and reached to twist the pistol from his mother's hand. He twisted it the wrong direction, as the two rounds she fired both struck his chest rather than the ceiling. Blood splattered on Pamela and she began to shriek in horror and grief.

The momentary confusion allowed me to draw my own pistol and motion for Mitchell to drop the pistol he was half-heartedly holding in his right hand. He did so and hastily locked his fingers behind his head. My aim turned to Pamela, who was still reacting to having fatally shot her only remaining child.

"It's over," I yelled. I didn't need to raise my voice to be heard, only to break her reverie. I knew what was coming next and resigned myself to play my part.

Pamela reached for the pistol at her feet. I let her grasp it and stand up before I shot her once, aiming just in front of her right ear and sending the round and her last conscious thought against the panes of glass behind her rather than through anyone else in the room.

I leaned over and tugged the pistol from Bradley's now lifeless hand.

"Thank you, Detective," Senator Donovan said and shoved a hand towards me as though that would make everything alright. I ignored him and glanced at Uncle Felix before I turned back to the senator.

"We aren't quite done, Senator." I raised my pistol and cocked the hammer before I aimed it at the bridge of his nose, leaving only inches between the still warm barrel and his trembling flesh.

"What the hell are you doing, Cooter?" Uncle Felix demanded. He was far more scared than curious.

"Here is how this plays out from here," I said without taking my eyes off the senator. His defiant expression had morphed into justifiable concern.

"Senator Donovan here is about to retire. His grief over his son's suicide has made attending to the state's business too much of a burden," I told the two men who would make it happen. "Belle is going to turn her research paper in for class credit and then burn it. She cannot sell the story because the senator would need to give his permission for her use the Donovan family's archives to publish the book now that Kirk is not here to give his permission."

I raised an eyebrow to let the senator know this was not a negotiation that either of them had any say in, because I was setting the terms both of them were going to accept.

"You are going to probate your son's estate make sure Gwendolyn benefits generously from the fortune your son made from selling this parish's children to strangers. I imagine she might want to take back her maiden name and move to New Orleans, never to return." I continued to dictate terms to everyone I was mentioning by name. Chester's eyes flicked past me to Uncle Felix and then back to mine once again. I am not sure what sign Uncle Felix gave him, but the senator frowned and nodded.

I dropped the handgun on the floor and turned to address Mitchell. "Put your hands down and get on your knees."

The relieved dupe wasted no time in doing as I instructed. Uniformed deputies began pouring into the house as soon as one of Tony's cooks opened the front door. I opened the sunroom door and waved Sheriff Mazant past me. He could do the paperwork and take all of the credit or leave me to explain what had happened.

I handcuffed Mitchell Ursin and led him past the local and state police officers until we were in the driveway. I shoved him against one of the state police patrol cars and unlocked his handcuffs.

"Go home," I said and busied myself with replacing the handcuffs on my belt.

"You're not arresting me?" he asked. His feet had still not processed the fact that he was being allowed to leave.

"For what? The level of stupidity you showed in being here after we told you to steer clear ought to be criminal, but it just isn't. You are the only one left alive, why should you pay for what those two have been doing for years?" I was sounding very philosophical, but honestly I just didn't want to have to come back to Saint Xavier Parish to testify against him. I wasn't coming back here ever again if I could avoid it.

Mitchell finally took off running. I saw no reason to believe he was not going to wind up in prison eventually. The dumb kid was as cursed by his family's history of crime as Kirk had been with his family's history of exploiting others.

H. MAX HILLER

Eighty-Four

Detective David Chance came by the bistro two weeks later. He wanted to thank Tony for getting him to the hospital, and to let me know he was returning to Houston. Bradley was inexperienced with a knife and had not known to twist the blade after he ripped into Chance's large intestine. Thankfully, he missed the detective's other vital organs. Houston's Police Department was willing to rehire Chance because the ballistics from Pamela and Bradley's pistols recovered in the sunroom matched the bullets taken from the two dead cousins, validating the obsession that had led to his being fired.

Chance arrived in the company of my Uncle Felix, whose facial expression was less friendly or grateful. He refused a drink and stood a couple of steps away as Chance and I said our farewells and only partially joked about never wanting to work together again.

"Can we speak? Alone?" Uncle Felix asked and tugged at my elbow.

"Let's step outside," I suggested and led the way.

"It's done," my uncle declared as soon as we were alone on the sidewalk. I made sure we were out of earshot of the valets parking cars, but stayed within view of everyone at the bar who watched us through the large plate glass window. "Senator Donovan has informed the Speaker that he is stepping down."

"Then we are good," I assured him. I was not entirely sure that I could have enforced anything I invoked in the sunroom. I was counting on shared trauma to make things happen.

"You cost me a client," he complained. This was the full extent of his concern over the end of a long-standing state senator's career and a political dynasty.

"Did Chester recommend anyone?"

"No. He is still afraid you are going to show up and kill him. He was afraid of that crazy woman who killed Kirk, but he is absolutely terrified of you. That's a good thing, because he would destroy you if he wasn't." I had no doubt that Uncle Felix knew his client this well, nor that neither he nor the former senator realized how little the badge I carry directs my actions.

"Put Gabouri's name in the hat," I suggested.

"Why should I consider doing something like that?" Uncle Felix all but laughed.

"The guy is a waste as a district attorney. He is not going to be any better at his job now that the senator will be in Donovan pulling strings there full time," I said as I began walking back towards the bistro. "He would also probably need a stable and experienced hand to guide him, don't you think?"

Uncle Felix started to say something, but the words were lost as my own turned on the light in his head and he saw the advantage in what I suggested.

I knew Gabouri was waiting on the Governor's phone call and he had an agenda which bore no resemblance to his predecessor's whatsoever. He was especially anxious to vote in favor of the bill Senator Donovan had managed to block for so long.

"Everything alright?" Katie asked after my uncle and Chance left us alone at the bar. I took a sip of my third Manhattan and chewed an ice cube before I responded.

"Don't let me leave town again."

"Fine by me," she said and leaned in to kiss me.

H. MAX HILLER

Postscript

We live in a society which has long accepted May-December romances as being normal. The 1979 motion picture *Manhattan*, about a romance between a forty-two year old man and a seventeen-year old girl was nominated for three Academy Awards and considered 'culturally significant' by the Library of Congress. But times do change, as Judge Roy Moore of Alabama discovered when his history of dating young women in the 1980s was considered to be a disqualification for public office in 2018.

While this story is entirely a work of fiction, it is estimated that 248,000 girls under the age of sixteen were married in the United States alone between 2000 and 2010. That figure does not account for the eleven states which did not even bother to track their own statistics.

Child brides are statistically up to five times more likely more likely to encounter complications while giving birth. The majority of child brides will never finish high school, which means they are then economically dependent upon their husband for support and less likely to be able to support themselves, much less themself and children were they to leave the marriage. Child brides are also statistically more likely to live in households below the poverty line, and to be subjected to spousal abuse.

In the years it has taken to research and complete this novel, the percentage of women who marry below the age of eighteen has dropped from a figure approaching thirty percent of all marriages in the world to a figure closer to barely twenty percent. At the start of the millennia, the figure approached twenty five percent. In 2018, researchers from UCLA found that six out of every thousand children surveyed in the United States were already married.

There are numerous organizations with in depth information and opportunities to become involved in the effort to change state laws and Federal immigration policy related to this exploitation of young women. Please consider adding your voice to the international outcry by contacting one of these groups:

Unchained At Last: www.unchainedatlast

Girls Not Brides: www.girlsnotbrides.org

Tahirih Justice: Center: www.tahirih.org

Humanium   (International Organization):   www.humanium.org

www.ingramcontent.com/pod-product-compliance
Lightning Source LLC
Chambersburg PA
CBHW020235110726
47898CB00004B/1274